LINGERING FLAMES

LINGERING FLAMES

ANNA AUGUST

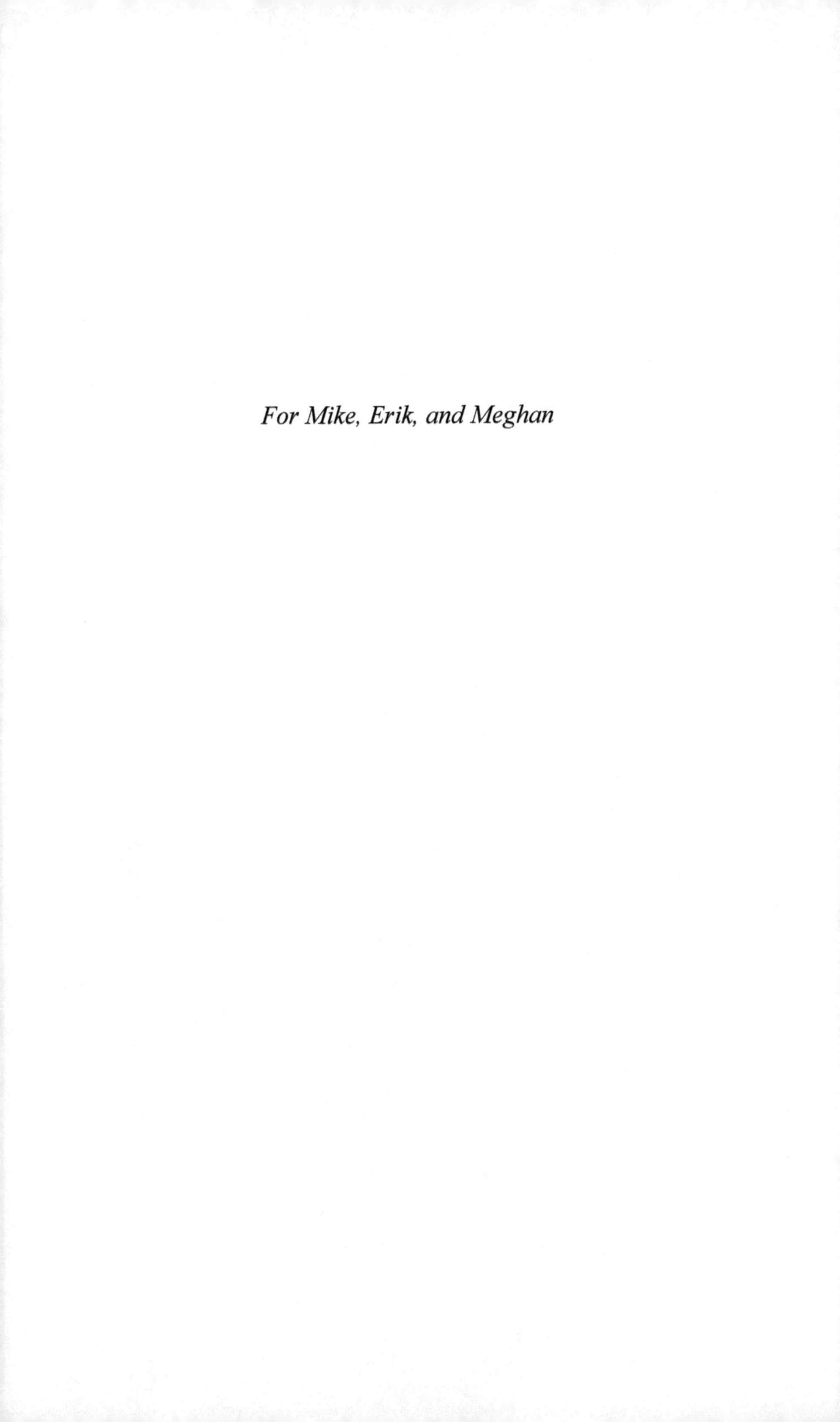

For Mike, Erik, and Meghan

Contents

"Love is like a friendship caught on fire."

— Bruce Lee

Prologue

With an exhausted sigh, Clara took a cautious seat behind the nurses' station to call Charlie to tell him she would be late getting home.

Her husband cursed a wild streak from his end of the call. His worry about her increased each day that she continued to work.

"You shouldn't be on your feet so much, *Acushla*." His voice sounded pained, shamed that his job didn't pay more.

But they couldn't get around the fact that it didn't. They needed her income. Better she work now so she could stay home some after the baby was born.

She tried to calm him, tried to hide the exhaustion from her tone. "I'm feeling fine. I'll come home as soon as May gets here. She got a flat. You know that takes time to fix."

Clara hung up the phone in the middle of another of his colorful curses, shaking her head.

Charlie would have to learn to watch his language. Unless he wanted his mouth washed out with soap. He knew she'd do it. She'd threatened him before. The thought of attempting it made her smile.

Beside her, another nurse, Nick, raised one dark eyebrow. Her husband's words would have carried to his ears.

"Charlie's upset."

"I got that."

With one hand pressed to her lower back and the other on the counter, she stood, attempting to rub circles through the fabric of her maternity scrubs to ease the ache. The weight of her protruding stomach didn't help. Not that she blamed the baby growing inside her. Carrying wasn't easy.

Nick studied her, his blue eyes sharp with assessment. "Roadside Assistance is with May now." He twirled a pen between his fingers. "When's your maternity leave? Not to piss you off, but you don't look so good."

She grimaced. "It's a hard thing, growing a child. It'll be worth it, though." Just a bit longer. She pushed herself away from the counter and walked around to the other side of the desk. The maternity ward doors swung open.

An intern wheeled a woman in, her dark hair mussed, her eyes full of terror. Her pants clung to her legs, soaked through. Her hands clung tightly to the arms of the wheelchair. Pain etched the lines of her pale face.

Her voice came out breathy with fear. "It's coming. I can't stop it anymore."

Nick was already in motion; he took over pushing the chair.

Clara moved toward a birthing room, and they went to work.

An hour and a half later, the woman's new daughter lay asleep in the nursery. The baby had come fast, less than fifteen minutes after they got her in a gown and took her vitals.

Luck was with the woman. Dr. Schroeder had been asleep down the hall and delivered the child. Clara had delivered plenty of babies on her own, but with her own three weeks to full term, her belly in the way, it would have been awkward.

The newborn had been difficult to soothe. Clara understood too well. The world was a harsh one. Sometimes, a new life needed a bit more care than others. Clara rocked and swayed the little one while the mother slept. In a soft voice, she sang lyrics from a lullaby until the babe's tiny eyelids drifted closed.

She kept rocking.

Adoption. This baby was up for adoption. Her future parents would be here in the morning to meet her.

The birth mother held the infant for a brief time. She'd needed extra care as well. She'd torn badly in the process of delivering her daughter. With tears on her cheeks, she said, "My situation. She'll be better off without me."

Clara wanted to offer the woman a hug. Sorrow wept from her eyes. She'd seen it on too many faces—that wish that things could be different. This woman hadn't been the first to want something more for her child.

Pain moved through Clara's back, enough to make her catch her breath, to make her stop rocking.

Charlie was right. She needed to be off her feet. Maybe he could rub her back before bed.

The pain dissipated when May entered the nursery.

Clara's heart ached as she moved toward the nurses' station. She'd tried not to watch the mother as she studied the newborn's face, the hand that smoothed over the wisps of dark hair gracing her head. How she held her breath when the woman pressed her lips to the babe's forehead.

She shuffled toward the nurses' station to clock out, the last of the patient's files in her hands. Nick stood as she approached. "Take my chair. It's more comfortable." He moved, held out a hand to help her. "I called your man to come get you. You shouldn't be driving."

She didn't argue. With a nod, she moved one foot forward and then stopped.

Pain. Sharp. Ripped through her.

It slashed through her back, across her middle. A harsh cry

tore from her throat. Papers fell from her hands as she reached for Nick.

Her eyes met his as he took a firm hold of her. Another pain. Fluid rushed out of her. A cry came from deep inside her.

Nick's voice was sure and calm. "Clara, I've got you." He held onto her with strong hands; his arm came around her for support.

Her baby was coming. "I'm in labor."

He gave her a gentle smile. "I noticed." He turned his head and hollered at the top of his lungs. "I need a nurse and Dr. Schroeder now!"

The contraction lessened, but another one would come soon. It hurt more than she expected. No wonder some women screamed.

She couldn't wait to meet her son, hold him in her arms, but she was scared too. Her baby was only thirty-seven weeks. "It's too early, Nick."

"Trust us, Clara," he said. "Breathe. Scream if you need to. I'm not leaving you."

She felt the rise of the next contraction. "Charlie—"

"—On his way. He's going to get one hell of a shock when he walks in."

She focused on her breath, Nick's calm blue eyes, and the strength of his firm voice as she heard the sounds of rapid steps on the tile floor.

Chapter One

Rose ran her fingers around the edges of her latest Criminy Mystery novel while she waited. The squeak and scoot of seats being taken and murmurs amongst the audience filled the front section of Brick Wall Books. Rain pattered on the storefront windows while she studied her book cover, marveling once more at the artist's rendering. A boy with straggly red hair and a girl with two black braids down her back perched on the branch of a tree. Above them, on a higher branch, sat a raven.

From beside her on the makeshift stage, Alec Kincaid cleared his throat. She looked up.

"You ready?" His eyes held questions.

She glanced at her audience. Eight rows of middle-grade children sat on metal folding chairs between her and the new release tables. Every pair of eyes was on her, including the adults, waiting for her to start. Her stomach flipped.

He'd already introduced her to the crowd. She hadn't noticed.

"I'm ready."

"Good luck." He stepped off the stage. He'd be nearby if she needed him.

With a nod in Alec's direction, she read the first pages of her latest book aloud. Each of her words brought Ruby and Jed to life.

Within minutes, her audience sat on the edge of their chairs, their eyes and ears caught as she gathered them into her character's latest adventure. Fingers trembling, she turned a page, the twist inside her loosening as she continued.

There were no whispers or mutters among those seated. Even the parents and guardians accompanying the children kept quiet. Not a fidget among them.

That was a good sign. She took a slow breath and continued.

With the turn of another page, the feel of paper beneath her fingertips became the texture of tree bark with crevices wide enough to stick her fingers in.

It had been some years since she'd climbed trees, but writing these stories, reading them aloud, made her remember how it felt to do so. A glance at the adults around the room told her they might remember, too.

As Ruby and Jed perched on the favorite branches of an oak tree with a set of binoculars, the very image the artist captured on the front cover, she ended her reading, setting the audience up for the next chapter. A warm feeling moved through her as she closed *The Mystery of Lost Time.*

The rain hadn't eased. A gentle drumbeat tapped against the windows. Alec, the new owner of Brick Wall Books, appeared beside her once more, looking as transfixed as the children.

In a low voice, just for her ears, he said, "That was incredible."

Then he turned to the audience. "Thank you all for joining us this evening. Let's hear it for the first chapter of the latest Criminy Mystery by Miss Everson Briar."

The children cheered. He cupped his hand over one ear and raised his voice. "I can't hear you. I heard some of you think this is a library."

The children stood, jumping up and down in front of their chairs. The volume of their voices tripled.

"That is more like it. Who's ready to ask Miss Briar some questions?"

Hands raised.

Rose thanked all of them. She called on a tall, gangly boy with spiked hair in the back row.

"Which of the Criminy Mysteries is your favorite?" He spoke slowly, as if he were sounding out each word from a card he held in his hand.

She held up her latest. "*The Mystery of Lost Time.*"

"Why?" he added.

"I climbed trees in the woods as a child. I forgot how much I loved it until I started this book."

What she shared was the truth. Coming home to Evers Hollow two years ago, back to the house she'd grown up in, had sent her imagination into the trees, onto the forest paths of her childhood.

The boy gave her a thumbs up and sat down as she motioned to another child. A younger reader with light blonde pigtails and hot pink glasses stood up. "Why is there a raven on the book cover?"

Rose shook her head and laughed. "Nice try. You'll have to finish the book to find out."

The girl flopped into her seat with a frown.

"Anyone else?" A few hands went up.

Rose called on a redhead in the front row. She looked like a high-school student.

The girl stood, her posture ramrod straight, as if readying for battle. "Colette Cooper, Weekly Warbler, Evers Hollow High. Are Ruby and Jed getting married someday?"

Rose curled her fingernails into her palms. It never failed. This question was asked at every reading.

She forced a smile. "Ruby and Jed are eleven. They're not old enough to date yet."

The redhead folded her arms, glared, and spoke in a defensive tone. "I think they get married when they're older." She flipped her hair as she turned and sat down. Her statement caused a reaction. Some of the other girls nodded in agreement. A few of the boys scowled.

"What's your next book about?" asked a dark-haired Black girl from the fourth row.

Rose winked. "A mystery."

The children groaned. Pleas for hints followed until she held her hand up for silence.

"You are a fantastic audience. I love answering your questions." Except for that romance one. "How about I share something from the next book?"

The room quieted. Many of the children leaned closer.

She said, "Ruby and Jed need something different for their next mystery."

The questions came all at once.

"A real magnifying glass?"

"A ladder?"

"A metal detector?"

She held her hand up again. The sound of shushes filled the space.

Rose said, "Ruby and Jed need a sidekick."

Exclamations burst out of the children. It took more than one effort to calm them back down. There were at least a dozen hands in the air. She called on a few.

"Is it a copperhead snake? Jed could carry it in his pocket."

Another voice. "Or around his neck."

"It's not a snake." A poisonous snake as a sidekick would not go over well with the parents of her readers. Many snakes in North Carolina were poisonous.

"Is it a dragon?"

She shook her head. Children often asked if she could add a dragon to her books.

A child off to the side with a tiny voice asked, "What about a bear? They like berries. I like berries."

Rose couldn't help but grin. "I like berries too. Blackberries especially. It's not a bear, though. Ruby and Jed's new partner is a dog, a brown one."

As the children celebrated this reveal, her gaze connected with Alec's. He held up two fingers. Time for one more.

She called on a young woman, perhaps a college student, who stood off to the side.

"How do you get your ideas?"

Rose rubbed her wrists together and tilted her head.

"I grew up with a forest behind my home. The trees were my playground. When I started college, my imagination returned to the forest. I started writing. Ruby and Jed's stories came to life on the page. My dear friend, Mr. Munstead, encouraged me to publish them."

A small whisper of a voice came from the front row. "Like magic."

Rose smiled down at a little boy with missing front teeth and nodded. "It is."

Alec moved to stand beside her and spoke again. "Thank you again for attending our book reading. We have a special treat for you. Miss Briar brought Ruby and Jed's favorite mystery solving snack. If you could all make your way upstairs, we have every-thing set up."

Excited voices and the scramble of footsteps up the staircase filled the bookstore.

With her fingers, Rose traced the threads of the new patch her sister Willow had sewn over the latest tear in her favorite tartan plaid skirt, a hazard of walking in the woods and working in the garden alongside her grandmother, Magnolia. The patch had small pink flowers on it. Her fingers fluffed her long hair before she followed everyone upstairs to the coffee loft. Halfway up, she pressed her hand against the infamous three-story brick wall that inspired the store's name. It felt cool against her palm, almost damp, like the weather outside.

She loved the bookstores she visited for her readings, but this one held a special spot inside her heart.

Brick Wall Books had been a treat to visit as a child. Magnolia made a point of shopping here for books back when Alec's grandparents ran the store.

Rose moved about the loft, talking with her readers. A black pen stayed between her fingers so she could sign copies of her books as she wound through tables and chairs. Some children hugged her; others had more questions. She posed for photos when asked.

Alec made his way toward her from the other side of the loft. He was an attractive, lean man with piercing blue eyes, dark hair, and a light amount of facial scruff. Rose watched as he answered every question from each potential customer. It was the way his grandparents ran the store. Since he'd taken over, he did the same.

He pushed his black-rimmed glasses up his nose when he reached her, a look of astonishment in his eyes. "I can't believe you brought the actual cookies."

She nudged him and smiled. "Only for your store, Alec. I've got a special bond with Brick Wall Books. I've told you that."

"They'd never know the difference."

"But I would." She glanced around the cheerful space, at young faces with cookie crumbs stuck to the corners of their mouths. "That matters."

"My gran is going to lay into me all over again."

"Because your gran loves me."

"And wants you to have her great-grandchildren."

"That'll never happen." There was no regret in her voice. One date had made that clear.

"It'd be easier if it could."

She shrugged.

He folded his arms, a serious expression on his face. "Someday, I want to meet Jed. Give him a solid fist to the face."

She had to fight a smile. "Jed is an eleven-year-old fictional character."

"Bull—"

She smacked him on the arm. "Language."

He offered a quirky grin. "Like they haven't heard it before."

She lightly smacked his arm again.

An hour later, Rose rubbed the ink stains on her fingers as she waited for Alec to lock up the store. They always went to dinner together after her readings. The store smelled of paper and wood now that all the customers were gone. Beneath the dimmed lighting, she could make out the comfortable chairs set throughout the first floor.

She heard Alec's shuffling gait moving toward her.

"All set?" He jangled his keys while his fingers hovered over the final light switch for the downstairs.

Rose nodded and lifted her canvas messenger bag over her head and shoulder as they stepped into the night. Rain coated the sidewalks and streets.

Alec slung his arm around her shoulders as they crossed the road. "Tell me again why you won't give us a second chance?"

"Because you can't kiss worth a damn." She poked him in his side. He flinched and let go.

"You're the only one who's complained. I've got skills and really long fingers." He held up one hand to demonstrate.

She laughed and brushed past him when he opened the door into Mad Dogs Brewery. A cheerful hostess bedazzled in suspenders and Hello Kitty badges seated them at a high-top table. Steel-gray light fixtures lit the place. A wooden bar ran the length of the closest wall. Customers filled the row of round red barstools.

When the server came by, Rose picked a beer off the menu, along with chicken fingers and sweet potato fries. After her pint of porter arrived, she took an inch off the top of the frosty mug.

Alec said. "We'd be perfect together, Rose. An ideal relationship."

She wished he would let this go. It was never going to happen. "Without love? Without chemistry?"

It was his turn to shrug. "Less complicated."

She tapped one pink-painted fingernail on the table. "I told you—I want chemistry. I want love. Our one kiss said everything. We have no spark."

"Damn. That's not a cool thing to say." He drank two inches off the top of his own beer.

"Not to mention—you're chaos—how many piles of books do you have in your apartment now?"

He ran a hand over his scruff and narrowed his eyes. "Sixty-two?"

"Case closed."

"I own a bookstore. I'm a writer."

"Buy some bookshelves already."

He stabbed a French fry in a circle of ketchup. "Fine. Tell me about Jed."

"There is no Jed."

"I'll figure it out. Nobody writes stories like that without having inspiration from real people. Ruby is you through and through."

She ate another chicken finger.

"What about your dedication in every book?" Alec said. "*For my best friend, a little boy who once thought girls were disgusting.*"

She may have growled at him. Her words sounded corny coming from his mouth. So what if she dedicated all of her books to the same person? The stories wouldn't exist without him.

Her cell phone rang. A quick glance at her watch made her frown. It was after nine o'clock. She slipped her phone out of her bag's front pocket. She sucked in a breath when she saw her phone screen.

Four missed calls. Multiple texts. All of them from her siblings.

Hands shaking, she slid off her chair and said. "I'll be right back."

Her fingers touched the screen to call her brother, Broome.

He picked up immediately. "Rose?"

"What's wrong?"

Chapter Two

F inn raked his fingers through his hair as he left his bedroom. He shuffled barefoot into his tiny, outdated kitchen. One streetlight lit up the small space through the window over the sink. All else was dark. He glanced at the oven clock. Three-thirty. Only four hours since he'd left his shift at the hospital and crashed on the rectangle he called a bed.

He pulled the pot out from the coffeemaker. At least a cup's worth of yesterday's sludge sat at the bottom. He tilted the pot toward the streetlight. Nothing floating. He grabbed a mug from the cabinet. Ninety seconds later, he removed a steaming mug from the microwave.

Finn took the few steps from the kitchen into the area that management called a family room in their floor plans. The space barely housed the green loveseat he'd taken from his parents' house and the darker green recliner he'd purchased when he'd moved in. A twist of his fingers clicked a crooked twenty-dollar floor lamp on. He should have left it off.

Cardboard boxes filled the space in front of him, stacked two and three high. All were from the attic of his childhood home, most of them his mother's. He pressed one hand to the back of his neck as he drank from the steaming mug.

Three months ago, his pa decided to move into a retirement community. His reasons were smart ones. He'd struggled back home in Evers Hollow after a broken hip didn't heal right. Finn lived an hour away and was in the middle of his medical residency. The neighbors had helped, but it hadn't been enough.

Beau from Pa's old bowling team had been the one to pitch the idea. Great food, no home repairs, and no cleaning. The kicker—he could play cards all day, Pa's favorite pastime.

More recently, Pa brought up the idea of selling the old house. He asked Finn to handle it.

"I've got it all worked out. You can take care of everything."

Lucky Finn. As if he had free time.

Ridding the house of its remaining contents to get it ready to put on the market took what little he had. Finn was an only child. He'd spent days off driving to Evers Hollow to empty and sort what was left in the old place. Multiple runs to local charities had rid him of his pa's car magazines, paperbacks, and old clothing. He found an awards shop that recycled shelves of dust-ridden bowling trophies. The attic, though, was full of his mother's things.

His last trip, he'd brought back a load of her boxes here to his small apartment.

Each box waited its turn.

"It's up to you to decide," Pa had said when Finn asked him about her things. *"I'm too old to revisit the past."*

Pa was only fifty-eight. His attitude was probably how the boxes ended up in the attic. Pa was an emotional sort—his grief still too painful to deal with in the years since his Clara had passed.

The faded black of his mom's handwriting beckoned in the lamplight. His hand returned to his neck, as if the pressure would somehow lessen the list of things he needed to deal with. So many boxes.

Bed beckoned. The streets outside were quiet. They'd remain so for a few more hours. Instead, he sipped murky liquid until only the dregs remained, foul and gum-like on his teeth.

Finn brewed a fresh pot and poured himself a new cup. It didn't taste much better. He turned a second lamp on before setting the mug on the old wooden trunk centered in the room, another relic from the old house. He grabbed his pocketknife off the top and directed the blade through the tape on the closest box.

Nursing books. He took them all out, then put them back in to be sure. He labeled it and put the box by the door. The next one held his soccer trophies and his old soccer jerseys. He left it open, moved it to an empty corner of the room.

He opened another. A single piece of newspaper lay on top. Beneath it sat a stack of photos, a red ribbon tied in a knot around them. Caught by the top image of himself as a baby in his mom's arms, he lifted the bundle out. His fingers slid the ribbon off as he moved to his recliner. A smile lit up her features, her strawberry blonde hair secured by a knotted headband. Even in a photo, her brown eyes sparkled. Her smile, her love, and pride rang clear in every line of her face.

She'd carried a subtle beauty that drew people to her, especially in her work as a pediatric nurse at Hollow's Hospital. Everyone who'd met her loved her. He trailed a fingertip around the edges of her face. Fourteen years since they'd lost her to stage IV breast cancer. It still twisted his heart.

Finn shuffled through the next prints, came across one of him and his pa beside an old Chevy truck, his motorized blue baby. He'd spent hours working on that truck. Finn and his mom took turns bringing him glasses of sun tea and handing him tools on long ago weekends.

The last photo was a family one, taken before she got sick.

Finn carried a worn copy of this one in his wallet and kept it as his screensaver on his laptop. They'd been a happy family of three.

He tied the ribbon to secure the photos and reached for the next item in the box.

Another bundle of photos, also tied in red. His fingers froze when he saw the top one. He sank farther back into his seat as a different sort of ache squeezed his heart. The image of his own gangly, mop-headed self next to a dark-haired little girl with two long braids.

His best friend.

In the picture, his own freckled face faced the camera. The girl looked sideways at him. She often had.

Emotions assaulted him—the good, the bad, and the part of him he still considered broken. He hadn't figured out how to put himself back together. Had she?

He took a long sip of coffee.

Six years old. They'd become friends at his first Memorial Day barbecue at Briar House.

Finn and his folks had just moved to Evers Hollow. Locals told them the barbecue was tradition to honor the soldiers who'd fought in the wars of long ago. He'd looked for boys to play with among all the pine, cedar, and oak trees. He'd only found Rose.

Friends with a girl—as a six-year-old—the idea had been disgusting. Dressed in a frilly pink dress and shiny black shoes, Rose sat on the top stair of her grandmother's porch and stared at him. Her two braids framed her face as she propped her elbows on her knees.

He'd looked everywhere but at her until she'd marched down those steps, grabbed his hand, and shook it like a cooked noodle. It felt like fireworks inside his arm. He wasn't sure he liked it, but she held on tight.

Her older frilly sisters sat in chairs, also in pink, with sour frowns. He could still hear the oldest one's voice in that tone that said she was better than everyone else. *"Rose, you promised not to get dirty."*

Rose had flipped her braids around and glared up at them. *"You promised I wouldn't get dirty. I said no such thing."*

Then she'd pulled him with her away from the house.

"Come on," she said. "We have to hide from the soldiers."

"Soldiers. What soldiers?" Finn looked around, seeing no one in uniform.

"The Redcoats are coming." She tugged on him as she crouched down.

Girls didn't play Revolutionary War, but...

"I got shot in my leg." He limped a bit. "I can't crouch down."

"Criminy, we'll have to find another hiding place."

Finn looked around; she still held his hand. "What about that big tree over there?"

Rose popped up like a jack-in-the-box. She nudged him, offered a toothless grin, and whispered, "Great choice, quick, let's run for it."

"I can't run; you go ahead. I'll catch up." Maybe he could still find some boys to play with.

"I won't leave you behind. Here, lean on me." Rose wrapped her arm around his waist.

He tried to back away; his clothes were covered with dirt. "I'll get your dress dirty." He didn't like girls, but he didn't want her getting in trouble.

"There's no time to argue. Our lives depend on it." She put his arm across her shoulders. "Let's go."

Once behind the tree, she let go of him, and they sagged against the foot-wide trunk, breathing hard.

"I'm Rose Everson Finch." Her voice was soft, cheerful as she looked him up and down. "This is my grandmother's house. What's your name?"

"Finn. Finn Murphy." He peeked around the tree. His

parents were talking with other folks. His mom was holding a baby.

"I never heard that name before." Her face scrunched up like a dried prune.

His face felt hot. "My pa picked it. It's Irish."

"My mom gave me my name. She's not here anymore."

"Oh." He knew that from Mr. Hal, but he didn't know what to say, so he looked at his shoes. Streaks of mud ran across the tops, caked the sides. "How do you know about Redcoats?" He tilted his head and studied her. Her face looked different, like her tummy hurt.

"My dad told me stories—he was a history teacher. He's gone too."

"Mr. Hal told me about your folks. It's a sad thing." It's what his pa would say.

"Thanks." Rose gave him a gentle smile. "You know Mr. Hal?"

"I do. Met him last week." He hoped he sounded important.

Rose sat down against the tree, folded her legs like a pretzel. He did the same.

"Mr. Hal's a vet. He takes care of Grandmother's horses. Want to meet them? Lady is beautiful. You have to see her."

Finn met the horses that day. He and Rose ate homemade strawberry ice cream and hot dogs. Then they'd caught frogs in the creek that ran through the woods.

Rose's grandmother had been angry about the mud on her dress. Ms. Magnolia's words and tone rang clear in his ears even after all this time: *"Young ladies do not play with frogs."*

The mud on Rose's dress proved otherwise, but a warning look from his mom kept him from talking back.

Finn moved to the next photo, another of the two of them, a little older. The porch swing at Briar House on a rainy day, Rose with her floral rain boots and her two braids. She'd always worn floral rain boots. His were dark blue.

He shuffled through the rest of the stack. Their entire friendship sat in his hands as a stack of two-dimensional photos. He reached into the box again to discover a second identical set with a note tucked beneath the ribbon.

For Rose.

Clearly, his mother intended to give these to her.

Mom was sweet like that every day of her life. She treated Rose as if she were one of her own. Called the two of them *inseparable adorables,* a name she'd coined that he found a bit embarrassing and difficult to say.

Finn picked up the duplicate stack, set it away from the other. His mom would want her to have them, even if his last conversation with Rose formed cracks between them. They hadn't spoken since.

Today was a day off. He'd made plans to visit his pa around lunch and meet with a real estate agent in Evers Hollow around dinnertime. He could find time to drop by Briar House and figure out how to give Rose the photos.

Surely someone knew where she lived. He hadn't been to the house in years, not since the day after the last Everson New Year's Eve party he'd attended.

He reached into the box again. His baby book. He'd forgotten about it. His mom had added his school photos and awards to its pages through the years. It would take a while to go through. He set it aside for later.

A couple of leather bound journals lay at the bottom. He flipped through them. Mom's handwriting filled the pages along with photos stuck in between. He set them on top of his baby book. They would have to wait as well.

If he was going to drive to Evers Hollow today, he needed to get a run in, shower, and get on the road. He'd call Pa to remind him he'd be dropping by Wylder Ridge Community.

Chapter Three

It was late afternoon when Finn turned his SUV onto the straight gravel drive of Briar House.

He climbed the few wide steps to the wraparound front porch and knocked on the large, faded maroon door. His last visit, he'd been turned away. That had been six years ago.

A young woman he didn't recognize answered the door. Was it possible the battle-axe housekeeper had retired? With a soft Southern accent, she welcomed him in and then showed him to the morning room. The late afternoon sun came in through all five windows in the octagonal-shaped space.

Furniture seemed randomly placed, with chairs, small tables, and a strange yellow couch that reminded him of a kidney. He'd never sat in this room. He and Rose spent their time outdoors, in the kitchen, or in the house's library.

He heard voices and turned back towards the door. Magnolia Everson-Brooks, matriarch of the Everson family and Rose's grandmother, walked into the room with the help of a cane while the young woman stood watchful behind her before leaving them alone.

As a boy, he feared this woman. As an adult, she looked frailer and smaller than he remembered. She wore black slacks and a white silk shirt. Silver jewelry decorated her throat and wrists. Her hair still looked like that of a sorceress, dark like Rose's, but with silver streaks throughout.

She paused in front of him. Her eyes, green like Rose's, narrowed. "You."

Her voice was exactly as he remembered—crisp, sharp, and a tad scary.

He nodded. "Good morning, Ms. Magnolia. How are you?"

She took a seat in a blue upholstered chair, both her hands on top of her cane as she looked him up and down. "It's been a long time."

"Yes, ma'am, it has." He stood still, waiting for her to finish her appraisal. Her eyes had always been like a bird of prey's. They missed nothing when he was a child playing with her granddaughter. He suspected that ability hadn't gone away with age.

"How are your studies?"

The question shouldn't surprise him. His recent trip into town had fed the gossip vine. "Going well. I'm in the middle of my residency."

He'd avoided the town he'd grown up in. For some time now. Only his trips to visit Pa brought him close. Until recently, those visits had been rare. The retirement community Pa lived in sat on the southern outskirts of Evers Hollow, eleven miles from the town center.

With Pa's sudden decision to sell the old house, they'd needed a real estate agent. There was no better source of info than the small group of men and women known as The Elders. Finn had driven in, stopped by their usual table at the Cracked Egg Cafe last week. Although Ms. Magnolia was one of them, she'd been absent.

She laid her cane against her chair, one hand still on it. Her lips pursed as he shuffled his feet.

"You're too tall." She motioned towards the odd-shaped couch. "Be seated. Tell me what brings you to my door."

He dropped himself onto the piece of furniture she indicated. It felt like a brick. Her tone reminded him of long ago lectures on *journeys into misconduct,* as she'd termed his and Rose's childhood adventures. He still had the scars on his right hand from when they decided to capture a raven to train as their own. Not their smartest idea.

"Well," she prodded.

"Ms. Magnolia—"

"You're an adult now. Call me Magnolia."

He nodded and continued. "I'd like to get in touch with Rose."

She turned her gaze towards the five windows.

"It's important." He caught the wince she gave as her head turned back. He pressed his hands to his knees to keep them still. What if she said no?

"I know you and she had a falling out of sorts a bit ago." There was a hardness in her eyes when she looked at him, a biting edge to her tone.

"That's true." He had to be honest.

"Did you know, the summer I took her to England, after her high school graduation, Rose mailed you a postcard from every village and city we visited? She spent more money on postage for you than on souvenirs for herself."

That was likely true as well. Every postcard and letter she'd sent still lay in a metal tin inside a drawer of his nightstand. When she'd returned, she'd sent regular letters, along with cookies, throughout his military training, his first assignment, and his first deployment. He had not been as good a correspondent.

He tightened his jaw and met the older woman's gaze.

There was something unreadable in her expression. Her next words were softer. "You still have them."

He didn't look away. "Yes, ma'am." The letters meant something to him. As did Rose. There was no point in denying it.

His answer seemed to satisfy her.

"Your mother was a wonderful woman. Cancer is an elusive evil. I imagine this is why you study medicine."

"It is."

"Clara did something significant for me once. I hoped I would have the opportunity to return the gesture."

She stood. He did the same.

"Rose is more of a private person now." She offered an apologetic smile before she moved toward the faceted array of windows. "I'll take your information down. I'll make sure she receives it." She paused in front of a large writing desk.

His shoulders slumped. He knew this might happen. After all, Rose was married. Her husband wouldn't like Finn reaching out. Especially after their last conversation.

"Take heart, young man. I've always liked you. Even that scandal causing father of yours. I'll make sure she sees your details. I suggest patience. She hasn't forgotten you, but contacting you will be up to her."

He should have expected this. He took in the view, saw one of many paths that went into the woods along with the rose garden. How many times had he walked over while Rose worked amongst her namesake, a large straw hat shading her face?

The older woman rummaged through the shallow desk drawers, muttering. "Where's my box of pens?"

Framed photographs sat on the corners of the desk. Wedding ones. He couldn't help himself. He moved closer.

He recognized the family one from Broome and Simi's wedding. He'd attended that one, stood and waited for Rose while the family posed for a ridiculous number of photos. Rose was beautiful in a pale pink dress, her happiness for her oldest brother and his new wife infectious. They'd danced together more than once that night. He'd wanted to kiss her.

It hadn't happened.

His gaze moved to the next frame. The bride had dark hair. He held his breath as he took in the image, then let it out.

It wasn't Rose. Instead, her oldest sister Aspen stood in a frilly, fluffy, white dress, her hair swirled on top of her head, a bouquet of yellow and orange flowers in her hand.

The scent of floral perfume and cherry cough drops drifted towards him as Magnolia straightened. "Do you remember my oldest granddaughter? Aspen married the oldest Roche son, Gavin. Do you know the family?"

"I do." He didn't elaborate. His acquaintance with the Roche's wasn't a nice story. She looked at him as if she expected more.

He forced a nod. "Congratulations. I hope their day was a happy one." He meant what he said, despite the fact that he'd never gotten along with Rose's oldest sister. Of all the Finch kids, Aspen had always been the one to look down her nose at him.

The older woman touched the top of the frame. "They had a May wedding. They're expecting their first child."

She picked up another of the whole family and handed it to him. It would be rude for him to refuse. He forced himself to take the frame. Rose stood at one end in a dark yellow dress, her hair up. He couldn't hold back a slight smile at the memory of her hatred of yellow clothing. She must have been furious, yet she still looked beautiful. He could admit that to himself, even if it felt like a torn hamstring.

He realized Ms. Magnolia was talking, likely had been for the last minute.

"Simi is pregnant again. She told me last night. Hard to

believe." She took the frame from his hands and set it back in place. "Due in April."

"Glad to hear it." His eyes found Broome, Simi, and three children in another frame attached to the wall. Two girls and an infant boy, each a blend of their parent's features. Simi's straight black hair adorned their heads. He looked at the other pictures on the wall, but didn't see—

Ms. Magnolia gasped. He turned and narrowed his eyes. She stood unmoving in front of the windows. She'd been so animated a second ago.

"Ms. Magnolia?" Her face had paled. She didn't respond. Her stillness, her lack of color, forced him closer to see what affected her so. Out the window, beyond the rose garden, a man moved along the edge of the surrounding woods. He had white hair. Finn didn't recognize him.

He looked back at her. She hadn't moved. He heard a rasp of words from her lips before she swayed.

"Ms. Magnolia!" He caught her as she slumped towards him and carried her towards the kidney-shaped couch. Her eyes fluttered as she looked up at him, tried to speak.

"The lights—in the woods." Her voice strained with effort, more of a rattle, with a tone that made his skin crawl.

"What lights?" He set her down gently. His fingers moved to her wrist as he glanced at the second hand on his watch, counting. Her skin felt hot, feverish. "Ms. Magnolia—who was that man? Talk to me. Tell me about the lights."

Her eyes drifted shut. He called her name again. She didn't respond. He hollered for help. The young woman who'd shown him into the room rushed in.

"Call 9-1-1. I need an ambulance."

She pulled out her cell phone.

Finn cursed under his breath.

"Ms. Magnolia!" Her eyes fluttered, came open again.

Wheezing sounds came out of her as if each breath was a struggle.

"He's back." Her hand swung up, grabbed hold of his arm. Her eyes held a desperate look. "Promise me."

Finn nodded.

She blinked and took a rattling breath. Her grip lessened. "You—have to—protect Rose." Her head fell back as she lost consciousness.

Chapter Four

Rose rushed through a pair of sliding doors just after ten pm, pushing her hair out of her face. The smell of antiseptic and sterile air hit her as the doors whooshed closed behind her. This wasn't her first trip to Asheville Community Hospital. Two years prior, Magnolia suffered a stroke, which instigated Rose's move back to Evers Hollow.

A text came in from Broome. They were on the fourth floor. Rose hurried to the elevator bank, tapping her fingers on her bag as she waited.

One bay dinged as its doors slid open. Rose stepped aside as people unloaded. She adjusted her canvas messenger bag on her shoulder and looked up as the last person stepped out.

Her heart stuttered when he glanced in her direction. With a breathy gasp, his name slipped out before she could take it back.

"Finn?" She gripped her bag a little tighter.

The man stopped. When he turned around, a jolt went through her.

Finn Murphy stood six feet away. His eyes were the same as she remembered—dark pools of brown that drew her in, like her favorite brand of chocolate. His reddish-brown hair had darkened a tad over the years, but still carried that unkempt, windswept look. Her fingers itched. Was it as soft as she remembered?

He wore faded jeans and a navy sweater, its sleeves pushed up short of his elbows. A backpack rested on one shoulder.

It felt like forever since she'd seen him. A forever that shattered her heart. Otherwise, she would have hugged him. She couldn't decide if that was wise. Something twisted inside her, an odd sort of pressure in her chest.

She wasn't sure which of them moved first, but she found herself within reach of him. It would be easier to look the other way, pretend the man who stood before her meant nothing. She needed to get to Magnolia.

Manners though, they were in her somewhere. Ingrained by the woman who lay upstairs in a hospital bed. She should say something. Anything. Before she rushed to the fourth floor.

Her thoughts faltered. What could she say? The last time, words had broken everything.

He spoke first, with sympathy in his eyes. "Broome, the rest of your family, they're upstairs. They'll tell you what you need to know." He shifted on his feet. "I'm sorry. I can't stay. Got to get home—I have an early shift."

She couldn't help it; the exhausted part of her questioned if he was even real. She reached out to touch his forearm, found it warm and muscled. Again, her insides twisted.

"It's good to see you, Finn." There. She said words. Courteous ones. Whether she believed them, whether he would, she'd think on that later.

He didn't move, merely looked back at her with unreadable eyes. "It's good to see you, too."

She let go. The elevator had left. She turned and pressed the button to call it again. She wouldn't watch him leave. Or think about how she felt seeing him after so long.

Her goal: get upstairs, see her grandmother, and ignore the

somersault extravaganza inside her. A glance told her he hadn't moved. Hadn't he said he needed to leave? He stood close enough to rub against if she wished. His attention was on his backpack, his hand inside, as if searching for something.

She tried to focus on the closed elevator doors, willing them to open.

Finn pulled a small rectangular parcel out of his bag and held it out to her. "Here. This is for you."

Rose hesitated. Talk about weird. "What is it?"

"It's how I ended up here. I found these this morning. Take them, please. My mom wanted you to have them despite—"

Despite what happened between them. Her throat felt clogged. She took the package, but he didn't let go. Instead, he moved his other hand over hers and squeezed. "I hope your grandmother will be okay. I'll see you soon." He stepped back.

"How do you know about—" But he was gone.

The elevator opened. She stepped inside and looked down at the parcel. Rectangular, flexible, and close to the size of her hand. Whatever was inside—she couldn't deal with right now, not when she knew nothing of Magnolia's current condition. She slipped it into her bag.

Rose pushed the circular number four as the doors slid closed. She leaned her head against the back wall as the elevator moved upward.

Finn Murphy. Here. The last person she needed to think about.

When she stepped out, Rose spotted Willow pacing up and down a tiled hallway in front of an ivory and light blue wall. Clad in yoga pants and a faded green hoodie, Willow had one thumb shoved just inside her lower lip, her nail likely bitten down to the quick with the amount of worry on her face.

In a loud whisper, Rose said her name. Her sister looked up.

Willow rushed towards her and threw her arms around her. "You made it."

Rose hugged her back. "What happened? Is she okay?"

Willow eased away. Her eyes were glassy, concern prominent in her expression. "She had another stroke. She has a fever. They're running tests."

"Is she awake?"

She shook her head. Rose followed her to the waiting room, where most of the family sat.

Broome stood first and hugged her. His voice was low when he spoke. "Glad you made it safe. I won't sugarcoat things. She's not well. High fever. They're trying to bring it down. I sent Aspen and Gavin back to Briar House to sleep in her old room. She's too close to her due date to sit in these chairs. She spent some time with Grandmother, though. Thorne's in with her now."

Rose pulled away from him, a knot of disbelief formed inside her. "But I just saw her. I had tea and scones with her this morning. She looked tired, coughed some, but insisted she was fine. Sassy and stubborn. She practically kicked me out the door to go to my readings."

"I only know what the doctors have told me," Broome said. "Grandmother's a stubborn little warrior. She'll fight as best as she can."

Rose stepped back, wiped her fingers beneath her eyes before she took a seat near Willow. This was all wrong. Magnolia had to be okay. There was no other option.

An hour later, she traded places with Thorne. His hug conveyed his worry, his fear. Hers, concern and panic.

She stepped inside the room as quiet as she could. The whir of machines filled the room. Magnolia looked small in the hospital bed. Her dark, silver-streaked hair had been brushed to one side, and each of her arms lay atop the blankets covering her. They had her on supplemental oxygen through her nose, and there was an IV in one arm. Hesitant and frightened, Rose took a seat in the chair beside the bed and wove her fingers gently between her grandmother's.

This wasn't her first stroke, but seeing her here like this, something felt different.

She didn't wish to wake her, but wanted to let her know she was here. In soft tones, she said, "Hey Gran, it's Rose. I'm going to sit with you for a bit. We need you to wake up and give us some sass."

There was no response. She watched her for a bit, comforted by the sight of her chest rising with each breath. A nurse came in to check her vitals. When she left, Rose leaned her head on the side of the bed and kept her hand intertwined. "I'll be here when you wake up."

Finn's image came to mind. She willed it away. All her mental strength needed to go to Magnolia. She needed to concentrate in order to do that.

But it had been a long day. Rose read at two school libraries in Asheville before coming back toward Evers Hollow. She drifted off with the memory of how warm Finn's arm had felt beneath her hand.

A kink in her neck woke her. A hint of sunlight lit the room enough for her to see that Magnolia's eyes were open and blinking. Rose stood up from her seat, wobbly from rising so fast.

"Magnolia? Can you hear me?"

"Of course I can hear you. I'm not deaf." Her voice sounded raspy and frail, yet still carried the bite she was known around town for. "Where the hell am I?"

"Asheville Community Hospital." Rose wiped away the tears that filled the corners of her eyes. "It's good to see you awake, Gran." She emphasized the last word.

"Impertinent child. You call me Magnolia."

Rose smiled through her tears. "I know. I'm checking to see if you know your name."

She gave her one of her infamous glares that said her humor was not appreciated.

Rose didn't ask how she felt. She was a woman who despised such questions. The doctor would have a hard time when they dropped by next.

She squeezed her hand gently. "I need to tell the others you're awake. We've been so worried."

"They can wait." She coughed and winced, accepting a sip of water from a nearby cup with help.

Rose said, "It's beautiful out—sunny. When you're better, we'll get you back to the rose garden, get you some fresh air. I'll just be a second."

"Rebel." Her nickname for how often Rose had gotten into trouble as a child. "Sit down."

With the words came that look, one that made her sit immediately.

"We need to talk." Magnolia paused, sent her a look of regret.

Rose swallowed. The fear she'd felt when she walked into the room came back.

Magnolia's gaze settled on hers. "First, Clara's boy, Finn. He dropped by."

The twisty feeling inside her returned. "He came by the house?"

"Yes, he caught me."

"Caught you?" Clearly, she was missing vital information about what happened yesterday.

"Brigette saw him last week, spoke with him…"

"I saw him. Downstairs." Rose's fingers curled in her lap, twisting into the fabric of her skirt.

"Excellent."

She shook her head as if she were a small child. It had been six years since she'd laid eyes on Finn Murphy. Days, months, years had gone by without an apology, with no attempt at amends for how he'd acted the night of her family's New Year's Eve party, after Caleb had proposed.

Finn should have been happy for her. He was her best friend. Instead, he'd been the opposite. His actions, his words that night—no one had said his name in years.

As if sensing her turmoil, Magnolia reached out. Rose placed her hand in hers.

"Did you never wonder why you broke your engagement to Caleb?"

She couldn't answer. Magnolia knew well why she broke things off.

The hand around hers tightened. "You care for Finn Murphy; you always have."

Rose looked down, an attempt to hide the truth from her discerning gaze.

Magnolia squeezed gently. "I've read your books. All of them. It's in there, this last one especially—love letters, every single one."

Rose's next words came out tight, pained. She could not allow her to think—

"My books are not love letters. We were friends."

Magnolia gave her a wane smile before she continued, her voice still raspy. "You broke your arm after climbing that tree to find the raven's nest, just like the girl in your book. The blanket sling the boy made—that yellow blanket is still in your closet upstairs."

"Inspiration from real life—that's all. You would do the same if you wrote books."

After another cough, this one sharper, Magnolia said. "Do not get me started—" She coughed again. "—your previous four."

"He's never apologized for the things he said to me."

"He will."

Rose wouldn't say his name. Once tonight was enough. Instead, with calm, she said, "I haven't seen him. Not since—"

"I know." Understanding hung between them.

Rose let go and leaned her head on the bed. She felt the brush of Magnolia's fingers on her hair, just like the night she'd finally shared what happened between her and Finn.

They hadn't spoken of it again until now.

Magnolia's voice sounded off, but her words were clear. "Not everyone gets a chance to fix their misunderstandings, Rebel. I want you to have your happy ever after."

Her fingers tightened on her scalp. She coughed again. Rose sat up. It stopped after a long sequence, but the sound concerned her. There was a wheeze and a rattle to it that hadn't been there yesterday. Surely a stroke couldn't aggravate a cold.

Rose helped her with more water, raised the head of her bed some. "Do you want me to get the nurse?" Her finger hovered over the call button.

She shook her head. "No."

Her grandmother was one of the strongest women she knew, the head of the Everson family. A woman who'd lived through more sorrow than most yet still raised five grandchildren to adulthood.

When she met Rose's eyes with her own, tears gathered in her eyes. "I'm not ready."

Rose wasn't sure if she meant getting the nurse or something worse, something she didn't want to think of.

"I have things—to take care of. Promises. Confessions. My own apologies." Her face was serious, as if her words meant something.

They made little sense. They were, in Magnolia's own words, dramatic. Unlike her.

"Rebel. Be careful. The woods—stay out." She coughed. "Lights, evil, you must be—"

The next cough stopped her words. Rose helped her with more water, fear and dread filling her. Evil? Lights?

When Magnolia spoke again, her voice sounded even weaker. "I need—"

"Anything." Rose took hold of her hand again. Her fingers felt so cold. She looked at the monitor, alarmed. Her temperature was 103.4 degrees. She needed to get the nurse.

"Call Brigette and Jeremy. I need—" Another cough broke her speech. She wanted her closest friends. Rose moved her hand to her back as she curled upward, with the hope it would help.

The door to the room opened. A nurse entered. "Ah, our patient's awake."

Broome followed close behind.

Rose held her till the coughing stopped, then leaned over her. "I'll call them. In the meantime, I—we—need you to get better."

Magnolia held fast to her hand and gave a slight pull. Once more, she struggled to get her words out. Rose leaned closer to hear better.

"Get me some proper—"

Rose finished for her. "Tea—I'll take care of it."

But she wasn't done. She still wouldn't let go.

It was clear the nurse needed to step in, do something for her, but stubborn as Magnolia was, she held on while she tried to catch her breath and her strength to speak again.

Rose glanced at Broome and didn't like what she saw there. His expression was grim.

She liked nothing she saw in this room. If only there was a wall of windows she could open and bring in the fresh air her grandmother loved to take in every morning after breakfast.

Magnolia gave a scratchy exhale, her words hard to hear. "Rebel—I love you. Remember."

Her words sent tears down Rose's cheeks. She tried to blink them back. She had to be strong. And follow through with what

Magnolia asked. She leaned forward and kissed her on the fore-head. "I love you too."

The nurse spoke. "Miss, I need you to step away from the bed. I need to see to my patient."

With one more kiss to her forehead, she eased away from Magnolia. Her hand felt empty as she stepped back.

With a nod to Broome, she slipped out. The waiting area, its soft light and uncomfortable chairs, stood quiet ahead of her. She walked past her dozing sister and other brother. When she found an empty space down the hall, she pulled out her phone, took a breath, and dialed Brigette and Jeremy Conroy, two of Magno-lia's closest friends.

It took less than two minutes for her to tell Brigette what happened.

"I'll bring the tea. Jeremy will bring the other Elders."

Rose didn't know what to say, but Brigette must have heard it in her voice. "You hang in there now. If there's a way for Nola to beat this, she will."

Rose hung up the phone, leaned against the wall, and wiped her eyes with her sleeves.

Chapter Five

The man in the mirror bore little resemblance to the face he remembered. He ran a lean hand through his sparse shock of white hair. Noted how loose his clothes hung.

He'd dreamt of her again, his redheaded fire-girl.

She'd been there, his first time, at seven years old. An accident.

It had been the start of a lifelong love. The lure, the beauty, the striking figure the flames made.

Fire-girl's face was smudged with soot. She removed her helmet, her curls a cascade of red against her yellow-striped black uniform. She looked beautiful, much like his mother. He told her so.

She snorted, "Yeah, kid—I look like a frigging princess."

He nodded. "A Princess of Fire. Your hair, it's pretty."

She cocked her head and studied him. "Princess of Fire, huh?"

He swallowed and nodded. "Your castle's built of fire. I'll build it for you."

She squatted down. Her tone was no longer playful. Instead, it was serious, like his mother's.

"I'd rather be a Wizard of Fire. I could control the flames then, keep them from hurting and scaring the animals that lived here."

He looked beyond her and all around. Wisps of smoke rose from the black-dusted ground. Skeletal black fingers reached upward as if in celebration. So thin, unsure whether they'd fall or stand, but excited all the same.

Fire-girl's voice was sharp. "Do you understand what I'm saying?"

A fist pounded on the bathroom door, an angry voice. "I gotta take a piss."

A reminder that he'd lost the freedom to make his own choices.

He cursed the image in the mirror, cursed those who brought him here. Then opened the door. The burly asshole shoved past him, forced him out. The door remained open. The sound and smell of dehydrated piss followed him to the kitchen.

This place was not for him. Neither was prison. Bitterness burned inside him as he thought of the years wasted. He'd been forced to live with men that were no better than dogs.

There were flies in the kitchen. One of the screens had a hole. In and out they flew.

The two skeletal men at the table made no move to close the window or clean up the dishes stacked in the sink. The flies hovered over the dried-on food as they would over a deer carcass.

Mom wouldn't like this.

He muttered about the vice of laziness as he marched over to the window above the sink and slammed it shut. They didn't notice. Not even when he yanked open the dishwasher and shoved the sink contents into the racks, poured soap into its compartment, and started the machine.

Living here had been his only option. His decrepit has-been

father said so. The cops who'd brought him here agreed. His probation officer also echoed their words.

The same probation officer who said if he slipped him twenty-dollars, he'd look the other way if he needed to take a walk or something.

It was the *or something* that drew him.

The others took advantage of the deal, came back reeking of perfume, sex, and sweat. He had other plans. Paid the twenty, took walks, did his own version of *or something*. Reveled in the news coverage of flashing lights, shiny red trucks, and uniforms.

He'd waited years, pacing the perimeter of the rectangle of grass he'd been permitted to walk on. He promised the man he'd once been that he'd finish what he started back when his hair held color and his shoulders weren't so stooped.

No one on his parole board saw that he still dreamed, had plans. They believed every word he spoke about the past.

I'm aware of the pain I caused.

Even the shrink declared him rehabilitated, safe to return to society.

Crackling crowns, hissing trees. His dream, a high like no other.

The fine aftermath sifted through his fingers. A cascade of shiny black waves over his hands.

He would have it all.

Especially his unforgotten dark muse. He'd pay another twenty dollars, take a longer walk, another bus ride. He'd deliver another gift, watch her reaction, from the trees. It had been too long since he'd heard the chorus she brought to his work.

His dream came to mind. Fire-girl's last words echoed as she crouched at eye level with him.

Tell me something, little guy. Do you still have matches in your pockets?

His hands went to his pants. His pockets itched. Only the key to this shithole met his fingers. His wallet in the back one.

That was about to change.

Chapter Six

You have to protect Rose.

Five words. Such power. Significance.

Each one hit a beat inside Finn's head as his shoes struck the dirt on the trail. The heavy metal music in his headphones couldn't drown it.

Was Rose in danger? Or had her grandmother been imagining things? In the ambulance, Ms. Magnolia clocked a fever over 103 degrees. Had her words come from a clear state of mind?

His promise wound in a loop inside his head as he ran his usual trail through the Bent Creek Experimental Forest. He noticed the mountain ridges in the distance, the beginning changes in color amongst the trees, the glimpse of the Biltmore. He didn't pause and take it in like he normally would.

He ran fast, as if speed could ease the worry over the last words Ms. Magnolia spoke to him.

Who was the white-haired man who'd trespassed onto Everson land? The things Ms. Magnolia said before she collapsed. What did they mean? She'd been frightened enough to cause her life-threatening stress.

He didn't know what to do. He'd planned to visit Briar House again on a future day off, after she was released from the hospital. Check on the matriarch and ask her about the promise he'd given.

Three days had passed. Last night, Pa called with the news that Magnolia Everson-Brooks had died.

Finn increased his pace.

Poor Rose. She'd been close to her grandmother. The child and teenager he grew up with would be devastated.

You have to protect Rose.

What had Ms. Magnolia meant? Protect her from what? He wouldn't get to ask now.

Was the old man they'd seen the threat? He'd been trespassing, but Finn hadn't recognized him. She'd mentioned lights, but he hadn't seen lights out the window.

Whether Rose needed protection or not, he had to be realistic. There were obstacles.

Where did she live? Her gran hadn't shared her address. She could be local, somewhere in North Carolina, or in Europe for all he knew. He wiped away the sweat on his forehead with the hem of his t-shirt. Europe was a stretch—she'd been at the hospital the night of her grandmother's stroke. Maybe she lived closer to Evers Hollow or in it. She'd still consider it home.

Finn didn't live in Evers Hollow. He lived in Asheville, not far, but how could he protect her from seventy miles away?

How would Rose react if he turned up to warn her she was in danger? He had no proof, only a plea from a woman who'd suffered a stroke. He knew how that conversation would go.

Rose hadn't listened to him the last time he'd tried to warn her. Sure, it was a sensitive topic. She'd gotten engaged to an asshole. He'd tried to talk her out of it. She'd gotten angry, especially when he'd asked the wrong question.

"Why didn't you tell me you were dating him?"

Her eyes flashed, her tone clipped. "Tell you. Why should I tell you anything? You never call or email. You couldn't even take the time to send me a stinking postcard."

She'd been right. He was crap at communication. While he'd created accounts on social media, he never took time to look, much less engage on the platforms.

He slowed his pace to a walk. Shook his head as if he was back in the conversation.

Guilt swept over him at her long-ago words. He shouldn't have interfered with her engagement to Caleb *fucking* Brentwood. Should have trusted her to figure things out for herself.

His interference had ended their friendship. He recognized that now.

Rose was married. For five plus years. She might have a child. A dog.

His pace slowed.

Something wasn't right. Rose was married. Why would Ms. Magnolia ask him to protect her? Shouldn't the prick she married be the one keeping her safe?

He walked out of the arboretum back to his SUV. He grabbed coffee and a breakfast sandwich from a corner cafe.

He pulled into the parking lot of his apartment complex, shoved the memories aside. He showered and dressed for his next rotation.

After his shift, he called Pa. The man hadn't been close to the Everson matriarch, but he wanted to attend her funeral. Finn offered to drive him. They both should be there.

Finn would reach out to Broome, Rose's oldest brother. Maybe he would know what Finn was supposed to do regarding his promise.

Chapter Seven

Rose turned her filthy Jeep onto the gravel drive towards the only place she considered home. A fresh layer of rain and mud coated her side windows. She parked in front of a white cottage, one of three that stood in a row. Hers had faded pink roses out front. All had been homes for on-site staff of the Briar House estate years before. Only the gardener's cottage, now hers, was kept up enough to live in. The one beside it had a tree branch growing out a window. Ivy and thorny vines engulfed the one on the end.

Rose's peony print rain boots sank a half-inch into mud when she got out of her Jeep. Rain hit the top of her head. She leaned back in to grab her damp raincoat from the back of the passenger seat. She slipped it on over her black dress, pulling her hair out from beneath its collar. Both hems hit just above her knees when she straightened.

She lifted her face to the gray sky and closed her eyes. Raindrops ran down her cheeks in skinny rivulets. She needed this. Just a few seconds.

She opened her eyes and faced Briar House. Swaths of rain sliced across its faded blue siding, making it look as if it too mourned. Its maroon front door held a large white wreath that underlined that feeling. Passed down through four generations, the three-story blue Victorian trimmed in white had stood since 1917. Overgrown yellow roses planted between the World Wars wound upward over the wraparound porch. Those that climbed gave the house its name.

Rose brushed rain from her cheeks as she moved forward and walked through puddles she'd jumped in as a child.

Thunder rumbled as she climbed the three steps to the side porch. The kitchen screen door creaked with resistance when she pulled it open and stepped in. Closing it, she set her jacket and rain boots inside the door.

Silence greeted her, the counters and sink empty of freshly picked berries and baked goods. No Ms. Tess or Olivia this morning. They would be here soon alongside her brothers and sisters. Most of their small town would follow.

Rose stepped from the kitchen into the heart of the house, the three-story square chamber that connected every room on the downstairs level. The scent of Murphy's oil soap lingered from the last visit by the cleaning service. In the middle stood the dark, square-shaped staircase that held its own record of all comings and goings through the years.

In the opposite corner, the morning room stood open. Sunlit triangles entered the hall via the open room. Rose stepped inside. Her fingers touched the back of Magnolia's favorite blue chintz chair. The tea tray sat in place on the inlaid table close by, waiting for guests to entertain. Rose didn't dare sit down. She swallowed tears back.

Nine days since Magnolia passed. Eleven since they'd had tea and scones together.

The doctors had been confident she would recover. They'd also assumed that she would survive pneumonia once they diagnosed her. They'd been wrong.

She pressed her palms to the corners of her eyes as she took the dark-stained rails upward. On the second floor, the double doors to Magnolia's suite stood open. She made the sharp turn to keep climbing, careful to avoid the phone table in the corner and the functional corded black telephone on top.

Memories of childhood, the lingering floral scent of Magnolia's perfume, chased her.

Rose had only been six years old when their parents died in a car accident during an ice storm. She remembered her own hand in one of Magnolia's, her brother, Thorne, on the other side as they climbed the stairs. Both their rooms were on the third floor. Grandmother showed Thorne to his room, then Rose to hers. There was a room between them, likely for a nanny generations before. Hers was a small squarish room with one angled wall, all bright from the array of windows opposite. Magnolia had opened a half-sized door on the angled wall to show her the cubby that was big enough to sit in.

Rose's bedroom door stood open now. She stepped inside, the woven wool rug beneath buffered the creak of the wooden floor. Her rose-patterned quilt lay atop the twin bed. A vase of flowers sat on the white antique dresser. She hadn't slept here since she'd fixed up the old gardener's cottage.

A new burgundy cushion padded the window seat where she'd once gazed at the stars and watched for her best friend's arrival on summer days.

Rose pulled open the half-sized door on the angled wall and pulled the string for a light that Magnolia's own father had put in years before. She crouched down to climb inside, pulled the door closed behind her, put her head in her hands, and wept.

Later, Broome found her standing in front of her window. The floor creaked as he entered.

The sky above had blended into dark smears of gray. Below, a parade of dark-clothed figures approached the house, many carrying umbrellas.

She turned. Her brother stood tall and somber beside her, his tie loosened, the top button of his white shirt undone. He was the oldest of their lot, with a fierce sort of face, hazel eyes, and hints of silver in his brown hair. Only his wife and their three children softened the prominent lines around his eyes.

"Do they need help downstairs?"

He shook his head. "Livie's got it. Some other women from town are helping."

His hands disappeared inside his pockets, a habit that precluded serious conversations. "We need to talk."

"What's going on?"

He hesitated, then said, "The reading of the will."

Rose knew what he was about to say. Briar House wouldn't go to Broome as expected. She'd known that when he and Simi custom-designed a 4,000 square foot home with an architect on the northern edge of Asheville. Darling Simi called it their dream castle. Broome called it *The Fortress.* He'd added a six-foot wrought iron fence and security cameras to make it so.

With Magnolia gone, based on their birth order, the house and the acreage surrounding would go to Aspen.

Rose blocked thoughts of what Aspen and her husband Gavin would do to make this property their dream residence. She'd seen their house up at Opal Point. It lacked a soul.

That brought up other things she didn't want to think about. She'd need a new place to live. Those thoughts needed blocking as well.

Today was about Magnolia.

Her voice sounded flat when she said, "I understand."

Broome swore. "You understand nothing." His tone was harsh. "I expect things to go to hell."

This was news. She met his riled eyes, saw his concern. "Oh."

"The lawyers will be here at three," he said. "Our guests will be gone by then. We'll meet in the dining room. Dinner will be delivered at five-thirty."

His hands remained in his pockets. She bit her lip. Rose felt as if she were a young child again. As the oldest, Broome served as more of a father figure to his siblings after their parents died. Six years her senior, he took the role seriously, determined to be their role model and mentor. That hadn't changed when they reached adulthood.

His next words seemed forced, as if he'd rather speak of anything else. "This evening will be—it'll be difficult. If you need to talk Rose—" He paused, but didn't meet her gaze. "Call me or come to dinner. I'll do what I can to help."

He left the room. Uneasiness filled her. Sincerity, stammered words, and hands shoved deep in pockets? Broome never stammered.

What had Magnolia done?

Chapter Eight

Finn stood beside his pa as they spoke with other locals in the parlor of Briar House. Every chair was taken. Many more stood. Damp clothes, sweat, and heavy perfume filled the remaining space.

Rose had been the last Finch grandchild to arrive in the parlor, a good half hour after the others, but she hadn't stayed in the room for long. Finn hadn't been able to reach her to offer condolences. She'd been surrounded.

At the service, she'd sat in the front row, on the end, beside her brother, Thorne. Finn hadn't been able to take his eyes off her. She wore her hair down. It was longer than he remembered, but still wavy and dark. Like midnight. That's how he thought of her hair when they were kids.

She'd once told him his was like the setting sun.

Pa's voice called him back to the conversation. "Isn't that right, my boy?"

Finn nodded, unaware of what he'd agreed with. He needed out of this stifling room.

"I'm going to get some air." It looked like it had finally

stopped raining. Finn made his way through the gathered mourners into the front hall. He wandered the first floor.

The library was one of the few rooms Finn was familiar with. He and Rose had spent rainy days looking at old atlases, planning adventures around the world. Bookshelves climbed to the ceiling along every wall. A set of wooden desks sat in the middle, back to back.

Broome stood by one of them, talking with two men. Two faded navy armchairs still occupied the space in front of the single large window. The room smelled as he remembered: polished wood, a hint of orange, and old books.

Quietly, Finn moved around the room, studying the full shelves as he waited. Broome might have answers he didn't about what happened the day of Ms. Magnolia's stroke. They'd spoken briefly at the hospital. His conversation with Thorne had been longer.

The discussion across the room ended. Handshakes were exchanged. The men left.

Broome turned to face him. "What can I do for you, Finn?"

The oldest Everson grandchild looked older than Finn knew him to be. Exhaustion shadowed his expression. As an only child, he'd looked up to Broome, seen him as the older brother he'd never had.

Finn reached out, shook his hand, offered condolences, and then said, "I need to talk to you about your grandmother."

"Is this about the old man?" Broome folded his arms and leaned back against the desk.

"It is."

"Did you see him?"

"I did," said Finn. "So did your grandmother. Her reaction to him—I believe it may have triggered her stroke."

Broome stood, turned away a moment, pressed one hand to his desk.

When he looked back at Finn, he kept that hand on his desk.

"Grandmother mentioned him. Her doctors figured he was a hallucination. Sheriff Hutchins said the same. There's been no sign of him in the woods or in town."

He couldn't help it. "He's real. I saw him. Edge of the woods, trespassing."

Broome rubbed the side of his jaw as if he were thinking. "I believe you."

"There's more."

Worry etched Broome's face. "What's that?"

"Rose is in danger. I promised your grandmother I'd protect her."

Broome's expression hardened. "From what?"

"Don't know. That's why I'm here. I wondered if you knew what she meant."

Broome's next words carried a bit of astonishment. "You promised to protect Rose?"

He swallowed. "Yes. Your grandmother insisted."

"Two of you fell out a while ago."

"Your grandmother—we talked about that."

Broome looked skeptical. "Did you and Rose talk about it?"

"Not yet."

"Where do you live?"

"I have an apartment in Asheville. I'm working on my residency."

"I heard you were in Chapel Hill."

"I was. When Pa broke his hip, I thought it best to apply for residencies that would be closer to him."

Broome pulled out his wallet. He took a business card from it and handed it to him.

"My cell's on there. Send me a text so I have you in my contacts."

"What about Rose? Her safety?" He'd given his word.

"I'll speak with Reggie MacShane. He's the sheriff's deputy and a friend. More likely to take me seriously."

Finn knew what he meant; he'd heard things about Sheriff Hutchins. Many at Wylder wanted him voted out.

Broome must have seen his worry. He moved closer and put a hand on Finn's shoulder.

"Don't worry about Rose. She'll be safe. My family is my highest priority."

"But—"

Broome held up his hand. "Let me handle it. You don't live here. I'll talk to Reggie. I'll let you know if he finds anything."

Finn left the room with Broome's card in hand. He sent him a text.

Broome would handle Rose's safety. He should feel relieved.

Instead, he made his way down the hall, feeling as if he'd swallowed mud.

He found himself in the kitchen, another familiar room. Ms. Tess sat at the end of the table, a younger woman beside her. Her mouth split into a grin.

"Finn Murphy, I heard you were back." She opened her arms. "Come give me a hug."

Dear Tess, a treasured pillar from his childhood. This woman had spoiled him. She made the best damn cookies in the world.

He bent down to hug her. He took a seat on the bench closest to her.

"How are you, Ms. Tess?"

Her expression changed. "Heartbroken." She clutched a handkerchief in her hand. "It's not right what happened to Magnolia."

"I know. I'm sorry about her passing."

She dabbed her brown eyes with the cloth and reached out a hand to the mixed race young woman beside her. He recognized her as the one who'd helped him the day of Magnolia's stroke. "This here's my granddaughter, Olivia, or Livie, as I prefer to call her."

"Nana." The young woman shifted in her seat as she took her grandmother's hand.

Finn nodded. "Nice to meet you. You were a big help with Ms. Magnolia, the day of…"

Livie looked down, wiped her eyes.

"She's my replacement," said Ms. Tess. "I've been training her."

Ms. Tess had been the cook in the Everson kitchen for as long as Finn had lived in Evers Hollow.

She dabbed her eyes again. "I'm not sure what happens now. With the house. The kitchen. Livie's job. All of it breaks my heart."

Finn hadn't thought about the house. He assumed it would be Broome's.

He glanced at the clock above the sink. "Have you seen Rose?"

Ms. Tess' eyes gentled. "Why haven't you married that woman?"

Finn shifted his feet. Marriage to Rose? Wasn't she…?

"She's married."

Ms. Tess snorted. "Where'd you hear that?"

"She got engaged. Six years ago. You were there. At the New Years party."

She waved a hand in the air. "Pish posh, she dumped his ass."

"Nana."

"Well, the man's an ass. In no way did he deserve her."

Rose wasn't married.

His shock must have shown. Tess watched him closely.

"You didn't know."

"I didn't."

"A little bird told me you were part of the reason."

More shock. Surely Rose hadn't listened to him. She'd been

clear about where she stood when he'd near begged her not to marry Caleb *fucking* Brentwood.

Don't marry him. Anyone else. Not him. Please.

Ms. Tess said, "I knew you'd come back. I didn't expect it would take you so long."

"I've been busy." He tapped his knee, knowing she would not condone his lame excuse.

She snorted. "I'm sure you have. She's been busy too."

Too busy to let him know she'd broken her engagement. Why hadn't she told him? Why hadn't anyone else told him? Pa had to know.

He looked around the bright kitchen, its whitewashed cabinets. There'd been lots of cookies at this table, PB&J sandwiches, and glasses of lemonade.

He hadn't knocked on the door of this house since the day after her engagement, after they'd had their argument. Six years ago. He hadn't gotten past the front door.

"I want to see that girl with babies of her own." Ms. Tess often gave direct looks when she spoke her mind. Her gaze focused on him.

He couldn't think of Rose with babies. His mind was still working on the not married part.

He stood. "Where is she?"

Tess pointed at the side kitchen door. "It's been too much. You know where she's run."

The rose garden. He should have thought of it already.

Sure enough, Rose stood alone in one row, still dressed in black. Her hair now hung in a loose braid down her back, her face turned away from his view. She was a contrast to the splattering of colors and green on either side of her. She took his breath. It had been too long.

What he'd felt before, and never shared with her, it lingered. Finding the photos from their childhood brought things back. He could tell himself it was nostalgia, but it was damn far from the truth.

Rose must have heard him approach. She wiped her face before she turned.

Their eyes met. Hers were glassy; her cheeks the sort of wet that only comes from tears.

He stopped an arm's length away from her. They'd grown up together. He'd offered condolences to the rest of her family, but for her, it was different. They'd once been the closest of friends. Until they weren't. The right words wouldn't come.

Instead, his mother's funeral slipped into his mind.

Tears ran down his face. Pa sobbed beside him. His shoulders shook with his own grief. His hand held tight around Finn's as they stood before her casket.

Then he felt Rose's small, soft hand slip into his. He'd glanced sideways, just able to make her out through his tears. She looked back, her face a mirror of his, shiny and wet. Her hand squeezed his in a long, gentle hug, a secret message. She stayed beside him even when someone told her to take her seat.

No one else tried. Not that day or in the days that followed. She stuck to him like a shield, quiet and ready to listen—a solid friend. He'd never forgotten.

The pain he'd felt that day. The same swirled in her green eyes now.

Instinct sent him closer. He slowly reached out to wrap his hand around hers. He couldn't look away. With a slow, cautious breath, their fingers intertwined. Gently, as she had fourteen years before, he squeezed, hoping it would say what his words could not.

She closed her eyes as fresh tears drifted down her cheeks.

He wanted to pull her against him, let her cry against his chest as he'd once cried on her shoulder for his mom. The past made him hesitate.

Rose launched herself toward him. He caught her, wrapping

his arms around her when he felt the impact of her body against his. He held her while she cried.

She fit still, as if nothing had changed between them. She smelled of rain, but also roses and lavender, another echo of the past. He had no idea how long they stood there. He could have held her for hours. The sky disagreed.

Cold raindrops hit the top of his head, the back of his neck. When he felt her shudder, he knew their hug was over. She stepped back with the smallest of whimpers, as if her retreat hurt her. She looked away, her hands twisting together. He hadn't forgotten what that action meant.

It was another moment before she seemed to gather herself and face him. Her hands separated, moved to her sides. Her shoulders and her spine straightened as if someone close by reminded her to correct her posture. With that movement, the two of them became strangers.

Her voice was soft, pained, and husky when she spoke.

"Finn—um, sorry for…" She motioned to his shirt.

He shrugged. The falling rain would make it all blend in. "Don't worry about that." He wanted to pull her back against him, comfort her more.

Her hands came back together, as did her fingers.

He said, "I'm sorry about your grandmother. She was something special. She did a lot for this town and for families like mine. Unforgettable." He sounded too formal.

As a child, he'd called her a witch behind her back, something Rose once found funny.

Magnolia's not a witch. She's got rules. That's all.

Super strict rules, especially concerning public displays of rowdiness. Ms. Magnolia scolded him as if he were one of her own grandchildren.

"My pa shares his condolences as well."

Rose folded her arms. "Thank you." Her fingers splayed on her elbows as she studied her floral rain boots.

She looked back up, sincerity in her eyes. "Thank you for what you did for her."

Why was she thanking him? He swallowed. "I'm sorry I couldn't do more."

"I think we all know that. You did what you could."

He couldn't respond, couldn't find the right words.

A sad smile graced her face. "Each of us spent time with her before the end. Not everyone gets that chance."

She tapped the toes of her boots together. As if she were as unsure as he was.

"How are you holding up? For reals?" They'd once told each other everything.

"I'm managing. I have things to think about." It was all she said, but she looked at him when she said it, studying him as if he were now a puzzle she didn't know how to solve. It was an improvement over her attention to the large flowers on her boots.

"Like what?"

She shook her head. He didn't press, but wished she'd answer. Ms. Magnolia had been tight-lipped about Rose when he'd visited.

She wiped her eyes again and focused on him. "Your dad, how is he?"

He was dumbfounded. She and her family had lost their center. Yet she asked about his pa. Such a small thing, but it pulled at him.

Chapter Nine

Willow came out the front door and joined Rose on the gravel drive. She asked, "Is that Finn Murphy?"

"Uh-huh." It was all Rose could manage as she watched Finn help his dad into a dark SUV.

"I don't remember him looking like that."

"No." She couldn't look away. Her sister was right. That scraggly, wavy hair he'd kept hanging in his face as a teenager was both managed and wind-tousled. She wanted to stick her fingers in it. The feel of his strong arms around her, his chest against hers, both comforted and weakened her knees.

"You should stop staring," Willow said. "We are in mourning. Although Grandmother would find your behavior amusing."

Rose didn't care if people noticed. Grief for Magnolia buried her. She'd cried more in the last week than she had in years.

Watching Finn help his dad into a car soothed her. It was so everyday.

He gave her one last glance before he left.

"Looks like he hasn't forgotten you either."

Rose stood there till both taillights disappeared.

Willow took her arm, tucked it in hers, and pulled her toward the house. "I always wondered if you and he were in love. Now I know."

A frisson of alarm went through her. "Know? Know what?"

Willow shrugged her shoulders. "That you and Finn had a thing."

Rose forced Willow to a stop. Her words were a whisper. "We did not have a thing. We never even dated." They hadn't, but she didn't want the rest of the family to hear speculation. Like Willow said. They were grieving. All of them.

This wasn't the time or place to discuss such things, despite Magnolia's belief in living towards the future instead of sinking in the past. Hadn't she given her that very advice the last time they'd talked?

Willow said, "By the way—your friends, Ada and Becks are looking for you. They're in the kitchen with Tess."

She'd spoken with her college roommates at the cemetery before the graveside service. Ada had been a huge help to the family. Her family owned the local florist. She'd set all the flowers up and brought the white wreath that currently hung on the front door. Becks had flown in from New York yesterday.

"Thank you, I'll slip in and talk to them." They were likely thanking Tess for all the cookies she sent when they'd lived in the dorms together at New York University.

Rose slipped into the kitchen. She was right; they were talking about cookies. She hugged Tess first; she'd taken Magnolia's death hard. The two had been as close as sisters.

After hugging her roommates, the four of them sat down at the table, talking until Thorne appeared in the doorway.

"Broome wants us in the parlor," he said. "Uncle Tamarack and crew plan to leave soon."

"Of course." She stood and thanked her friends for coming. Another round of hugs ensued, with promises to check on her in the coming days.

She entered the parlor beside Thorne. Uncle Tamarack, his

wife Cora, and their son, Oakley, stood in the middle with her siblings. Their granddaughters played with stuffed animals by the array of windows.

Uncle Tamarack said, "I'm sorry I couldn't get Cherry to come. She despises this town."

Rose knew Broome had tried to convince Aunt Cherry to fly out from England for her older sister's funeral, but she'd refused. At least Uncle Tamarack and his family were here. They sat together in the parlor for a time. He shared his favorite memories of his sister. Their granddaughters told them about their new kitten, named Posey.

When it was time for them to leave, Rose and her siblings followed them out, promising to stay in touch. A gray sedan entered the driveway as they said their farewells. This must be the lawyer Broome mentioned.

They were an hour into the reading of the will at the large claw-footed oak dining table when Aspen erupted out of her seat. She slammed her hand on the dark-stained surface. "What do you mean Rose gets the house?"

The lawyer, a Mr. Simon Winslow, flinched.

Rose too, wondered if she'd heard wrong. Magnolia loved her, loved all of them, but she would never choose her, the youngest, to inherit this house.

Seated across the table with his muddy blonde hair slicked back, Gavin's smarmy smile flatlined. "There must be a mistake."

Aspen sat back in her chair, shoulders stiff above her prominent baby bump. Her words were clipped. "Briar House is mine."

Mr. Winslow, a gaunt man perhaps in his fifties, cleared his throat, removed a yellow pocket square from his gray suit and dabbed his forehead. Then repeated his words. They came out the same.

I, Magnolia Eleanor Everson-Brooks, leave the property

known as Briar House and the grounds that surround it to Rose Everson Finch.

Rose gripped the edges of her chair.

Beside her, Thorne's eyebrows rose.

Rose glanced at Broome. His expression gave away nothing. His cryptic words earlier came to mind. Was this what he referred to?

Gavin's jaw jutted out. He and Aspen had been married four years. Magnolia required him to sign a prenuptial agreement. Despite that, he looked unreasonably pissed.

The lawyer's face carried a pinched expression as he adjusted his papers. He looked pointedly at Aspen and Gavin. "Ms. Everson-Brooks was clear about her wishes. She wished Rose to inherit the estate."

Her stomach churned as if the words had been said for the first time instead of the third.

Briar House.

Magnolia wanted her to have Briar House.

Her hands twisted beneath the table.

Rose loved everything about this gentle old place. The window in her bedroom, its tiny reading cubby. The brightness of the morning room, the library with towers of bookshelves around the edges. The forest perimeter, the rose garden, even the row of worn cottages, one of which she'd lived in for the past two years.

When Magnolia suffered her first stroke, it made sense for Rose to move home. Of all the Everson descendants, as long as she had power, an internet connection, and a phone, she could work anywhere.

Worked, she had. More than she had in New York City. She'd indie published three more *Criminy Mystery* books since she moved home. Her sixth was under edit with Elise, her developmental editor.

Briar House and the surrounding forest fed her mind. Her

books revolved around this house and the nearby woods. Her settings came more alive after she moved back.

But she'd always considered living on the estate temporary. She'd known the house would never come to her. In the past month, she'd decided that when the time came, she would buy a small place in Evers Hollow so that she could continue to walk through the woods and find inspiration.

But now…

Rose looked around the dining room. Took in its faded cream floral wallpaper, original to the house. Generations of scuffs and light stains marked the lower perimeter. The tattered ceiling above could use a bit of love. The chandelier caught her eye, its many prisms radiating light throughout the once glamorous room. A single wisp of a spiderweb hung from one of them.

Of all the chores, the chandelier had been the most time consuming and tedious. Magnolia felt that no Everson descendant should take the household staff for granted. Each of them had been tasked with doing every chore at least once, so they knew the effort it took to maintain such a place.

The lawyer said her name. Everyone looked at her. She'd missed something.

She leaned forward. "I'm sorry, I didn't—"

Slap.

Aspen's palm hit the table. "She's not even listening to you, Winthrop."

The partially balding man looked affronted. "My name is Winslow."

Aspen waved a hand as if in dismissal. "Do you really think this is who my grandmother had in mind when she wrote her will? She's the youngest. This house has stood for a hundred years. Rose will run our family's legacy into the ground."

Her emotions bubbled. Why Aspen would think such a thing, Rose couldn't be sure, but this wasn't the moment to whip out her financials to prove she wouldn't. She folded her arms and glared at Aspen.

In agitated tones, Willow said, "Would you lower your voice? Grandmother wouldn't want us to argue."

Thorne rocked his chair back on two legs, one hand on the table as he turned his head towards the lawyer. "Bet this happens all the time."

Rose watched as the lawyer met Thorne's eyes. If the slight inclination of his chin was a nod, it was the most subtle she'd seen. Aspen and Gavin had their heads together.

Aspen leaned over the table with a twisted, desperate look about her face, her voice shaky. "Rose. Give me and Gavin the house. It should belong to me. I was Grandmother's favorite."

Across from her, Willow's eyes narrowed, but Aspen pressed. "I went to all her social events with her, all the way to the end. I'm pregnant. You don't even have a boyfriend."

An impolite noise came from Thorne, his chair still off-balance, a contrast to the faded formality of the room.

"It's true," Aspen said.

A catalog of ugly words perched on the tip of Rose's tongue. Her teenage self would have said them, every single one. None would do any good. Not with Aspen. Not today.

Willow was right; they shouldn't argue. Their grandmother had been buried only hours before.

Yet Aspen tried again, her tone placating as if she were speaking to an irate child. "Please Rose. You could stay in the cottage. We'll hire you to be our nanny."

A privilege indeed.

As if she would ever agree to live on the same property with them, not with what she knew about Gavin.

Rose glanced back at the chandelier. She'd near forgotten. Aspen had never cleaned it. Rose couldn't remember what excuse she'd used. The rest of them each spent their two hours removing every prism and cleaning it with the housekeeper's homemade cleaning solution with cloth diapers. It had taken another hour to hang every prism back in its place.

Something drifted down from above, landing in front of her. A spider? Willow would freak.

No. Something white. A tiny piece of plaster. She looked up as if doing so would give her answers.

Was this normal? Could it be a gauntlet thrown down by the house itself? It might as well be.

Rose sat taller, her shoulders back, infusing her spine with the strength of Magnolia's love of Briar House and the Evers Hollow community.

"Magnolia loved all of us. She never had favorites. I love Briar House and its grounds. She knew I wanted to restore her. If this is what she wants, then I accept."

Her stomach turned as she glanced at her siblings around the table. Were they okay with this? Willow's eyes sparkled, and Rose knew. Willow didn't want the house, had never wanted the house. She had her own dreams.

Whatever Thorne felt, he hid well behind his unreadable eyes as he maintained his balance on the tilted back dining chair. Magnolia never tolerated the way he sat. He kept quiet. Perhaps he was still shocked at what had been left to him in the will.

Broome, his face ever steady and a bit fierce. He'd been named executor. He'd likely known all of this ahead of time.

Aspen's next words carried the strike of a copperhead. "I don't give a damn if you love the house. It should be mine."

Thorne rocked his chair to the floor with a thud. "So you can dig up Grandmother's rose garden and put in a pool?"

Aspen reeled back in her seat and sputtered. "How did you—"

"I heard yours and Gavin's plans while Magnolia was still on her deathbed. You should have closed your bedroom door."

Aspen slammed both fists on the table. "This isn't fair."

The lawyer averted his eyes and cleared his throat.

Broome said, "Stop. All of you. Every word in these documents is Grandmother's. Briar House belongs to Rose."

Aspen opened her mouth, but Broome cut her off with a look. "We need to move past this, Aspen. There's more to cover."

Fury blazed in her eyes. She closed her mouth, but the twist of her lips said the fight wasn't over.

Mr. Winslow continued his recitation. Rose heard his words, but didn't absorb the tiny details of who got the silver, the china, and the various antiques in the house.

It was well past dark when Broome walked the lawyer out of the library. Mr. Winslow met with each of them briefly in private in the library after the reading. Rose had been last.

She fell back in her chair, clutching a bulky manila envelope to her chest. Magnolia's signature lay across the seal to indicate no one else had seen its contents.

Broome returned and closed the door behind him. He'd sent Simi and the kids home before the private meetings.

"Still in shock?" His voice was gentle. Sweeping shadows underlined his hazel eyes.

Rose ran a hand down the braid she'd woven earlier. Her fingers clutched its tail, pulling on it a tad, a leftover nervous habit from childhood. "I never thought..."

He gave her a wry smile as he sat on the edge of his desk.

She clutched the envelope. How could she say this? "Aspen has a point. I'm single. This is a huge house just for me."

"You won't always be single, Rose."

Objections rose, but she stayed quiet.

Broome folded his arms. "It's a hundred-year-old house that needs extensive work. Grandmother believed you were up to the task. We talked about it after her first stroke. She kept me updated about what you've done since you moved back. I've noticed the improvements to the house, the grounds, as well as the new roof you paid for."

Her efforts made a small dent in all that needed to be done.

Rose said, "Magnolia took all of us in after Mom and Dad's car accident. She didn't have to. She could have sent us to foster care. A new roof is a pittance to pay for everything she's done for us. My books sell well."

"It's right that it's yours. She showed me a list a few months ago of other projects the two of you discussed. You've familiarized yourself with some of the local contractors. Let me know if you need other suggestions. I recommend an overall inspection. I assume Grandmother wouldn't have thought of that. As for the grounds, you know them like the back of your hand. You know how neglected everything is."

Rose had done what she could in the time she'd been back here. Broome was right, though. Everything had been neglected. It would take time and money to bring the house back. "She told me stories of how it was when she was a little girl. I had hoped —" She paused. She couldn't let grief overwhelm her here, not with Broome. He could never deal with his sister's tears. "I'd hoped she would still be here to see it when it was finished. It was to be my gift to her for everything."

Magnolia, the house, and the woods provided her six-year-old orphan self with a loving home and stability. The first months hadn't been easy. Especially for a grieving forty-nine-year-old woman suddenly in charge of five children. They'd each provided a challenge for her. Broome, with his interminable silence. Aspen, with enough attitude that became armor. Willow, with her tears and the nightmares that plagued her. Thorne, with too much anger to be contained in a seven-year-old. And her. The woods became her haven, a place where bad things never happened in its magical branches.

She had one more question she needed to ask. No matter what the answer.

"Broome, why me? Just because we made a list together didn't mean—"

He nodded toward the large envelope in her hands. "She'll tell you herself. Everything you need to know."

Rose frowned.

Broome walked around to Magnolia's desk, opened a drawer, and reached in.

"Here." In his hands lay a letter opener, one she'd never seen before. The handle was a dragon. He handed it to her. "Use this. She'd want you to have it. It was her favorite."

Rose took the blade from him, her gaze caught by the elaborate details and the dragon's jeweled green eyes. She ran her fingers over the dragon-shaped handle. The blade looked sharp. Magnolia liked dragons? She'd never even hinted.

He said, "Take some time to go through the contents. We'll talk more tomorrow."

The library door opened. Willow walked in. She looked at each of them with worry, her arms around her waist so tight that her clothes puckered. "Aspen and Gavin went home. Thorne's outside; he's planning to stay over. Everything okay here?"

Rose noticed her red-rimmed, swollen eyes. She'd been crying again. The words exchanged around the table over the will had gotten to her, on top of the grief she suffered.

She nodded to her oldest brother. "We're good."

Turning, she reached out to hug Willow. "Everything will be okay."

Broome said, "It's time to call it a night."

Rose linked an arm with her sister's as they left the room.

Willow said, "It's raining again. I've been through every room in the house." They reached the base of the staircase. "Little has changed since the day we moved in. You have a lot to think about, Rose."

Rose didn't get to comment. A loud crack and a horrendous wrenching sound drew their heads around.

Broome's voice hollered behind them. "Move behind the

stairs! Get down! Close your eyes!" He pushed them down and tried to cover them with his own frame.

Sounds of continuous impact trembled through the floor they crouched on. With her eyes closed, Rose clung to Willow. Willow clung right back.

When the shaking and noise stopped, Rose dared to open her eyes. Dust hung in the air around them. As Broome pulled her and Willow to their feet, a cloud of white bellowed out of the room they'd all sat in hours before.

The dining room.

Broome ushered them outside and pulled out his phone.

Chapter Ten

Pa snored from the passenger seat as Finn drove. The funeral and reception had tuckered him out.

The near silence took him back to the garden. He'd talked to Rose. Held her. His collar still bore the tears she cried into his neck.

He'd once called her *Evie*. His own idea. When they'd been close, when they'd shared almost everything.

She'd loved having a secret nickname—a play on her middle name, Everson. Not a girl's name. A legacy name, her grandmother's maiden name.

She'd tried to give him one, too. He refused. He liked his name.

Summers had meant free time back then. They'd been too young for jobs, too old to need constant minding. They had the run of the forest and the town as long as they followed the rules set by his parents and Ms. Magnolia.

With that freedom, they'd been adventurers when they'd been young. On the lookout for potential mysteries to be solved.

Sometimes the mysteries were small ones.

The first time, they helped Mr. Hanover find his glasses in

his own hardware store. He'd removed them to help a customer read some fine print on a package and couldn't see well enough to find them. He laughed when they found them in the paintbrush section and gave them a five-dollar bill as a reward. Enough for two ice cream cones.

They'd found lost dogs, lost cats, even a lost pet snake who'd thought an extension cord was part of its family. Not that they'd questioned the snake. Rose had been the one to pull it away from the cords, though. He'd feared snakes. Wanted nothing to do with them.

Don't worry, I won't tell anyone.

She never had.

Sometimes, their investigations resulted in phone calls.

The time they'd returned someone's cat only to learn they didn't own a cat, especially one covered in fleas and ticks.

The adventures paused when Rose fell out of a tree and broke her arm.

It had been the raven's nest. An unwise quest. Absently, he rubbed the back of his hand against the steering wheel, the scars there a reminder of the sharp pains he'd endured while trying to help her.

Pa let out a snort and shifted in his sleep.

The view on the two-lane highway changed. Gray fog hugged the road ahead. Except it wasn't fog. The stark scent of burned brush and wood seeped inside his car.

Red firetrucks sat either side of the road, lights flashing. He drove around a curve and pressed the brakes to slow down. Pa stirred and opened his eyes.

Finn said, "There's a fire in the woods."

"What?" He sat up. Low sounds of exclamation came out as he looked around. His father loved an emergency spectacle, especially one that involved flashing lights.

A black Evers Hollow Police Department SUV blocked their

side of the road. A pair of police officers held small stop signs up.

As the car drew close to one officer, Pa rolled down his window. Finn tasted the smoke on his tongue.

"Pa, this is not the time," Finn said even as he stopped the car. He knew better than to argue.

The closest uniformed officer was one they knew well.

"Officer Sheffield," Pa said as he rested his arm on the door.

Finn nodded at the broad-shouldered man, who'd once been a linebacker for the local high school team and a good friend. "Zane."

Zane nodded back. "Mr. Murphy. Finn."

"What happened here?" Pa asked.

Zane touched the bill of his EHPD cap. "There's a fire. It's under control."

"How'd it start?"

Zane shook his head. "Can't tell you that right now."

Slow oncoming traffic passed them from the other side of the road. Zane and the other cop waved the cars out of the burned area.

Zane spoke into the radio on his shoulder, then flipped his sign to *SLOW*, waving Finn's car forward.

Finn said, "Thanks, Zane."

Pa rolled up the window as Finn was directed to drive on the opposite side. Smoke hovered. Through it he saw scorched trees and a blackened forest floor. Nine firefighters in full gear moved among the trees, likely looking for hotspots.

He glanced at his pa. "Well?"

Pa frowned in displeasure. "Been awhile since we had a fire, especially this far out of town."

Finn wouldn't know. The only time he spent around trees was running on the trails around Asheville when he had time. Those trees were far from here.

"Damn shame about Magnolia," Pa said. "I can't say she liked me all that much, but she was one classy lady."

Finn slid him a sideways look. Random statements from Pa didn't bode well. Never before had he given an opinion on Magnolia Everson-Brooks.

As for whether the woman liked his father, he knew she liked him just fine, but he would never share. It would go straight to his head.

Finn said, "She wouldn't have let Rose play with me if she thought ill of you."

"Maybe it would have been better if she hadn't."

There it was. This wasn't about Ms. Magnolia.

"Pa, don't." They exited the burned area. Finn sped up as the line of cars thinned out.

"What about my grandkids? I'm going to be fifty-nine."

"That's got nothing to do with things here. I've been busy."

"I want a chance to spoil them rotten. Before I'm bedridden."

Finn sent him a glance. "Really, Pa? Bedridden?"

"Never know. It could happen. Along with drool."

Finn wiped a hand over his face. Fifty-eight wasn't old. Not in his eyes. How was he supposed to respond?

"You know I'm proud of you, son, but I thought a lot about this. I want grandkids."

"Pa—"

"No, I've made up my mind. You need to find a woman, get that Finch girl out of your system."

He should have known. Death reminded people of their own mortality.

"Rose isn't a girl anymore."

"I know. My body parts might not work so well, but I still got both my eyes. That girl's damn pretty. That's the problem. Maybe if her face got covered in warts."

Finn couldn't help it. He smiled. Rose hadn't been pretty when he'd met her. Her large, soulful eyes carried sorrows that most didn't as a six-year-old. Those eyes drew him along with her odd obsession with floral rain boots. He didn't know why. He only knew that as the years passed, her legs lengthened, her body developed the slightest of curves, and her soulful eyes…became damn captivating.

Even now, once he'd seen her, it was hard to look away. Especially when he noticed she still wore floral rain boots, as if she weren't so different from the girl he remembered.

"What's that face for?" Pa said. "You think I'm crazy?"

"No, not that. It's hard to imagine any member of that family covered in warts."

Pa swore. "The whole lot of them—too pretty for their own good. I heard even Magnolia had the student body tied in knots back in her high school years."

"What's your point?"

"You talked to her. After I asked you not to. I saw you."

"She lost her grandmother."

"Maybe you should have sent me to do it."

Finn shook his head as he directed his car around the gentle curves ahead. "It wouldn't be the same."

"Son," Pa said in a serious tone. "She broke your heart. You said it yourself. Why would you give her the chance to do it again?"

Finn bristled. "I never said she broke my heart. We had a disagreement."

"You had a fight. You found out she liked someone better than you, someone she planned to marry. It hurt you."

Finn said, "That's not—"

"I know what I saw. Hard to miss the mood you were in then."

Finn shook his head. He couldn't admit that some of what Pa said was right. Rose's eyes, the night of her engagement. Large and dark with anger, hurt, and disappointment. He'd hurt her. She'd said so.

He'd tried to see Rose the day after they'd argued. He'd stood at the front door of the big house, waiting. The housekeeper, Mrs. Haskell, hadn't let him in. Aspen had been the one to tell him Rose didn't want to see him. He'd tried once more later in the day. Aspen had opened the front door and repeated her earlier words.

He'd had no choice after that. His military leave was about to end. He'd flown back to his assigned military base, then received orders to deploy.

For six years, he'd avoided Evers Hollow except for visiting Pa. He couldn't bear the thought of running into Rose alongside her husband.

Rose now lived in Evers Hollow.

According to Tess, it had been Rose that broke her engagement to Brentwood. The very issue that caused the rift between them.

"Son?"

"I know what I'm doing."

Pa grimaced and muttered a curse. "Is that what you call it? I may not live in town no more, but I hear things. That girl's still single, beautiful, and the town's darling. You're going to fall like an axed tree."

Finn had no words that would contradict him. He'd fallen years before. He'd dated other women, tried to have relationships. All of them had failed. They weren't her.

"I don't think you have anything to worry about. Rose never saw me that way."

"Her mistake."

Finn glanced at him, wondered what ran through Pa's mind. "Why didn't you tell me she broke things off?"

Pa shifted in his seat. "I'm sure I said something."

Finn frowned. "You didn't."

"Huh. Too late to change that now."

It was.

"Ms. Magnolia mentioned something to me the day I spoke to her." Finn slowed the car when he saw the reduced speed limit sign.

"What's that?" Wariness lined his words.

"She said Mom did something for her, said she meant to repay the favor."

Pa sighed. "She won't get to do that now."

"Do you know what she meant?"

He shook his head. "Your mom didn't talk about that. Was a long time ago."

"Pa?" Finn took the next right turn, slowed to the posted fifteen mph speed limit. He stopped his car beneath the welcoming archway at the entrance to Wylder.

Finn engaged the emergency brake. Pa opened his door and grabbed his cane from the side of the seat.

Finn swore and jumped out. "Pa, let me help you."

With a few flavorful curses on Pa's part, together they got him upright with his cane in hand, supporting his weaker side.

"What did Mom not talk about?"

Pa double-tapped his cane before he took a step forward. "Bingo's starting soon. I need to get inside."

"Pa."

He shook his head and gave him a single glance that held firm. "It's not your business. Leave it alone."

The words only made Finn curiouser, but he nodded, letting it go for today.

He needed answers though, soon.

He'd made a promise to a dying woman. Despite Broome's assurances on Rose's safety, he had to find a way to keep it.

Chapter Eleven

No one would sleep in the main house tonight. The dining room ceiling had collapsed. EMS had come along with the fire and police departments. All power to the main house had been shut off.

As they ran out of the house, Rose got a glimpse into the dining room. Debris lay like a thick blanket over everything in that direction. The chandelier no longer hung from the ceiling.

It was after midnight before all emergency services left. After a shower, she climbed into her bed at the cottage. Willow slept in its guest room. Thorne had taken the couch. Broome had gone home.

Rose lay in her bed, waiting for sleep to come. Thoughts of the day's events wouldn't let her. The clock beside her bed ticked past one o'clock. She sat up, turned on her lamp, and reached for the large envelope Mr. Winslow had given her.

Folding her legs beneath her, Rose reached for the afghan Magnolia's closest friend, Brigette Conroy, crocheted for her when she'd graduated college. She used it to cover her bare legs.

Rose picked up the dragon-shaped letter opener that belonged to Magnolia. Its emerald eyes winked at her in the lamplight. She slid its blade beneath the flap, then reached inside. She wiggled the contents out. A stack of papers, a slightly smaller manila envelope, and a wrapped rectangular box emerged.

The stack of papers intimidated, at least a finger's width tall. Two loose pages sat on top. One displayed the Winslow and Barrow Law Offices letterhead, a brief letter addressed to her. The other listed the contents of the envelope. A pink binder clip held a copy of the will. It was quite thick. She set it aside.

Magnolia's signature scrolled across the seal of the envelope. She ran her fingers over the calligraphy-style signature, but felt only the edges of the flap it covered. Once more, she used the letter opener. Paper-clipped pages and a letter-sized ivory envelope with her first name fell out.

The paper-clipped pages confused her. The top page was her birth certificate. She set it down. Broome had given her a copy years ago when she'd left for college. The second document gave her pause.

The words across the top made no sense.

Certificate of Adoption.

Had she received someone else's documents? She checked the envelope. It still had her name on it. She examined the certificate, saw the name of the child.

Rose Everson Finch.

What the hell?

Her father was Clark Finch, her mother, Daisy Brooks. She'd come early while her parents were on holiday.

No way was she adopted.

Her birth certificate would prove it.

She picked up the document she'd set aside. Her breath caught as she studied it. This wasn't the birth certificate she'd been given when she'd left for college. Her birthdate was different, a month earlier than what she celebrated; she noticed the same was on the adoption paper. The names for mother and father were not Clark Finch and Daisy Brooks. The line for father was blank. And for mother…

Rose flung aside the afghan and stood. Her bedroom was small. There was no room to pace, but crud. She sat back down and ran her hands through her hair.

Aspen's arguments during the reading of the will, each word questioning why the youngest grandchild should inherit a house that had been in the Everson family for over a hundred years.

Rose knew the answer.

Bloody hell.

The tips of her fingers grazed the raised seal on the birth certificate. It was official, unlike the copy she had in her firebox, the one with Clark and Daisy Finch's names on it. Their names were nowhere on this new birth certificate. She read the name on the line designated for her birth mother.

Magnolia Eleanor Everson-Brooks.

Could this be true?

Her grandmother was her birth mother?

Why had she never told her?

Needing a minute, she picked up the afghan and held it against her chest. Then, she caught sight of the small ivory envelope.

Her fingers shook as she reached for it. *Rose* scrolled across the front in Magnolia's calligraphy style script. The letter opener sliced through the flap. She pulled two pieces of paper out. The familiar feminine handwriting invited tears to her eyes. Shaky words filled the page, a sign that this letter was more recent, perhaps after her first stroke. She pulled the afghan higher, wiping her eyes on its soft yarn. Then she began reading.

My dear imaginative Rebel,

If you are reading this, you have learned the truth

of your birth before I found the courage to tell you. This stubborn woman thought she had more time.

Perhaps in a different place, one not named for my great-grandfather, I could have kept you and raised you as my daughter.

I was alone and frightened. Fearful of what might happen if I acknowledged you as mine.

Evers Hollow will always be a small town. With its own woes and history. With all its ghosts, none more so than my ancestors. I ignored the stories passed down through generations before mine.

There came a menace to the woods, one that lurked, watched, and waited. I saw it, the glow of the lights, felt its icy fingers linger each time I lost someone. My father, my Devin, my precious Daisy and Clark.

When the accident happened, all five of you came to me. I feared keeping you. I feared sending you away.

In the end, I couldn't let any of you go. Each of you deserved love and the best upbringing I could provide. I love each of you.

For a time I thought I'd won, pushed back the dark. But if this letter is in your hands before I have told you its truth, then something has failed. If the lights in the woods have returned, I've failed. My father once told me that a knight can only stop evil for so long.

Briar House, her grounds, her woods, were always

going to be yours. I've heard your words, your poems to her, and the forest surrounding.

She speaks to you. You hear her as I do, as my father did when he was a boy. Not everyone has this gift. Your first time up the stairs, even amidst your grief for those you called Mom and Dad—the first time you touched the handrail, I saw it in your eyes. The hearing her, it's a gift.

Listen to her. Take care of her. In turn, she will take care of you.

Love, Magnolia

Chapter Twelve

Light peeked around the edges of the curtains on Rose's bedroom window. She lay on her side. Her eyes felt worn and dry. Too many tears. Her throat carried a lingering soreness for the same reason.

She sat up.

The papers she'd studied into the early morning hours still lay on her bed, along with their truths. Beside her pillow sat the wrapped box she'd yet to open. The letter, the truth of her birth, was enough. She couldn't deal with more shocking news. She slipped the box beneath the journals in her nightstand.

Rose got out of bed and swapped her sleep tee for jeans and a clean shirt. Unsure of the outside temperature, she reached for her dark green cable-knit sweater. This time of year, layers were a wise choice. The soft cotton sweater felt right as she slipped it over her head. After a visit to the bathroom and a glass of water, she gathered her hair with a scrunchie, then shoved the papers back into their envelope and into her messenger bag.

Morning walks had been absent from her schedule these past days. Fresh air would refresh her mind, maybe clear her lungs of any lingering dust from last night's disaster. A damn good coffee would also help.

She stepped outside her room. The guest room door remained closed. Hopefully, Willow still slept. She'd been just as wrung out. Yesterday had been—yesterday. Difficult, but they'd made it through.

The couch was empty; the blankets Thorne used sat folded on one cushion. A note lay on the kitchen counter. He'd gone for a run. She scribbled her own *gone for a walk* beneath his words, her *R* below it.

The trails would be muddy. She shoved her feet into her peony rain boots. Then grabbed a crocheted scarf from the basket by the door. Its softness comforted. She stepped outside, easing the cottage screen door closed to prevent its usual rattle.

Rose entered the woods that wound round and beyond the Everson estate. She needed the subtle snap of autumn, the scent of the forest, and its sounds of stirring life. This was her equivalent of Magnolia's precious rose garden, the place most likely to give her peace after all of yesterday.

Her boots were quiet on the trail. The fallen wet leaves cushioned her steps. Images tapped the edges of her mind, each one a memory of Magnolia. She tried to ignore them. Hadn't she cried enough?

Narrow streams of light shot through the branches above her as the sun climbed a little higher. An illusion of fog teased from the depths of the forest. The scent of damp tree bark and wet leaves surrounded her.

She thought of the words inside her bag. Why hadn't Magnolia told her the truth? It didn't matter that she read the letter, knew her answer. Her heart hurt. Magnolia's explanation left something amiss inside her.

A branch snapped close by. She froze, then spun and waited. Only silence followed. Not even a slight breeze shook the surrounding loose leaves. She startled once more when she heard the scramble of squirrels up the bark of a pine tree. The chattering argument between them encouraged her to let out a breath.

Despite her relief, a chill shuddered through her, a reminder of Magnolia's other words, about a menace amongst the trees, her cautionary warning in the hospital. She gathered the ends of her scarf and tucked them snug around her neck. It didn't make her feel better.

She walked until she came to a fork in the path.

The path to the right was neglected and overgrown with thorny vines and poison ivy. Sadness filled her at the sight. The number of times she'd traveled that fork as a child and teenager to see Finn. Those days were gone.

Rose took the left path, avoiding its fresh puddles. Within minutes, sounds of car engines reached her ears. As the trees thinned, she could see a line of cars to her left, bumper to bumper. She never came into town this early, but she knew from Broome that this was Evers Hollow's version of morning rush hour, an entire eight blocks' worth.

The path divided again. Straight on, the woods continued north a few miles. She turned left and took the first crosswalk across Ash Street. A right turn and a slight left led her inside a little coffee house she'd discovered when she'd moved back.

Firebrew.

No one would look for her here.

The hand-painted mural of a dark green dragon over the coffee counter drew her gaze. A burst of flames came out of its mouth as it curled its claws around a mug of coffee, its horde of beans nearby. Warmth misted through her as if the dragon itself caressed her with its fictional breath.

The owners, Shirley and Molly, both dressed in jeans and dragon logo'd black tees, waved at her from behind the counter. Mother and daughter, both had blemish-free golden skin and black hair. Shirley kept hers short while Molly kept hers shoulder length, embracing its tendency to curl with attitude.

Both were busy taking and completing orders for a line of suited professionals. Each person waiting looked to be a copy of one another. Only their hair and skin color varied. Rose recognized no one. To her, that meant anonymity and no prying questions.

She stepped behind the last person and waited to place her drink order.

"Want anything out of the case?" Molly asked as she pressed the screen of an iPad. "Mom is working on some new recipes. She needs customer opinions."

At the mention of food, her insides gave a tiny rumble. She'd barely touched the catered dinner the night before.

The glass case beside the register offered choices—some with glaze, some with streusel topping. "The lemon-blueberry muffin." She couldn't resist its streusel topping.

"Excellent choice—one of my new favorites." Molly told Rose her total.

She used her debit card.

"It'll be a few minutes," said the younger woman. "Mom's got a few ahead of yours."

The sitting area was near empty. Rose chose a seat in her favorite cozy corner, away from the windows. A fire burned in the old stone fireplace. She loosened her scarf and curled her sweater sleeves around her fingers.

Molly brought her order over. She seemed to hesitate a moment, but set the muffin and steaming mug down, then returned to the counter. A new line of Asheville commuters waited to place orders.

Warmth from the hot mocha stole into her fingers as Rose wrapped them around the burgundy mug. She inhaled the scent of espresso and chocolate before taking a sip. The flavor was a desperately needed hug. She drank more. Liquid warmth filled the chilled spaces inside her.

She broke open the large muffin, warm on her fingers.

Taking small bites, she glanced at her messenger bag. Another line of customers arrived and disappeared. Only two remained.

Rose looked around the seating area. Privacy rarely existed in Evers Hollow. A couple of men conferred at a nearby table over their laptops.

With a deep, decisive breath, she pulled the manila envelope out of her bag. She opened the flap and pulled its contents out. She turned her body to shield the papers while she read through them again. Each sentence remained as it had last night.

Magnolia Eleanor Everson-Brooks was still her birth mother. Not that she'd doubted what she'd read last night. But seeing it again cemented it.

She'd always loved Magnolia. Whether as grandmother or mother, none of that would change. She'd come to that realization as she lay in the dark, digesting what she'd learned.

Was this the reason behind Magnolia's preference that Rose call her by her given name instead of Grandmother?

It sounds pretty when you say it. Like flowers are flying out of your mouth.

As a child, she'd thought that silly. Since it made her smile, Rose stuck to Magnolia and rarely called her Grandmother. All of them were told to call her one of the two, nothing else. The others called her Grandmother, except for Thorne, who went back and forth between the two, depending on his mood.

Emotion threatened again. She wished she could stop, take a break from her thoughts over what she'd learned. She moved to slip her birth and adoption certificates back inside the envelope. Something prevented her from doing so. Reaching her hand in, she pulled out a flat hand-sized parcel, the one Finn had given her at the hospital. With all that had happened, she'd forgotten.

She unwrapped it and found a stack of photos. All of her and Finn. From childhood to eighth grade graduation, all taken by his mom. She smiled at the first picture. She'd wished for a distraction. This was certainly that. Her fingers flipped photo after photo, studying each one as memories assailed her. He'd been the best part of her childhood.

The scrape of a nearby chair made her look up. The two men were leaving. Rose tucked the photos back in their envelope and stuffed everything back into her bag.

Molly wiped the abandoned table. Then she came over.

With a visible swallow and glassy eyes, she said, "Mom and I. We're real sorry about Ms. Magnolia. She was one of our favorites."

Favorites?

"Magnolia? You knew her?" A potentially stupid question. Most townsfolk knew Magnolia. She'd been heavily involved in the community. But how did these two know Magnolia? She wasn't one to frequent coffee houses.

A gentle smile touched Molly's lips. "We knew her."

Rose straightened and looked around the space: its dragon decor, its cozy setting, the chalkboard menu behind the register. The inside looked rugged, cabin-like, not at all what she'd associate with the woman she'd previously known as her grandmother.

"Did she come here?"

Molly put a hand on one hip. Her smile broadened. "Like clockwork. Every Tuesday, sometimes with your oldest brother."

Magnolia in a hipster, fire-breathing dragon-themed coffee house. The image of the dragon letter opener flickered in her memory. Broome had told her it was her favorite. The urge to cry evaporated.

Molly said, "She talked about all of you when she came. Mom sat with her when we weren't busy."

Rose's face must have said what she couldn't fathom.

"You don't believe me," Molly teased.

Rose shook her head even as a smile came to her lips. "I'm trying. It's just…"

The younger woman turned. A hint of laughter rang through

her words. "Mom, Rose doesn't believe that Ms. Magnolia came here."

Shirley chuckled and blew her a kiss. Rose drank to cover her expression, whatever it might be.

Molly shook with laughter when she turned back, her curls bouncing around in subtle mirth. "Your gran—she could be a grumpy one. Scared us both the first time she came round. We'd been warned about her, you see. No disrespect, if you get my meaning."

This Rose could believe, but all she could do was nod, eager for more.

"She railed at us something fierce the first time she came in. Said we served compost for tea."

Rose indicated the adjacent chair. She had to hear this story.

Molly sat down. "Mom and I were in absolute tears. We knew her reputation. We feared she'd blackball us, that our coffee house would fail."

Not even Magnolia had that kind of influence.

Rose said, "She was very particular about her tea and wasn't timid about letting people know." Using past tense, she'd have to get used to that. "Her sister sent her tea from England."

Her eyes widened. "We didn't know. Funny thing is, she came back the very next day—then once a week after that."

Rose nodded. "That sounds like her, too. She loved small businesses."

Magnolia also liked to test people, evaluate their reactions.

"She came every week till she had that first stroke, sometimes with Broome." Molly's cheeks flushed. "After that, Broome brought her in or picked up to-go orders. He's really sweet, your brother."

"I would have brought her here if I knew she liked it."

Molly shook her head, a hint of a frown grazing her expression. "I think it was their thing. She mentioned you and the others plenty, and was so proud of all of you."

Interesting that neither Broome nor Magnolia ever mentioned this place.

The bell on the door jingled. Molly turned and jumped up. "Speaking of—I better get back to work."

Her abruptness took Rose by surprise until she turned and saw Broome enter *Firebrew,* a backpack over one shoulder, a somber expression on his face. Molly beat her mother to the register and took Broome's order. So the young barista had a crush on Broome. She wasn't the first. Both her college roommates described him as hot. She hadn't wanted to hear it.

She watched Molly point a finger in her direction. So much for anonymity. With his own burgundy mug in hand, he turned towards her table.

Broome slid out of his jacket and hung it on the chair opposite hers. He sat, took a long sip from his mug, and studied her.

"Thorne wanted to be the one to find you," he said. "I asked him to let me do it."

For Broome to seek her out was unusual. To say he volunteered over another was worse. Then it all made sense.

"You know." It wasn't a question.

Another sip.

"Yes." He didn't look away, focused on her.

She broke eye contact first. Damn. She wasn't ready for this conversation. Because if he knew...

Rose straightened, dug her fingers into her knee. "Do the others know?"

"No."

"Why you?"

"I've always known you weren't my real sister," he confessed in a low voice, his voice stark with a sadness she hadn't heard before.

A tightness gathered around her chest hearing the truth spoken aloud. Not his real sister. He'd always known. "How?"

"I remember when Mom and Dad brought you home. I was

six. A neighbor stayed over to watch us. She thought all of us were asleep." He shrugged. "When I heard the garage door, I got out of bed. I sat at the top of the stairs and listened while they talked with the neighbor. I had a new sister. Yet I knew Mom wasn't pregnant."

Things between them. His lack of patience towards her. She couldn't help it.

"All these years…" she said in a hoarse whisper. With one hand, she motioned between them. "That's why…" She couldn't finish.

He swore. "Whatever you're thinking, stop." He leaned forward, meeting her eyes with earnest. "You are my sister in every way that matters. I was six years old when they brought you home. I was told never to lie and was punished for breaking that rule. They told people Mom gave birth to you. I didn't know what to think."

"You kept their secret all these years."

He nodded. "Truth was, it scared me."

"They never knew you knew?"

He shook his head. "Not Mom and Dad. As for Grandmother, it took me years to figure out she was your birth mother. Long after we moved in. She never spoke of it, not till after her first stroke."

Her lips parted. Another question. The blank line on her birth certificate. Was it even appropriate to ask?

"Any idea who my father is?"

"It's not on the birth certificate?"

"No."

He pushed his fingers through his hair and sighed. "No idea. Is it important that you know?"

She rubbed her hands up and down her arms. "I don't know. All of this—it's overwhelming. I feel different, like I'm not sure who I am anymore."

"I would worry about you if you didn't feel something. Truth is, you're exactly who you've always been. Rose Everson Finch. Details behind that are a little different than you thought. You know the truth now."

"I do, made it hard to sleep."

"You're calmer than I thought you would be. I expected you to be upset, even angry."

"I'm a plethora of emotions. Why didn't she tell me? I have so many questions that will never be answered."

Rose looked at him, a man she'd called big brother as long as she could remember. She couldn't think of him as anything else, but… "Can I still call you brother?"

His expression gentled. The lines around his eyes softened. He leaned forward, placed both his hands over hers. His words came out strong and sure. "I told you. I'm your brother in every way that matters. Always. We've got the documentation to prove it."

"What about the others?" Nausea edged at the idea of telling the other three.

"Tell them when you're ready."

"Magnolia kept her secret for a reason."

He shrugged. "The truth is yours now. Do with it what you wish."

What did she wish? Part of her wanted to just tell them, get it out there and be done with it, but…

"Aspen is still angry about the house. She sent me three texts last night. This might send her over the edge."

"The house is a symbol to her, nothing more. In time, she'll understand." He let go of her hands. "Grandmother knew what she was doing. Briar House is a part of you."

Rose mulled his words over. His words rang true. The house and its woods were part of her. It was one reason her books were successful. She cocked her head. Had Aspen ever walked through the trees, pressed her hands against their bark? Did she know all the hidden secret places inside Briar House? Had she even looked?

I've heard your words, your poems to her, and the forest surrounding. She speaks to you.

Briar House was hers. She'd signed the paperwork last night. Her fingers had trembled when she'd put pen to page. Wild things tumbled inside her stomach.

"Are you and Simi still hosting the next family meal?" she asked.

"Yes."

"I'll tell them then."

"If that's what you want."

She'd never liked the cliché about ripping off Band-Aids, but in this situation, it fit. "It is."

Chapter Thirteen

Finn spotted the pile of unopened mail on his kitchen table when he entered his apartment. Kendra, his neighbor, must have used her key to bring it all in.

He left the door open to air out the place, then tossed his keys and wallet into a basket in the middle of the kitchen table. He set his cell phone on top of its charger on the kitchen counter.

Within minutes, a boy appeared in his doorway. An almost nine-year-old with dark hair trimmed close to his head. The boy was skinny except for a small tummy around his middle. Clad in dinosaur pajamas, he stepped in.

Behind him, a very pregnant Kendra stood.

"You're back," she said. "I thought I heard the squeak of your door. Landon has been checking the window every five minutes since he saw your last text."

"Mom." The word carried a pleading tone with it. "He's teaching me soccer. I'm going to the World Cup."

She rested her hand on her belly and threw her son the look. "The man just got home. He drove a long way. Leave him be."

Finn couldn't ignore the plea on the boy's face, but he knew

Kendra. She was trying to teach Landon patience. He needed to support her efforts.

"Tell you what, little man. If it's okay with your mom, I can take you to the park after school on Wednesday to practice."

Kendra looked back at him. "He can go if he gets his homework done when he gets home."

Landon pumped both his fists in the air. "Yes."

Her eyes narrowed. "I can change my mind if you don't quiet down. Your baby sisters are sleeping."

The kid said, "Sorry, Mom, I'm excited. I can't wait to tell Dad."

"Go brush your teeth, then you can call him from the kitchen table." She emphasized the last. These apartments didn't have the greatest insulation. Sound carried.

Landon gave another silent double fist pump as he walked back into their apartment.

Kendra brushed her hair out of her eyes. "Appreciate that. That one keeps me on my toes."

"He's a great kid."

A worn smile brushed her lips. "He is. He does so much to help me with the girls."

Finn asked, "When's Dare getting home?" Kendra's husband transported cars throughout the country. He was often gone for days at a time.

She said, "Thursday. Hopefully, before dinner. Otherwise, I'll never get that one to bed on time."

"Like Landon said, he's going to play in the World Cup."

Within days of Finn moving into his apartment, Landon asked him if he knew how to play soccer. When Finn said yes, he'd asked for help with his corner kicks. Knowing Landon had twin sisters and another sibling on the way, Finn agreed. Scrambling for attention with two toddlers in a place was difficult. He tried to make time for Landon when he could.

Concern rimmed Kendra's brown eyes. She put a hand on Finn's arm. "You okay?" She knew he'd gone to a funeral.

"Yeah. More tired than anything."

Kendra looked at him as if she doubted his words. He needed to say more.

"The funeral was a nice tribute."

Broome had spoken for the family. Not a surprise. As had Brigette Conroy, one of the town's elders. Locals filled the big house after the graveside service, many reciting stories about Ms. Magnolia.

"And your pa?" Kendra had never met him, but knew Finn visited him once a week.

"Wore him out, but otherwise he's fine."

Her expression relaxed. "Okay then. You should come to dinner when Dare gets back. Text me with potential dates. We've also got Landon's birthday coming up. He'll want you there if it works with your schedule."

"Sounds great."

A few nights later, he walked down the hill to the local sports bar. He'd told Decker, a fellow resident, he'd be there. Every TV broadcasted football. There was no such thing as a bad seat, but it was crowded enough to make it hard to find his friends. He made his way through a group of Carolina fans, then spotted Decker and Walt in a back corner. Decker wore his Panthers jersey and had a blonde on his lap that he recognized from the lab at the hospital. Her name escaped him, but she, too, wore the Panthers' colors. Walt wore Kansas City red and kept one arm around his girlfriend, Avery, dressed in Miami's colors.

A pint of Guinness in hand, he sat down on a stool with the lot of them, nodded to Decker and Walt, exchanged handshakes with Avery and the blonde. It was too loud for conversation.

He spotted the curvy redhead he'd been interested in right after he'd moved to Asheville. She was leaning over the bar, trying to get the bartender's attention.

He'd asked her to coffee. She'd been lukewarm on the invitation but seemed interested by the end. He'd hoped to see her again. She'd said maybe when he asked, but they hadn't set a date.

Now he knew he wouldn't.

Rose wasn't married.

No matter what Broome said, Finn had been the one to make the promise to Ms. Magnolia. It would be difficult for him to keep his word. He didn't live in Evers Hollow. His rotation schedule was tight. He hadn't been able to get back up there since the funeral.

Later in the week, he'd have three days off. He planned to spend the time at the old house. Pa's birthday was this coming Sunday.

There were things he needed to say to Rose. He owed her a better explanation, and an apology. Another sip, larger than the last. He'd never felt connected to anyone like he had with her. That hadn't changed with distance or time.

He should have found the courage to do it years ago. Been honest with himself, and with her. Their friendship was important, more important than any other he'd had. Fear that she didn't feel the same way kept him quiet. The last thing he wanted was to lose her as a friend.

They'd gone six years without speaking.

He should have told her he wanted more. Asked her out. What would she say if he asked her now?

Chapter Fourteen

Brody Bates showed up at Briar House in worn jeans and a logo'd blue polo shirt. A ball cap sat backwards on his head atop collar-length wavy brown hair. He stood a tad taller than Rose in leather work-boots. It took him an hour to go through each level of the house, walk the roof, and wriggle through the crawl space. His father had been the one to inspect the dining room days prior, per Broome's recommendation.

Brody was doing what his father hadn't had time for. A full home inspection. After the dining room disaster, it was needed.

Rose tried to take notes on everything he told her. He spoke fast. It was hard to keep up.

He said, "Rot's common here with our weather and all the trees. Did you know you've got a chimney pulling away from the house? In the parlor."

"Seriously? That can happen?" How had no one noticed this after the roof replacement fifteen months ago?

He caressed his scruff of a beard. "Yeah, it happens. Looks like there's a nest of some kind up there in the gap."

"Great." She grimaced and wrote in the small notebook in her hand. Spiders, snakes, she could handle. It came with the territory they lived in. This sounded like more. Something she couldn't deal with on her own. In capital letters, she scribbled *NOT MY TASK* across a line.

Brody led her past the stairs and into the ballroom. Even though he'd already gone room to room looking for issues, he seemed transfixed by the space as he studied the trio of large crystal chandeliers overhead. The room looked like a film set from a Regency mini-series.

He said, "My grandparents told me stories about this place. They loved coming here, said the New Year's Eve party was the event of the year."

He glanced at his clipboard and motioned to the longest wall, the part of the house that lived in permanent shade. "We need to treat for termites. All the drywall needs replacing, along with some of the support beams. The moisture rating in this room is higher than the rest of the house."

She made a frustrated sound, but wrote it down.

"Termites are common here with all the rain. Had them in my own house two years ago. We're on a yearly maintenance plan."

"So, termite treatment and annual plan." She wrote the words down, her penmanship jagged and harried.

"Old houses are great until they're not taken care of." He looked regretful. "I wish Ms. Magnolia had called us years ago. We could have prevented some of these things."

Rose said, "I don't think she could have known these things by looking at the house. I had no idea, and I've been back for two years."

She took another look around the ballroom. Had any of them walked the rooms of the house during holidays and family events with the thought of maintenance? How could one tell a wall needed replacing when it looked like every other faded wall in the house, especially those covered with wallpaper?

The man she'd thought of as her grandfather had likely managed these things. After he passed, Magnolia might not have known the level of what was needed. When she lost her daughter and all of them moved in, termites were likely the last thing on her mind.

Downstairs, Brody showed her how some windows were painted shut. "People thought it kept the house warmer in the winter."

Her brows furrowed. Tess often had the windows open in the kitchen, but the rest of the downstairs, she'd never noticed. What moron did such things? Magnolia would never be so impractical. It must have been an ancestor.

He chuckled. "It makes no sense, but people do funny things to save money."

They moved upstairs. He explained more of his findings, including the integrity of the remaining ceilings. He explained the plumbing issues that contributed to the dining room collapse. The info was familiar. His father had gone over that yesterday by phone.

He flipped a few pages as they took the stairs back down toward the front entry. "I checked the electrical as well."

She supposed that was a normal inspection thing. "And?"

"You hadn't noticed any problems?"

"No."

More scribbles. "Amazing you haven't noticed. Not all the outlets work. I recommend a full update of the electrical, including the wiring on the ballroom chandeliers. It would be tragic to see a fire spark after all the improvements you'll be thinking of. I'll give you the name of an electrician. He's worked on a bunch of the older homes in Asheville. Does solid work."

Rose swallowed. This was going to be expensive. It was one thing to inherit the house she loved, another to consider whether she could afford to keep it. She had some money saved, with more coming in from her latest book release. She needed to meet with Broome to get his thoughts on all this.

Brody stowed his camera and put his clipboard back in his bag. "I'll have a full report with my photos in a few days."

She opened the door for him but hesitated. "If she were yours, would you spend the money to fix her?"

He didn't answer at first, studied her as if trying to figure something out. He clicked his pen a few times and said, "She. That means she's not just a house to you. I've heard other stories, not just from my grandparents."

He pressed his palm on the door frame as if the contact provided additional insight. "She's got memories, this one. Harbored her share of ghosts through the years. She won't go easily—she'll put up a fight."

Rose wrapped her arms around herself, unsure of what to say. She didn't believe in ghosts. But she'd grown up with the stories, too. Everyone considered local had. They shared stories of old Macintosh Everson roaming the grounds with his shovel, digging holes for more trees. Of Magnolia's favorite horse, Lady, galloping around the edge of the property after the barn fire. Even the sons who never came home from Europe during World War Two. They marched through the forests more often than she did, if the rumors were to be believed.

Magnolia had called the stories ridiculous, but said if it kept people from trespassing, she'd tolerate it. She preferred her privacy.

Brody looked pensive. "I won't lie to you. She'll be a significant investment. I'd prioritize safety. Then I'd go with what's important to you, shop around on the restoration and any updates you're interested in. I know Dad gave you a list of fully licensed and insured contractors we recommend."

She nodded.

"Any of those names would compete to fix up this old place. They all do fine work."

"I'll remember that."

"You'll want to look into grants, too. There are a few historical societies in the county and the state that might support your efforts.”

She said, “I didn't think of that.”

“In the long run, my opinion doesn't matter. I'm guessing there's a reason she's yours, that she means something to you. I'd keep her, fix her. It might take years, but she's worth it.”

She opened the door the rest of the way, followed him onto the porch. Dry leaves crunched beneath her shoes.

Brody clicked his pen again. “You might consider turning it into a bed-and-breakfast. People love old houses and will pay to stay in them. You'll make your money back.”

He slung his backpack over his shoulder and gave her a half-smile.

She thanked him again and closed the front door when she heard his truck start.

Briar House as a bed-and-breakfast. That would never happen. The ghosts she didn't believe in would protest for sure.

Chapter Fifteen

It was ten past nine when Rose approached the doors of the Cracked Egg Cafe. She welcomed the opportunity to get away from the house for a bit. Brody's recommendations, multiple phone calls, and estimates had provided her a template for an overall plan. Two days had passed since she'd met Broome for coffee to go over the report.

A disaster specialist crew showed up early this morning to start work in the dining room. Over the weekend, family and friends, masked and covered in old clothes, helped load debris into a dumpster Broome ordered for delivery.

The leaning chimney repair was scheduled for next week. As for the termite issue in the ballroom, there was a three-week waiting list. Her name was on it. Brody's contact for the electrical was out of town for a family wedding. His secretary promised to follow up as soon as he was back.

Magnolia's letter, her confession, Rose's true parentage—all of it weighed heavy on her mind whilst she made phone calls, set up appointments for the house, then drove into town.

Rose put her hand around the handle of the Cracked Egg

Cafe's glass door. The Elders would be inside, among them, Magnolia's closest friends. She had questions to ask them.

The diner was a town favorite, open for breakfast and lunch. Their menu carried a selection of hearty breakfasts, classic sandwiches, and soups. The waitstaff wove around tables as if in a choreographed dance.

From the checkout counter, Florence, owner and server, greeted her with her usual, "Mornin' sweetie. Seat yourself."

Rose bypassed the empty booths and tables around the perimeter, then approached the large round table in the middle, all but one chair taken. Brigette Conroy and four men, known as The Elders, occupied the rest.

Each of them was a bridge, a connection to Magnolia's past. They'd attended school together. Breakfasted here every Thursday morning for years.

Rose greeted the group with an overall *hello*.

The Finch children had grown up knowing all The Elders, some more than others. Jeremy and Brigette Conroy, the Finch kids' honorary aunt and uncle, saw her first. Both stood and gave her a hug.

Brigette said, "It's wonderful to see you."

Rose put her hand on the empty chair at the table, the one that had been Magnolia's. The place was set with silverware and a yellow coffee mug. She swallowed. "Do you mind if I join you?"

Jeremy motioned toward the empty chair. "By all means."

Rose sat.

Across the table, Mr. Hal looked up and studied her. "You're Nola's youngest grandchild, Rose. The writer, the one who drove her here every Thursday."

The Elders called Magnolia, Nola. They were the only ones in town who had permission to call her something besides her given name and Grandmother.

She said, "Yes, I'm Rose. I remember when you took care of our horses."

He nodded. "It's been a bit. You remember well. No need to be formal. Call me Hal. Makes me sound younger."

"All right."

Hal Lawson had worked as the local veterinarian for as long as she could remember. Time and sun had aged his face. As a child, it hurt her neck to look up at him. She'd likened him to a tree more than once. He was the sort that kids and animals gravitated to, even though he and his wife never had children. He'd retired a few years prior.

To her right, Dr. Cook nodded at her. Magnolia called him the quiet one. He was a stout man with close-cropped light gray hair. He'd been the only pediatrician in town for years, an irony since he never seemed fond of children. Despite retiring, Magnolia said he still served those in need on a volunteer basis.

Beside him sat Clyde Winston, the mayor. Sunlight bounced off the flattop of his white hair as he grinned. He said, "Good morning. You look fresh as sunshine."

She greeted him back.

Florence came by with coffee. Her brown hair was wound into a bun at her nape. She said, "It's been a while since you dropped in for a bear claw, Rose. I hear you're cheating on us with that dragon coffee house."

Rose stammered, "I—"

Florence winked and laughed in a way that lit her entire face. "I'm just messing with you, girl."

She filled Rose's mug. "I gotta wonder what they put in those beans, though. Even I have to stop by there on the way to my mother's. A jolt of caffeine is safer than what we all used to call liquid courage."

Dr. Cook muttered, "I still call it liquid courage."

Rose wasn't sure everyone heard him, but she sent him a small smile.

Florence pulled a sharpened pencil from behind her ear and a notebook from the apron she wore over her jeans. "I've got the others in. What will you have? Besides a bear claw."

Rose grinned. "Blackberries and a scrambled egg."

"I'll get this put in with Stan." Florence walked back to the kitchen.

From her left, Jeremy asked, "What's the latest on the ceiling collapse?"

Both he and Brigette had shown up masked and ready to help with the debris cleanup earlier in the week, along with two of their sons, Aidan and Ethan.

"Brody Bates did the full house inspection," Rose said. "He brought his father's report regarding the ceiling. A crew started on things this morning. The insurance adjuster will be out later to fine-tune some numbers."

Jeremy nodded. "The Bates run a solid business. You can trust their findings. They helped us with some damage from a leaky air conditioner years back."

"I'm thankful Broome knew who to call. He's been an immense help. I hadn't even had the house an hour before disaster struck."

True enough, Broome had done more than she had this past week with his local connections. Ordering the dumpster that sat outside the front of the house, asking local friends to help clear the debris out.

Brigette said, "Don't fret, hon, you'll figure it out."

Hal spoke next. "What brings you by?"

Rose said. "I miss her. I wondered if you had any stories you could share. It would help."

Brigette's blue eyes filled with understanding. She reached across Jeremy, put her hands over Rose's. "Of course. She was my dearest friend. I miss her too."

She dabbed the corners of her eyes as Jeremy moved closer to put his arm around his wife.

The rest of them nodded. Hal leaned forward. Magnolia always said he was the storyteller of the group. "What would you like to know?"

Now that she was here, she couldn't think of a single question. She couldn't exactly lead with the fact that Magnolia was her birth mother. Not here in the middle of the Cracked Egg Cafe.

"Anything." She could get more specific later.

Beside her, Dr. Cook muttered a few words.

Brigette turned to him. "What's that, Sam?"

He cleared his throat. "She used to tutor me back in school. Mathematics."

Brigette's expression eased as her voice softened. "In the library. I remember."

He nodded, looked at both of them. "Equations were hard for me. Word problems too. Nola made them clear."

Brigette said, "She was a genius with numbers. She got an award, end of her junior year."

Dr. Cook said, "I passed Algebra because of her. Along with geometry and trigonometry."

Rose never knew that. Broome had always been the one to tutor them in math.

Brigette spoke next. "Nola and I ironed our hair for the homecoming dance. It was a disaster, smelled something awful. Her hair was so dark it was hard to tell that it was burnt, but mine, these blond locks—so obvious I had done something bad to it. We both ended up wearing our hair up. And hoping no one could smell how we scorched it."

Jeremy's shoulders shook as if in silent laughter. "You cut your hair, so did Nola."

Brigette's hand went up to her long blond and silver strands. "Six inches. It broke my heart, but the burned parts were breaking away. I looked like a scarecrow."

Jeremy's long, tanned fingers played with his wife's hair.

"You never looked like a scarecrow." He kissed her until she giggled and pushed him away.

The two of them acted like newlyweds. They'd been married for over forty years and had five children.

Even after their kiss ended, Brigette's gaze flitted to her husband, her love for him clear in every glance of her bright blue eyes.

A glance told her the mayor was watching her. He'd been silent since his initial greeting. She didn't know him well. Only that his father had served as a senator for years in the state legislature. From Magnolia, she knew he had two children, a son and a daughter, both in their forties. His wife, Louise, was not one of The Elders. Brigette had once let it slip that Louise Winston despised their little group, but never elaborated on why.

"You should date my Jesse," he said. "He's my oldest, a handsome devil with a ten-thousand dollar grin."

Rose got the sense he meant that literally.

Dr. Cook cleared his throat. Hal and Jeremy straightened in their seats as if preparing for something. Brigette's eyes narrowed.

The mayor continued, "I'm retiring end of my term. He'll take my place."

Rose hadn't met his son, only knew he had gone to an Ivy League school.

"A pretty young woman on his arm, especially someone with the Everson name, would help with the votes. An engagement would be—"

Brigette slammed her coffee cup on the table, hard enough to crack it. Coffee leaked onto the surface. No one moved at first.

In a menacing voice, Brigette said. "Hear that? Nola just rolled over in her grave. We're telling stories about her. This is not the time—"

The mayor held up his hands. "No offense. I was just thinking."

Her eyes flashed. "Then stop. Rose and the rest of her family lost someone precious to them. She wants to hear cheerful stories about Nola, not your politics."

The argument drew attention. Other customers looked their way.

Rose curled her fingers against her jeans. Wished for a quick escape. A trap door beneath her chair.

The mayor guffawed, then looked at both of them. "I apologize. I meant no harm to you, Rose, nor you, Brigette. You're making me look bad."

Jeremy leaned forward. "You're doing a good job of that all by yourself, Clyde."

His face reddened as he sucked in his cheeks.

Florence bustled over with a towel, dropped it on the coffee spill, her voice agitated. "Everything okay over here?"

Hal raised his head. "It'll be fine, Flo. Clyde shoved his boots into his mouth. Brigette's—"

"I'm pissed, Florence." Brigette helped wipe up the spill.

Florence raised an eyebrow, removed the cracked mug, a few empty plates. "I can tell sugar. You're all drawing attention, though."

"Sorry, Florence," said Dr. Cook.

"Just pipe it down. I don't need drama in my place."

"Of course. We'll behave."

"You do that. Maybe you'll all get a cookie for it."

Dr. Cook cleared his throat and looked across to Hal. "You got a story about Nola?"

Hal nodded. "Chock full of them. Would you like to hear?"

As if the question was a lifeline, Rose said, "Yes."

He launched into one.

Chapter Sixteen

When the white-haired, wiry, pale-skinned man sat down to eat breakfast at the dirty kitchen table, he noticed the folded local newspaper in the middle. The date was over a week old. Its headline stood out, along with an enlarged photo below it.

Local Matriarch Dies

Her. He snatched the newspaper up even as his hands shook. The picture—Maggie, his muse for all his work. Dark hair, inviting eyes. Both green as new growth, begging him to impress her.

This couldn't be real. Some sort of sick joke.

He set it down, glanced around to see if anyone was watching. The kitchen was empty. Both doors down the hall were still closed.

Of course, they'd want him to think his muse was dead. No one appreciated his work, or understood the beauty she brought —the soundtrack.

He'd seen her last week, watched her shadow flicker across the closed curtains of her bedroom as she moved about.

He read the rest of the page.

Magnolia Everson-Brooks, seventy-two, of Evers Hollow, NC, passed away on September...

The newspaper trembled in his hands, dampening as he continued to read.

This couldn't be. It had to be a lie.

He stood.

Did they think they could keep him away from her?

Everything he'd done was for her.

Before he ripped it down the middle, he read the last lines of the supposed obituary.

Evers Hollow Cemetery

Chapter Seventeen

F inn set the large paper bag he carried down so he could sign-in at the front desk of Wylder Ridge. Through the glass wall behind the front desk, he could see at least a dozen residents on the back patio basking in the midday sun. Wylder Ridge was a smaller retirement community, aged fifty-five and over. The main building held studio apartments. Half a dozen cabins with full kitchens sat in back for couples who wished more independence, who drove regularly. No fancy programs, no arts director, but it was clean, and the staff cared about their residents as if they were family.

An unfamiliar thin man with tortoiseshell glasses sat behind the wooden counter. This must be the new hire Pa mentioned. No name tag yet.

He looked up and said, "Who are you here for?"

"Charles Murphy, room 52B."

Pa's favorite Black nurse sat nearby at a computer, her long dark braids pulled away from her face as she typed. When he spoke, Stella raised her head and rose, her full lips curving into a gentle smile.

She came around the counter and gave him a hug. "Finn Murphy. It has been a spell."

"It has," Finn said. "You were on vacation last week. How was Disney with Ty and the kids?"

She beamed. "We had a fantastic time. My kids can't stop talking about it."

"That's great. It's been a bit since I've been down there." Finn scrawled his name on the clipboard atop the counter.

"Charlie's birthday's today. You got a cake?"

Finn nodded as he picked up the bag. "And berries just the way he likes."

Stella stepped back as if to evaluate him. She'd worked with his mom at Hollows Hospital in town for years, long before its doors closed.

A single line of worry appeared across her forehead. She tsk'd. "You've lost weight since I saw you, in a bad way. Your pa's going to notice."

"Long hours in rotations. Studying. How is he today?"

She frowned and held her hand up. "You did not just try to distract me. I made a promise to your dear mama before she passed. She would want you to put some meat on those bones."

He folded his arms. "I started my rotations two months ago, Stella."

"What happens when you're skinny enough to walk through cracks?"

He cocked his head and fought a grin. "It's not that bad."

"I'll be keeping my eye on you. A promise is a promise. Your mama was an angel." She tugged his arm toward the hallway on the right. "You'll be having a large piece of that cake if I have to feed it to you myself."

"Yes, ma'am."

Stella walked alongside him; her shoes squeaked along the tile floor. "Charlie's in the game room, on a winning streak." She lowered her voice, her southern accent dropping into the pronunciation of her words. "It's a good thing you're here. He's acting like he's the one who drove ten hours to see Mickey Mouse."

"Cards?"

"Mm-hmm. No one's beat him today."

They passed open doors on either side of the hall, a lingering scent of hospital grade disinfectant in the air.

Pa loved cards. He often won and celebrated with enthusiasm. His opponents, though, felt downright resentful. Finn glanced at the bag in his hand. Maybe he should have brought a bigger cake.

As if she could read his mind, Stella said, "Half of them can't eat sugar. I'll stash it in his room, bring you some plates and silverware."

He followed her into the game room. The walls were painted sky blue. Framed photographs of the Great Smoky Mountains hung along one wall. The windows opposite brought light in. Small sitting areas filled the corners of the room, some occupied with residents visiting loved ones. Square wooden tables stood in the middle with chairs around. Two women worked a puzzle at one. Pa sat at another, cards in hand, across from a man in a wheelchair with a long white beard.

Stella's voice rang out like a musical note. "Charlie— brought you a visitor."

Pa turned. A broad smile broke across his time weathered face. "Finn, my boy."

With the help of his cane, he rose and gave Finn a back slapping hug. Smiles broke around the room.

Finn wasn't a stranger at Wylder. Most of the residents had lived in Evers Hollow before they ended up here. Pa worked on their cars at Ferris' Garage before opting for an early retirement. Finn himself worked alongside him for three years back in high school.

He walked around the room to greet the men and women who'd watched him grow from a scrawny boy to an adult back in the Hollow they all called home. He'd developed visible muscles in the time since, but knew they only saw the boy he had been.

The sight of familiar faces reminded him how long it had been since he'd left Evers Hollow to seek his future.

Finn made his way back to his father's side and gave him another hug. "Happy birthday. How's your day?"

"Not bad. Won myself a handful of *get out of jail free cards* from Cartwright here." He motioned to the man he'd been playing with. The bearded man clasped Finn's hand in greeting.

A few Monopoly cards lay on the table. Wylder often used objects from the past to energize their residents. "That's great. Ready to celebrate?"

"Four letter word?" Pa had a childlike hope in his eyes.

Finn nodded.

"Let's get to it then. Tell me it's from Betsy."

"It's from Betsy's, with custard filling."

Pa rubbed his stomach. "Ever consider asking her out?"

"I think her wife, Alessia, would have something to say about that."

Pa chuckled as they moved down the hall. "You can't blame me for asking. She's an artist with cake."

The couple opened Lightning Cakes five years ago. Betsy made the cakes and Alessia made the pastries with the help of their employees. The bakery was a huge success.

Stella met them in Pa's room. Each room at Wylder was a small studio apartment with kitchenettes. Regular meals were served in the facility's dining room. Pa's held a small table with chairs, his favorite recliner, and his bedroom set from the old house.

The small, round decorated cake sat on the table. Stella took a picture of the two of them before they sang *Happy Birthday*. She cut the lemon-flavored cake. She handed Pa the first piece with a spoonful of berries on top. Then cut an enormous second piece and pushed it at Finn.

"Eat."

He sat down and ate. His mom taught him long ago that Stella was not a woman to be argued with. At his insistence, she cut herself a sliver and joined them for a bit.

The leftover cake was stowed in the mini-fridge in the room. Pa was still licking his fork when Stella left.

Finn said, "I brought a surprise for you."

"What's that?"

He pulled a box out of his backpack. "Found a Battleship game that could fit in my bag."

Pa's brown eyes lit up. "It's been forever since we played."

"It's been forever since you won."

"I'm glad you don't play cards."

"You refused to teach me. Afraid I'd beat you." He set up the two halves of the game.

Letter and number pairings filled the minutes. Finn looked at the number of ships he'd lost. Four. This was not a game he lost.

"Rough time at work?"

It had been, but Pa didn't want to hear about last night's car accident. He didn't like bad endings. The ER rotation was difficult. These past weeks showed that no matter how hard he tried, there were some people that couldn't be saved.

"Work is the same," Finn said.

"You meet with Ray yet?"

"Had to reschedule."

Pa swore. Finn ignored him. Ms. Magnolia's stroke took precedence over a meeting with a real estate agent. Plus, he was the one doing all the work on the house. The inside still needed a fresh coat of paint, which he'd be doing himself. The quote he'd received from a local painting company was too high.

"I went through more boxes. Got some questions. G-4."

"Miss." Pa's voice sounded gruff. "I told you, all decisions are yours."

"I found your wedding album." Finn reached into his bag and pulled it out, setting it on the table between them.

Pa didn't even glance at it. "H-7."

He glanced at his board. "Hit—destroyer." He stuck a red peg in one hole of the tiny plastic boat.

Pa leaned forward, his eyes narrowed, focused on an obvious victory. "Make your play."

Finn studied his board. "A-10."

"Miss." His glee was obvious. His fingers rifled through the pegs compartment in celebration.

"I figured you'd want the album here."

"You figured wrong. H-8."

Finn sighed. "Hit and sunk—destroyer."

"About time." Pa started pulling pegs off his board, putting them away.

"I'll leave the album here on the shelf for you, just in case." Finn leaned over and placed it near the bed.

Pa snapped his game board closed and set it back in the box, his mouth now a thin line. "You leaving the game here or taking it with you?"

"It's yours. I noticed it wasn't in the game room." Finn put his half away.

"I'll keep it in here. Harley Conti chewed up all the Parcheesi pawns."

"I hope he didn't swallow them."

"No, he spat them out," said Pa. "It's been hard on him, giving up tobacco. Stella lectured him."

Finn grimaced. He'd had a few lectures from Stella as a child. She and her husband, Ty, lived next door to them for a few years before they had kids. She babysat him several times back then.

"Delicious cake. Good birthday." Pa leaned back and rested his hands on his stomach.

Finn watched Pa distance himself. His normal routine every

visit. He'd talk about how much he loved his Clara, tell the stories of long ago—how he'd wooed her with wildflowers and hikes in North Carolina's state parks. The tangible though: the photos, the Irish double chain quilt she'd sewn for her hope chest as a young woman—Pa refused to touch them.

Finn pressed a hand against the back of his neck. What could he say? Every person had their way with grief. He glanced at his backpack, at the other thing he'd brought. There was no putting it off.

He pulled out his wrapped gift and handed it over. "I came across these last week."

The wrapping came off easily. Two frames sat in Pa's hands. He held the top frame by its edge as he looked at the long ago image of Finn and himself in front of his old truck. "Old Blue. You were just a pup then. You couldn't even lift a tire."

Finn's biceps contracted as if in defense, as he rested his forearms on the table. "I can lift one now."

Pa nodded, his gaze still caught by the old photo. "That you can, although you could use some fattening up. You're forgetting to eat."

Finn wouldn't call it forgetting. Meals were long hours apart when multiple ambulances rolled in.

Thankfully, Pa didn't press the issue while he studied the image of father and son. "You made a wonderful mechanic."

"It was good training for my hands." He'd spent hours under his and Riley Pierce's tutelage working at Ferris' garage.

"I know. Your mom would be proud of you becoming a doctor." Pa set the frame down. "At the big house after the funeral, I heard it was you at the house with Magnolia when she had her stroke."

"It was, but…"

Pa ran a hand over his face, glanced at Finn. "You gave the family time to say goodbye."

"I know—it doesn't mean I have to like it."

"They said the pneumonia took her. I never thought..." He looked away.

Finn didn't know what to say. His pa wasn't one for emotion. This was the closest he'd come to discussing a difficult topic in a while.

The second frame lay facedown on the table. Battered from years of working on cars, his fingers touched the back gently. "This other one—it's your mom, isn't it?"

Finn nodded. "Thought it would make you smile."

Pa hesitated. Would he hand it back to him? Finn held his breath.

He turned the frame over. "I'll be."

His parents stood side by side dressed like pirates, his mom's eyes alive with laughter. A gentle smile took over Pa's face. His eyes crinkled at the corners as he took the image in.

"That was the best Halloween we shared. I miss her. Makes it hard some nights even after all these years."

"I know. I miss her too." Finn laid a hand over Pa's and squeezed. "She'd be proud of you."

He looked wistful. "I suppose she would. Twelve years dry. Thanks to you and Riley."

Finn took the moment for what it was. Enjoyed it. His mom's passing made for some rough times when Pa decided to self-medicate his grief with whiskey. He forgot himself for a time, along with his job and his son, who needed him.

It had been Riley Pierce, the new owner of Ferris Garage, who'd had words with Pa after he ended up in the local lock-up for a night. Then again, after he found Finn one night, bloodied and bruised behind the garage, a victim of local bullies.

Riley was the one to get Pa enrolled in a treatment program and then drove him there. No longer did Finn receive phone calls late at night to walk into town, collect the truck keys from the bartender, and drive Pa home. Finn didn't have his license; he was too young. Every bartender who handed over the keys knew, but he'd never been pulled over.

Riley took Finn in while Pa was in the initial program and again when he went through a second time. Made sure he ate, taught him how to defend himself, and hired him on at the garage once he was old enough.

He'd done what Finn couldn't. Riley restored their family.

Pa set the frame down, face up. "This thing with Magnolia—word is you were there to visit. That you rode in the ambulance."

Finn's muscles tightened. Damn gossips.

"I found some photos in one of Mom's boxes. A stack of me and Rose. Mom made doubles. She wanted her to have them. I dropped by the big house, thinking I could get them to her."

"You didn't see her?"

"No, Ms. Magnolia wouldn't give me Rose's info."

"Good. I wish you told me you'd gone to see her. Bad enough you spoke to her at the funeral. Two of you never had a chance. I knew. No matter what your mom said."

Finn leaned forward. He hadn't heard this before. "What did Mom say?"

Pa grumbled as if realizing he'd said too much. "Think it'll rain?"

"Pa—what did she say?"

"Fine." He grimaced. "Clara called her your *acushla*."

"Loved one." Finn reeled. His mom didn't use Irish words lightly. "What else did she say?"

He shook his head. "I'm not doing this. I can't watch you fall for her again. She doesn't deserve you."

How could Pa know how he felt about Rose back then? He'd never shared with anyone.

Pa pushed his chair back and stood. "Sell the damn house."

Chapter Eighteen

R ose turned her car onto Ash Street, the main road that went through town. Before she departed last night's family dinner, Broome asked her to drop by the cemetery to look at Magnolia's headstone in the family plot. He'd been notified that the engraving had been completed.

She drove past the garage where Finn had his first job. The *Ferris Garage* sign still hung from the eaves even though Riley Pierce had purchased it years ago when Joel Ferris retired. A newer one beneath said *Riley's*. Many a summer afternoon, she'd watched Finn work under the hoods of cars.

Hanover's Hardware across the street was still the only place to buy generators in town. The lumber shop stood behind it.

Farther down, close to the river, the raised platform sidewalks showcased tourist shops complete with logo'd Smoky Mountains gear. She smiled as she drove past the old-fashioned ice cream parlor.

New shops and services had popped up on the northern edge. New housing and new residents had driven demand for a third gas station and a second grocery store. All stood a mile past the Center Street hub.

As the road curved, she thought of last night's meal at Broome and Simi's house. Everything had gone well until she told Aspen, Thorne, and Willow the truth of why she inherited Briar House.

Aspen hadn't taken the news well. Her words were harsh.

How could she do this to me? To all of us. We'll be the town pariah.

Then she'd broken down in tears.

Rose didn't remind her what year it was, even though her words about the town were accurate. If this secret got out, there would be those who'd censure Magnolia's past choices, and also censure Rose.

Beside Aspen, Gavin looked downright scandalized. Rose had hoped he'd be absent, but he attended most of their family meals. Hopefully, his fear of scandal and her fierce warning to keep the information private would silence him.

Thorne had shrugged, acting as if she'd shared a weather forecast. His lack of reaction concerned her. As they'd walked to their cars, she asked him if he was okay. He'd shared what he really thought.

It doesn't matter who gave birth to you. You're my baby sister.

And Willow was Willow. She'd looked pensive, but kept quiet. Rose knew how Willow's mind churned. She tended toward slow digestion of information. The questions would come when she was ready.

She turned right onto Cemetery Road. Street names here weren't creative. The road wound up toward the hills; a foggy mist permeated the trees on either side with the slow increase in elevation.

Rose's black boots ground on crushed rock as she stepped out of her vehicle. Gentle slopes full of headstones bracketed the road she'd parked on. Farther up, mist clung to the trees that bordered the cemetery.

A text from Mr. Castor, a representative of the funeral home, told her he was on his way. She'd rolled her eyes when she read it. Old money and a generational legacy. As if she needed help to find Magnolia's headstone. She knew well where the Everson family plot lay.

Rose locked her car and began her ascent up the hill. She tugged the hem of her black sweater down as she climbed. The Eversons were buried in the oldest part of the cemetery, which meant no path existed. Watchful of her footing, she stepped carefully. The older plots tended to be uneven.

Rows of headstones dotted the level areas of the slope, some small and some more elaborate with carvings. Debris and the first layer of autumn leaves lay in a random pattern over the ground after the recent storm.

The climb to the family plot took more than a few minutes. An odd sound made her stop partway and look up. She held her breath as she took in what she saw.

Someone, a man, crouched inside the low wrought iron fence that bordered their family's section. It was not Mr. Castor who'd arranged Magnolia's funeral.

From this distance, the man looked to be dressed in rags. A shock of white hair topped his head.

A sliver of unease went through her. This man was inside the fence of her family plot, on the ground, in the section that held Magnolia's grave.

Disturbing sounds reached her ears. She took an automatic step back in reaction. He spoke words, tortured-like ones she couldn't make out.

She shuffled another foot back. Maybe it would have been better to wait for Mr. Castor.

She needed to get back to her car and lock the door.

More unnatural sounds.

Another careful step back. Then another, afraid to take her eyes off the scene before her.

A twig snapped beneath her boot. She froze.

His head swiveled around, and he stood. Mud covered his face and the front of his clothes. His eyes, they looked straight at her. She felt cold.

Had he slept here? On Magnolia's grave?

Then his eyes widened. A single word broke from his lips in a raspy voice. He jumped over the low fence and rushed towards her.

Instinct screamed.

She turned and ran. The wet grass was slick, her attempt precarious, a half slide with every step.

The smell reached her before he did. Human filth.

A desperate shout, "Maggie! Stop!"

Rose didn't stop.

Pain spiked through her elbow as a hand grabbed her arm. A cry burst from her lips as he wrenched her around to face him. A wave of nausea hit.

Words fell out of him in a monotone. "Don't be scared. It's me, Maggie."

Who the hell was Maggie? And where the hell was Mr. Castor? The legacy extras suddenly appealed.

With her free arm, she worked to break his grip the way Thorne had taught her. He grabbed that arm too, his fingers like manacles of ice.

"None of that now, pet. They tried to keep me from you, but we're meant to be together." His eyes were glacial, the sort of lifeless cold that couldn't be reasoned with.

She forced the words out through clenched teeth. She wouldn't cry out again. "I'm—not—Maggie."

His eyes narrowed. He pulled her closer as if to check. His lips formed a garish smile, revealing decaying teeth. "You're her all right. I've waited a long time. No escape this time."

Who was this creep? Anger flared inside her. She yanked her arms in another move Thorne taught her. It didn't work.

His grip tightened. A whimper escaped her.

His voice was harsh. "You hear me?"

Sudden shouts came from below. She dared to look, a glimpse before his hand twisted more, forcing her to look back at him.

Help had come, but would it be in time?

A well-dressed man, two others in security uniforms, raced uphill towards them.

Rage filled the man's eyes.

Help might not make it in time.

Spittle hit her face, his breath was foul. He said, "You teasing bitch. It's my turn. I've waited long enough."

The suited man, the guards drew closer.

His eyes flicked back and forth between them and her, calculating. Unless he had a car within arm's reach, he wouldn't escape with her in hand. She tensed, though. He could still hurt her.

He snarled. More spittle. "I'll be back for you. Next time I'll bring a shovel." He pushed her and ran. She didn't have time to break her fall. Pain radiated through her left arm as she fell onto the damp grass.

The security guards changed direction to chase him.

The suited man reached her. It was Mr. Castor. He paused a few feet away, his hands braced on his knees as he breathed heavily. His mouth hung open in shock, his eyes wide as if he'd never seen a person on the ground before. He didn't offer his hand as she pushed herself to a seated position. Instead, he mopped his brow with a handkerchief from a pocket before straightening.

Her attacker disappeared into the woods atop the hill. Both guards kept up their pursuit.

Mr. Castor wrung his hands. His speech carried a slight accent. She couldn't place it. "I'm so sorry, Miss Finch. I had no idea. That man. I swear. My secretary saw him on the security cameras."

Rose wiped her wet hands on her jeans, pushed her hair behind her ears.

"We've never had this happen before. I promise you."

She doubted that. The cemetery dated back to the late 1800s.

"Your clothes. They're muddy." His disgust, as if she were covered in dog poo, assured her he would be no help. It was a struggle with the pain in her arm, but she got her legs beneath her and stood.

She looked down. Definitely muddy. Not for the first time, but her elbow hurt like hell. She cradled it against her as a cold drizzle began to fall.

The slim Mr. Castor began a fresh round of apologies. He looked so clean, rain resistant in his light blue suit and white shirt. Magnolia would have dressed him down for his lack of manners, but Rose couldn't get a word in amongst his apologies. She was tempted to flick one drop of mud his way even as she cradled her arm.

Rose glanced upward to the wrought iron fence that surrounded the Everson graves. She hadn't seen the engraving on the tombstone. Once more, she wiped her hands on damp denim. It didn't help.

"Mr. Castor, please stop. My clothes will be fine." Magnolia despised effusive apologizers. Rose thought she might share the feeling.

He flinched as if she'd hit him and began again. "So sorry. Nothing like this has happened before. I don't want to get fired. I love my job, working with people…"

Did he mean dead people?

Rose was tempted to give him a solid shake. She was cold, wet, and getting wetter.

Two police cars entered the drive below, lights swirling without sirens. Mr. Castor quieted at the sight.

Two uniformed officers climbed the slope. She waited where she stood.

Deputy Reggie MacShane reached her first, his long strides eating up the damp ground. Dressed in a black uniform, with his badge and name on his chest, he looked her over, his eyes widening at her appearance. He was older than her, Broome's age, if she remembered correctly. He was broad shouldered, tanned, and tall with an athletic build. His hair was short, almost to his scalp. Had he served in the military? She couldn't remember.

The second man she'd met before, back in high school. His name was Mack, one of Finn's old soccer friends. He was slightly taller than Reggie, Black and more muscled.

Reggie said, "Mack, run down and get a blanket out of the back for Rose. Then we'll figure out what happened here."

He turned to her. "Are you hurt?"

"My arm."

Reggie stepped closer. "May I take a look?"

Rose nodded. His hands were gentle as he eased the sleeve of her black sweater upward to get a look. He gave a low whistle at the bruises forming. "We'll want pictures of this. I bet it hurts like the devil. We'll get some ice on it as soon as we finish up here." He eased her sleeve back down.

She didn't argue.

The light drizzle stopped. Not one word came out of Mr. Castor's mouth.

The deputy returned in minutes and laid a thick wool blanket over Rose's shoulders. She thanked him and held onto it with the hand of her good arm, keeping the pained one close to her body.

Sympathy reflected in both officer's eyes.

"Can you tell me what happened?" Reggie asked. "As best you can. Then we'll get you down the hill. Maybe Trudy can make you something hot to drink."

He looked pointedly at Mr. Castor, who reacted like he'd

been hit with a stick. He nodded vigorously and pulled out his cell phone. "I'll text her right now."

Reggie said, "Perfect." He pulled out a notepad and pen. "Just the basics. We'll talk more inside, where it's warm and dry."

Rose nodded, pulling the blanket tighter. "I came to see Magnolia's headstone. Broome got word that it had been placed. He asked me to check on it and make sure everything was correct. I parked my Jeep and walked up there." She pointed toward the Everson plot.

"Are you okay to walk back up there with us?"

Another nod before she walked beside them, with Mr. Castor tiptoeing behind. Reggie stayed close as they climbed. She stopped and looked at them. "I was here. Then I heard a sound. Stopped, saw a man. He was inside the fence. I know it's short, but the gate stays locked."

"Go on," Reggie urged in a gentle voice.

"He didn't look right. Sound right." The fear she'd felt pressed on her again.

Reggie didn't push. Neither did his partner.

"I think he was crying. I've never heard anyone make those sorts of sounds before. I backed away slow. Mr. Castor was supposed to meet me."

Mr. Castor nodded.

"Can you describe him?" Reggie scribbled.

"The man was tall, taller than me—baggy clothes, muddy. White hair. His face, long and narrow."

Reggie interrupted. "White hair, you said?"

"Yes."

He and Mack exchanged a look, but before she could ask, he said, "Continue."

"His eyes, ice blue." Glacial. Without compassion, especially while angry. She shuddered. "He saw me. Jumped the fence. Chased me. His grip—I couldn't get away."

Reggie gave her an encouraging nod as they continued uphill, his hand a light touch on her uninjured elbow. "You're doing great, Rose. What else?"

"He smelled bad. I thought maybe he'd slept there. He turned around, and—" She broke off and gasped.

Reggie swore beside her. They'd reached the Everson plot. She closed her eyes then opened them in the hopes what she saw wasn't real. Tears burned her eyes as she took in the sight of Magnolia's grave. Reggie put an arm around her shoulder as if to steady her, as if she'd swayed. Perhaps she had. She had reason to.

Magnolia's grave looked as if an animal had tried to dig its way down to her. Long, narrow furrows carved through the mud and grass. Had that man done this? Why?

She couldn't look away. She wished she could.

Reggie kept his arm around her while he turned to Mack. A current of anger underlined his words. "Get Quincy and his team up here. We need whatever they can find ASAP."

Reggie gentled his voice. "Rose, let's get you inside. We'll finish our questions there."

She didn't argue, letting him herd her down the hill while Mack stayed behind and spoke into his radio. A fretful Trudy waited for them in the chapel, a large Ziplock bag of ice in one hand. She gave it to Reggie before taking one pale Mr. Castor by the arm and urging him through another door.

Rose sat in one of two leather chairs inside a room off the small on-site chapel. Reggie wrapped the bag of ice gently around her elbow and pulled the blanket around her shoulders.

Trudy, a rail-thin woman with dark green cat-eye glasses and upswept pink streaked blond hair, came in with a cup of hot tea for Rose. Curiosity rimmed the secretary's eyes, but she didn't pry. "Let me know if you need anything else. I'm taking some coffee to Lance."

Reggie sat down in the other chair. Mack entered. "Quincy and his team are here."

He snapped some photos of Rose's arm with his cell phone. After, he leaned his frame against the doorway, ready to listen.

Rose told them the rest.

Mack asked, "You have no idea who he is?"

"I didn't recognize him. His face was muddy. He called me Maggie. Said we'd be together. I don't know anyone named Maggie."

"Your grandmother?"

Rose vehemently shook her head. "No one called her Maggie. She despised nicknames. Considered them lazy. We couldn't even call her Gran. Grandmother or Magnolia, nothing else."

Reggie tapped his pen on the notebook, his lips pursed. "You should see Doc Mason about your arm. It's not broken, but it'd be good to document it."

"Doc Mason's still here?" She hadn't needed a doctor since she'd moved back. All of Magnolia's were in Asheville.

"Yes, he took over Dr. Cook's practice on Poplar Street. He's not so young and cocky now. He even got himself a wife."

Rose remembered the young man with the prominent Adam's apple fresh out of medical school. He'd lectured Magnolia with his *expertise* after a horse kicked her the night of the barn fire. Rose herself had been eight years old at the time.

"Magnolia called him an imbecile to his face."

The corner of Reggie's mouth lifted. "Your gran inspired fear in anyone who didn't know her better."

"True."

Footsteps sounded in the hall. A female officer with short blonde hair stepped in. "Still no sign of him, sir. We've got Lance and Trudy's statements."

"Thanks Ashley. We'll head out shortly."

She left the room. Reggie turned back to Rose. "You okay to drive? We can give you a ride."

She set the ice aside, moved her arm a tad, and nodded. "I'm okay."

He studied her and shook his head. "Your grandmother will come back from her grave if something happens to you. We'll follow you home."

She nodded. "Do you have any idea who he is?"

"I'm working on it." He reached out a hand to help her up.

Her brow furrowed. Unusual comment for something that had just occurred. Had she missed something?

"I'll see if Doc Mason can stop by your place to look at your arm. I'll also send a sketch artist out to you."

Chapter Nineteen

Sunlight filtered through the surrounding trees, not quite filling the cul-de-sac with light, when Finn pulled into the cracked driveway of his childhood home. He'd woke early, filled his coffee mug, and started driving north towards Evers Hollow. He made a quick stop in town before continuing.

He turned the car off and stepped out of his SUV.

The sun topped the trees, highlighting the chalky yellow exterior of the house. Cracks and chips were prevalent on the wood siding. Rot edged the bottom all the way round. Green scuzz adhered to half of the front and one side. He tried to scrub it off as a teenager. It never worked.

He studied the other houses in the cul-de-sac. All stood in similar condition. Several residents lost their homes after the lumber mill north of town closed. One-hundred-forty-five jobs gone overnight. The recession hit the people who lived in this neighborhood hard. Made it difficult to renovate and repair.

He walked around to the back. The siding looked the same. Years ago, Pa added a small screened porch for summer evening meals. Jagged gashes in the mesh left the screening cloth hanging. Pa's foot had gone through one, years before, as if kicking it would make his grief over his wife's death lessen. He'd never repaired it.

Finn walked back to the front door and let himself in.

Linoleum cracked beneath his feet as he walked into the kitchen. Out of habit, he toed the crack in the floor that ran parallel to the counter Mom used for baking. He remembered sitting on a chair, forming cookies beside her and sticking them on a cookie sheet in a random manner. How she always rearranged them to allow the proper spacing. Over and over again. Different t-shirts, different heights, and often a second chair for Rose.

He took a deep breath, glanced around the room. The yellow table sat where it always had. It had been one thing he couldn't remove. It belonged here, along with its four yellow chairs, in front of the yellow wallpaper behind it.

Finn took his time to check things over, opened all the now clean cabinets. His neighbor, Norah, had arranged a house cleaner. Even the yellow table seemed to shine. The smell of bleach and lemons permeated the rooms. In the family room, depressions in the faded gold carpet still marked where the furniture once stood. Not even a professional steam cleaner could change twenty-something years of that.

A knock interrupted his train of thought. Finn glanced at his watch. Right on time. He opened the front door. "Morning, Raymond."

Raymond Alvarez, a local real estate agent, stood on the small stoop. His slicked back dark hair and trimmed mustache crossed the middle of his face. He was shorter and thicker around the middle than Finn. He carried a clipboard in one hand and held out his other. "Good to meet you, Finn. Please call me Ray."

"All right. Thanks for coming out so early." Finn shook the man's hand.

"Not a problem. We accommodate everyone's schedules."

Ray stepped into the house from the front stoop. Whatever he thought, his face remained neutral.

Finn looked at the man apologetically. "I'd offer you coffee, but the coffee maker here broke."

"No worries. I've had a cup."

Finn had never put a house on the market before. "How does this work?"

"First, let's walk through it together. I'll take some measurements, make some notes, and then we can talk."

He gave the man a tour. It didn't take long. The small home hadn't changed since his childhood. All the furniture was gone except the kitchen table, its chairs, and a small dresser in Finn's bedroom.

"You mentioned painting?"

Finn nodded. "I've got a few days off. Figured fresh paint might brighten it up."

"It's not a bad size house for a small family or a couple. I'll get the measurements."

While the real estate agent went room to room, Finn busied himself by bringing in his painting supplies.

Once finished, he found Ray in the kitchen, making notes on his clipboard.

"If you and your pa decide to move forward," he said, "I can arrange for a photographer to take pictures."

Finn knew what Pa wanted—the house sold ASAP. "I'll talk to my father." He'd spent most of his childhood in this house. It carried memories of his mom. He needed to make peace with Pa's decision.

Ray pulled out a black wallet. "Here's my business card. I'll call you later just to touch base. I won't hound you about the place. It's a big decision. I'm here if you need me."

"Thanks. I appreciate that."

They shook hands. Finn walked him out.

As Ray got into his car, Finn asked, "Where do you get a good cup of coffee here these days?"

Ray lifted his chin. "Firebrew. It's on Second Street and Maple. Great coffee and evil baked cakes." He patted his stomach as if it were the reason for the padding around his middle.

"Thanks, I'll check it out."

He unloaded the rest of his car: the air mattress he'd purchased, a single pillow, a duffel bag filled with clothes, and his sleeping bag.

Finn laid drop cloths down in the family room. Filled nail holes and other dents along the wall surface. It took time to run blue tape along the stained wood baseboards. Rather than dirty the clean kitchen, he put on running shoes and ran into town to pick up a breakfast burrito from a tiny takeout place. Fed and energized, he picked up a roller and got a coat of primer on the walls. A few hours later, the first coat of paint went on.

The sun disappeared as he drove into town. Rain hit his windshield as he searched for a place to park. He looked at his maps app to find the place Ray mentioned. Second Street. He passed a red and orange dragon sign that spelled Firebrew in red. Found a small parking lot just after. Once he was out of his SUV, he dashed through the increasing rain to the door below the sign and entered. To think he'd considered walking.

Chapter Twenty

With one fist, Rose tightened her rain jacket around her neck as she hurried into town, her rain boots kicking water up with each stride. The patch of blue sky she'd seen when she'd left the cottage had been a lie. The storm wasn't supposed to hit for a few more hours.

The sky became grayer, the raindrops harder as she walked the path through the woods. When she broke from the trees to cross Ash Street, the wind shoved the rain into drifts that wove and battered everything in its path, including her. She forced one rain boot in front of the other.

Why hadn't she checked the battery supply earlier? She'd known the storm was coming. The weather forecast declared there was no hiding from it. High winds were expected. She should have thought about the possibility of a power outage, but she'd been too focused on the rendering of her attacker by the sketch artist Reggie sent. An image real enough to haunt her thoughts.

Rose held up a hand as if she could divide the rain to create a clear path for herself to walk through. Rain snuck in beneath her collar where the top button had fallen off long ago. With every gust, her jacket flapped, exposing her messenger bag beneath. At least she'd had the sense to use her old bag, the one without her laptop inside.

Her destination came into sight. The bell on the door of Hanover's Hardware bounced with a strangled jingle as she fought to push the door open. It slammed closed behind her before she could stop it.

She removed her rain jacket; it was dripping. With stiff fingers, she hung it on the coatrack by the entrance. A small puddle formed beneath it on the floor. With her boots, she adjusted the towels on the floor to catch the drips. She reached up to scrape the rogue strands of hair out of her face. The wind had done its best to dismantle the braid she'd woven before tackling this idiotic errand.

"Who's that there?" An older man, hunched and weathered by time, appeared in the main aisle that ran through the middle of the store.

"It's Rose Finch, Mr. Hanover." She moved forward so he could see her clearly. "I need to buy some batteries for my lanterns."

He looked her up and down, his expression skeptical. "Just batteries?"

"Yes, sir, that's it for today." It would be best to let him help her. She'd get home faster. He was a lifetime fixture in Evers Hollow but a cranky, suspicious one, always on the lookout for shoplifters. She'd learned that lesson in her childhood.

"Sure you don't need any kerosene or lamp oil?" His wrinkled face and coke bottle glasses came into better focus as he shuffled towards her.

"If I was in the main house, I would, but I'm in the gardener's cottage still. The lanterns will be fine." She pressed her hands together. She should have worn gloves.

"Candles?"

"I stocked up last time I came in." She hoped that was true.

He harrumphed, took off his glasses and cleaned them with a bandanna from his chest pocket. "What size?"

"D batteries. I need at least an eight-pack."

He brightened and motioned for her to follow him. "I keep them by the register. Had an issue with theft. Everybody wants AAs. Makes it hard to keep them in stock. Only time people buy C's and D's anymore is cuz of storms like this and them hurricanes that come through."

The last hurricane caused significant damage. It had downed trees, damaged homes, and flooded the storefronts closest to the river. Asheville had gotten it much worse.

Evers Hollow received its share of problem storms. There was a solid chance a tree would fall somewhere and take the power with it. She didn't fear the dark, but she liked being able to see her surroundings, especially when she was working on a book.

She said, "I try to keep batteries on hand. All the sizes. When I looked this afternoon, I only had two Ds left." Her lanterns each took four.

"Mayor said there might be sleet and snow." Mr. Hanover moved to the back wall, past the long register counter. The scent of metal and oil grew stronger as she followed him back.

"That would be unusual." It was sixty-one degrees outside, but stranger things had happened in their little nook.

He showed her the battery display. She pulled her selections off their hooks, cradled them against her without moving her injured arm. Her dose of ibuprofen was wearing off. She followed him to the counter. The scrapes and dents along the thick wood stood testament to how long this store had been here. He rang up her purchase while she took in the view of tall shelves with small engine parts behind him. The faint sound of a television came from the back of the store.

She paid in cash with exact change from the damp bag beneath her rain jacket. He preferred that. A long ago memory, maybe something Magnolia told them. She was surprised his wife hadn't come out to say hello. She always greeted the customers.

Rose opened her mouth to inquire about Mrs. Hanover.

A scrawny black cat jumped onto the counter between them. She flinched. "Cat."

The single word came out of her as if she'd never seen one before. She'd never seen a cat like this.

Mr. Hanover reached out and stroked the feline. "A stray. Keeps me company. Young Rose, meet Smokie." The man almost smiled as his hand ran over its ragged back.

Rose wanted to say something complimentary about the cat. It was a struggle. It looked like someone had removed half its fur and tried to glue it back on. One of its ears was damaged enough to appear missing. Straight out of *Pet Sematary*. The cat stared at her. Its yellow eyes held no offer of friendship. One of them oozed. Rose took a half step back.

"I found him covered in mud in that last storm we had. Somebody set him on fire. Teenagers today got no respect for animals."

Rose broke eye contact with the cat and looked at him. "That's horrible. It's a good thing you found him."

"Me and Smokie are friends now. He wasn't too trusting at first." He held up his forearm. Half-healed scratches crossed his flesh. "We got an understanding now, don't we, Smokie?" His voice softened as he rubbed the feline's head, its undamaged ear straight up as it emitted a mangled meow.

"I took him straight to the veterinarian, had to wrap him in a towel to keep him from harming me."

She listened as his story continued, but the storm divided her attention. Repetitive sounds came from the metal roof above. Was that hail?

When the overhead lights flickered, he said, "You best get home. It's getting darker."

Batteries in her bag, jacket back on, she left the hardware store. It was hail mixed in with icy rain. Both pelted her back and the top of her hood with an overzealous tune. Her rain jacket repelled most of the water. Between it and her peony rain boots, parts of her remained dry. Her jeans, however, did not. They clung to her legs uncomfortably as she moved away from the store. The wind pushed at her.

Why hadn't she driven?

After a few blocks, an illuminated open sign came into view. There was no hesitation. She reached for the door and stepped inside. She forced the door shut behind her and leaned against it, her breath loud in the absence of wind.

Rose looked up to see red and orange walls—Firebrew. Not a bar. Somewhere familiar and warm. Her hands pushed back her hood as Shirley came towards her.

"Rose Everson Finch, have you lost your mind? Out in this hell of a storm!" Shirley looked her over, obvious shock in her eyes.

She forced the words through her teeth before they chattered. "Batteries. Had to buy batteries."

Molly came into view, her mouth gaped open. Rose winced as Shirley's voice came out again, shrill. "Did you walk here?"

Both mother and daughter stood with their hands on their hips, glaring at her. They looked so similar in appearance—dark hair, dark brown eyes, ageless. She imagined they were often mistaken for sisters rather than mother and daughter.

Rose said, "It was sunny when I left the cottage. Mr. Hanover delayed me some. Told me about his horror cat. I didn't even know he had a cat." Her chilled fingers moved to the oversized buttons of her raincoat. Slipped one free.

They continued to stare.

"I need to warm up some before I head home."

A sound of disgust came from Shirley, her voice still shrill. "Young lady, you will not walk home in this."

Another voice broke into the conversation. A masculine one. "I'll take her home."

That voice. She knew it. Rose whirled around.

Maybe Willow was right.

Finn Murphy was back in Evers Hollow again, his eyes dark in the low light of the coffeehouse as he sipped something steamy from a burgundy mug. He sat in her corner, the one she always claimed as hers.

In her favorite Firebrew cozy chair.

At her favorite coffee house.

Wearing a cable knit fisherman's sweater.

Damn.

So not fair. She loved cable knit fisherman sweaters, especially on him.

He stood. She heard a tiny whimper. It may have come from her. He, too, must have been caught in the storm. Not as long, though. His clothes looked dry. Light caught the nestled raindrops in his wet hair as he moved towards her. Shirley and Molly spoke. Their words were cloudy, as were their movements around her.

Her fingers stalled over the next button. Her throat felt tight, rejecting her attempt to swallow. A shiver went through her as he stepped within reach.

"Let me." His voice sounded like flannel, the cozy kind she could snuggle up to. His fingers moved slowly as he pushed the large buttons through their slots. She let him help her, too stunned to argue otherwise. Her heart beat a little faster, a small ball of warmth inside her waiting for more.

Molly appeared with towels in her arms, dropping one on the floor to sop up the small puddles forming around her.

Buttons undone, Rose removed her jacket, forgetting about her injured arm. She winced as it slipped the rest of the way off her shoulders. Finn took hold of the jacket and hung it beside his own on the wrought iron coat rack by the door.

Molly handed her a towel. With one hand, Rose rubbed it on her saturated jeans. It surprised her how much water the towel took in. She was lucky she'd had the sense to wear thick wool socks. Snug within her rain boots, her feet were the only part of her that felt warm and dry.

When she straightened back up, she met Finn's gaze. His eyes held concern and something new. That small warmth inside her twisted into an ache. She licked her lips.

His fingers came up and smoothed back the rogue wet strands of her hair as if he'd done it a million times. She couldn't look away.

Shirley came out of a door with a blanket and cleared her throat. Her eyes flicked back and forth between them. Finn stepped back as she put it on Rose's shoulders.

"Thank you, Shirley." Rose pulled the blanket around her as best as she could with one hand. It felt warm, as if it had been hung in front of a fire.

She smiled, her expression still darting between them. "That's better. Take a seat by the fire. Molly will make you something hot to drink. Usual mocha with almond milk?"

"A mocha would be great. Let me get my wallet." She snaked her hand into her bag, still hanging across her body.

Shirley pressed her hands on Rose's shoulders and turned her toward the fire. "Have a seat. Free drinks for everyone needing shelter from the storm. Go on now. Your grandmother would want us to take care of you."

Finn put a hand on the small of her back. "Let's get you warm." He urged her to take the seat he'd occupied, closest to the fire, the one she considered hers.

Rose sank into the chair. Finn crouched down in front of her and tucked the blanket around her. The smell of rain and forest filled her nose. She held back a groan. In all this time, his scent hadn't changed. How did he do it? Even when he'd worked in the garage as a teenager, beneath the smell of grease and oil, he smelled of the woods.

"Better?" He sat down in the other chair and scooted it close to her, their knees almost touching. A wisp of a smile played on his face as if he found something funny.

Molly appeared with a steaming mug. "Guessing you two know each other?"

Finn said, "We grew up together."

Rose accepted the mug. Her fingers wrapped around its warm sides. "Thank you, Molly. Your red sign saved me."

She smiled, perched herself on the arm of another nearby cozy chair. "Got waylaid by Mr. Hanover, I heard."

"Forty minutes to buy batteries and leave." Rose took a sip and almost closed her eyes. Perfect.

"Cat story?" Molly asked.

She sat up a little straighter. If she ignored the clamminess of her legs, she felt almost warm. "How did you know?"

"Last week, we bought lamp oil. It took us forty-five minutes to escape."

"That cat is scary."

"Can you believe he found it like that?" Molly shook her head as if in disapproval. "What kind of person sets a cat on fire? It's amazing the thing survived."

Finn leaned forward, his expression one of concern.

Rose sipped more. "Is his wife still around? I didn't see her like I usually do."

"Her health is poor. She's in that old nursing home near the church."

"Caring Hands?"

Molly nodded.

Rose shook her head. "Magnolia never liked that place, complained about the conditions more than once. She had friends there."

"I gather they had no choice."

Finn said, "I heard that place is bad. Pa decided on Wylder Ridge."

His pa was in a retirement community? He hadn't mentioned that. Not like they'd had much resembling normal conversation yet.

"I'm sorry, Finn, I didn't know. Is he okay?" She resisted the temptation to reach out. Her hands stayed where they were.

He shrugged. "Broke his hip awhile ago. He spent a few weeks there. A few months back, he decided he wanted to make it permanent. It's more independent than Caring Hands—small apartments with kitchenettes, medical staff on hand if needed. He gets to play cards everyday."

She tilted her head; the image of Charlie Murphy's jovial face came to mind. "I remember he loves cards. Still, I'm sorry."

Her fingers pressed harder against the outside of her mug. His eyes, his voice, made her remember how close they'd once been.

It had been almost six years since their argument over her engagement to Caleb Brentwood, at her family's annual New Year's Eve party. She hadn't needed anyone telling her who she should and shouldn't marry. Least of all, Finn. She'd lost her closest friend that night.

If only Finn had apologized. In-person, a phone call, even a freaking postcard with *SORRY* would have worked. She would have given him hell for the single word, but she would have accepted it. They'd never had an argument they hadn't talked through afterward. Instead, Finn had disappeared from her life. Was it too late to hope for words of apology now?

Hail pelted the front windows, loud enough to hear over the crackling fire.

Finn's knee bounced a little. It meant only one thing. This was awkward for him too.

"They're saying one to two inches tonight." Shirley voiced

from behind the counter. "Molly, we need to prepare for closing."

Molly glanced at her watch. Then jumped up. "Gotta help Mom. Hope we don't lose power."

Finn said, "Hell of a mess out there. I wonder if there'll be flooding."

Great. The weather had taken over the conversation. A bold underline as to how weird things were between them. Was she supposed to respond with her opinion of the storm?

She didn't want to. She'd rather watch him. It served as a pleasurable distraction from the damp jeans on her legs, the ache in her arm. His neck and collarbone fascinated her in a way they hadn't when she'd been a teenager. Her face had been against that very spot when he'd held her while she cried after the funeral. It had felt warm on her tear-washed face. She hadn't wanted to move away. Even in grief, she'd wanted to press her lips into his warmth, against his skin.

His voice broke into her thoughts, low and still cozy.

"Finish your coffee, then I'll drive you home."

She nodded, trying to stifle the thoughts she shouldn't be having about the man who once claimed the role of *best friend*.

Chapter Twenty-One

R ose didn't look at him while they drove. Neither did she speak. Unusual, since she used to tell him everything, whether he wanted to know it or not. He missed that. She was in fact unnaturally quiet.

It made him think of the texts he'd received earlier, minutes before she entered the coffeehouse.

MACK

"You still keep up with Rose Finch?"

FINN

"Why?"

MACK

"Someone attacked her at the cemetery. Perp's still at large."

FINN

"When?"

MACK

"This morning."

FINN

"She okay?"

MACK

"Yeah, Doc Mason dropped by and examined her. Her arm's messed up. She's going to be sore. Figured you'd want to know."

FINN

"Thanks."

Was the attack related to the warnings Ms. Magnolia had given him?

He'd slipped his phone back in his pocket, questions in his head.

Seconds later, Rose stormed inside the coffeehouse, escaping the rain.

They'd talked over their coffees, the conversation stilted, uncomfortable. She hadn't mentioned the incident or her injured arm. She was hurting. He'd seen the wince when he helped her back into her coat. Even now, in the passenger seat, she cradled her left arm against her. Good thing her place was only seven minutes from town by car.

The continuous rain resembled a carwash. He slowed, focusing on staying on the road. Frustration coursed through his fingers as they tightened around the steering wheel. His tires found every pothole beneath them.

This storm, too much rain at once. In a mountain town. It created a landslide risk. Hollows Hospital had closed four years ago. There was no urgent care, only a day clinic with limited emergency means. The closest hospital was more than an hour away, with a mountainous road between them.

Finn had hoped to return to Evers Hollow after finishing his medical residency. He'd wanted to work in the same hospital his mom had, provide care to the people in this town. That was no longer an option.

He pulled into the long straight driveway of the Briar House estate, the water-logged gravel loud beneath his tires. The house was pitch dark. Had the power gone out? An illuminated porch light on one cottage suggested otherwise.

Rose said, "Pull in next to the gardener's cottage. I live there."

He parked his SUV in front of the small white house and turned toward her. "Why are you living in the cottage?"

"Magnolia suffered a stroke awhile back. I offered to move home. She agreed. We decided I'd stay here though instead of the house. Give her the illusion of independence."

"Did it work?"

The porch light lit the wistful smile on her face. "Not really, but she and I excelled at pretending. She never admitted it, but she needed my help."

"What happens to the house now?"

Rose was quiet a moment. Her fingers fiddled with the hem of her rain jacket. Then she said, "Magnolia left it to me." She opened the passenger door and slid off the seat, hurrying through the rain to the tiny porch.

It wasn't his business, but he opened the door to follow her. What she said made no sense.

"Why you? There must be a story there." The words came out before he could stop them. His curiosity tended to rise around Rose, even in bad weather.

She unlocked the door, tried to open it. Pain flickered across her face.

He asked, "Need a hand?"

"Door's a bit warped. Sticks when it rains." She stepped back as he moved forward. "Shove it up and to the left. It'll open."

He did. The door swung open with a creak.

She entered and flicked a switch, illuminating the inside. "You want to come in? I have soup in the crock-pot. It'll be ready soon. I can make us something hot to drink while we wait."

Her invitation was unexpected. He couldn't resist accepting it. He wanted, needed, to make things right with her. Was there a chance they could be friends again? Maybe something more?

"I'd like that." He followed her inside, set his boots by hers. Before she could object, his fingers undid the buttons of her rain jacket. She'd already removed her bag, set it on a nearby bench. Mindful of her left arm, he slipped it off her shoulders.

With a murmured thanks, Rose stepped away, slid around the main room in wool socks. An array of lamps came on.

She said, "Lock the door, will you?"

He did.

The cottage was small, smaller than the house he'd grown up in. An older green couch with a ridiculous number of pillows, flowered armchairs, and a scarred coffee table crowded the small sitting area. A tattered rug covered the old carpet.

Rose disappeared through a door and hollered. "Be right back. I need to get my wet jeans off."

He was tempted to offer help.

Lightning flashed. Thunder sounded. With a yelp, she came out of her room, still hiking faded yoga pants up her hips with one hand.

Finn asked, "You okay?"

Rose ran her right hand over the long braid of her hair. "Fine. Only thunder. Took me by surprise."

He recognized the unease in her eyes. Connected her silence in the car. How had he forgotten? It had been a weather event that took her folks.

The lights flickered.

"Crud." Rose moved to her kitchen.

It was tiny with little counter space. Whatever was in the crock-pot smelled delicious. His stomach rumbled.

She said, "If we want something hot to drink, I better get the water started." She got the kettle on, pulled out a can of hot cocoa mix and a bottle of Bailey's Irish Cream. Marshmallows followed.

"What can I do to help?"

She had her head in the refrigerator, but straightened. "You can find the lanterns. They're in the closet by the front door. If they don't work, the new batteries are in the bag I was carrying."

"On it." He headed toward the door.

"Do you want your drink spiked?"

"Sure."

The kettle gave out a piercing wail once he returned with the lanterns, all ready to go. She moved the kettle to a different burner, its wail decreasing in pitch. He watched her add a shot of Bailey's to each mug.

After a thorough stir and the addition of hot water, she handed him an oversized mug of hot cocoa. The smell of vanilla and whiskey reached his nose. Mini-marshmallows floated on top. He studied the black mug, a dark bird along its surface with the words: *Once upon a midnight dreary, while I pondered weak and weary...*

Poe. Appropriate. Thankfully, he wasn't weak or weary.

Rose had a thing for poetry back in high school. She'd often recited from books as they walked the woods together as teenagers.

With her right hand, she carried her mug into the family space. "Can you grab the Cadbury tin off the counter? It's got shortbread inside."

He did. The lid was off. His mouth watered at the sight of the cutout hearts. Could it be Tess' recipe?

She flicked a switch, which ignited the small gas fireplace in the room. "Let's sit. The soup is almost ready." She took one armchair, folded her legs beneath her. "Help yourself to the shortbread. Tess and her granddaughter, Livie, made it. Brought it by yesterday."

He sat carefully to avoid spilling his drink. He reached for the shortbread, took a bite. It tasted like childhood.

She studied him as she sipped her cocoa, then said. "Word around town is you never come home."

"That's right. I'm in the middle of my residency. I've been busy."

"Why are you here now?" Her expression was neutral.

"Pa wants to sell the house. I'm helping him."

"Of course." She blinked. "With your dad at Wylder, he won't need it. And you, you've made your life elsewhere."

He raised an eyebrow.

"You live in Chapel Hill. That's a good four-hour drive."

He shook his head. Local gossip sucked. It was never accurate. "I transferred my residency to Asheville. I drive up on my days off, at least once a week, to see Pa."

She frowned. "Since when?"

"Four months ago." He'd worked himself ragged trying to be both in Chapel Hill and here when Pa broke his hip. Their friends from Ferris Garage and his neighbors had done all they could to help, but it wasn't the same.

It had taken time, loads of paperwork, and multiple conversations with his attending physician to find a vacant residency program slot closer to Pa.

Rose asked, "How is it we haven't bumped into each other?"

The fireplace fan clicked on, warming the small space.

"I thought you were in New York. With him." He didn't need to say the asswipe's name. Or tell her he avoided town.

Her face sobered. She took a long drink. "I didn't marry him. You know that. The gossip was all over the town's social media."

He shook his head. "I didn't know. I don't do social media. Tess told me after your grandmother's funeral."

"Seriously? Your pa didn't tell you?"

"No, he didn't." He frowned.

"Oh." She looked away, took a long sip from her mug.

Thunder rumbled again, lower this time, the sort one could feel through the floor. Silence followed, creating discomfort in the air between them.

His own sips of cocoa seemed too loud, the bit of shortbread an echoing crumble on his teeth. He wanted to ask what had happened, but the two of them hadn't been close in years. He wished they could magically return to what they'd once been. The closest of friends.

Not that simple, not after the things he'd said about her asshole fiancé.

"You want to know what happened," she said. "I see it on your face. Go ahead and ask."

Her friendship had been the most important in his life. He wanted that back.

"I do, but first…" He cleared his throat, washed down the last bit of shortbread before he looked at her. "I need to say something to you first."

Her face changed; her jaw seemed to tighten. She put her mug down and folded her arms. "Go ahead. Lots of people have said things about my broken engagement."

A frisson of warning moved through him, made him hesitate.

"Maybe you want to tell me you were right about Caleb," she said, "now that you know I didn't marry him? Say you told me so? Or state how naïve I was to believe he loved me? Or maybe the opposite, that I'm stupid for cancelling the wedding? That I'll never find anyone better. I've heard them all, both here and in New York."

Her words. What the fuck? Fiery anger lit through him. Someone, multiple someones, had said all those things to her. Probably worse. The curse of having a large family, of living in a small town. Everyone had an opinion, especially regarding Rose's engagement to Caleb *fucking* Brentwood. Including him.

He swore again, ran both his hands through his hair and looked across at her.

The anger, the hurt were all there, in her dark green eyes. She'd grabbed an afghan from a basket, hugged it to her like an oversized stuffed animal.

He put his mug down and stood. He grabbed hold of the coffee table and dragged it so he could sit closer to her.

Wariness filled her eyes as he sat on its edge, close enough for his knees to touch hers.

His mom used to say that an apology was never too late as long as it's meant.

Finn took a long breath, then said, "I said things to you I shouldn't have that night. When I found out you were engaged, I reacted badly."

A sound of protest came out of her. "That's a century's worth of understatement."

He nodded. "I know. The things I said. I didn't want you hurt, especially by Brentwood."

Caleb *fucking* Brentwood was a piece of shit.

She nodded. "I got that. Your opinion of him was crystal clear."

Rose lowered her legs, sat up, and narrowed her eyes. "The irony, Finn, is that you were the one to hurt me that night."

He knew that too. The moment he was *encouraged* to leave the party by security, he knew he'd screwed up.

Finn said, "I know. I'm sorry. If I could take the words back, I'd do it. I never wanted to make you cry."

Her eyes glistened. "You didn't trust me to make my own decisions, to make my own mistakes, and to learn from them."

"You're right. I didn't think of things that way that night. Brentwood's not a good person. He used girls like toilet paper."

"Did you ever hear me criticize your girlfriends back then?" Rose asked. "Even the ones that were ridiculous."

"I know. That was different. I was worried about your future. Your happiness."

She shook her head. "It's not different. Some of those girls you dated were poisonous snakes. What you said that night wasn't right."

"Agreed. I regret all of it. I—"

"Lost your mind?"

He nodded. "Yeah, I did. I care about you, Rose." Too much.

She reached out with her fingers. He grasped them lightly.

"I care about you too, Finn. Friends since we were six. I thought nothing could tear us apart."

"Brentwood went to high school here, not even a year. He got a friend of mine pregnant, left her in a shit situation. Rumor was, she wasn't the only one."

She didn't look surprised. "Thorne said something similar when he found out about the engagement, mentioned he broke Caleb's nose in the locker room back then because of something he said about me. Thorne tried to defend your behavior that night. I'm sorry about your friend."

Too bad Thorne's tactics hadn't worked permanently. How could they have known the asshole would end up at the same college as Rose?

"Caleb played a part with me," she said. "He was good at it. I don't know why. Maybe he wanted my family name; maybe I was a challenge to him. He probably did the same to your friend, but I figured it out in time. I know the person he is now, and he's not a good one."

He traced her fingers with his own before he met her eyes again. "I should have believed in you, trusted you to figure it out. I'm sorry it took me six years, but I mean every word. Can you forgive me?"

She squeezed his hand. "I've tried to do that. But I needed you to say these things to me, in person. I figured it would never happen. Thanks for saying them now."

Chapter Twenty-Two

Over soup and bread, Finn confessed he'd been told about the cemetery attack and her injured arm. Probably Mack Daggett, the other cop at the cemetery.

Rose told him the whole story. Better that it come from her. By tomorrow, the local gossips would have her fighting a slew of undead with a set of car keys.

She also told him about Caleb, the abbreviated version of why she'd ended their relationship.

"I learned Caleb never planned to move to Evers Hollow. Never planned to give up his condo in New York."

That had been a rough night. She and Caleb had argued. She'd returned to the apartment she shared with her friends, Becks and Ada, who'd listened to her over pasta and red wine.

"Despite my love of New York City, I knew I couldn't be happy there forever. I'd always planned to come home. I missed our woods, the quiet here, and my family."

Finn nodded even while he looked on edge. "I get that. This is home."

He understood the pull this place had. She threw him a small smile and rubbed her hands over her legs.

She said, "We'd talked about children. He lied about that too. Suddenly, he didn't want them."

Finn's eyes blazed. "That's a Rose deal breaker. You've always wanted kids. The number of times you made me play house. Didn't you have names chosen before third grade?"

She nodded. She missed how he understood her, knew the way her mind worked.

"The children thing wasn't the only deal breaker." She inhaled sharply. She'd tried so hard to be blasé about it, but never succeeded. "Turned out he had a child with someone else. A baby girl. With one of his interns. I knew she was pregnant, even gave her a gift, but had no idea the baby was his."

Her next words felt choppy, rushed. "I broke things off, cancelled all the wedding arrangements."

Finn reached for her. "You did the right thing." His hands slid over hers and held on like he didn't plan to let go.

"Even though I was the one who broke things off—"

Finn's fingers tightened. "He never deserved you, your trust, or your love."

"He blamed me. Said I was a prude. That it was my fault he'd gone elsewhere for sex. I never slept with him."

His hands loosened. "Never? Even though you were engaged?"

She shook her head. "No. I was twenty years old when I met him, twenty-two when he proposed. I thought it'd be romantic to wait until my wedding night."

"You're a virgin." His tone held a bit of shock.

Before he could speak again, she leaned forward and placed her hand over his mouth.

"Would you stop?" As if someone would hear.

He pulled her hand away. "Sorry. It's not my business."

"You're right. It's not. And I'm not a virgin."

His attention returned to her. "Say again?"

She held her fingers up and did air quotes. "I'm twenty-eight years old. After my being romantic crap, I got tired of waiting."

"Got it." He looked flummoxed as he rubbed the back of his neck. "Can I please look at your arm now?"

Rose agreed. When Finn sat down on her coffee table again, in front of her, she realized she shouldn't have spiked their second cocoas. His woodsy scent made her brain muzzy. Yet here she sat, halfway through her second mug, leaning back in her favorite cozy chair, her legs folded in front of her. Finn sat close.

His expression was grim when she pulled her left arm from her sweater to show him. It looked worse than it felt, all the darkest colors of the rainbow. The dull ache had lessened with more ibuprofen. His touch ran gentle over the finger-like bruises on and around her elbow. His warm palms, his callous's felt better than the ice pack Doc Mason insisted she use every few hours.

"X-rays?" he asked.

"Doc Mason said nothing's broken."

"You using an ice pack?"

"Yes." The word came out breathy. She couldn't help it. Her pulse responded to his touch, something that hadn't happened when they were kids. Finn didn't stop at her elbow. His touch ran down her forearm, traced the back of her hand, outlined each finger, then her palm. She closed her eyes. Desire exploded through her insides, like a cracked pen. Could she just apply him every few hours?

The second cup of spiked cocoa was definitely a bad idea.

He let go suddenly, stood, his gentle fingers gone. "I'll get the ice."

The dull ache in her elbow returned.

While she held the damn ice to her arm, he sat back in his chair, drinking his cocoa. His knee bounced. The intense way he looked at her made her fidget in her seat. His chair was large enough for two people as long as she was the one straddling him. Not that she'd ever used it in that way. She had an excellent imagination, though. It wasn't the first time she'd fantasized about a scene involving that piece of furniture. Images of what they could do outside of drinking hot cocoa for the rest of the night clicked like a slideshow in her mind.

The lights flickered again, more than once. The lantern sat between them, ready.

He leaned forward in his seat. "I have a confession."

"Really?" Was he thinking of sexy chair activities?

"I made your grandmother a promise."

Rose sobered some. That line of desire she'd been so focused on thinned.

"And?" She closed her eyes.

She heard him inhale. "I promised her I'd protect you. Keep you safe."

He'd what? Her eyes flew open. "That was—you don't live here."

"I know. I wish I did. If so, maybe today wouldn't…"

"I'm fine." She was more than fine. "People don't usually camp out on graves."

"I told her I would."

Every stubborn bit of her rebelled at the idea she needed protecting. Evers Hollow was a safe place. Crime existed, of course, but not in the numbers large cities experienced.

"Why didn't you say something last time I saw you?"

"It was your grandmother's funeral."

He had a point.

He said, "I talked to Broome."

"You spoke to him about it, but not me."

"He's the oldest, the head of your family now. Figured he might know what I didn't, why you'd need protecting."

"I don't need protecting." She sat up, winced at the twinge in her arm.

"Your bruises suggest otherwise."

No wonder Broome added more cameras around the place, including the cottage. "The cemetery thing was random. They think it was a homeless person. He's probably moved on. If not, the cops will find him."

The man had called her Maggie, though. That worried her. What if he did mean Magnolia?

Finn's lips pressed into a single line. It was clear he didn't like her words. What the hell was Magnolia thinking, asking this of him? She may not know the details of his life, but knew what a medical degree demanded. Thorne completed his residency last year at Duke University. It was like he'd gone overseas to live. They rarely saw him until he finished, until they could call him Doc Finch.

When she lifted the ice pack from her elbow, he sprang up, took it from her and returned it to the freezer.

He stopped a few feet away, facing her. "There's something else I'd like to tell you." His tone was serious. Something flickered in his eyes. Guilt, maybe more—

She curled her fingers into her afghan. "Okay."

"We've established I was a jerk at that party six years ago. Did you never question why?"

"Because you were an awful friend, and I didn't realize it until that moment."

His voice pitched lower. "I was a terrible, jealous asshole friend."

Her heavy eyes fully opened at his choice of adjectives. "What?"

"I was jealous. And pissed I never asked you out."

Was he saying he was attracted to her? She glanced at her

empty mug on the end table and stood. This didn't seem like the kind of conversation one sat down for. She folded her arms, ignoring the twinge in her elbow. She tipped her chin up. No way did she believe him.

"That is impossible," she said. "I overheard when Thorne suggested you ask me to prom. You said no." It still bothered her, those overheard words.

I'd never ask Rose out. Definitely not to prom.

The use of *definitely.* He'd dated half the females in their grade. Why not her?

He moved closer. The scent of pine and cedar fluttered her insides.

"You were my best friend," Finn said. "I had to say no. I was eighteen." His face was so close to hers. "I would have kissed you, more than kissed you. The way I felt about you then…"

Something eased inside of her, made her want to reach out, but she held back. "Finn."

His words sounded sincere. "I didn't want to lose you as a friend."

But he had lost her—for six years.

His minty breath mingled with her own. He lifted one of his hands, brushed a few strands of hair behind her ear. "I wish I'd asked you. I'd have kissed you, more if you'd let me. Your soulful eyes, your legs. Evie, they haunted me, they still do."

Her nickname. The one he'd given her forever ago. She'd missed hearing it. Too much.

His eyes reflected what she felt. He wanted to kiss her. Truth was, she wanted that too. But she didn't want to be hurt again.

"I don't know Finn. It's been six years. We should focus on our friendship." Her hand reached out to push him back. Her entire palm found itself against his chest. The warmth of him through his shirt made her feel as if she touched his bare skin. His heart beat against her palm. What had she planned to do?

Had he somehow moved closer? His lips hovered over hers.

"You feel it too," said Finn. "The connection we had before, but different. I see it in your eyes—the way you look at me. I've tried dating other women. None of them come close to being you."

Her breath caught. "I don't think—what I feel now—it doesn't mean we should do something about it."

They shared another breath. "We should. I've learned some things since I was fifteen. What about you?"

She nearly groaned. He was referencing the only kiss they'd ever shared, which had been awkward as heck.

"This isn't a competition."

He moved a tad closer. "You sure about that?"

Damn, he would use that. She couldn't resist a challenge, even one that might work against her. Unable to say no, she inched towards him. Her sexual experience might be limited, but she knew how to kiss.

"One kiss."

The smile on his face lit something inside her.

Her fingers curled in the cotton of his shirt. His other hand slipped around her waist. She pulled. So did he.

Their lips touched.

This time, there was nothing awkward or inexperienced about his lips on hers. She cursed. This kiss was everything she feared it would be. Warm, soft, firm, all at the same time. An ember sparked to flame. Damn wonderful. Her hands circled to his back, still pulling him closer as she moved her lips against his.

His hand threaded through her hair while the other skimmed her skin just beneath the hem of her shirt. His lips slanted over hers again and again; his tongue teased her breathless.

Everything about this felt right. Finn wanted her. He actually wanted her. The evidence was hard to miss, pressed up against her middle.

Once more, her lips answered his. Her fingers curled tighter against his back, her nails pressing hard enough to leave marks. One kiss became many. It made her want more.

The distant sound of thunder nudged her common sense, reminding her that their friendship was more important than this moment of…desire. Weeks ago, she'd still been angry at him, hurt by him. Was it that easy to forget and forgive?

The kiss needed to end.

It hurt to let go, but she did so, unwinding her arms and using one of her hands to remove his from her hair. He released her, leaned back, his eyes heavy-lidded.

She looked away. "You should go. The rain's letting up." She hoped that was true.

He needed to leave. Before she did something she might regret. It had been awhile since she'd been intimate with anyone. None of her previous sexual experiences felt like that kiss. A homecoming. It would be easy to step back into his arms and take things into her bedroom.

She should focus on his socks. That'd be safe. Wool socks. Gray socks. Strong lips. Perfect amount of scruff on his jaw, imagining it other places on her body. The muscles on his back, how they felt against her palms. His socks were definitely gray. He probably looked amazing shirtless. This wasn't working. She had to get away from him. Leave the room.

She pushed herself away, sidestepping around him. Their bodies brushed. She couldn't help her sharp breath.

He brushed his fingers through his hair and followed her to the door. Her hands shook.

She hugged herself as he put his boots on, then reached for his rain jacket.

Only when she heard the slide of his jacket's zipper did she dare meet his eyes with her own. Despite being covered from head to toe in cozy clothes, she felt exposed. She needed to think away from him, digest the butterflies slamming against the inner walls of her stomach and the desire she felt for him.

His eyes held something different from what she'd seen before, like he might want to kiss her again, maybe more. If he did, she wouldn't be able to resist. He looked too damn savory for her peace of mind.

He didn't kiss her again. Instead, he hugged her tight, all of him pressed against all of her, his hand against her nape. Her own hands curled into his back. The words were on the tip of her tongue.

Stay.

But she'd never been a person to jump into bed with someone on a whim, even someone she'd known forever.

He let go, eased back. "Thank you for dinner. I—" He swallowed. Looked how she felt. Scattered. "I'll come by next time I'm in town. Maybe we can get coffee. Talk more."

"Night, Finn." She needed him to leave. Now. Even as part of her wished for a tree to fall on the driveway, blocking him in. He opened the door and walked out to his car. The driveway was clear. The rain had stopped, as had the wind. Stars were visible now.

She turned the deadbolt, fastened the chain. Then sagged against the door as she heard his SUV start. Her knees were weak from his touch. She touched her fingers to her lips. If one kiss did that to her, what would it be like to do more?

Chapter Twenty-Three

After breakfast and a coat of paint, Finn stopped by Wylder on his way back to Asheville.

Stella was happy to see him, but she looked perplexed. "It's not your usual day to visit Charlie. Everything okay?"

"I took care of some things in town yesterday. Figured I'd stop by, spend more time with him."

Ask him more questions. Update him on his meeting with Ray.

"He's in his room. He caught a cold, probably at that funeral you all went to."

"Is he okay?"

"Just grouchy, telling me too much about his snot." She shook her head in disgust.

"I look forward to hearing about it."

"I assume you're seeing plenty of it at the hospital."

Flu season had started. He'd been told the urgent care was overrun, but he spent his time in the ER dealing with more severe health issues.

Stella walked him down to Pa's room. They entered. He was sitting at the table eating breakfast off a tray.

"Morning, Pa."

Like Stella, he looked surprised to see him. "What are you doing here?" His voice was hoarse. "Don't come in. I'm sick."

Pa picked up a wad of Kleenex and blew his nose into it.

Finn stood just inside the doorway. "I'll keep my distance. I was in town taking care of things. Figured I'd see you on my way home."

He sounded pitiful, like a child. "I'm full of snot, that's what. Stella won't let me play cards with the others."

Stella remained in the doorway, her arms folded in front of her. "You know the routine, Charlie. We have to keep whatever you have from spreading."

"Humbug."

He was definitely grouchy if he was quoting Scrooge. Best keep his visit short, let him rest.

"I'll be brief. I met with Ray. He thinks the house is the perfect size for a couple or small family. He's confident it will sell if you want to put it on the market."

"I told you I want to sell. I don't need the house. You need to stay out of Evers Hollow."

Damn. What did he think would happen?

Exactly what had happened. He'd kissed Rose Finch. Wanted to do it again. He wouldn't share that with his father.

Instead, he said, "I've been painting. Got the family room done. It looks nice."

Pa stabbed a sausage link with his fork. "Painting. Why the hell are you painting?"

"The walls look like crap. The paint brightens it up. It'll make it more likely—"

"It's fine the way it is."

"I can't un-paint it."

"Dammit son. I want the house gone."

"It will be. I'll give Ray another call, let him know what you said. He'll come by with the paperwork."

"Let's get it done."

Chapter Twenty-Four

Rose met Alec upstairs in the coffee loft at Brick Wall Books. He'd made caramel lattes for both of them. She took the seat across from him, then pulled out her laptop, opened it, and logged in.

She said, "Thanks for rescheduling."

"Of course. How are you holding up?"

"Each day is a little different. I miss her."

"I guess so." He looked away from her, cleared his throat. Did her honesty make him uncomfortable? Perhaps he didn't expect a real answer. Was she supposed to lie and say she was fine?

"You ever lose anyone close?" She'd wondered about his parents. He never spoke of them.

"No."

Alec was a good friend, had a talent for lattes and selling books. He avoided more personal topics.

She picked up the coffee in front of her and took a tentative sip. The hint of caramel accented its coffee flavor.

"I remember meeting your grandmother," Alec said. "You brought her to see your books on our shelves."

"Magnolia loved books, read every night before bed. She might be the only family member besides my oldest niece to read all of mine."

"That's a compliment."

A wistful feeling tugged. "I'm aware. She told me what she thought about each one."

Something must have shown in her expression. He motioned towards her face.

"Why do you look—?"

She hesitated. Alec was a good friend, almost like family, but he didn't seem a fan of emotion. How would he react if she teared up? "She left me the house."

His eyes widened. "The house? The Victorian that's over a hundred years old."

"Yes." She swallowed.

"Shit. Bet you didn't see that coming."

"Not at all."

Alec asked, "What are you going to do?"

"I thought about that for two minutes. Me being single— antique house that needs lots of work, even more so since the dining room ceiling collapsed."

"You agreed." Alec sat back, his coffee in hand.

"Yes. I love the house."

"Isn't it haunted?"

Rose thought of Magnolia's letter, her words of warning. The local gossip.

She said, "Briar House has personality. Anything else you hear is speculation."

"I heard a bit of that at the funeral reception. Some said the library is haunted. That the books shelve themselves."

She smiled. "They don't."

He raised an eyebrow. "What about the dumbwaiter? The wailing spirit within?"

Mirth flickered around her heart. "Only when it's windy."

So many stories among the locals, about the house and its grounds.

"You spoke to someone at your gran's service. I saw you on my way out. Outside. Looked intense."

How like him to notice and exaggerate. Alec noticed everything.

"I spoke to many people. Magnolia was well-loved."

"Nice try. I know what I saw. You in his arms." His eyes lit with amusement. "It's him, isn't it? The boy from your books."

An unpleasant sound escaped her in response. Why was Alec fixated on her character, Jed? She knew it irritated him that she'd refused a second date with him, but she also knew it wasn't because he'd fallen for her. Dating her would be a convenience for him, nothing more. A way to get his matchmaking gran off his back.

They were supposed to talk about website improvements and marketing. Their meeting had been scheduled for last week, but she'd had to cancel. Magnolia's funeral, inheriting a house, a falling ceiling—all of that changed things. Discovering truths she hadn't known, random cemetery attack—the list kept on.

Rose hadn't decided which thing was easiest to accept.

She drummed her fingers on the table. "We should talk websites."

"I called to you, said bye. You didn't hear me."

She hoped she was delivering her harshest glare. "Alec."

"I've never seen you like that. Oblivious to others." He narrowed his eyes. "It was enlightening. I understand now why you always turn me down."

"Alec, please don't joke about this. It's been a heart-wrenching week."

"I'm not joking." His voice, his expression, both turned serious. "He's your one."

Astonishment filled her. "My one. You don't believe in that sort of thing."

He shrugged. "I don't believe in that sort of thing for me. I lived my parents' marriage. Saw how it ended. I won't go down that road. But you, you should go for it. You're a forever girl."

He meant what he said. It made her sad to hear the stark sincerity in his tone. Questions came to mind, ones she'd never had the courage to ask. About his parents, his childhood, what had made his attitude so. What sort of person might change his mind, make him want love for himself?

What could she say? "Things are complicated." She didn't want to be hurt again.

"That look on your face. Why are you upset? Is there something wrong with him?"

Something wrong with Finn? Despite her caution, her heart felt like a fluttering moth in her chest when she thought of him. She hadn't forgotten the kiss that felt more like a soul searing dozen.

"Whatever you call it, it's all over your face." Alec closed his laptop.

She closed hers too and shoved it in her bag. Their non-meeting was over.

"Does he live here? In Evers Hollow?"

"No."

"Haven't kept in touch?"

"Of course not. We sort of broke." Yet they'd talked about that, maybe more.

"Then why did you write an entire book series about you and him as kids?"

"I thought it would help me to write them down. Make me stop thinking about him. They started as journal entries. I hadn't planned to publish them."

"Someone held you at gunpoint and forced you?" He mocked.

"Mr. Munstead, our gardener. No gun involved. I helped him tend the grounds when I was younger. I used to tell him about our adventures. He loved hearing about them and convinced me to give it a shot."

"Does your guy even know about your books?"

"No idea." She stood and put her bag over her shoulder. "And he's not my guy."

F inn studied the bookshelves in front of him in the children's section. How did anyone decide with so many choices?

Pa's nurse, Stella, had recommended this family-owned bookstore. He'd asked her if she knew of a place and ended up driving back into town after. The name was familiar.

He'd come here as a child with Rose a few times, but back then, he preferred comic books. The bookstore didn't disappoint, but the large variety made choices difficult.

Finn stood beside a brown-haired young woman whose name tag read Kinsey. She crouched in front of the bookshelf, perusing its titles.

"You said he likes soccer?" She had one fingernail between her teeth as she scanned the shelves of middle grade books.

"It's all he talks about."

"We had a series. Looks like they're sold out." She stood. "I'll go look it up. It'll be a minute."

He should have asked Kendra what else Landon was into. It was a lucky thing he'd be able to attend the kid's party. She'd left an invitation on the center of his dining table a few days prior. A handwritten note from Landon in marker said, *"PLEASE COME!"*

Kinsey returned minutes later. "We're sold out of the soccer series, but we have some nonfiction books. About the game itself and some of the better known players."

Finn listened and considered. Knowing Kendra, anything that

didn't involve fart jokes would be fair game. She'd complained about the number of poop references happening at their apartment. It didn't help that she was in the middle of potty training her twins.

"That would be great."

Ten minutes later, he held two books in his hands. One about little known soccer stories and the other, an overall reference to the game. He headed toward the register. A dark-haired man and woman stood close together at the base of the stairs. They looked like a couple. His next step hitched. He recognized her. As if she sensed his notice, she looked up. Their eyes met. They were at least twenty-five feet apart, but he saw the moment she spotted him. Her lips parted in surprise.

Evie. His mind whispered it. He'd stopped using his nickname for Rose after the argument they'd had when she got engaged, hadn't even thought it till he'd seen her in Firebrew last week. Quickly, he moved toward her. He'd often run through the woods to meet her as a child.

He stopped in front of her. "Hey, Rose."

She said, "Finn."

The tall guy in glasses slung an arm around her and pulled her close to his side as if he had some sort of claim on her.

Who was he? Why did Finn have the urge to pull her away from him?

The man looked between them. "So, this is Jed."

"Alec." Her voice held exasperation.

Finn couldn't help himself. "Who's Jed?"

The guy raised an eyebrow and gave him a once over. "Maybe you're not Jed."

She poked him. "Ease up, Alec."

Finn's jaw tightened. They were familiar with each other. They'd had sex. The way he'd pulled her into him, protective like. His arm still hung over her shoulder. Only four inches separated their sides. He'd like to make it a solid four feet. Especially when Rose poked the guy again.

She motioned between them. "Alec, this is Finn Murphy. Finn, Alec Kincaid."

Alec removed his arm from around her and offered his hand. "Good to meet you. I've heard stories."

He'd heard about him? Finn looked at Rose.

She looked at Alec. "I've told you nothing."

"I know enough."

Rose's eyes narrowed. Her expression changed. She took a step away and folded her arms.

"Can I get my check?"

Alec's face changed as well. "I thought we were doing lunch."

"Only if you stop the immature crap." Her face showed irritation.

"Of course." His manner changed to one of business. "Did you bring more books? I can send Jack out to get them."

"I did."

Alec turned and called for Jack. A younger man, college-aged, red-headed, appeared.

"Can you get the box of books out of Rose's car?"

"Sure. Emmie's got the register."

Alec nodded. "Great. Glad to hear Gran made it in."

She pulled her keys out of her bag and handed them over. "They're in the trunk. Thanks."

The young man took her keys and disappeared out the front door.

Alec put his hands in his pockets. "Clarinda's place?"

Rose looked at her watch, then looked at Finn. "Do you have time to join us?"

He didn't. He needed a few hours of sleep before tonight's shift, but… "For a bit. Let me pay for these first."

Finn walked to the register. An older woman with long silvery hair and a kind, wizened face greeted him. "Welcome. I'm Emmie. I haven't seen you in here before. Did you find everything okay?"

"Yes, ma'am. Kinsey helped."

"She's a doll, that one. Especially in the children's section." She picked up the books he'd set down. "Great choices. Are these for your son or daughter?"

Her question reminded him that everyone in Evers Hollow knew everyone's business. "For my neighbor's kid. He's having a birthday."

She beamed. "Splendid. We have stickers for birthdays. I'll put one in the bag."

"Thank you." It was a beautiful bookstore, tall paned windows, lots of dark bookshelves, and the infamous brick wall Stella mentioned. It had been around a lifetime.

Emmie placed the books in a logo'd paper bag. "Saw you talking with my grandson and our precious Rose. So cute, those two." She had a wistful look on her face. "I keep hoping the two of them will get married. Give me some great-grandchildren to spoil."

Hell no. Finn hoped his expression was neutral as he finished with his purchase.

Once Rose had her car keys back, they crossed the street together to a corner cafe on the next block. The owner, a woman with short dark curls, greeted them with an enthusiastic welcome.

They all ordered and seated themselves.

Finn asked, "How long have you two known each other?"

Alec looked at Rose. She looked back at him, her face scrunched as if she were thinking.

Rose said, "Four, no, three years?"

Alec nodded. "About that."

"We officially met at a conference, but I'm guessing we met

when we were kids and ignored each other. His grandparents started Brick Wall Books."

How fucking cute. They had history.

Rose continued with warmth in her gaze. "Alec bought the place from his grandparents."

Alec shrugged and pushed his glasses back up his nose. "I told you, it's not a big deal. I practically grew up here. Taking over—it makes sense."

Rose patted his hand.

Finn wanted to retch. No wonder she'd pulled away from his kiss the other night, told him to leave. She was already involved in a relationship.

Chapter Twenty-Five

Briar House's kitchen screen door creaked as Rose pulled it open for Willow. Her arms were full.

"Morning. Sorry I'm late. I figured we could use caffeine and something delicious." She set a coffee carrier with three lidded cups and a pink pastry box on the kitchen counter. The box displayed the iconic Lightning Cakes logo.

Rose turned the coffee carrier to find her name. "You're amazing."

Willow shrugged as she removed a faded denim jacket from her shoulders and laid it over the back of a chair. She wore a faded tie-dye tunic, likely homemade. It covered a portion of the jeans she wore underneath. A fabric headband pulled back her brown hair. "It took a bit. Betsy and Alessia were overwhelmed. Two of their employees called in sick." She peeled the tape off the pink box and lifted the lid. She took out an iced cruller, then turned the offerings toward Rose.

More iced crullers, custard-filled cream puffs, and glazed cinnamon donut holes stuffed the box.

"Why'd you bring so much?"

Willow shrugged as she pulled a few small plates from a

cupboard and napkins from a drawer. "Today's lots of work. Aspen's very pregnant. She'll eat at least two, maybe three."

"Aspen cancelled. Doctor appointment. She might come later." Rose pushed up the sleeves of her lavender hoodie and pulled out a cream puff. The first bite—damn delicious. She mumbled her appreciation.

"I hope everything's okay," Willow said.

"She didn't say. Maybe she forgot she scheduled one."

Her brows furrowed. "That's not like her. Did you speak to her?"

"Text." Custard leaked onto her fingers. A drop fell onto her jeans.

"Here." Willow held out a napkin.

Rose licked the custard off her fingers, then took the napkin, dampening it to wipe her jeans. Willow frowned. She didn't do messy. Especially if it involved licking fingers.

She added a couple of donut holes to her plate.

Willow did the same, then said, "You and Aspen still need to talk." A statement, but Rose knew it was also a question.

"I know." It'd been almost two weeks since the reading of the will. Magnolia would have anticipated strong arguments mixed with emotion, but would have expected reconciliation.

Aspen knew this. They all did. Magnolia had reasons for everything she did.

"Has she talked to you?"

"Once or twice." Willow paused before continuing. "She's still upset. She was shocked to hear about the ceiling. At least she wasn't here for it."

"And the reason I inherited?"

"I think she's still trying to wrap her head around that." Willow ate another cruller. "It's a little weird that you're both our aunt and our sister. Aspen will come around though, realize we're still the same family who loves each other regardless of pesky details."

She didn't share Willow's confidence. "I hope you're right." She and Aspen didn't get along well—never had. Maybe it was the five years between them. Maybe it was the fact that Rose would rather write books and stick her hands in garden soil than mingle, dance, and sip champagne at the town's only country club.

She toyed with the last donut hole on her plate. "What about Thorne?"

Willow sent her a gentle smile. "The silence is his way."

"He bottles emotions, always has."

"I've never seen it the way you do. Must be because you two are closer in age."

Rose finished her coffee. "I want to make sure he's okay."

Willow nodded. "I'll call him tonight, check on him. Maybe you can do the same."

"I'll wait until tomorrow. Don't want him to think we're hovering." She popped the last bite of cinnamon enhanced evil into her mouth before loading her plate into the dishwasher. Willow followed suit.

Within a half-hour, the pastry box sat inside the fridge and the counter was clear.

Assembled boxes sat empty on the long wooden table beside stacks of newspaper and packing paper. All the cabinet doors hung open on both sides of the kitchen. The sight was over-whelming. One cabinet held everyday dishes. The rest were crammed with fine earthenware and crystal ware. All in various designs and sizes. Rose swallowed. This would be a lot of work. Where even to begin?

Willow held her copy of the list Mr. Winslow provided of who inherited what.

Rose said, "All those generations. Why did they all buy their own set of dishes?"

"Because they wanted to."

"How are we supposed to know which set is which?"

"They should say on the bottom."

"The Spode is the blue and white?"

Willow set the list down. "Yes, but so is the Burleigh."

The Burleigh would go to Rose. Most in calicos and chintz patterns.

Willow left the room and came back with a six-foot ladder. "I'll start with the Spode since I know it's mine."

Once Rose consulted the list, she glanced at the cabinet opposite where the crystal sat. "The stemmed crystal is the Waterford?"

Willow nodded. "All Aspen's."

She retied the laces on her sneakers, then grabbed a sturdy chair from the table. "I'll pack the crystal, get it out of the way. Aspen shouldn't be on a ladder."

"I'll designate a shelf for any Burleigh I find for you."

They worked as quickly as wrapping fragile items allowed. The sounds of packing tape, cardboard and the crinkling of paper created their own music, with snippets of conversation in between.

Willow said, "I ran into Carina Wellington at Betsy's."

Rose offered an unladylike snort as she reached for a champagne flute. Carina ran the town's social media. Rose avoided it. Gossip and vitriol. The sixty-two-year-old encouraged it all.

"Who's she looning about now?"

"You, of course. Word's out that the house is yours."

"Crud."

"I know. You've been back for two years. It shouldn't be that big of a deal."

Rose shrugged. "Now I know why Lucas Bowers asked me out when I got gas yesterday."

Willow turned to look at her from the ladder. "Tell me you turned him down."

Rose nodded. "I sat next to him in ninth grade World History.

I never got past the way he dug into his nose in class and wiped it on his jeans."

"High school?" Willow didn't wait for her to confirm, but visibly shuddered. "That is so unsanitary."

It was.

"There's more," Willow said.

"More about me and the house?"

"No, about you and Finn Murphy."

Damn. She placed another crystal flute on the counter below her.

"I wasn't the only one who saw you talk to him after the funeral."

Rose stared hard at the few remaining flutes on the shelf. "Don't people have other things to do besides gossip?"

A small sigh escaped before Willow said, "It's the way you look at him."

Rose climbed off the chair, ire rising inside her. "How do I look at him?"

A subtle grin formed as Willow came down off the ladder. "Like he's a piece of Betsy's seven layer chocolate cake."

"I don't—" She swore. Betsy's seven layer chocolate cake was pure sin.

The grin was full force now. "I know what I saw. Even in grief, I saw it. You liked seeing him."

She didn't want to talk about this. "I'm taking a break. I need some fresh air."

Rose opened the screen door, walked to the short set of steps, and sat down. Willow followed a few minutes later. She took a seat beside her and handed her a glass of lemonade.

"Rose…word is Finn will be around more. Some wonder if he's moving back."

"He's not. He's here to help his dad."

Willow gently bumped her shoulder and said, "When you moved back here, I worried about you."

"It was the idea that made the most sense."

How many times did she have to explain her willingness to move home? The choice had been lifesaving.

Willow sighed. "I worry the memories here haunt you."

"Life is full of memories. This place is part of mine. So is Finn. I can't undo that." Better the memories here than what she'd gone through in New York.

New York City changed after she broke her engagement with Caleb Brentwood. Her temporary fiancé had destroyed her confidence, her trust, and her ability to read other's sincerity. She'd fallen for someone who'd been acting a part. He'd only revealed his true self after he slipped a ring on her finger.

The friends they shared there had taken his side. Whatever reason Caleb told them for their break-up worked. No more book club, no more Friday morning coffees with girlfriends. Only one woman had bothered to return her text messages, letting her know her loyalties lay with Caleb.

Thankfully, she had her own friends. She'd known Ada almost as long as Finn. They'd roomed together in college. Becks made them a trio the year they rented an apartment together. Both of them helped her heal, helped her move past the fact that she'd fallen for someone who didn't exist. With their emotional support, she found her confidence again, excelled in her job at the magazine, and found the courage to write her and Finn's childhood adventures.

She'd poured her creativity into writing. Within a year, she published her first book and enjoyed a bit of celebration because of it. When she published her second, her success made her long for home. When Magnolia suffered a stroke, she volunteered to return to Evers Hollow.

The sounds of squirrels on branches, the sight of multicolored leaves, were restorative after packing boxes full of fragile crystal.

"I love it here. It helps me think. Every morning, I walk in the very woods my books come from. It's like coffee."

Willow lifted her glass as if to toast. "You've always been more attached to Briar House than the rest of us."

"I still can't believe she chose me over all of you."

"You're her daughter. That there is reason enough."

Once they finished their lemonade, they returned to the kitchen. Rose carefully pulled down a stack of plates with dark pink flowers on them. A glance at the bottom and the reference paper told her these also went to Aspen, that they'd belonged to the first bride of Briar House, Aurelia Sophia Hughes.

Her thoughts drifted to Magnolia's letter, her words of caution.

Willow might have some insight.

"In the letter Magnolia left me," said Rose, "she warned me to be careful. She wants me to avoid the forest. Something about lights at night, in the woods."

Willow tilted her head and pursed her lips as she wrapped a teacup. "She wants to keep *you* out of the woods?"

"Yes." Another dinner plate went into the box.

"That's like telling a bird not to fly."

Rose said, "I know."

"Why would she say something like that? And lights? That makes no sense."

"I know. That's why I'm telling you. She also asked Finn Murphy to protect me."

"What?" Willow shrieked as she lost her grip on a saucer she'd just removed from the cabinet. She caught it just before it hit the granite counter.

"That's what he told me," Rose said. "She told him to protect me. He agreed."

"But he doesn't live here." Her brow furrowed. "At least not yet."

"Their old house is going on the market."

"Maybe you can change his mind?"

Rose climbed up on the chair to reach the next shelf. "It's Charlie's decision. He wants it sold."

"I heard Charlie's at Wylder."

"He is. Finn visits him once a week."

"And he visits you as well?"

Rose shrugged.

Willow beamed, slightly bouncing on her feet. "He does visit you. I'm right."

Rose focused on her packing efforts.

Willow bounced again. "Spill. I need happy news."

What could she say? Willow's eyes looked so hopeful. "The storm the other night. I got caught in it. He gave me a ride home. We talked."

Willow's smile faded. "That's all you're going to say?"

Another shrug.

"You have a better vocabulary than that. I want adjectives and verbs."

"Fine. We talked about my engagement. He apologized for being an ass, and…"

Willow leaned over. "And?" There was so much excitement in her voice.

"And we kissed." Until she'd pushed him away.

"Then?"

"Nothing else happened."

Willow put a hand to her forehead and leaned against the counter. "Was the kiss bad?"

Rose felt her cheeks warm.

Her sister's grin was too big. "So it wasn't bad."

"No more questions about Finn." She'd tried not to think of him these past few days. She'd pushed him away, but all she could think of was the way he looked at her, the sincerity of his words. And their kiss, the knowledge she wanted more—it kept her awake at night.

Willow laughed. "I don't believe it. You're blushing."

Shaking her head, Rose put one of her music playlists on the Bluetooth speaker Ms. Tess kept on the counter.

"Party pooper."

She ignored her sister and reached for more packing paper. There were whiskey glasses to wrap for Thorne.

Two hours later, Rose heard the click of heels in the inner hall. It had to be her oldest sister. Willow had left after they ran out of boxes.

Aspen entered the kitchen, looking like a model for maternity wear in fire engine red and three inch black heels. She didn't seem to notice the boxes labeled with her name in dark Sharpie. There were eight of them now.

"Hi Aspen, how was your appointment?"

Her expression was pinched. "I need to talk to you."

Worry nudged her. "Are you and the baby okay?"

She waved a hand, her tone snippy. "Yes, fine. That's not why I need to—"

"What about Sunday dinner? Are we—"

Aspen made a sound of frustration, folded her arms over her baby bump, and glared. "We're fine. I'll still call you sister. To call you aunt would be creepy and create gossip this family doesn't need."

Relief overcame her.

Rose had interrupted, inexcusable, in Aspen's eyes, but she needed to clear the turmoil within the family over her parentage.

Aspen asked, "Are you crying?"

Rose didn't miss the sarcasm. She wiped her thumb under her eyes. "Not really. It's worried me, this change."

"Well, it's fine, all fine, water under bridges." She patted Rose on her shoulder twice. "Can I talk now without interruption?"

"Of course."

Aspen refolded her arms. Her expression turned serious. "Be honest. Are you seeing Finn Murphy again?"

Didn't the townsfolk have anything else to talk about? "We've bumped into each other a few times. He came to the funeral with his dad."

Aspen's eyes flashed. "I know. Carina Wellington saw you in his arms."

Carina Wellington again. Witnessing what should have been a somewhat private moment. She was an interfering hag, but that wasn't the issue.

"I hugged many people at the house."

Her eyes narrowed. "You hate him."

Not this again. "I never said that. I was angry with him for not supporting my engagement to Caleb. Turns out he was right to withhold it."

"That's an excellent reason to hate him."

It wasn't, but Aspen had her own ideas about friendship. Rose shook her head. "Not in my book."

"But you said—"

"I was twenty-two. And hurt."

"But—"

Rose held up her hand. Whatever issues Aspen had with Finn —she needed to nip it now. Her friendships were her own decision. No one else's.

"What is your problem with Finn?"

Aspen lifted her chin, her words sharp. "He's not good enough for you."

Honesty at last. Like Magnolia, Aspen said nothing she didn't mean.

"You think Caleb was?"

"His family had money. He had money."

"I'd rather have honesty."

Aspen flinched, but straightened as if she hadn't done so. What happened with Caleb was common knowledge amongst the family. Aspen studied her, then looked down with a visible swallow. "I don't want you struggling. Ever. I've seen things, circumstances that made me angry. I—" She shook her head as if shaking ghosts away. "Financial security is important. Then there's his father. He spent a night in jail for what he did."

"That was a long time ago. He'd just lost his wife."

"The mayor's wife brought it up at the Women's League luncheon yesterday."

Rose wanted to roll her eyes, but such an action would make things worse.

Besides, there was more. She could see it. Aspen's face, her gestures were wooden. As if a wrong word would break her. Her remarks might carry venom, but they were sincere, something she wasn't known for.

"Don't worry about me, Aspen. I know what I'm doing."

Despite what Willow suggested, what Finn told her, she doubted she'd see him anytime soon.

Aspen did the unexpected. She burst into tears.

Rose pulled her in for a hug. "There now. We're going to get through this."

Aspen pushed away and shook her head. "It's not about Grandmother. Or the Murphys. Gavin—he's not happy about the baby."

Any calm Rose felt dissipated. Sympathy and quiet rage replaced it. It took effort to keep it out of her voice. "I'm sorry to hear that."

"He wants a boy."

Of course, he did. "I thought you were having a girl."

Aspen's eyes looked glassy. "I am. Both ultrasounds confirm it."

Rose couldn't help it. She hugged her sister once more.

For a woman who avoided affection, this time, she clung back.

When they separated, Aspen pressed her hands to her eyes.

"He said both ultrasound techs are wrong, that the baby will be a boy."

Gently, Rose said, "When she's born, he won't be able to deny it."

"No, he won't." Worry creased her eyes along with deep sadness.

Was there anything Rose could say to ease her anguish?

Aspen bit her lower lip. "Please don't tell the others. Or him. We've got family brunch coming up. I'd like him to attend. Be around our nieces."

It wouldn't help. Her brother-in-law cared only about himself. She refrained from sharing her opinion. Instead, Rose offered a single nod. "Of course. Mum's the word."

Chapter Twenty-Six

Rose pressed her fingertips into the cinnamon and brown sugar crumbs on her plate. She gathered as many as she could and pressed them to her tongue. The bear claws were her favorite, but the coffee cake at Cracked Egg Cafe also bordered on evil.

The place was noisy this morning with many tables occupied.

The Elders' table in the center of the room sat empty.

Rose sat in a booth. She had her notebook out, hoping to get some words down. So far, all she'd done was doodle on an empty page and exchange texts with her friends, Ada and Becks. They'd asked about Finn.

Florence came round to her booth with a pot of coffee. "I'm not sure you got them all."

Rose glanced at the plate. "Fine. I'll just order a bowl of the topping next time."

With a sparkle in her eyes, she said, "I'll see if Stan can add that to the menu."

She refilled Rose's coffee cup before moving to another booth.

Stan's voice barreled out of the kitchen. "Order up."

Sadie, another server, collected the array of steaming white plates from the order counter. Dishes clattered close by as a busboy cleared a table.

Rose sipped her refilled mug, glanced at the clock over the register. She'd have to leave soon. She needed to buy groceries before she headed home.

Someone approached her table. It wasn't Florence. Black sneakers, beige slacks. She looked up. A man stood at her side. A musky odor emanated from him that made her want to hold her breath.

"I hear you're fixing up the big house," he said.

A smattering of saliva hit her arm. She struggled to hide her disgust as she wiped her arm with her napkin.

"Can I help you with something, Mr—"

"Don't be like that, Pet. You know my name. I worked for your dad, in the garden."

Something about his voice, his tone, made her cringe. It wasn't the pervasive cologne or the manner in which the man presented himself. Something inside her said to get away from him.

His words made little sense. She looked up. He turned the corners of his mouth into a gruesome semblance of a smile. "Hello, Maggie."

A shiver went through her. The man at the cemetery. Without the mud.

The fear she'd felt that day flooded her, froze her in her seat. She remembered his grip on her elbow, felt an echo of the pain. The bruises hadn't faded.

This man thought she was someone else, possibly Magnolia. She recognized that now. In all her years of living with Magnolia, she'd never heard anyone call her Maggie, but this man possibly had.

She glanced at the two servers. Florence was helping another customer. Sadie stood at the register. The busboy had just taken another table's worth of dishes to the kitchen.

Rose tried to remain calm. "I don't remember you." She herself had worked alongside Mr. Munstead, the head gardener, during her teenage years. There'd been no other gardeners.

His jaw slackened and his eyes narrowed, studying her as if in confusion. "Don't toy with me."

"Everything all right, Rose?" Florence came over, glanced at the man beside the table. A wariness flickered in her eyes.

"Can I get the check?" Her voice sounded shaky. She hoped her eyes conveyed everything she felt. Forced calm and panic.

Florence nodded and headed toward the kitchen with quick steps.

The man, however, remained. "I want my job back." He curled his fists, stood straighter.

Her common sense stressed caution. "I'm sorry. I can't hire anyone right now." She shoved her notebook into her bag and stood. She'd pay at the register.

He grabbed her wrist. "I need the work. For our future."

That same grip of ice. The nonsense he spouted, like before.

Her voice shook. "Let go of me. I told you. I can't hire anyone."

His face changed again, his eyes edged with cruelty. "You're lying. Your pa's got plenty of money to pay me."

"Stan!" Florence yelled.

The hand around her wrist tightened. Customers watched from their seats. Cell phones extended upward, clearly filming.

"Let—me—go." Rose's eyes watered.

A large hand came down hard on the man's shoulder.

With menace, Stan said, "Let go of the girl."

The creep let go.

Stan hauled him back away from the table, anger in his eyes. "I told you what would happen if you caused trouble again. Apologize to the lady."

"She's no lady." He snarled.

"Now. Before I call the cops."

Rose's fingers gripped her bag tighter. She didn't care about apologies, only wanted to get away. She forced herself to stand still, to take a breath. Stan was with her. This was a public place.

"Sorry." No sincerity. Rose didn't care.

Stan used his grip to turn him, guide him to the door. "You need to leave. You're not welcome here."

He resisted. "I need a job."

"She's not hiring."

"Her pa can pay me."

Stan shook his head, his grip still firm. "You've been gone awhile, George; this girl's pa died a long time ago." He sent her an apologetic look. "This here's one of Daisy's girls."

The accusatory look on the man's face said he didn't believe him.

Stan pushed him towards the door. His next words echoed through the cafe as he propelled him outside. "Don't come back here—I'll call the sheriff."

"OMG!" Sadie rushed over to Rose, her eyes huge. Every word came out with a Southern slang. "I thought he was going to hurt you. Are you okay?"

Florence was there too, looked like she wanted to pull Rose into her arms and rock her like a child. The other customers didn't bother to hide their gawking.

Rose nodded. "I'm okay. I want to go home." Forget the groceries she'd made a list for. She wanted to go home and throw punches. All her training, her self-defense class she'd taken in college, the things Thorne had taught her. All for nothing if she couldn't get away from a scary old man with a handcuff grip. Her hands shook as she pulled her wallet out.

Florence's hands stopped her. "Breakfast is on us."

"I can pay." Her hands shook as she pulled out a twenty dollar bill. Keep it together. She could do this.

She pressed it back towards her. "No argument."

Kindness. It choked her. She nodded without meeting her eyes. She refused to cry.

Florence addressed the room. "Rest of you, stop it. She's all right. Eat your food while it's hot."

Then she pointed a finger at a table behind her. "You. With the cell phones. We'll send what you have to Deputy MacShane. Then you'll delete that footage you've been taking. And prove that you have. Otherwise, I'll call your parents and have a conversation."

The phones lowered. Teenagers. Red flushed their cheeks. "Yes, ma'am."

The man was gone when Rose stepped out the glass door. Stan stood on the sidewalk, his muscled, tattooed arms folded over his white apron. Concern hung heavy on his face. He insisted on walking her to her car.

"I'm sorry about him. He's never been quite right. I had hoped they would help him in prison, but he's the same as before, maybe worse."

Her eyes widened; a sliver of alarm went through her. "Prison?"

"You didn't know?" Stan prodded. "That George Hindley was in prison."

"No. Why would I? I don't know him." They reached her car. She unlocked it.

Stan opened the door for her and held it as she climbed in. A long sigh escaped him. "I forget. You were just a kid."

He took a step back. "Years ago. That barn fire that sent the Murray's son to the hospital and killed your grandmother's horse —he set it."

Chapter Twenty-Seven

Rose's run-in at the cafe left her feeling vulnerable, on edge. She ran a hand over her left arm, then her wrist. Her skin was a fading mix of dark and yellow. The feeling that she wore a bracelet of ice hadn't gone away.

All she'd wanted to do was go home. Common sense kicked in, though. She now knew who'd attacked her at the cemetery. This needed reporting.

Sheriff Darin Hutchins' eyes held no warmth when she walked into the Evers Hollow Police Department. He looked her up and down. Perhaps he didn't recognize her.

She held out her hand. "Hello Sheriff, I'm Rose Finch. I filed a police report a few—"

"I know who you are." He didn't take her hand. Instead, he turned and walked away from her, past his secretary, who watched with wary eyes.

He snapped at the middle-aged woman behind the desk. "Coffee. Now!"

Rose lowered the hand she'd offered. She'd seen the sheriff around town, but had never spoken with him. He was a broad, heavyset man, and quite tall. She imagined some voted for him based purely on his height and breadth, along with his expression. It was pure menace.

He looked back at her, his words clipped. "You have five minutes."

She followed him into his office, took in the utilitarian combo of gray and black furniture. He didn't invite her to sit. Instead, he leaned back against the metal desk and looked at her expectantly.

She began describing what had happened. One minute into their conversation, he cut her off. "You're wrong, Miss Finch. George Hindley is up in Gray Mountain at a transitional residence. No way he's down here, walking around my town."

She struggled to use a respectful tone. "Stan identified him, called him by name this morning. I watched him force him out of the cafe for what he did to me."

He frowned. "Not possible. Stan's got some of them cataracts, needs glasses."

Rose matched his frown. Glasses didn't fix cataracts. "I will go on record with this new information."

His jaw clicked. "You always were a troublemaker." He picked up his phone. "Who's in the corral?"

Rose folded her arms.

"I see." He hung up the phone and sneered. "Mack Daggett will take down your new information. But see here, little lady, I'll prove you wrong."

She sat down with Mack, then drove home.

Mack called her late that night, just before bed. They'd found George Hindley. He'd been nowhere near Gray Mountain.

Chapter Twenty-Eight

This time, Finn didn't get a text. Mack left him a voicemail on his phone—to call him back ASAP.

He did so as soon as he got a break between patients.

Mack said, "If I were you, I'd get up here. There might be something to Ms. Magnolia's worries about protecting Rose."

"What happened?"

"You remember the barn fire way back? I know we were just kids, but—"

"I remember." He'd had nightmares. It had taken years for them to go away.

"The guy who set them—he's out of prison. He's the one from the cemetery. Rose confirmed it. He approached her again in public at the cafe this morning."

He pressed a hand to his neck. "Mack—"

"She's okay. Stan took care of it. Threw him out, but he didn't know about the other incident."

"Damn it."

"She came in. I took her statement. I followed her home, checked out the property. All clear. We've got someone keeping an eye on the grounds. Patrol cars are out looking for him."

He'd planned to head up to Evers Hollow early in the morning. "I'm on nights. Let me see if I can get someone to cover my hours for me. I'll text you when I head up. I'll have to come back for tomorrow's night shift. Then I'll have a few days off."

"I wouldn't have bothered you, but I remember you two seemed tight way back. Something tells me she'd appreciate seeing you. In the meantime, we'll keep an eye on her."

Finn hung up the phone. Sent a message to Kendra. He'd have to cancel Saturday's dinner with them. He knew they'd understand. Especially Dare, who would do anything to keep his family safe.

Next, he sent a message to Broome. Letting him know they needed to talk again. Another resident agreed to come in to cover the rest of his shift. Finn was on his way within two hours.

He'd never seen the man who set the barn fire years ago, only his picture in the paper when he'd gone to trial. Something about his eyes, even in black and white, said evil.

An hour later, on the northern outskirts of Asheville, in the dark, Finn drove through a set of wrought iron gates. It was hard to miss the security cameras and spikes on top of the wrought iron fence.

Broome hadn't been joking when he said he took his family's security seriously. This was a fortress.

Were there guards as well, walking the perimeter? It wouldn't surprise him. Even if he didn't understand why this level of precaution was necessary.

He directed his SUV up the lamplit circular driveway and pulled it around to the right, as Broome requested. He left his vehicle and approached the front door, the porch light illuminated.

A note covered the doorbell with the words, *text upon arrival, toddler sleeping.*

He sent a text.

The door opened. Broome stood in a worn metal band t-shirt,

faded jeans, and bare feet. His hair stuck straight up. Finn didn't think it was intentional. He held a finger to his lips and motioned for him to enter.

Broome led him toward a hallway on the right. Large windows lined the walls of the house, displaying what looked like an inner sanctum of greenery.

He was tempted to ask if the windows were bulletproof. It wouldn't surprise him.

They reached a room with a solid wooden door. Broome motioned him in. The inside held bookshelves. It smelled of leather. One wall alone looked to be professional books with dark covers.

Broome spoke first. "Future parenting advice. Never put a baby's room over the front door. Especially when they're teething."

A strange comment, especially to him. "Noted."

He motioned toward two leather chairs grouped at one end of the office beside a large desk. "Have a seat. Let's talk about Rose's safety."

The conversation was brief. Broome looked over the security footage from the Briar House cameras. They both watched Rose return from town after the Cracked Egg incident, along with Mack Daggett. The cameras caught bits of him checking out the property, but nothing else since.

Finn felt like he was spying on Rose, but it comforted him to know she'd made it inside the cottage safely. That Mack said they'd keep an eye on the place.

It was past midnight by the time he got to Evers Hollow. A truck hauling a trailer overturned, blocking the small two lane highway. It had taken over two hours to get the right equipment to open one lane. Once inside his old house, he realized he didn't have Rose's cell number.

He texted Mack.

Mack texted right back.

MACK

We got George. He's in a holding cell for at least twenty-four hours.

FINN

"I'm at my old place. Should I check on her?"

MACK

"No. I spoke to her earlier. Let her sleep. She's safe now."

Chapter Twenty-Nine

George Hindley was in custody. The news from Mack should have made her feel better as Rose readied herself for bed, made it possible for her to sleep. The day's events, though, the memory of her encounters with him, the nagging ache at her wrist, woke her up repeatedly, each time with a gasp.

When her clock displayed five am, she got out of bed and pulled on leggings beneath the oversized flannel shirt she wore.

She sat down at her desk, a cup of tea in hand. Pressing pen to page, Rose rewrote the problematic sections of her next Criminy Mystery. A glance at her paper told her the words still weren't right. Bleary-eyed, she didn't know how to make them so.

Her editor's feedback so far hadn't been surprising. She'd felt it too.

"Something's missing with this one, sweetie."

The true story involved a homicide. It was a struggle to adapt it for a middle grade audience. How could she add humor to its sad reality?

Rose stood and stretched before making herself a second cup

of English breakfast tea. She moved back to her desk and picked up her pen again. She worked for another half-hour until the sky lightened.

George Hindley was locked up. This knowledge should have forced her outdoors to walk the paths she loved. It was her morning dawn ritual. Her boots remained by the door.

She slipped her sneakers on instead and left the cottage, keys in hand. She unlocked Briar House's kitchen door and walked its floors, room after room, floor by floor. A heavy plastic barrier blocked off the dining room and the second floor bathroom, to keep the dust from the rest of the house. The crew had made progress, but the repairs would take time.

She stood in front of Magnolia's bedroom windows on the second floor, studying the grounds below. The rose garden still thrived, but the cooler temperatures meant lesser blooms. Beyond that, grew the spiral herb garden, in the spot where the barn once stood. Fog clung to the forest perimeter, as if warning her to stay away.

Broome had asked about her plans to move into the house. She'd been reluctant to name a date. Especially about moving into this bedroom. The four-poster bed, its heavy brocade coverings, and its bedspread were all Magnolia's along with the elegant antique dresser, vanity, and the small chaise lounge in the corner. All beautiful but different from Rose's simplistic mishmash of cottage styles. She wasn't sure how to go about discussing such things, to ask the others if they wanted any of the bedroom furniture. Would such questions upset them?

Rose's gaze fell on the bedside table, on the book Magnolia had been reading. How many times had she come into this room while Magnolia read?

Too many to count.

Her eyes twinkled each time Rose handed her a new Criminy Mystery. Her joy inspired Rose to keep writing. It was a privilege to bring that spark to her eyes, hear her comments on a book.

"I should be appalled by what these two get up to. There's truth in here somewhere. I shudder to think which parts."

Most of the chapters had a backstory in truth. Each book reflected what it was like to grow up in a town such as Evers Hollow alongside a best friend. The woods were their very own playground, the eight blocks of town their amusement park.

She thought of Finn as she left Magnolia's bedroom and headed back downstairs. Seeing him at the bookstore was a surprise. The memory of his lips on hers ignited her insides, made it difficult to stand still while they'd conversed. Even worse, when they sat at a table for lunch. His knees had brushed hers. Her heart beat a bit faster in those seconds.

After Finn left to head back to Asheville, Alec had grilled her again and joked about needing a fire extinguisher before his voice grew serious.

"Remember what I said. He's your one."

She returned downstairs. Boxes stood in short stacks by the stairs, waiting for their relocation via Broome's and Thorne's pickup trucks.

Moving to the kitchen, she perused the pantry, noting what groceries she'd need to buy for the upcoming family brunch. She'd never hosted a family meal despite her love of baking. They'd rotated between Magnolia, Broome, and Aspen. They were the ones with large tables and plenty of space.

Her specialty was scones. She'd bake two kinds, and maybe a quiche.

With breakfast plans in mind, she returned to the cottage. Seated at her desk once more, she reviewed her work and found sentences she could work with. A new idea came to mind, a way to circumvent the murder and make it a smaller part of the story. She filled a few pages before setting her pen down.

This would be the first book Magnolia wouldn't get to read. That bothered her each time she thought about the draft being complete. Perhaps that was part of her problem. Her fingers traced the new lines she'd written.

This story was one of hers and Finn's last. They'd been twelve when it happened. Their adventures grew farther and farther apart. When they started high school, they ended.

She'd worried about high school. Worried about all the expectations that went with a new school—more homework, social things, even kissing.

At fifteen, on a summer day at the creek, she and Finn had shared an awkward melding of lips and tongue that resulted in bumped noses and shy smiles. She couldn't remember whose idea it'd been, only that it had seemed a good one at the time. They'd had so many firsts together. Why not this one too?

Her stomach felt strange during and after. She'd actually feared she was allergic to kisses. She knew now that it was her first experience with desire. Mere stones skipping on the surface of what was possible.

Their recent kiss—they'd gone from a babbling creek to a cascading waterfall. She'd responded like she needed him in order to breathe. Not what she planned. She'd meant to focus on restoring their friendship. A new beginning. He'd apologized for the things he'd said to her in the past. She'd shared life things. So had he.

Back-to-back knocks came from the cottage door, startling her. Curses. She hesitated when she reached the door. After what happened at the cemetery and the cafe, she needed to be cautious. "Who is it?"

"It's Finn."

She looked at the clock. Eight o'clock am. She looked down. Not what she'd call put together in her yoga pants and ratty flannel shirt. She hadn't brushed her hair when she'd gotten out of bed; she'd wound it in a messy bun.

She opened the door. "You should have texted first. It's early."

With a raised eyebrow, he said, "I don't have your phone number."

She tried not to look at him, but her eyes had other plans. Shadows of sleep deprivation underlined his eyes. He wore paint-splattered jeans and a long-sleeved t-shirt. He'd showered; the scent of soap clung to him. His hair was still damp on the ends. She wanted to reach out, touch the strands.

He studied her, his gaze traveling from her head to her toes. "Want to get a cup of coffee?"

So he'd meant it, coming back here and asking her to coffee. Even with talk of his promise to Magnolia, she hadn't expected to see him again so soon after the bookstore. Was that why he was here?

She motioned between them. "Is this about your promise?"

He pressed his hand to his neck. "It's coffee, Rose. This doesn't have to be anything more than that. I'd like to spend time with you, catch up on the past six years."

Magnolia's words came to her, along with her tone of wistful regret.

You care for Finn Murphy still; you always have. Not everyone gets a chance to fix their misunderstandings, Rebel. I want you to have your happy ever after.

Was such a thing possible? After what happened with Caleb? She thought of Brigette and Jeremy, Broome and Simi, her best definitions of what love was.

She took a breath and another. Caffeine. "Coffee's good." She looked down at her clothes. "Should I change?"

His eyes had that look she remembered from his last visit here. One that stole her breath. One that hinted *coffee* meant something more. "You look perfect."

That was doubtful. Why had she asked his opinion? "Give me a few minutes."

As he waited just inside the door, she slipped back into her bedroom and brushed her teeth. Then slipped a bra on beneath her shirt, grabbed a sweater, her keys, and her wallet. Her navy floral rain boots went on last.

Chapter Thirty

He and Rose sat in a corner, on gray chairs, a square table between them. Finn liked this corner. It made him feel he had her all to himself. It was warm in here. The sweater she'd worn now hung behind her.

Her phone rang while they walked through the woods. When the call ended, she told him about yesterday's incident at the cafe, that she had to go in later, identify George Hindley in a line-up.

He didn't share that he knew about yesterday.

Rose was nervous, off-balance. It made sense, after what happened yesterday, but he dared to hope he was the reason, that the kiss they shared days before affected her as much as it affected him. Her lips, the taste of her skin, the feel of her—all kept invading his thoughts.

Was she dating the bookstore owner? He needed to know.

She told him about her initial move-in to the cottage. "I found a family of copperheads in the dryer vent. Can you believe it?"

Tiny wrinkles appeared at the corners of her eyes when she smiled. "You're not scared of snakes."

She lowered her voice to a whisper. "Older, wiser now. It was a whole damn poisonous nest."

Her eyes held that spark of memory, of too many great ideas that got them into trouble. Her lips were glossy. He caught a hint of floral each time she leaned closer to him.

"What'd you do?"

She sat back, tilted her head with a sly grin on her face. "Would you believe I charmed them into moving to the next county?"

He shook his head, fixated on the mischief in her eyes, glimpses of the girl he'd grown up with. The differences came through as well. There was thought and hesitation in her words —that hadn't been there before. She'd been the confident one, the more mischievous.

He couldn't resist her teasing, though. She could well kill a snake without help. He'd watched her do it at thirteen.

That floral scent again as she leaned forward over the table. The loose neckline of her flannel shirt caught his gaze, drew his attention to the slope of her breasts, now exposed by the angle. He remembered how soft they felt against his chest during their kiss. He wanted to explore them with his hands and mouth, along with the rest of her.

"I needed help," she whispered. "Someone stole the shovel from our shed. I called Brigette. Within an hour, all of their sons were there with shovels ready to behead the entire family."

At those words, he sat up taller and frowned. "All of them?"

"Yes. All four, plus Jeremy and Brigette with her own sharpened spade."

The thought of all four Conroy sons ready to rescue Rose spiked something he didn't like. He knew their reputation. Women flocked to them like bees to honey. "You're pulling my leg."

She leaned even farther. He swallowed at the hint of lace now visible. Pink lace, the same color as her glossy lips. He rubbed a hand down his leg. It was getting harder to follow her story.

He forced himself to look away, shifting in his seat. She didn't appear to notice his discomfort.

She asked, "Would you believe Brigette took pictures for the Evers Hollow Facebook page?"

"No." Brigette despised social media.

"You know her too well." She took a long sip from her mug, her eyes teasing over its brim.

He set his empty mug down and folded his arms to rest on the table. "Killing poisonous snakes is Brigette's hobby. I bet another cup of coffee she killed one and that you held one of those shovels yourself."

She set her own mug down, mirroring his arms. "You think I could drive a shovel through a snake?"

He lowered his voice. "Have you forgotten your first copperhead decapitation? If you'd had a shovel—you'd have taken out the whole family by yourself."

He heard her inhale. If he edged closer, he'd be able to taste the coffee on her lips. Her impish look disappeared. She studied him with what looked like interest in her eyes.

"I—"

Raucous laughter rang nearby. She sat up with a jolt, a hint of pink on her cheeks.

She grabbed his empty mug. "I'll be right back."

Rose wrapped her arms around herself as she waited in line. Time with Finn was exhilarating. He'd been absent from her life for too long. Who knew they could snap back together as if nothing bad had happened between them? Six years, they'd gone without speaking. So similar, yet different.

Of the two of them, he'd been the quiet one until high school.

Something changed after he lost his mom at fourteen. He made the varsity soccer team as a sophomore, got his first job at the garage, and his first girlfriend.

Rose kept her *best friend* status as he moved through his second, third, and fourth girlfriends. She'd always felt something for him but convinced herself it was friendship, nothing more. She'd heard it from his own mouth that he would never ask her out. But last week, what he'd said—the fear of losing her as a friend. It made her think.

They had undeniable chemistry. Hadn't she told Alec that was her top requirement for a relationship? After Caleb, was she ready for that sort of chemistry? Her ex had destroyed her self-confidence, her ability to trust. Would she ever be able to hear the words *I love you* and believe them?

She thought of Ada and Becks, last night's group text thread, their efforts to check on her. She cherished them both. They were the two who'd lifted her mood after the break-up and encouraged her to pursue her dreams outside of her journalism job. Becks still lived in New York, but Ada, she'd grown up here in Evers Hollow, lived with a cousin on the other side of downtown.

She placed an order for two more coffees. They drank them, then walked to his childhood home in what she referred to as the Hollows Eight. The street sign read Hollows Loop. Hollows Eight was a much better name.

Rose followed him inside. The house was small, all of it in a straight line. Two bedrooms, a family space, a narrow kitchen with a dining area on one end. The kitchen walls were still a cheerful yellow. The golden laminate countertops were stained and worn, as was the vinyl floor. Light oak cabinets sagged above the counters, matching the rest of the room.

She smiled when she saw the yellow table and its golden yellow chairs.

"You kept the table?"

Finn shoved his hands in his pockets. "I can't get rid of it."

She ran her fingers along its aluminum edge. Rose had loved the days they played at his house, sat at this table finishing homework or eating summer jam and peanut butter sandwiches. Mrs. Murphy made cookies almost as good as Tess.

Drop cloths covered the family room carpet. Paint cans sat in the corner along with a paint tray and an empty roller. The smell of paint hung in the air.

Finn said, "I've finished in here. I'll do the bedrooms when I come back."

She didn't ask when that would be. "Are you seeing anyone?" The question came out before she thought it through.

He folded his arms, appearing amused. "Do you think I would have kissed you if I were?"

"Oh." She hadn't thought of that.

He said, "I've dated some. Nothing long-term. Longest was five months. She wanted the whole thing—marriage, kids, two-and-a-half dogs. I didn't. At least not with her."

"Really?" She glanced up at him. Was that hope in her own voice?

"Yeah."

"And you went to UNC Chapel Hill."

"Yeah."

"Too bad the hospital here closed." She watched for a reaction. He didn't seem to have one.

Instead, he asked, "What about you and Alec? How long have you been seeing him?"

She and Alec. Did he think—

She couldn't help it. Laughter spilled from her lips. "No. We're friends. That's it. He's commitment phobic."

Did he look relieved?

She followed him down the hall. Finn's old room looked different. All his posters, the quilt his mother made, his twin bed, were gone now. As were the curtains. A lone dresser covered in stickers remained. Tack and nail holes marked out a dot-to-dot on the walls that made no picture. A partially deflated air mattress sat in the middle of the wooden floor with a sleeping bag and a blanket thrown on top. A zippered duffel bag sat nearby.

She asked, "When will the house go on the market?"

"Soon. I met with the agent last week."

"How do you feel about selling it?"

He shuffled his feet, nudged the air mattress. "It's not my house. It's Pa's. I'm dealing with it."

With the way his shoulders hunched, she wasn't so sure. She wouldn't pry.

Instead, she ran her fingers over the top of his dresser, studying the stickers he'd attached from long ago. She recognized many of them.

Finn walked her back to her cottage. She unlocked the door and turned to him.

"I have to return to Asheville for another night shift," he said. "I wanted to see you though—make sure you were okay."

She should have known her time with him would be short. He had a life in Asheville. She shouldn't be upset or sad. The words they'd exchanged these past days mattered. The kiss—that mattered too, but a restored friendship was her goal. "I understand."

He touched her arm and turned her to face him. His fingers slid into her hair, cupping her face in his hands. "Do you? Am I that easy to read?"

She met his gaze with her own. He was close, like before when they'd kissed.

How could she resist what she felt? More than friends.

If she moved just a tad, his lips would touch hers. They both moved. A sound left her when his lips caressed hers—soft, warm, breathtaking. He pulled away and let go of her. "I'll see you soon." He turned and disappeared into the woods.

Chapter Thirty-One

Identifying George Hindley in a line-up had been easy. Afterward, Rose returned to the cottage, grocery bags in hand. Her phone rang as she nudged the door closed.

From the other end of the line, Brigette said, "I heard about what happened. All of us are worried about you. We want you to meet us for breakfast tomorrow at Cracked Egg."

Rose agreed.

Willow had the morning off, so she came too.

The Elders had chairs out for them around the table. Serious expressions welcomed them as they took their seats. Florence poured coffee all the way around.

Jeremy cut right to it. "We heard about the trouble you had up at the cemetery and here at the cafe. Horrible thing when men think it's all right to handle young women without permission. Unacceptable. Especially with what you've already been through."

Rose assured them. "I'm okay. My arm's getting better. The cemetery set things right with her grave."

"We took flowers up there earlier," Willow said. "They

replaced the sod over the damaged areas, cleaned her tombstone."

Brigette's eyes narrowed. "Any news on who it was?"

Rose said, "I identified him in a line-up. It's George Hindley. He set the—"

Hal cursed. "Hell. How is he out of prison?"

The mayor cleared his throat.

With hesitation, Rose continued. "The sheriff said he served his time."

Jeremy shook his head. "He was sentenced to life."

"Life with parole," said Dr. Cook. "I remember the shock I felt when the sentence came down."

Rose shook her head. "I'm no lawyer. Broome's checking into it."

Jeremy looked at the mayor. "You know anything about this, Clyde?"

The mayor reddened a bit, adjusted his collar as he cleared his throat. "Of course not. I'll make some calls. We want a safe town."

Brigette reached across Jeremy and patted her hand. "My goodness, girls, what a scare, so soon after your loss. You let us know if there's anything we can do."

Rose said, "Thank you. We will."

Florence came over and took their orders. Jeremy and Brigette ordered an omelette to split.

Hal wasn't ready to let the topic go. "Hindley's a monster. Not a speck of goodwill in his blood."

Brigette said, "Hal, this is not the place. Florence is watching you. Let the law do its work."

He muttered. "Like it worked last time."

Their plates were half empty when Deputy Reggie MacShane walked in. He came right to their table.

"Morning. How are all of you this am?" He didn't give

anyone a chance to answer. "What about you, Rose? Heard you came by the station."

She nodded. "I did. It's him."

Hal put down his fork. "Reggie, I got to say, Hindley being back here, it's no good. We need to protect the citizens in this town. That man's rotten to his core. Always was."

Reggie set a hand on his shoulder. "I hear you, Hal, but it's not up to me. He'll go before a judge. He'll be tried. Rose here, she's pressed charges."

They all looked at her as if in surprise. Mayor Winston paled.

Dr. Cook nodded. "Good on you, Rose. I don't care who his father is."

Confusion filled her. "Who's his father?"

Mayor Winston answered, his words slow. "Franklin Hindley. He served four terms as the mayor of Gray Mountain."

Reggie said, "I heard stories about how he ran things up on Gray Mountain. He had power and the finances to go with it. When he retired, he hand-picked his successor. No one ran against his candidate."

Rose asked, "What does that have to do with anything? He's not the mayor now."

Reggie shrugged. "No, he isn't. Franklin's in his nineties, in hospice care. I called the facility up there to see if I could talk to him about his son, but he's in and out of consciousness. I'll try again, but I'm doubtful I'll be able to question him."

Dr. Cook asked, "Is that how Hindley got out? Favors?"

Reggie said, "I have no evidence indicating such. Franklin Hindley was a cop before he became mayor."

Hal and Dr. Cook looked like they wanted to say more, but Mayor Winston spoke first. "Franklin's stance on crime won him the election in Gray Mountain. People thought that if he was willing to send his own son to a ranch for troubled boys, they'd have a safer community."

"Rose looks too much like Nola," Hal blurted. "They should deny him bail."

All eyes turned to Hal, even Florence's, who'd appeared beside Reggie with coffeepot in hand.

"Have you forgotten, Clyde?" Hal continued. "He caused trouble here long time ago with Nola. Was obsessed with her."

Reggie sobered. "Did he hurt her?"

Jeremy said, "He tried."

Rose reached beneath the table and gripped Willow's arm. This was the first she'd heard of this.

"George Hindley's older now," said Mayor Winston. "I don't see how he could be a threat."

Rose couldn't help it. She glared at him. "Would you like to see the bruises on my arm?" She'd worn long sleeves to hide them.

The mayor blanched, shook his head. "I think you misunderstood the situation."

Hal said, "His age doesn't matter. His heart's full of tar. The only thing he wanted that he couldn't have was Nola."

Dr. Cook straightened in his chair. "Only because we stopped him."

Rose and Willow exchanged horrified expressions. What had happened all those years ago?

Reggie hooked his fingers into his gun belt. "Shit Sam. You would have to say something like that."

Hal said, "One of us has to. It's the truth."

"I'll do my best about the bail hearing. They've set it for early next week."

Reggie squeezed Rose's shoulder as if to reassure her before he grabbed coffee-to-go and left.

Chapter Thirty-Two

The floor was dirty. Strands of dark hair stuck to the bars in front of George. His pockets were empty. They'd taken his matchbooks.

He wanted them back. He'd made plans.

His time in prison kept him from their heat, their sparks that made his insides sing. He needed a new playground, a new castle of his own making.

At eight years old, he remembered following his uniformed father through a blackened forest, over the soft grey ash surrounding them. He'd been forced to plant baby trees, a consequence of the fire he set in a state park. Community service. They thought it would fix him. He only thought about how he'd burn the trees when they got tall.

Inside his pockets, the matches never stilled. Their whispers never quieted. They demanded freedom.

At fourteen, George's matches took the Quick Mart on the corner. Someone saw him do it. His dad took him to the station.

Time for you to face consequences, son.

He could still hear his mother crying at his sentencing.

Forced to wear pants with no pockets, the music in his head diminished.

They sent him to a working teen ranch in the middle of nowhere, one with boys like him, all damned to hell.

He returned home at seventeen. Mother welcomed him back with tears and open arms. Two days later, Dad drove him to the bus station.

"I'm running for mayor of Gray Mountain. I plan to win. I can't have you causing trouble for my campaign."

He'd handed him a one-way ticket and a piece of paper with an address on it.

"I've enrolled you in a state run employment program for young men like you. A friend of mine found you a job in Evers Hollow that qualifies for the program. You'll learn skills that will help you find a job after your probation ends. I've got a deputy in Evers Hollow that'll monitor you."

The bus ride took over an hour. It dropped him off in a small mountain town. The deputy, a Darin Hutchins, met him at the bus station. The cop studied him with a sneer before taking him to the group home he'd live in. Nosing into his business, like his father.

George saw the most beautiful girl on his third day there. Hair black as soot, pearl-like skin, she stood across the street from the stretch of lawn he cut. Music rushed into his head. It replaced the silence drilled inside his mind.

She'd be his. He'd find a way.

A buzzer sounded. The small jail's main door swung open. A younger cop came into view, a blonde woman. She carried a chair. He grinned at her from inside his cell. "Such a pretty morsel. Come to keep me company?"

She didn't smile, gave him a hard stare. "You've got a visitor."

A visitor. He stood. Could it be his Maggie?

Blondie placed the chair in front of his cell. "Keep your hands in your own space."

She stepped back, motioned with her hand. "Come on in, ma'am. I'll be just outside. Call for me when you're done."

It wasn't his Maggie. Long, stringy red hair. Fire girl?

No.

He took a better look. The hair was a wig. Even with the fake hair and a solid layer of make-up, he recognized his half-sister's skinny body, her pinch-tight expression. She took a seat.

"Hello George. I see you're in trouble again."

Chapter Thirty-Three

Rose tied the last piece of twine around the linen wrapped silverware and placed it on the final floral plate atop the kitchen table. She stepped back, took in the ten place settings plus the old high chair for Broome's youngest, Freddy.

Today would have been Magnolia's seventy-third birthday.

Cloth napkins covered both scone filled platters down the center of the table. Cinnamon crumb and orange vanilla. She'd stayed up late baking the orange-flavored ones. Empty spaces waited for the fresh fruit and yogurt, keeping cold in the fridge. Two trivets sat ready for the Quiche Lorraine cooling on the counter.

The three vases evenly spaced on the table were empty.

Crud. She glanced at the clock. She had forty minutes left. In a fluid motion, she untied her apron and slipped off her pink flats. She walked to the side door. Her leather gloves and her pruners sat inside the large basket that should have been filled with roses. She shoved her feet into her peony rain boots, grabbed the basket, and slapped her straw hat on her head.

The screen door slammed behind her. The skirt of her dress

swished, disrupting the light blanket of leaves around her as she rushed toward Magnolia's rose garden.

When she reached the five rows, she noticed the number of blooms had lessened with the cooling temperatures. She'd have to choose carefully. She cut every available pink rose on the outside row before she moved to another.

Seven yellow ones went into the basket. She moved to the next row, slightly narrower, careful with her dress as she made her way to its middle. Full-petaled white roses.

Fourteen cut before she stepped right for more. A tearing sound stopped her. She turned to look, felt the telltale pull on her clothes, saw the long stems snared in her dress.

Curses. Of all the days. Why hadn't she grabbed her rain jacket on her way out? It would have protected her new dress.

A quick glance at her watch made her fret. Twenty-five minutes. All her efforts last night, early this morning, would be wrecked if the family found her stuck in the middle of Magnolia's prize-winning flowers again.

Magnolia once said that if curses existed, Rose's involved a lifetime of ruined clothes, especially when thorns were involved. Willow's talent with needle and thread covered years of snags and tears, enough so that the patches on Rose's garments appeared intentional.

She reached her gloved hand back. If she could free her skirt from the little barbs, she'd have time to change, start the kettle, and brew coffee. Another inch of her dress tore. Hell.

A whistling tune reached her ears—a familiar one. Criminy.

What was he doing back here? Shouldn't he be in Asheville doing doctor things?

She tried again to free herself. Rip. This was worse than a member of the family finding her. Trapped, she nibbled on her lower lip. Maybe he wouldn't notice her.

The whistling cut off. Damntastic.

He moved closer, then stopped. "Morning Rose. You okay there?"

"Fine."

He wore a t-shirt and paint splattered jeans. His eyes narrowed as he studied her. "What are you doing?"

"Cutting roses for the house." It should have been obvious. She held pruning shears in one hand.

"In a dress? You might get stuck."

It took effort not to grind her teeth together. "I'll be careful." She didn't dare move. He might hear if her dress tore anymore.

His eyes narrowed. He moved closer until he stood at the edge of the outside row. "You're stuck."

She looked skyward. Why couldn't he just walk away, go back to his house in Hollows Eight?

"Rose?"

She glared at him. "Fine. I'm stuck."

"You could have said so."

She didn't answer him.

"Would you like me to help you?"

"Not really."

"Stubborn woman." There was more tease than menace in his tone as he slipped sideways into the row next to her. It was wider and allowed him space to move.

"These roses are the best ones," she said. As if that explained everything.

"You're definitely stuck."

With gritted teeth, she asked, "Can you get me out? Without ripping my dress more?"

He looked behind her. "You're caught in multiple places. Your dress is ruined."

"It won't be the first time."

A quick laugh escaped him. "That's true. Why aren't you in jeans? I never knew you to garden in dresses."

"I didn't plan this."

He bent over the row again. "Hold still."

She did. She could see the top of his hair, still just as full as it had been when he was younger. That hint of a curl had stuck around too. Even though the color had darkened some, it caught red beneath the sunlight. Her fingers curled in on themselves, itching to sink her fingers in again.

"Turn to the left a bit."

She moved left. Rip.

"Sorry. Other left."

She turned the other direction.

"There. Stop. Hold still."

She felt the gentle tug of his fingers, caught a sound of frustration before he straightened.

"I could only get one." He looked apologetic, but serious. "I got an idea."

How many times had she heard him say those exact words in their youth? How many times had they been really bad ones?

"I'm afraid to hear it."

"Nonsense. I'm more mature now."

"Out with it then."

He held out his hand. "Hand me your pruners."

She cradled them to her chest. "What are you going to do with them?"

"Cut you loose." He reached for the tool. She gave it to him. "The stems are snarled in your dress. I have to trim each one. You can pretend you've been shot by multiple arrows."

He leaned over. She heard the open and closure sound of the shears. She held her breath as she heard another snip. And another. The gentlest of tugs on the last rose stem felt like a caress, as if the movement of her dress against her thigh were his knuckles against her flesh.

He straightened. Shoving the pruners in the back pocket of his jeans, he held out his hand. "The roses are too tall to pick you up and carry you out of there. If you hand me your basket, you should be able to hold your dress close and get out."

She passed over the basket.

"Mind the stems. The thorns are still in the fabric."

She carefully pressed the skirt against her legs and inched out of the row, angling towards him as they left the rose garden.

Rose stole glances at him. He wore a faded black concert t-shirt. She didn't have to touch it to know it would be soft between her fingers. The slight humidity encouraged it to cling to muscles he hadn't had back in high school. She swallowed. His triceps stood out more than she remembered. Smudges of white paint touched his knuckles and his forearms.

His worn, paint streaked jeans hung low on his hips. The knees sported gaping holes, along with a small one on his backside above a back pocket that gave just a hint of the dark blue he wore beneath. Did he still wear boxer briefs, or had he gone to something different? And of all the things that could come to mind, why was she thinking of his choice of underwear?

She held her gloved hands out. He put the shears in one and the basket in the other.

"Thank you." She glanced at her watch. "I have just enough time to change and put these in water."

"Glad I could help." He shifted his stance. "First time I met you, you wore a pink dress."

She tilted her head. "I was. I forgot. You remember well."

"Hard to forget. You were covered in dirt by the end. Your grandmother was furious."

She had been. One of many transgressions that earned Rose a lecture.

He flashed a smile as if in memory of that day.

Their recent time together during the storm almost made her forget the past. Their conversation felt natural, as if their argument never happened.

They'd kissed, more than once.

He said, "You had that word you used. It wasn't a real word."

Her heart felt a pinch. He'd forgotten her favorite make-believe word. "Criminy."

His eyes twinkled as he repeated it as if the word had flavor. "Criminy. That's it. Still use it?"

In every single book she'd written. "When I need to."

Her fingers tightened around the basket handle.

He glanced back toward the woods as if something waited for him there. "I should get back. I'm still painting. I needed a break from the smell."

His words shook her train of thought. She'd been staring at him, had even caught the scent of him when he'd handed her the basket. Pine, the something else on top of it—all him. He'd always reminded her of the woods. The woods always reminded her of him.

She felt the flush move over her skin as she thought of pressing her face into the skin of his neck to plant open mouthed kisses from his collarbone to his jaw, maybe nibble his ears too.

"Rose?"

He stepped closer. Said her name once more.

Her lips on his skin. His lips on—

She clutched her dress. A bad idea. A thorn pierced her palm. The pain broke the spell she'd been under.

She needed to change. Cut the quiche. "Quiche," she muttered.

"Did you say *quiche*? Is that your latest curse word?" His voice had a bit of tease in it. He was so close. They could share air. Her insides fluttered.

She should invite him. It might be a horrible idea. He might say no. But here, now, with him, it felt like it used to be. And she missed him.

"I'm serving quiche." She stammered. "Sc-scones…for brunch."

He only nodded, looking at her like she'd been in the sun too long.

Her words rushed out. "Come to brunch. Please."

Surprise filled his expression. And wariness. He motioned downward. "I'm not dressed for brunch."

"You look delicious." Had she really said that?

"Thanks." The spark returned to his eyes.

Backpedal. "Fine, I mean. You—clothes. It's casual." Another flush. Was fine a synonym for delicious? She shifted on her feet.

"You're serious."

Why would he think she wasn't? She nodded.

"I don't know." He took a step back. Put his hand on his neck, his expression one of debate. "Your family's coming, aren't they?"

"Yes." His reminder snapped her back to reality—the time.

He looked hesitant.

"Tess' pink lemonade. I made three pitchers' worth."

"You would use that." He sighed.

"It's your favorite." Her tone changed, quieter. There was so much she didn't know about him now. "Or it was."

"Still is." He nodded. "I'll see how fast I can get the second coat on."

"I'll save you a glass."

"Save me two."

"Deal."

Chapter Thirty-Four

Finn walked back through the woods to his home and picked up the paint roller he'd left wrapped in foil.

He'd rather pick Rose up and kiss her senseless after her attempt to bribe him with pink lemonade. Not just any pink lemonade, but Tess' own top secret recipe that she swore she'd never share with anyone.

Somehow Rose had it, and he wanted to know what made it so damn delicious.

She'd blushed during their conversation. Who knew she was capable of that?

Her dress felt soft beneath his fingers. When he'd cut the rose stems, he'd found her legs distracting. Her toned calves and a hint of the same above her knees made it hard to focus. He'd wanted to run his palms over her calves, the backs of her knees then continue farther up. Everything about her messed with his concentration.

In their teens, she'd spent summers in cut-offs and t-shirts. How often had she sat on the hood of a nearby car at the garage, putting her legs at eye level as he worked? He'd fantasized many times about pulling her to him, wrapping her legs around his waist and putting his mouth to hers like in the movies.

When Thorne suggested he take Rose to prom, he'd been tempted. The thought of her in a dress, showing off her legs that he tried too hard not to stare at. He couldn't do it, so he refused and asked someone else. He'd never known she'd overheard his long ago conversation with Thorne. It was something he couldn't undo.

Six years ago, Finn arrived late to the annual Everson New Year's Eve party because of a significant flight delay. Based off the cheers and sounds of glasses clinking, he'd missed Magnolia Everson-Brooks' traditional toast.

He'd moved through the crowd, searching for Rose. He wanted a quiet moment with her, outside under the stars. It was time to share his feelings for her.

The sight of her had him rushing towards her, ready to sweep her into a hug. The glittering, oversized diamond on her finger stopped him. It was a sucker punch he hadn't expected. He'd talked to her months ago. She hadn't mentioned being engaged.

Rose spotted him though, and ran to him, full of excitement.

"Did you see it? The proposal? Can you believe it? I'm getting married!"

He felt lost; he hadn't known she was seeing someone. Who was she marrying?

"I want you to be my man of honor," Rose said.

He'd seen a man slip up behind her, pull her back against him, a familiar smirk in place. Caleb *fucking* Brentwood. The last asshole anyone he cared about should be with.

Finn lost it that night and reacted unforgivably.

He had a second chance now.

Rose hadn't gone through with the wedding. She'd invited him to brunch. With her. And her family. He swept a hand through his hair. Her family. All of them.

The second coat went on so fast in Pa's old room, speckles of white covered his arms. He pulled off his clothes and took a quick shower. He pulled a clean shirt from his duffel bag and slipped it on along with his paint splattered jeans.

Whistling, he retraced his steps toward Briar House. Leaves crunched beneath his hiking boots. A glance around him said there were more waiting to fall. He'd spent recent hours covered head to toe, clearing the trail. He noted the thorny vines and poison ivy farther into the trees that still needed taken care of.

When he exited the woods, he saw two dark-haired girls playing on a grassy area in front of the old house. Both girls picked red, orange, and yellow leaves from the ground. Broome stood nearby, supervising while holding a toddler in one arm.

The crunch of his boots on gravel gave him away.

Broome lifted a hand in welcome. "Rose mentioned you might come by. Everyone's in the kitchen. I brought the kids out —minimizes the tantrums after the drive."

The oldest straightened from where she crouched, a bouquet of multicolored leaves in one hand. Finn recognized her from the photo he'd seen in the house.

With a hint of a British accent, likely from her mother, she said, "Dad, I'm seven years old. I don't throw tantrums."

Broome's expression changed to one of amusement. "That so?"

"Yes, tis so. I'm a little lady now. Mama said." She flipped her long ponytail over her shoulder and went back to picking leaves off the ground.

"Your mama is never wrong." Broome shook his head, then lowered his voice. "That one's Aliya, too smart for her own good."

Finn grinned. "I can see that."

A feminine voice hollered from the main house's porch.

"That'll mean food's ready," said Broome. "Aliya, Mara, time to go in."

The younger girl looked to be around three. She patted her stomach and said, "Cones go in my tummy."

Aliya walked over and took her sister's hand. "It's scones, Mara. Auntie Rose made scones. Like a snake sound."

Mara held onto her, wriggled her torso, and said, "Sssssss—"

The way Aliya corralled her little sister was cute and bossy.

"Can you tell who runs the house?"

Finn laughed. "Yeah."

"Let's go inside. I need to change Freddy. You know where you can wash up."

When he stepped into the kitchen behind Broome, Rose noticed him weaving through the others to greet him. She slipped her hands in his and pulled him farther in. Her voice came out in an excited whisper with a double squeeze. "I'm happy you're here."

She handed him a glass of pink lemonade with plenty of ice, then re-introduced him to everyone. Most, he knew well. Thorne and he played soccer together back in high school. Thorne slapped him on the back, near causing his drink to spill. "Didn't know you'd be here. Good to see you."

Willow sent him a gentle smile. "Welcome, Finn."

Aspen nodded, her expression neutral as she pressed a hand over a prominent baby bump. Her husband, Gavin, was in the next room, on his phone.

Simi waved as she helped Mara wash her hands and told Aliya to do the same.

It wasn't long before he sat down at the long wooden table in the kitchen beside Thorne, catty-corner to Rose, who sat on one end. Across from him, Willow sat beside Aliya, who obviously adored her aunt based on the giggles and whispers exchanged between bites of food. Broome sat at the head of the table, Simi near with the little one in a high chair and young Mara beside. Aspen and Gavin sat farther down on the bench.

Once everyone had full plates, Broome stood. He held out his hand to his wife, who took it and smiled. "We have an announcement to make."

Thorne's mouth fell open. "Another baby?"

Simi pressed a hand to her heart and beamed. "Isn't it wonderful?"

Thorne said, "You two are creating your own personal army."

Aspen scowled at her brother, the first sign of life from her since they'd all sat down. "Thorne, don't be a di—"

"—Diplodocus." Aliya finished for her. "Uncle Thorne, don't be a diplodocus. They have very mean tails."

Simi covered her mouth even as her eyes lit with mirth. "Aliya, dear, it's rude to interrupt."

"But I like dinosaurs."

Simi sent her daughter a look.

Aliya squirmed in her seat. "Sorry, Aunt Aspen, for interrupting you."

Aspen reached over, put her hand over her niece's, and squeezed. "Perhaps you can talk about your favorite dinosaur after we finish eating."

Aliya nodded.

Across the table, Willow asked, "What about you, Aspen? Did you decide what shade of pink you're using for the nursery?"

Before she could answer, Gavin leaned forward, authority in his voice. "Our son will not have a pink nursery."

Finn wasn't friends with Aspen, never knew her well, but even he caught the flinch after her husband's words. He looked toward Rose. Her green eyes flashed, her fingers white knuckled around her fork.

Willow looked down, toyed with her napkin. "I thought…"

"Excuse me." Aspen tossed her napkin on the table, stood, and left the room.

Simi rose too, touched Broome's shoulder. "I'll be back."

No one spoke. Everyone seemed to focus on their plates, forking bites of quiche, scones, and fruit into their mouths. It was maddening. Meals with his parents had never been quiet. Perhaps he needed to break the silence. He thought of his trip to the bookstore.

"Rose, what sort of books do you write?"

A fork clattered to the table. All eyes turned to Finn.

Willow spoke first. "You mean you don't know?"

"No."

With a smirk, Thorne chimed in. "You going to tell him, baby sis?" He exaggerated the endearment.

Rose's face flushed. Her voice stumbled when she said, "Adventure books—for kids."

Her tone sounded pained. As if she'd confessed to writing erotica.

No one said a word after her answer. Kids' stories. Cool. Yet everyone looked back and forth between them like spectators at a tennis match.

Aliya opened her mouth and said, "I love Auntie Rose's books. The new one is my favorite. Papa promised he'd show me the tree where—"

"—Anyone need more coffee?" Rose came out of her chair, walked toward the counter.

Aliya frowned. "Auntie Rose, you interrupted me. Mama said it's not nice."

When she came back with the coffeepot in hand, her face was flushed. "I'm sorry, pumpkin. I wasn't thinking. What were you saying?"

"Apology accepted." Aliya rubbed her nose. "I can't remember."

Rose took her seat again. "Maybe it'll come back."

Simi returned. Aspen followed soon after, silent for the rest of the brunch. The meal ended. Rose and Simi waved Finn off when he offered to help clean up. Thorne took the girls outside.

Finn followed. Gavin stood at the end of the drive, cell phone to his ear.

The girls ran toward the spiral herb garden, where the barn once stood. Finn walked beside his old teammate.

"You still like her," said Thorne.

Finn glanced over at him. "What are you talking about?"

"Rose, dumbass. Do you think I never noticed the way you look at her?"

"We're friends." Ones that shared kisses.

Thorne gave him a shove, shook his head. "You *were* friends. I'm her brother. I shouldn't interfere, but after Brentwood, I have to say it. I'll come for you if you hurt her again."

Finn looked at the trees ahead of them—the ones that outlined the property, the ones he'd spent hours in alongside Rose. "I'd sooner cut off my own arm."

Broome's girls ran the spiral through the herb garden, then back to the patch of grass in front of the house.

Thorne picked up Aliya. He spun her around and around on the grass in front of the house.

Mara came toward him and held her arms up. "Up, up."

Finn picked her up. She was lighter than he expected. She stared into his eyes like he was the most fascinating thing she'd seen. Her small hand reached out and pressed against his cheek for a moment. Then she wiggled while jumping within his arms. "Ing." She arched. He kept a firm hold, but wondered if it would be safer to set her down.

Thorne said, "She wants you to swing her around like Aliya."

"Okay." He held onto her even as she arched, hoping he wouldn't drop her. Around and around they went. Squeals of happiness erupted from her. Her hands wiggled in the air.

When he stopped and held her upright, she was still for all of a few seconds before she bounced and said, "Again."

He spun her again.

"Again."

Once more. Then she wanted down. Broome joined them, Freddy in his arms.

Aliya, done swinging, danced in front of her father. "Papa, I would like some cookies, please."

Broome shook his head. "I don't have any cookies, Aliya. You'll have to go ask your aunts."

Aliya held out her hand. "Come on, Mara. Cookies."

Thorne said, "I'll keep an eye on them." He followed the girls.

Broome set Freddy on the grass with some toddler toys. "Mack told me he texted you. About the cemetery. The incident at Cracked Egg."

Finn looked back at the house, the side door where Rose worked inside with the other women. "He did. Mack remembered we hung out together as kids. I heard the guy who attacked Rose is in custody?"

Concern crossed his face. "He is. It's George Hindley. He set the barn fire years ago."

He hadn't forgotten that night. Finn asked, "Isn't he supposed to be in prison?"

"Yes, for life. I'm looking into the details of his release."

"What's the sheriff say?"

Broome said, "Sheriff Hutchins claims Hindley is harmless, that he's rehabilitated. Otherwise, he wouldn't have been granted parole."

"He hurt Rose. I've seen the bruises."

Broome's hands went into his pockets. "Reg sent me the pictures of her arm. We're all concerned. George's bail hearing's in a few days."

His hands became fists. "Bail hearing?"

Broome shook his head. "I know. His priors should make him ineligible."

Finn said, "I don't like this."

"No one does. Reggie says strange things are happening around here. He's trying to figure out who's behind them."

"Like what?"

Mara came back outside, her hand in Thorne's till she got to the edge of the grass. She ran straight for Finn, crashing into his legs.

"Ing."

Finn picked her up.

Broome said, "I'll call you when I know more. We're adding motion sensors where we can."

Finn heard what he wasn't saying. Briar House sat on a sizable portion of land, surrounded by woods, some of which were public land. Cameras and motion sensors wouldn't cover everything. Knowing Rose's initial reaction to his promise to protect her, she wouldn't like the thought of being monitored.

Broome squatted down, removed something from his son's mouth. "Freddy, don't eat the leaves."

The boy fussed. Broome picked him up and brushed more crumbs off. "This one's about done."

Mara held up her arms. "Ing!"

Broome motioned to Mara. "Go slow with her. Otherwise, she'll toss cookies and lemonade on the way home."

Finn was careful.

Chapter Thirty-Five

From the windows of Magnolia's bedroom, in socked feet, Rose watched Aspen and Gavin drive away from the house. Neither looked happy once the meal ended. Gavin hadn't paid attention to his nieces and nephew. Rose couldn't help the strong, gentle embrace she'd given her older sister. As if a hug could fix things. Did Gavin even want children?

Broome and Thorne stood outside on the gravel drive talking while Mara and Freddy played on the grass. They'd loaded some boxes into each of their vehicles earlier. Both her brothers wanted her moved into Briar House. They'd grilled her to name a date so they could help move her belongings from the cottage.

"Briar House has better security than your cottage."

Rose felt conflicted. The idea of moving into the master bedroom still bothered her. Behind her lay too many things that reminded her of the woman they'd lost.

Once her brothers came back to move her things, there would be no going back. Maybe she'd move back into her own childhood bedroom instead until she felt more comfortable taking over this one.

She turned away from the multi-faceted window. Willow sat

on the floor with Aliya, going through Magnolia's jewelry. One of the many costume necklaces draped around Aliya's neck. The girl popped up to admire herself in the free-standing oval mirror in the corner.

Simi stood in the middle of the room. The fabric of her asymmetrical dress swirled as she slowly turned around. She moved as if digesting the full contents of the room.

Ivory brocade draped the four-poster queen bed and the room's windows. Claw-footed bedside tables flanked the bed. A large mahogany dresser, smaller vanity, and a burgundy velvet settee stood against its walls. They'd all seen the room many times before, but it felt different now.

Simi asked the question no one else had. "How do you feel about taking over the main bedroom, Rose?"

A glance at her sister-in-law told her Simi expected a genuine answer.

Rose took a breath. "It feels awkward. This is Magnolia's room. The brocade, the four-poster bed, the vanity—all represent who she was. I can't see this room as anyone else's."

Willow looked up. "What do you mean? It's a beautiful room."

Guilt pinched her. She'd forgotten. Willow had helped with the latest draperies and other soft furnishings.

She needed to be honest. "It's a beautiful room, Will. Magnolia told me it made her feel like royalty. What she liked, what she wanted, isn't me."

Willow stood, her brows furrowed.

Simi moved closer with a gentle smile on her face. Her hand swirled in an encompassing gesture. "It'll be difficult for Rose to accept this room as hers. So much emotion." She took Willow's hand. "I know how hard you worked to update this room. It's beautiful, but I think you'll agree this room needs to represent Rose. She'll be the one sleeping here. She'll never get a good night's sleep otherwise."

Willow nodded. "You're right, I see that. Rose needs a room that embodies her interests along with the outdoors."

Simi's fingers moved, gesturing towards the windows, the bed. "Perhaps remove the brocade, bring more light into the room, highlight the wooden bedposts rather than obscure them."

"We can use lighter fabrics, wistful ones, in the colors you prefer, Rose," said Willow.

"I suggest houseplants, many of them."

Willow said, "We could replace the vanity with a writing desk."

Rose marveled. What a wonder the two of them were. They knew her so well. She'd never been one to sit in front of a mirror and do her hair, but she had memories of Magnolia doing just that from the small cushioned chair tucked underneath the mahogany vanity. A writing desk would be perfect in its place. Maybe they could even swap her mattress for the one in here. Hers was only two years old, and it was amazingly comfortable. The tightness inside her eased.

"I like the writing desk idea," said Rose. "What will we do with the vanity? Magnolia loved it."

Willow moved closer to it and ran her fingers over its surface. "I might have a use for it if you're sure about letting it go."

Rose nodded. "Of course. I can already see it in your apartment."

She chuckled. "I'm not sure about that, but I have some thoughts."

She wanted to ask more about those thoughts, but before she could, Broome's voice called up the stairs.

"Simi, love, the young ones are ready to leave. Freddy's four minutes from a full meltdown."

Rose followed the three of them down the stairs and slipped her feet into the rain boots by the side door. She walked Aliya out to Simi's silver Volvo and helped her climb up to the back seat. She waved as they disappeared down the drive.

Willow took Magnolia's vanity with her. Thorne helped load it into her car. Both left soon after.

Rose locked up Briar House and took a seat on the old porch swing.

It wasn't long before she heard the crunch of footsteps on leaves.

Chapter Thirty-Six

Key in hand, Rose stood, sidling closer to the kitchen door in case she needed to get back into the house quickly. The sound of crunching leaves came closer.

She snuck a glance around the porch. It was Finn. Her grip on the keys relaxed.

He'd dashed home to put another coat of paint on. They spoke little during brunch, but he'd asked if he could stop by later.

He paused short of the trio of steps. "Want to walk?"

She stepped down to meet him and took the hand he offered her. Tiny sparks danced across her palms as their fingers intertwined. They walked the perimeter along the forest's edge until they came to the tire swing. Twin ropes secured it to the largest branch of the oldest oak tree on the grounds. No one had swung on it in years. Until Aliya noticed it a few years back. Determined to keep his daughter safe, Broome had replaced the old tire and the rope.

Nostalgia sent her toward it even though she had long outgrown the days in which Finn and she took turns spinning and pushing each other. He'd always sent her high enough to make her stomach fall.

Letting go of his hand, she climbed onto the tire and sat on its edge with her legs extended. She wrapped her fingers around each rope. Finn moved behind her, grabbed hold and pulled her back, as if years of habit forced his hands. The swing moved in a low swoop. A laugh escaped her.

The thick branch creaked overhead as he tugged the tire higher and let go. Flutters flickered inside her as she swung back down.

Once more, Finn caught hold, pulling the swing towards him above the ground. His chest, his upper arms brushed against her back, her shoulders. His breath wafted over her neck, stirring the strands of her hair.

She turned her head, met his eyes with her own. The color of dark chocolate and a hundred percent focused on her. His face was mere inches from hers. It reminded her of Willow's words, *Betsy's seven layer cake.* Would he kiss her? Her lips parted as she held her breath.

He let go. She flew away from him, the flutters inside her stronger this time. This time on her return, he kissed her quickly before releasing her. It wasn't enough to assuage the stirrings inside her. She wanted a kiss like the night of the storm.

She dragged her feet along the ground to stop the swing. Finn reached for her as she scrambled off the tire. His arms circled her waist as she stood, pulling her flush against him.

Her arms wound around his neck as she pressed her lips to his with a hunger she'd never felt with another. She wanted him.

He answered her with an urgency of his own, capturing her mouth in a searing way that made her restless.

He broke the kiss. "We need to go inside. It's getting dark."

She nodded. What they'd started here beside the swing crackled inside her, demanding more. She barely glanced at the main house as they hurried away from the oak tree toward the row of cottages.

They made their way through the cottage door. Once closed, she found herself against it, Finn's hands bracketing her waist. Her breath sharpened when his lips returned to hers, the sweep of his tongue mingling with hers. His hands moved up her sides, over her breasts, lingering before exploring the rest of her with cradling caresses. His mouth left hers, exploring her neck, her nape—his hands more urgent, slipping beneath her dress, sliding up her legs, pressing, teasing until his name escaped her lips—a whispered plea for more.

Rose felt lightheaded, her breath over loud in her ears.

His mouth, the scrape of his light scruff, another kiss behind her ear. His voice, a grated whisper, as if he was as caught up as her. "Evie, how far do you want to take this?"

"I—" Her mind clamored. The hallway that led to her bedroom stood in front of them. What happened to her focus on *friends?* Her fears of getting hurt again? Neither protest seemed to matter now. There'd always been a connection between them.

But if she invited him into her bedroom, it wouldn't be just sex.

There'd be no coming back from this. She'd felt possessive back in high school, maybe even jealous of the number of girls she'd seen him with, but she'd never fallen for him.

Until now.

Criminy—she'd fallen for Finn. Her heart trembled with the weight of her realization.

Finn's thumb traced her lower lip. It felt like understanding, as if he sensed the debate in her mind. "Rose, we don't have to—"

They did, they so did. She slipped her hand around the back of his neck, pulled him close, took a deep breath, and met his eyes again. "Make love to me, Finn."

The longing in his eyes seemed more as they kissed.

She led him to her bedroom, a cozy space of greenery and twinkle lights.

The backs of her knees hit her soft comforter. Finn's hands moved to the buttons of her dress. His brown eyes glittered even darker while his fingers moved, brushing over her skin as they undid the first one, as if he needed to savor the moment.

Need pulsed inside her, but she too wanted to cherish this.

He said, "I've thought about you, this, a long time."

His words stoked the fire inside her, a secret invitation to play, the sort they used to get in trouble for.

She'd loved getting in trouble with him.

She swallowed. "Care to elaborate?"

"No. I prefer to take things one button at a time."

She glanced down. Only a few buttons remained. "You're quick."

He paused. "Is that a question?"

"No." She didn't want to think about his previous experiences.

"Good." He undid the last three. His hands felt warm as they slipped over her shoulders to peel the bodice of her dress open to her waist.

His fingers stilled; he was staring at her breasts. "I never thought a bra could kill me."

Amused, she looked down. She was wearing her pink one. She wasn't large chested. To her, the bra looked harmless, some satin and pink lace. But his gaze was awfully intense.

"You wore this at the coffeehouse," he said in a low, sexy tone as his thumbs grazed over her lace covered breasts. "I could see all the way down your shirt."

"I didn't know you were—"

"You're beautiful, Evie." His hands moved lower, tugging her dress over her hips. It fluttered to the floor, leaving her in her pink bra and matching panties.

His gaze burned as he studied her. "This one's definitely my favorite."

The words made her insides curl, but she managed a small laugh. "As if you know what the others in my drawer look like."

"If you want to model them, I'll vote."

She pressed her lips back to his even as she reached back to unclasp her bra to remove it, murmuring, "No. I have other plans for you." She grabbed the hem of his t-shirt and helped pull it over his head. It landed next to her dress.

Her fingers found the front of his jeans, making quick work of the button and zipper. She couldn't help the smile that graced her lips when he slid his boxer briefs to the floor. As he had with her, she looked him over, her breath tripping over itself as she took the view in. Much better than seven layer cake.

She didn't know which of them moved first, but they came together in a rush. His flesh felt strong against hers—breathtaking, warm, and real. She began her own exploration of his body as they fell back on the bed. Her palms ran over his arms, his back, and grasped his backside as he settled against her. The shape of him, his weight over her, felt right.

Perched above her, he asked, "You sure, Rose? This is going to change—"

She threaded her fingers into his hair, raising upward to press her lips to his. "No backsies," she said, "I want you, Finn. All of you."

He kissed her then paused, pushing himself back up. "I have condoms in my jeans. I always use them."

Condoms. Plural. She raised an eyebrow even as her fingertips traced circles over his chest. "I'm on birth control. I've always required the use of condoms."

Finn's jaw tightened. She assumed he also didn't want details.

She ran her hands down his chest, his abdomen, lower,

circling, teasing. "If I were ever going to go without, it would be with you."

"I want." His eyes sparked, darkening as he lowered his body back to hers and kissed her with a passion that curled her fingers against his back. They rolled, touched, learned the feel of one another.

She whimpered and writhed beneath him as he slipped down her body, touching and kissing her neck, her breasts, across her midriff, and then lower still, to the most intimate part of her. His fingers, the caress of his tongue, had her clutching the strands of his hair and the sheets beneath her. He brought her to the brink and then over. Waves of pleasure crashed through her against his mouth, around his fingers. She felt like she'd survived her very own storm.

He moved back up her body, positioning himself over her, even as she reached for him, wrapping her legs around him.

Their eyes met as their bodies joined. She couldn't look away. The way he felt inside her. The connection between them. It was like nothing she'd felt before. Their lips brushed as he moved. Her hips rose to meet each thrust. A sound she didn't recognize left her lips when the pace of his movements increased. She arched in answer, tightening her grasp around his arms as if the strength in each was a tether. Her breath, her whimpers became desperate as pleasure built inside her.

Her hands slid down his body, searching for his. Their fingers touched. She cried out, his name on her lips, as her body quaked with release. He followed her in climax, his breath heavy against her neck as he collapsed against her. She locked her legs around him, reluctant to let go despite the sheen of sweat over her skin. They lingered, remaining wrapped around each other until he rolled off of her onto his back.

Finn kept hold of her hand as if he still needed to touch her. It centered her thoughts, her feelings. Her mind lacked adjectives for their lovemaking. The mattress shifted as he turned toward her. She glanced at him. He was watching her. His expression mirrored how she felt—wrecked in an incredible way. And when he lifted her hand and pressed his lips to her palm, she knew that if this thing between them didn't work out, the devastation would destroy her.

Chapter Thirty-Seven

The hoot of an owl woke Rose in the dark before dawn. She lay nestled in Finn's arms, his body curved around her backside. Each exhale of his breath caressed the nape of her neck, doing a little something to her insides.

As children and teens, they'd held hands, wrestled, and huddled as friends.

None of those moments felt close to what they shared last night. Too bad he was asleep. She'd like a turn driving him crazy.

As if he heard her thoughts, light kisses rained along her bare shoulder. His arm tightened. His words came out raspy, heavy with the lingering fog of sleep. "What time is it?"

"Close to dawn."

He grumbled. "Go back to sleep."

"No." She pushed him onto his back.

He threw a hand over his face. "We are not going for a hike this early."

"Don't be ridiculous. I have a different adventure in mind." She smiled to herself as she rose to straddle him. After last night, she'd be willing to stay in bed most of today. She moved his hand away from his face, right before she kissed him. He roused enough to kiss her back, his hands squeezed her backside before she moved down his body. Her hands and mouth reveled as they brushed over his flesh, exploring the shape of him. He flinched when she traced her fingers up his sides. He was still ticklish. Knowledge she'd save for another time.

A small groan escaped him when she slid slowly down over him until they were once more together, him inside her. She couldn't hide anything from him. He still knew her too well. Even in the dark. Her every breath, every reaction, was his to hear and feel as she moved over him. His hands gripped her hips, pulled her down to him again and again, until they both climaxed together.

Her body relaxed against his as their breathing slowed, her cheek resting against the beat of his heart. She eased off him, stretching out beside him and marveling over the past hours. His chest rose and fell in slumber while she remained awake, her internal clock saying it was time to rise. A glance toward her bedroom window told her the sun hadn't quite crested the trees.

She slipped away from his side, threw on a nightshirt, and walked into the kitchen to make coffee.

She glanced over her latest manuscript while it brewed, then returned to her room carrying two mugs. Finn was still asleep, on his stomach now, his face turned towards her, his eyes closed. She set one mug down on her nightstand and sat on the edge of the mattress, studying him while she sipped from the other.

Asleep, he looked more like the boy she'd grown up with. The lines she'd noticed around his eyes were absent; his eyelashes lay against his cheeks. She'd always been jealous of his lashes, longer than most, with a hint of red in them.

The blanket had slipped down, exposing his arms and his back. Everything in sight was defined more than she remembered. She'd watched him sometimes in the back of Riley's garage, lifting weights. He'd had muscular legs from soccer back then, but his upper body wasn't developed like now. She longed to glide her hands over the muscles in his arms, his back, press her lips to the warmth of his skin.

Her experience with morning afters was limited. She'd lost her virginity to a trusted friend a few months after she'd broken up with Caleb. There was no cuddling. The rest of her experiences followed a similar line. She hadn't felt emotionally involved, not like now.

Last night, Finn made love to her as if he'd waited years to do so.

In the early morning hours, she'd made love to him. Every bit was better than she'd imagined.

She looked back at his face. He was awake and watching her. Her insides fluttered. Was she supposed to say something brilliant or casual? Her cheeks warmed, a hesitation behind her lips.

One word escaped. "Hi."

He didn't speak. Instead, he turned to his side, rising enough to get closer to her until their faces were inches apart. The comforter came with him.

His fingers threaded into her hair as he touched his lips to hers. One kiss, then another before he eased back.

"Last night—" he said.

She stiffened. What if he said it was a mistake? They hadn't talked afterwards.

Maybe he sensed her unease.

He kissed her once more, then said, "Last night was everything I fantasized, but more."

His expression was earnest, his eyes serious. He'd fantasized about her? Her insides melted. She couldn't help the smile forming and set her half-empty mug down on the nightstand.

Finn had once known her better than anyone. It was uncanny to think that, after all this time, he still might be the one to know her best. She had other friends. But they never ran through the woods with her, climbed trees, and captured frogs along the creek. Neither had she been intimate with any of them.

She burrowed into him, pressed her lips against his neck.

His hand slid farther into her hair. "Evie?"

The way he said it. As if the two syllables took effort.

Rose eased back so she could see his face. "We used to tell each other everything. Why didn't you tell me how you felt?"

Finn traced circles on her skin. "I knew you didn't see me that way."

She hadn't, not then. Rose thought of all the girls he'd dated. Perfect hair, make-up, clothes that never snagged on branches or brambles on walks in the woods. Even if she'd felt something like this for him back then, she wouldn't have believed he'd want to date her.

She said, "You never looked at me the way you looked at other girls."

"Of course not."

She stiffened, felt his hand caress her neck.

"None of them were you."

It was a sweet answer. She hoped it wasn't a line.

"Were you really jealous of Caleb?"

"I told you I was."

"I wish we'd talked after that night." Even as she spoke the words, she knew. They hadn't had a chance. She'd been too hurt. He'd been too angry at her then fiancé. She knew that now. "Why didn't you come see me the day after?"

"I tried," he said. "I was told you wanted nothing to do with me. When I tried again, I was told the same."

"Who told you that? I was upstairs all day, hoping you'd come by."

He sighed. "Does it matter?"

"Which means it was Aspen," she said. "If it had been Thorne, he would have told me." She pressed her lips to his jaw.

It wasn't Aspen's place to interfere, but it wasn't the first time she'd done so.

His fingers shifted to trail up and down her spine. "I don't want you at odds with your family over the past. Your oldest sister doesn't look happy."

Oldest sister. In their recent conversation, Aspen had said Finn wasn't good enough for her.

They'd talk. Whatever Aspen said to Finn years ago couldn't be undone. But Rose needed to know why.

As for Finn, Rose decided to tell him her secret. They'd wasted enough time apart. She'd trusted him once. It was time to risk doing it again.

She leaned toward the nightstand, picked up the second mug of coffee, and held it out to him. "I made you coffee. I'm going to take a shower and brush my teeth."

He joined her in the shower. It was better than playing in the creek as children. Parts of her still hummed when she sat down at the table, the large veggie laden omelette she'd made halved down the middle between them.

He'd put his jeans back on. She wore an oversized flannel shirt and a simple gathered skirt. When the omelette was gone, she rose and retrieved the envelope of documents from her room. She took a breath and sat back down.

Trust.

"I need to tell you something."

Not sure what to expect, Finn leaned back in his chair, one hand around a mug of coffee. The envelope she'd brought lay on the table between them.

Rose's fingers picked at loose threads on the skirt she wore before she raised her eyes to his. "I'm not Magnolia's granddaughter. I'm her daughter."

I'm her daughter.

It took a moment to make the connection, to understand what she meant.

This was—not what he expected.

She continued, her speech faster than normal, as if she needed the complete story out.

Rose was Magnolia Everson-Brooks' daughter? Her parents were her adoptive parents. The woman she called mom was her older sister.

Silence filled the space between them as he took in her last words. Because hell.

Why hadn't her birth mother told her? In his mind, that was a shit move. What was he supposed to say?

He couldn't keep the grit from his voice. He touched his fingertips to hers where they curled into the black skirt she wore. "How long have you known?"

"I found out after the ceiling fell. She left me a letter and my real birth certificate." She tapped the large envelope she'd placed on the table.

A letter, a real birth certificate. He didn't need the proof. He believed her. She'd resembled Ms. Magnolia more than the rest of the Finch children. He'd figured it was family genetics, would never have guessed it was directly from mother to daughter.

He couldn't help himself. He pulled her against him, felt her face press into his neck. Her arms tightened. They were at an odd angle.

He stood with one arm still around her. His other pushed the table away. It swayed but didn't tip. He wanted her fully in his arms, all of him against all of her.

"Finn, what are you—"

"Making us more comfortable."

She turned her head. "What about—"

"Later."

He wanted her somewhere he could hold her. He moved to

the couch in her family area. Sat in the middle and stretched out with her alongside him, their faces inches apart.

It wasn't the time to think about how she felt against him, better than any other woman he'd dated. He ran his hand down her side.

Finn asked, "Want to tell me the rest?"

Rose nodded. "I don't know all of it. I'm trying to piece it together. She went to the Cotswolds in England. Our family has a cottage there, near her sister Cherry. But she delivered me in Winston-Salem. She eventually returned home. Magnolia must have arranged the adoption with Mom and Dad. They raised me with the others, as their own until the car accident. No one knew except Broome—he knew."

"Rose." He threaded his fingers through her hair. "How do you feel?"

She gave him a half smile even as her eyes glistened. "I feel…" She hesitated. "I feel lost without her, angry sometimes that she didn't tell me. That I'll never ask her the questions I have. I would have told her it was okay, that she had reasons for her choice. That I loved her."

"She knew you loved her."

He pressed his lips to hers briefly, then looked at her.

"Thank you for trusting me." He'd feared they'd have nothing resembling this closeness again.

When they got up off the couch, she showed him what the envelope contained. He picked it up, looked over the details, glanced up at her, then focused on a single line. "I thought your birthday was in February."

"They changed it. It was too close to Thorne's to be believable."

The new date. "Your real birthday—it's the same as mine."

She leaned over to look and shrugged. "I hadn't noticed that."

He pondered the piece of paper. The details were as clear as his own. There was something else. The typecast, the paper, all aged by time. He put the paper down.

She must have sensed his unease. "What is it?"

He brushed his fingers through his hair. "I don't know. Maybe it's nothing."

Later, after he returned to his house, he pulled out his laptop and opened his documents folder. He'd scanned all important paperwork into his files years ago. When he clicked on the line labeled *birth certificate*, he saw what bothered him about Rose's.

It wasn't nothing.

Not only did they share the same birthday, but they'd also been born in the same county, inside the same hospital. While he hadn't memorized every detail on Rose's birth certificate, he had a feeling that a Dr. Schroeder had delivered her too.

Chapter Thirty-Eight

Tuesday brought sunny skies, encouraging Rose to find an outside table at 828 Street Tacos. She set the numbered orange block down in the middle of the table, along with two bottles of strawberry soda.

Willow followed close behind; her eyes sparkling with undisclosed mirth. Between them, she placed napkins and silverware as if she was setting a formal table. She adjusted her fork's position as if she had a sight ruler in her head.

Both took seats. Curiosity overwhelmed her. Rose asked, "You're especially bright this morning." She picked up her soda. "Finally have a successful blind date?"

A single beat of laughter as Willow shook her head. "Haven't had time to date. I drove down to Asheville yesterday to meet with a real estate agent."

Rose lowered the glass bottle to the table without taking a sip. "Are you thinking of buying a place?"

Willow nodded. "My sales on Etsy are high. I can't sew fast enough."

"Why didn't you say something?"

She tilted her head. "It's always been a someday sort of

thing. I never thought I'd be able to buy my own place, much less my own store. My latest research says otherwise." Her eyes looked lighter than they had in weeks.

"This is amazing!" Rose knew little about opening a physical storefront, but Willow's excitement was catching. "How did it go?"

"Nothing yet. My ideal's a place with a loft apartment. The agent said it could take a bit."

"Of course, it'll take a bit. You want something with huge display windows. I can't wait. When you open your own store, it'll be an awesome success." The clothing Willow made represented a love of artistic creation.

Willow flushed. "Thanks for the vote of confidence. Time will tell. The winter lines are still coming in at Posh. So much overtime. Doesn't leave me lots of time to walk through buildings with real estate agents."

"Will, why are you helping me with the house? You should be with your agent. Or putting your feet up and—"

"It's fine. It wouldn't be right for you to pack up everyone's inherited stuff. Besides, it's nice to spend time at the house. Helps a bit."

Rose knew exactly what she meant. She reached out her hand.

Willow took it and squeezed. "We were lucky to have her."

Rose squeezed back, then let go. She had a feeling they all felt that.

"When you meet with your agent again, I could go with you. It'd be fun to do something for you instead of the house. We could make a day of it, invite Aspen and Simi."

"I'll think about it. I've talked to Simi, bounced some display ideas off her."

"She's a talent at interior design."

"She is."

"Aspen?"

Willow worried her lower lip. "Maybe. I haven't told her about trying to find a shop. She'll be angry after she helped me get the job at Posh."

Irritation ran up her spine. She'd never liked Willow's decision to work for the Posh family. Especially after she described the job as soul sucking. The small amount of make-up she wore never hid the shadows beneath her eyes. "You've given those parasites plenty of your time, especially after—"

Willow held up her hand. "Let's not go there."

"Sorry. I don't mean to crush your sparkle."

She tilted her head. "Sparkle?"

"You looked happy, confident when you walked in."

A young man with pulled back dark hair set large colorful plates in front of each of them. Each plate held an assortment of street tacos alongside black beans and lime cilantro rice. They each thanked him. Rose reached for her fork. Chipotle sauce zigzagged over the open-faced mixture of chicken and pork.

Outside of expressive murmurs over each delicious mouthful, they were silent.

Willow set her fork down, leaned back. "This tastes amazing, but I need a break." A smile accompanied her sparkling eyes.

Rose quirked an eyebrow.

She said, "I stopped for coffee earlier. I may have had a scone. Sketched some ideas for potential displays."

Needing a food break herself, Rose sat back, folded her arms. "Your day off. You paid it forward."

The lightest flush appeared on her cheeks. "I did. The customer behind me needed some kindness. I hadn't seen him before."

"Him?"

"Yes. Him. A bit grouchy, a little bit scary. Even more so after my gesture."

"Some have a hard time accepting gifts."

She nodded, picked up her fork again, poking at the

remaining rice on her plate. "Precisely. Molly, bless her, wouldn't take his money, whoever he was."

"Must have been one of the suited commuters."

"You misunderstand. No suit, he looked a mess, scruffy, as if he'd slept with his clothes on." Her voice lowered as if she was talking to herself. "Striking blue eyes, though."

Her description didn't sound like anyone she knew. But Willow was the sort to notice those who needed kindness or a little help.

They finished their tacos. Rose listened to Willow talk about her excursion into Asheville, heard her opinion on the storefronts she'd viewed with her agent so far. She hadn't taken photos.

"None come close to what I want."

After lunch, they went to Briar House. A truck from HK Renovations, the company she'd hired to do the renovations, sat in the driveway. Rose spoke with the three person crew working on the dining room. Inside, two stood on scaffolding, working on reconstructing the ceiling. Another confirmed her paint selections for the ceiling, the walls, and the trim. Rose could have gone with wallpaper, tried to recreate the previous appearance of the room, but she wanted something different. Something cheerful. The house deserved it after all the years of faded wallpaper.

After Rose finished speaking with the crew, she found Willow in the middle of the morning room, arms folded. "I've always found the furniture in this room strange." She nudged the fainting couch. "This especially."

Rose shrugged. "I like it. It's a relic from another time."

"It should be reupholstered. I can still see the wine stain from Aspen's engagement party."

Rose moved closer, leaned down, not seeing anything.

Willow moved toward the fireplace. The painted portrait of Magnolia's horse, Lady, hung above its mantle. The painting accurately portrayed the sheen of her dark coat, the dark strands of her mane.

Without a word, Willow backed away and exited the room. She returned with the house's six foot ladder and planted it in front of the fireplace.

"Will—what are you doing?"

"I think Lady's frame is cracked." From the third rung, she examined the painting, then ran her fingers all the way around its frame. Then turned to Rose. "Sadly, I'm correct. There's a sizable crack here." She pointed at an upper section of the frame. "It could fall off the wall, damage the canvas."

Rose moved closer. Sure enough, a long crack ran through one side. It was amazing it hadn't fallen. "What should I do?"

Willow carefully lifted it off the wall. "I know an archival framer. He'll be able to reframe it." She stepped off the ladder, holding the painting with careful hands.

The wall looked empty without it. "How long will she be gone?"

"I'll drop it off on my way home. They usually have a four-week turnaround time."

Rose nodded. She had a feeling Willow needed to do this. She disappeared once more, to set the painting on the kitchen table.

When she returned, she said, "Maybe we should tag the items we know go to the others to make moving things out of here easier."

It was a smart suggestion. The family was coming on Saturday to move boxes and furniture. Most of the items in this room stayed, especially the tea tray and its cart. Rose couldn't imagine them anywhere else. It defined years of memories and tradition within this room.

"That's a great idea. Let's get started. Then I can help you with the attic."

Part of Willow's inheritance included the entirety of the house's attic. It was an unusual thing to put in a will. Magnolia had known about Willow's dream of opening her own shop.

Perhaps she thought those items would be of use for such an endeavor.

A few hours later, they'd tagged some items and brought down others from the attic to load in Willow's Subaru Outback. Thorne had already agreed by text to help her move the bigger pieces into a local storage shed next time he was in town.

Willow left with the painting and everything else in her car.

Rose picked up her phone and called Aspen. Their conversation wasn't an easy one. Aspen's reasons for her interference were petty. By the end of the call, Aspen had apologized and promised to make amends to Finn.

Chapter Thirty-Nine

Finn heard the mallet strike the wooden post as Ray swung the tool again and again until the for sale sign was stable in the half-dead grass of the front yard.

With the help of his cane, Pa stood beside him. Finn had checked him out of Wylder for the day to get all the paperwork signed for the house listing.

A heaviness settled around his heart at the sight of the sign advertising his childhood home.

Pa cleared his throat as Ray attached a smaller piece advertising its availability. "You were right about the paint. Looks nice inside. Clean too."

Finn said, "Norah arranged the cleaning. She knows someone in the business."

As if the mention of their neighbor conjured her, a door opened across the cul-de-sac. Norah Fox stepped out of her home and headed towards them. Her niece Chelsea followed. Both women wore jeans. Chelsea wore a long sleeve pink tee, her red curly hair a contrast to the surrounding trees. Norah wore a bandanna around her hair and a long paint-splattered smock, with bits of something gray, perhaps clay, smeared on the front.

Norah wrapped her arms around Charlie and squeezed. "Charlie Murphy, I see you broke out. Want to go to Atlantic City?"

A whist of a smile played over Pa's face. "You should have asked me ten years ago, Norah. I might have said yes."

She frowned. "I did. You said no."

"That's right." He shook his head. "The answer's still no."

She put her hands on his shoulders and kissed both his cheeks. "Difficult man. How about some iced tea and a tarot reading instead?"

Charlie smiled and turned to Finn. "How long's my jailbreak?"

The light in his father's eyes. Pa's friends in the community. He hadn't seen them since he'd moved into Wylder. Finn had made plans to take him by the garage so he could see Riley Pierce and the rest of the men he'd worked with for twenty years. He should have thought of Norah as well, guessed she'd want to visit with him. They'd been neighbors for twenty-two years. He'd text Stella to let her know they'd be gone longer than planned.

Finn said, "I think you should spend some time with Norah."

Ever direct, Norah took charge. With a dismissing nod to Finn and her niece, she pulled Pa with her across the cul-de-sac.

Her words carried as they reached the weathered pink single-wide. "We'll have lunch. I made meatloaf last night. We'll have sandwiches and potato salad."

Pa looked back. "Son?"

"Don't worry, Pa. I can take care of myself. Have some fun."

He nodded. "I still want to see the boys."

"We'll have time for that. Let me know when you're ready."

The two older people disappeared into the structure that had seen better days, like every other home in the cul-de-sac. Mature trees surrounded, along with the eclectic metal sculptures Norah welded together when she wasn't working at her odds and ends shop in town.

Finn looked at Chelsea. "How's she doing?"

She folded her arms and shook her head. "Busy as ever. She's been at the wheel all morning."

"She still welding?"

"Not as much. She's not as strong as she used to be. She's focusing on clay."

He shoved his hands into his front pockets. "Pottery's a safer choice. As well as the Tarot readings."

Norah's shop in town offered an array of products. Metal art, tarot readings, and pottery were mere examples of what she sold. The glow of the shop's pink and purple tarot sign drew customers in. She made a living off the combination.

Chelsea said, "She's talking retirement. I'll believe it when I see it."

"Maybe Pa will convince her to move into Wylder."

Chelsea's expression changed to one of horror. "I'd never do that to Stella. She taught me most of what I know about nursing. I love my aunt, but she'd be a nightmare in that place."

"How's the hospital treating you?"

She shifted, swatting something on her pink sleeve. "All right. Still working in day surgery. Commute's a bitch, but where else am I going to work?"

He knew exactly how she felt. The commute to Asheville wasn't great. Chelsea made it for every shift.

She asked, "You okay with the house going?"

He shrugged. What could he say? A *For Sale* sign stood in the yard. "All these houses will change owners someday. Might as well be now."

"You practice that? I almost believe you." She didn't look at him. She wasn't one to make fun of someone. Subtle sarcasm, more her style.

Finn asked, "You hear anything about weird things going on around here, in town or in the woods?"

Chelsea folded her arms. "Does this have anything to do with Rose Finch?"

"Maybe. What do you know?"

"I hear the gossip. That woman at the grocery, she's got plenty to say. Most of it untrue. But people listen to her."

He said, "I remember her. Her last name, Wal—"

"—Wellington. Blessed Carina Wellington."

Finn kicked up a corner of his mouth. "You sound like a fan."

Chelsea shook her head. "The things she's said about my family…"

"I remember. She and Louise Winston still peas in a pod?"

"Smashed together under a child's thumb."

The info shouldn't surprise him. The combination of the two women's gossip never ceased. They always had something to say about someone else. Finn knew firsthand how such things could escalate.

He motioned to his vehicle. "I've got a couple of things to take care of while Pa's visiting."

Chelsea nodded. "I'll send you a text when they seem close to wrapping up. Aunt Norah's readings go longer than average."

"Sounds good." He headed towards his SUV.

"Finn."

He turned back. "Yeah?"

"Tell Rose I said hi."

How did she know?

"I…"

With a cheeky grin, Chelsea waved. "Small towns have large ears and open mouths."

He found Rose in a pair of patched denim overalls, a body-hugging t-shirt beneath and a large straw hat on her head. She wore sneakers for once. They looked small on her feet compared to her array of boots. Her knees rested on a cushion of sorts. Her body leaned over a section of the spiral herb garden that'd been planted during their high school years. She had headphones in her ears. Didn't seem to hear him. He moved within her line of sight, but she startled all the same when he got close.

She tilted her hat back and stood. Her face was flushed.

"Finn. I didn't expect you." She pulled gloves off her fingers. He hadn't noticed she was wearing them. He was too focused on the tinge of pink on her face, the light sheen of sweat on her neck, the strip of skin he could see along the edge of her t-shirt before the skin became covered in denim.

The memory of the last time he'd seen her sent him closer. He paused only a moment, heard the intake of her breath, then reached out and slid one hand into the hair at her nape, the other around her waist. He waited, ready to step back if she voiced an objection. She didn't. Her hand grabbed hold of his shirt as she came up on tiptoe to meet his lips as they touched hers. Her straw hat drifted to the ground as his fingers drifted farther into her hair. A tiny moan came from her as she kissed him back. He pulled her closer, slipped one hand inside her overalls, pressed his palm against her back. She moved against him.

He ran his fingers along that bare strip of skin he'd spotted. Soft and warm against his fingers. "I want my mouth here."

She took a wobbly half step back from him. His hand kept hold of her waist. Her eyes looked heavy as she blinked dazedly up at him. "I'd like that."

They made it inside the cottage. The need to touch, to put his mouth on hers, was hampered by her efforts to touch him, the brush of his lips against hers every few feet. He didn't know who opened the door, which of them closed it. The days since he'd last seen her, brushed his hands over her skin, seemed too many, too long. His lips pressed against her abdomen as the buckles from her overalls clinked on the wood floor.

Chapter Forty

Rose picked up her phone to call Aunt Cherry. She'd already done the math to make sure she wasn't calling too early or too late with the five hour time difference. Magnolia never said much about her sister. She hadn't attended Magnolia's funeral. Her health made it difficult for her to travel from England. Rose hoped Aunt Cherry might know answers to her questions about the past, concerning the months before she was born.

The line connected. They exchanged greetings and common niceties. The weather there and here was discussed. Her aunt asked about the memorial service and apologized for not attending.

As a child, Rose had noticed Magnolia pursed her lips more during Aunt Cherry's visits to Evers Hollow. She'd never questioned why, but when Aunt Cherry began talking about the aftermath of Magnolia's passing, she began to understand.

"I suppose Broome will have to deal with Briar House now."

Rose said, "Broome didn't inherit the house. I did."

Her tone came across as condescending. "Hogwash. Did my

sister lose her mind? What's a young thing like you going to do with that creepy old place? Are you old enough to vote?"

"Aunt Cherry, I'm twenty-eight."

A harrumph came through the earpiece. "I'll need to see your driver's license next time I visit."

Rose rolled her eyes. There was no way her aunt could see her. "Aunt Cherry—I need to ask you about the past, back when Magnolia was pregnant."

"Pregnant! Are you saying my sister was pregnant when she died? That's impossible."

Rose shook her head. This wouldn't be easy. "You misunderstand. I'm talking about before, twenty-seven years ago. She spent a few months in the Cotswolds cottage."

Only silence followed. Had the phone disconnected?

"Aunt Cherry?"

Her voice came through, tinged with authority and judgment. "You mean the illegitimate one. I remember. She got rid of it. Gave it away. What's it to you?"

Rose's mouth fell open. Her fingers gripped the phone. Aunt Cherry didn't know. Why wouldn't Magnolia have told her own sister that Rose was, in truth, her daughter?

Her aunt continued. "I told her to flush it. There was still time. The father sounded like a ne'er-do-well. Not the sort to hobnob with the rest of us Everson's."

Rose couldn't decide if she was more shocked or horrified at her words.

A semblance of laughter reached her ears. It held no kindness. "So the town darling's big secret got out. I told her it would. Nothing stays hidden in that rotten place. It's one reason I chose to live with our mum when our parents divorced."

Was that glee in her voice? She tried to speak, but Aunt Cherry wasn't finished.

"Bet Louise Winston is eating cake over this. She always hated my sister."

Rose frowned. Why had she thought this phone call was a good idea? Perhaps she should have called Uncle Tamarack instead to get information. The space behind her right eye throbbed. She tried to break into the conversation, tell her the secret remained hidden. The older woman rolled right over her attempts.

"Downright scared she was, to take you all in after that father of yours got him and Daisy killed. I told her she was a loon. Told her again when she asked me if I would help raise all of you. The nerve. Five children. In my cottage, at the same time."

Again, Rose tried to speak. She didn't get past opening her mouth.

"It would be safer she said—across the Atlantic. I refused, of course—told her she'd lost her bloody mind. I think she may well have."

Rose pressed her palm to her forehead.

"I can't believe she left the house to a girl. Do yourself a favor. Light a match and take it down to its foundation. Better that it never stood."

Burn down Briar House? What was wrong with this woman? One she was supposed to claim as family.

She had to defend this house, herself. "I love this—"

It was too late. The line cut off. A dial tone eventually sounded, followed by silence. There was no sense in calling Aunt Cherry back. Unless she wanted to compound her headache. She slipped her phone into her pocket, then pressed her fingers to the outside of her right eye.

Confusion and more questions filled her mind. Was she supposed to believe that Magnolia hadn't wanted them here? That she'd wanted them to live overseas? Because of fear.

She sank into her couch, clutched a pillow to her chest. Of course, she didn't believe the woman's words. No wonder Magnolia never told her the truth.

Aunt Cherry called Rose's birth father a ne'er-do-well. An

outdated term, but Rose got the message. The woman felt the father of her sister's illegitimate child was unfit for what previous generations called the Everson Legacy.

And why had she mentioned Louise? And cake?

She needed to take something for the emerging headache.

Rose did so, then made another call to her friend, Ada, asking if she could come over. She quickly agreed.

While she waited for her to arrive, she thought more about the things she learned from Aunt Cherry. Secrets often found their way out here in Evers Hollow. Why hadn't Magnolia's?

A knock came at the cottage door. Thoughts of the past disappeared.

Ada, her closest female friend, held a bottle of wine and a box of chocolates. "I'm glad you called. I bought these weeks ago. I knew you'd need me at some point. Phone calls and texts are not enough."

She wore yoga pants and a tunic style sweatshirt. Her curly blond hair was piled on top of her head in a messy bun. Gold metal rimmed glasses perched on her nose, accenting the gold flecks in her brown eyes. Rose ushered her in. Once seated, she told her everything she'd learned since Magnolia's passing.

A glass of wine later, Ada set her glass down and pushed up her glasses. "So, what you're saying is that your—what do you want me to call her?"

"Magnolia. It's easier. Anything else is plain confusing." The pain in her head hadn't dissipated. She sank farther back. The wine probably wasn't wise, but it paired too well with the chocolates Ada brought. She ran a finger around the rim of her glass.

Beside her, Ada folded her legs beneath her. "So, Magnolia got pregnant with you after her husband passed away. The woman who is technically your older sister, Daisy, had her kids already."

"Yes, except she was still pregnant with Thorne. I think that's why they changed my birthdate. We were too close in age for anyone to believe that my mom, Daisy, delivered me."

"Damn girl. That's a lot. No wonder you called." Ada held out the box of chocolates. "Have another one. It'll make you feel better."

Rose massaged her temples.

"You should take something for the headache," said Ada.

"I did. I'll take more before I go to sleep."

Ada ended up crashing in the cottage's guest room. They'd finished the bottle and most of the chocolates. At breakfast, over scrambled eggs, maple sausage, and cinnamon apples, Ada asked more questions.

"So, you don't know who your real dad is?"

Rose said, "No. No clue. It's why I called my aunt."

Ada pulled one knee to her chest. "She sounds lovely. I hope I never have to meet her."

Rose finished her breakfast. "No worries, we haven't seen her in forever. I couldn't even say when. She came to one of the weddings. Maybe Broome's."

Ada forked her last bit of sausage and held up a finger. "Tell me, why are you still living in this cottage?"

"We're figuring out a weekend to move me in."

"Good." She sent her an accusatory look. "Why didn't you tell your besties about the creep in the cafe? And the cemetery?"

"You heard about that?"

"I own a flower shop on Center Street. Of course, I heard about it. I would prefer to hear it from you."

Rose stood, set her plate in the sink. "I'm sorry. I—"

"Didn't think how worried we'd both be?"

Rose turned to face her. "Does anything stay private in this town?"

Ada cocked her head. "Becks would say no. That's why I can't convince her to give up her job in New York and move down here."

"I'll call her. I promise."

Ada stood, glanced at her watch. "Would you like me to help move some things now? I've got a bit of time."

"Sure, if you don't mind."

"Awesome. I'd love to see the progress in the dining room. I can't see much in the pictures you sent us."

Together, they filled a few boxes. Rose stuffed her suitcases with clothes and shoes she wasn't currently wearing.

After unloading the boxes, they climbed the stairs with the suitcases. When Ada wheeled one toward Magnolia's room, Rose said, "I can't sleep in there yet. We're still going through her things."

"Oh," said Ada, before she turned around. "I imagine that's difficult."

"Willow, Aspen, and Simi have been helping. We've gone through most of her clothes. Aliya loves the costume jewelry."

Ada pressed a hand to her chest. "A girl after my own heart."

"Willow will sort through the last of the clothes. Most will go to the women and children's shelter in town. Willow's got some ideas for the rest."

Ada followed her up the stairs to the third floor. "Knowing your creative sister, she'll come up with something cool."

They emptied the suitcases and set them back downstairs.

Rose walked Ada through the house. They peeked into the dining room through the crack in the plastic curtain the disaster team had hung. They'd be here later in the day.

She'd have to find a new dining table. Initially, the old one appeared to have held. Closer examination revealed a splintered crack through the oak top.

Most of the chairs made it through with minor damage. They'd been taken to the ballroom. Willow had offered to chalk paint them. Rose needed to find out what that meant.

Ada asked, "What do you have planned for today?"

"Since my call with Aunt Cherry was useless," she said, "I

need to visit the Conroys. Maybe they know something. Surely, Magnolia would have confided in someone."

Ada's expression turned somber. "I hope so. I hate to think of her dealing with all that by herself. Your gran—oops, I'll need to get used to that." She brushed a hair out of her face. "She was sort of scary, but also epic cool. Even when I shaved my head."

Rose smiled at the memory. Tess had actually screamed the first time Ada entered the kitchen with a shaved head. Magnolia hadn't so much as flinched. She had, however, gifted Ada a soft winter hat for Christmas.

"Did you ask Tess about it?"

Rose tapped her forehead. "I'm a moron."

Ada tilted her head with a grin. "So, that's a no."

Tess, a woman who'd worked inside Briar House since she was a teenager. A woman who was more family than an employee. She'd also gone to school with Magnolia in their younger years.

"You brilliant woman!" Rose hugged her. "Why haven't I asked her yet?"

"Cuz you're a moron," she teased. "And maybe cuz you don't see her everyday now that she's retired."

"I'll talk to Tess. I need to check on Livie too. I had to let her go since it's just me now. I wrote her a recommendation. Hopefully, she's found a new job."

Ada left an hour later, promising to help on the next scheduled moving day. Rose drank a glass of water and took more Tylenol.

Rose then drove to the Conroys and parked in front of their white ranch style farmhouse. Brigette and she sat indoors, mugs of freshly brewed coffee atop their scarred farmhouse table. She'd once said the dents and gouges were what came of having five children.

Rose blew across the top of the hot liquid before asking, "Did Magnolia date anyone after Devin died?"

Brigette pushed her heavy silvery blond braid behind one shoulder before wrapping both hands around her mug. "I don't remember. We all grew apart for awhile. The older boys were all sorts of trouble at the time."

Rose was well acquainted with the trouble her boys got into. She was four months younger than their twins.

"We all did what we could for her when she lost Devin," she said. "She knew she could call us anytime, but you know how stubborn she was." A perplexed look entered her cornflower blue eyes.

"What is it?" asked Rose.

She shook her head dismissively. "Nola was a private person. I never knew all her secrets, but I never shared all of mine."

Rose leaned forward. "What do you mean?"

Her expression changed. "It sounds crazy, but at one point, I thought she might be pregnant. Felt I recognized the signs. I was carrying the twins at the time. Her pallor matched how I felt."

This was it—the information she needed. She shifted in her chair.

"She never admitted it. She told me she was going to visit her sister. I thought that strange. She never got along with Cherry."

Rose swallowed. Her heart beat sporadically in her chest. Could she trust Brigette and Jeremy with the truth? "How long was she gone?"

"Months. I didn't keep track of how many. I wish I could tell you more."

Rose decided. "She was pregnant, with me."

Brigette's mouth fell open. "You—you're serious, aren't you?"

Rose nodded. "She wrote me a letter. Daisy and Clark adopted me. I read it after she passed."

"Of course she'd tell you in a letter. The emotional stuff was always hard for her." Tears filled Brigette's eyes as she reached for Rose, took both her hands. "Oh, honey, I never knew. No wonder you've come here. You want answers."

"She doesn't say who my birth father is."

Brigette's brows crooked as if in concentration. "I'll have to think on that. I was younger than her, only overlapped a couple of years in high school. She and Devin were true loves, though. Hard to imagine her trying to find that with anyone else."

The house door creaked open and smacked closed.

Brigette shook her head. "He keeps saying he's going to fix that."

Jeremy entered the kitchen dressed in Wranglers and a button-down plaid shirt. He was a tall man, at least six four in cowboy boots. His oldest son, Aidan, followed him. They were the same height, but the Evers Hollow Fire Department t-shirt Aidan wore emphasized the hours he spent at the firehouse gym.

Jeremy removed his cowboy hat, set it on a nearby bench, and dropped a kiss on his wife's lips. "Aidan's here to pick up the dinners you made for the firehouse."

He greeted Rose then went to wash his hands at the kitchen sink.

Aidan hugged his mom and greeted her. Then he turned to Rose and squeezed her shoulder. "Good to see you. Been awhile."

Brigette stood. "The lasagnas for the firehouse are in the garage freezer. Do you need help loading them?"

"Nah, I got it." Aidan hugged her once more. "We appreciate you, Mom and Dad. Stay out of trouble, Rose." He winked at her before he went back out the door.

Jeremy poured himself a cup of coffee from the pot on the counter.

Brigette sat back down. "Rose is here to ask about Nola. Did she date after Devin died?"

"You expect me to remember? That was what, thirty years ago?" He leaned against the counter.

"Not quite that long. Maybe we set her up?" She tapped her index finger against her chin.

He shrugged. "We took her to the range a number of times. She loved to shoot when she was angry. Crack at it, too."

Something else Rose hadn't known.

Jeremy shook his head. "I don't remember her seeing anyone other than Devin after high school. The others might know."

The image of Magnolia at a shooting range was still with her. It shouldn't surprise her, but she hadn't seen her with a gun outside the night of the barn fire.

Jeremy's eyes narrowed. "Why are you asking? She was your grandmother. Not like any of them are still alive except all of us."

Brigette chuckled. "I forget."

Both she and Jeremy looked at her.

"The whole lot of them asked her out at one time or another. Even my Jeremy."

A hint of color reddened the older man's cheeks. His boots shuffled. He looked as if he'd been caught stealing a whole pie off a windowsill.

"You can't still hold that against me, love." He cradled his hand around his wife's shoulder. "Besides, Nola turned me down."

Brigette gave a wry smile. She reached up and patted her husband's hand. "Nola was my best friend. She knew how I felt about you."

"You can't blame any of us for trying."

Brigette gave him a tender look, the kind that implied they forgot they weren't alone. "No, Nola's always been beautiful, but you saw me in the end."

This conversation was clearly over. The Conroys were making moon eyes at each other in front of her. No wonder they had five kids. It was amazing they didn't have more.

Rose slipped out with a subtle thank you for the conversation. An exchanged glance with Brigette said they would talk again.

She drove back to Briar House, pondering what she'd learned from their discussion.

Magnolia enjoyed shooting. That knowledge was unlikely to lead anywhere.

Brigette had thought she was pregnant.

All The Elder men had asked her out at some point. Dr. Cook, Hal, Jeremy? The mayor?

Aunt Cherry's words came to mind.

Louise always hated my sister.

Maybe that's why Louise Winston wasn't part of The Elders. Magnolia had mentioned years ago that she and Louise went to school together—that there was no love lost between them. She'd never mentioned details.

As for Magnolia, had she dated any of them? Perhaps Tess would know. She pulled out her phone and sent a text.

Chapter Forty-One

Finn stepped toward his tiny kitchen and switched on the overhead light. He'd showered, thrown on a t-shirt and sweats. Last night's shift had been difficult, on top of the two before. He wanted to make himself an omelette and sleep. His time in the ER solidified his desire to work in Family Medicine. He loved helping people, but he wanted the connection that came from seeing the same patients year after year. He wanted to make a difference in their health and longevity, to prevent visits to the ER.

A knock on his apartment door forced him to change direction.

Thorne Finch stood outside with a canvas grocery bag in one hand. "Hey."

There was no reason for Thorne to show up at Finn's without a text or phone call. Why was he here now? Unless—

A chill went through him. "Something wrong? Is Rose…is she okay?"

Thorne didn't answer. Instead, he pushed his way into the apartment. Finn had no choice but to step aside.

Something was wrong. Finn shut the door behind him, raked

a hand through his hair, and motioned to the couch. "Sit anywhere."

Thorne looked around the room. The stacked boxes were hard to ignore. "What a shithole."

Finn didn't defend the state of his place. "Tell me. Is she okay?"

He shrugged one shoulder. He set his canvas bag on the trunk in the middle of the room. It made a heavy thump on the old wood. "Do you have coffee?"

Thorne didn't wait for an answer. He found the kitchen himself. He returned, holding a steaming mug. Then headed to the nearby kitchen chairs and sat down backwards.

After a sip, he grimaced. "You need to buy better beans. These suck."

Finn had no response. Why was he here?

Thorne drank a bit more. His expression gave away nothing. He grimaced, then motioned. "Sit down, Finn. Let's talk about my sister."

Like hell he was sitting down. Not till he knew what this was about. Never had he felt threatened by Rose's brothers. He didn't now. He leaned against the closest wall, folded his arms, and waited.

Thorne eyed him as if he were something to be torn apart. He'd always been bigger and stronger than Finn, the most aggressive player on their high school soccer team. He wore that scowl that had intimidated many a player way back.

He lifted the mug again as if he were toasting his refusal. "Fine. I got a question. You're going to answer. No bullshit."

Finn moved both his hands to his sides, thinking keeping them free might be smart.

"What are your plans related to my baby sister?"

"Plans? Baby sister?" He knew now that Rose wasn't fully Thorne's baby sister. Did they still call each other—

Thorne seemed taken aback by his words. "Did she tell you —?" He broke off. "She did. She fucking told you."

Finn gave a nod.

"Didn't expect she'd want to see you, much less tell you anything, until you showed up at brunch."

"We've talked. She told me the truth about her mother." Thorne was the last person he wanted to talk to regarding Rose. He tended to get defensive about his sisters. Finn knew the man packed a mean punch. He'd witnessed it a few times back in school.

Thorne said, "She must trust you."

"I believe so." After what they'd shared, he hoped she felt more than trust.

"She also tell you we don't give a fuck what a document says?"

Finn got his own cup of crap coffee and took a chair, figuring it was now safe to do so. "She left that out. She was…"

Thorne closed his eyes, anguish clear. "She was crying."

"A little."

"My baby sis never cries. The other two could open their own waterworks, but not Rose."

Finn knew. He could count on his fingers the number of times he'd seen her cry. Most of them had been these past weeks.

Thorne looked at him directly. "I hate to see her cry."

"So do I."

"Then you'll understand why I'm here. Your plans?"

Finn knew there was no right answer. He knew how he felt toward Rose. Pa was right to worry. He'd fallen for her again. It was possible he'd never stopped. He didn't know how she felt about him, though.

Disapproval etched across Thorne's face. "I see."

"See what?" The need to defend himself rose alongside annoyance. It was a familiar feeling back when Thorne took his team captain role too seriously. He'd told them there was no space for losers on the trophy stage, to play their damn positions with everything they had.

There was no stage inside his apartment. As for plans, and Rose…

"It's not your business, Thorne."

His hands formed into fists. "After Brentwood, I made it my business."

"Don't compare me to that asshole."

"I'll ask again. Why do you keep coming back to town?"

"Pa asked me to get the house ready to sell."

"Sure." Thorne quirked one eyebrow, waiting.

"I'm not talking about her with you," said Finn. "It's Rose. She's not just any girl."

"She's not, which is why I give a shit. I told you before—if you hurt her, I'll break more than just your nose."

"I said I would never hurt her."

"You got one strike against you on that."

He did. He and Rose had had that conversation. She wouldn't have slept with him if she was still upset. "That's between me and Rose."

He eyed the bag sitting on the trunk. "Why are you here, Thorne?"

His unwanted guest smirked and slapped the side of the canvas bag. "I'm here to make things clear for you, one of those Christmas ghosts from the creepy Scrooge book we all had to read in school." He pushed the bag towards him. "Take a look."

Finn stood and peered in. It held multiple books. The top one had kids on the cover. "You brought me books?"

"I brought you Rose's books. I suggest you read all of them."

He knew she wrote books after their encounter in the bookstore. Learned at her family brunch that she wrote for children.

Finn pulled out the top book, read the title, then the author's name at the bottom. *The Mystery of the Hidden Playground by Everson Briar.*

She'd used her middle name. He then saw the smaller words at the bottom—

Criminy Mysteries

She hadn't…

Thorne's smirk said it all. "I didn't believe her, but I can tell by your face. You didn't know what she wrote."

Finn shook his head. He pulled out four more. All hardbacks.

"You need to read them."

Finn could only nod. He'd find the time, between shifts and studying the latest writings assigned by the chief resident.

Thorne left soon after. Finn made his omelette. In between bites, he laid the books out on the old trunk on top of all his medical textbooks. They barely fit. All five hardbacks.

Criminy Mysteries

Had Rose really written these? Stupid question to ask himself when the evidence lay in front of him. But why?

He put his plate in the dishwasher, poured the remaining coffee into his mug, and nuked it. He scratched the back of his neck as he drank his bad coffee and studied the books, their covers. One had a fence on it.

The Mystery of the Hidden Playground.

He sat, placed his mug by his feet, and reached for the book.

The playground had been fenced all the way around with no gate. A couple of boards had been loose. Enough for them to slip through. He remembered holding onto the merry-go-round, running as fast as he could, then pulling himself on, spinning round and round alongside a toothless, grinning Rose.

His fingers stiffened as he opened the cover, turned the first two pages. And then swore.

*For my best friend, a boy who once thought girls were
    disgusting.*

Three hours later, he was halfway through the second book. Her words made him laugh.

The broken windows they hadn't noticed until an older man walked by and accused them of breaking them. Phone calls had gone to his folks and Ms. Magnolia.

The two of them denied it, of course. Innocent until proven guilty. It's what Rose always used with Ms. Magnolia. The two of them would never break a window. But they had to prove it. That had taken a bit of work since they'd both been grounded for a week after.

He finished the second and went to bed.

After his next shift and another round of sleep, he picked up the third.

Chapter Forty-Two

George breathed in the freedom of night air as he left the police station. Someone had paid his bail.

When he spotted a woman with red hair standing beside a battered gray minivan with muddied license plates, he knew who.

His half-sister studied him a long while before she opened the passenger door.

"Come on, I found you a better place to stay."

They never hugged. Tonight was no exception.

He got in the car and shut the door. "Crap wheels."

She settled in the driver's seat and started the car. "My handyman's. I couldn't drive my own."

Of course not. His half-sister would never acknowledge him, or be seen with him in public. She was too much like their shared father. A relative in jail was always bad for politics.

As she drove, he asked, "Who gave you the bail money?"

She glanced at him. "That's not relevant. You're out. That's what matters."

"Was it Dad?"

"No, he's taken a turn for the worse." Her voice choked. "He's under hospice care now."

Their old man was dying. Finally. "About time."

Reprimand was clear in her words. "You can't mean that. He's our dad."

George shook his head. "He turned against me, used me to win an election."

"You committed crimes. You set things on fire, repeatedly."

"I fell in love. The flames call to me." Just like his Maggie. He studied his sister, wishing she'd remove the stupid wig. It reminded him too much of fire girl. He'd dreamt of her again last night, her soot dusted face. Always the same question.

Tell me something, little guy. Do you still have matches in your pockets?

His sister continued, her tone too much like their father's. "You've ruined your life with this obsession. You went to prison for it."

He shrugged. "True passion has consequences."

To his surprise, ten minutes later, she drove through monogrammed wrought iron gates onto the grounds of her own home. A brick wall surrounded a stately old house on a hill. Despite the darkness, he saw the wealth surrounding his sister and her husband.

Holding power paid.

George asked, "Here?"

The engine shut off. "You need a place to lie low until your court date. Dad's moved to the hospice center in Asheville. His quarters are empty. It's clean, just how you like."

She led him through a side entrance, around the back of the house. The suite inside was large, decorated in white and gold.

Hands folded in front of her, she said, "I had your things brought from Gray Mountain. My staff won't reveal your presence here, but you're to remain inside the walls."

Conditions. She'd never visited him in prison. Too bad for her public image. He opened drawers, found the clothes he'd purchased since his last release.

He said, "Tell your husband I need a talented lawyer."

"I can't do that. He's unaware that you're here. You weren't supposed to return to Evers Hollow, little brother. Dad said—"

"I had to come back. I'm getting married." He put his hands in his pockets. Empty, both of them. His fingers curled.

She paled. "George. No. You can't still think—"

"I love her."

"Magnolia Everson-Brooks is dead. I attended her funeral."

He laughed. "I've seen her, talked to her, even touched her."

She pressed her hands together as if in prayer. "Magnolia's gone. You accosted her granddaughter."

"You lie, just like our father. Maggie's alive and mine."

His half-sister drew closer, putting her hand on his arm. "She was never yours. It's time to face the truth. Let her go. Magnolia was never worth this."

He stepped out of reach. "You never liked her."

Her eyes teared up. Her fists clenched. "I beg you to stop this. Live the rest of your days in peace."

He curled his fingers. He wanted to hurt her for her words, but she was his half-sister, married to one of the most powerful men in Evers Hollow.

"Let me help you, George. Our father's dying—I don't want to lose you, too."

A pawn. He'd always been a pawn. So others could have what they wanted. It was his turn.

"George, please."

"Why'd you bail me out? The truth this time."

She held her chin high despite the tears in her eyes. "Very well. I made your mother a promise before she passed, that I would take care of you."

His mother. Gone some years now.

"I need a lawyer. Tell Clyde I'll tell everyone you're my sister if he doesn't help me. The truth will sour your son's chances for his mayoral run here in Evers Hollow."

Her hands flew to her face. "You wouldn't."

"Test me and find out."

Chapter Forty-Three

Rose exited the woods, her messenger bag across her body. The workshop she'd done at the elementary school had been fun and emotionally rewarding. The students had been excited to design their own character. Next week she'd go back, work with them again.

They'd offered her the title of *writer in residence*, a once a week position where she'd rotate through the fourth and fifth grade classrooms during their language arts timeframe. She'd accepted.

Her time with Tess after had been lovely as well. To ensure privacy, Rose had picked up deli sandwiches in town and gone to her place. They'd talked for over an hour on her screened-in porch.

I knew. I've always known you were hers. We spoke of it then, and a few times through the years, but she never told me who your father was. I didn't press. We each had our pockets of personal things we kept to ourselves. We respected that about each other.

Briar House came into view. Rose paused. The white wreath Ada had placed on the front door was missing. Something else hung in its place, a piece of paper. Most people didn't come onto the property, simply shoved their flyers into the old newspaper slot on the mailbox out at the street.

Curious, she climbed the steps to see what it was. She stopped, took a half-step back.

Anger whirled up inside her. Who would do such a thing?

The wreath lay haphazard at an angle on the welcome mat. Its dried white flowers lay crushed and muddied as if someone had stomped on the blooms.

She looked back at the door and felt a little sick.

A folded piece of paper was attached to the door with a tack. It was rude to mark someone's front door with a sharp object, but that wasn't the problem. Whoever had done this had shoved the tack through a large cockroach first, as if it were an accent to the paper beneath.

She raised her phone and snapped photos. One of the wreath. One more of the note on the door. In seconds, both were on their way to Reggie and Broome. A typed explanation followed. She rummaged through her bag. Perhaps she should wait, but damn if she'd let this remain on her front door. She pulled a red bandanna from her bag, forgotten after her last cold. Using the cloth like a glove, she removed the tack and the insect, then separated the paper. She opened it enough to see the words.

MUCH DEPENDS
ON THE MATCH THAT SPARKS
THE
FIRE.

FALLING TREES
NEVER FEEL A THING.
ASHES
TO DUST.

ALL I BURN

IS BECAUSE OF YOU
SKY
AND GROUND.

IN THE DARKNESS
A RIOT OF FLAMES.
ME
ON YOU.

DARK CANVAS
PAINTED BLACK FOR YOU
JUST
FOR YOU.

Bile rose in her throat. Was this supposed to be poetry? A gesture of affection?

All she saw in the words was death.

A fiery one.

Rose backed away, turning toward the side kitchen door. Her fingers shook as she opened it.

She barely made it inside before she became sick.

When she exited the half bath off the kitchen, she went straight to the sink. Her hands shook, part fear, part rage.

Why would anyone torment her like this? She pulled out her phone, checked the security camera app on her phone. The footage was dark and unfocused. She looked up at the camera. It hung at an odd angle, an obvious crack on its front. She texted Broome and Reggie MacShane.

It wasn't long before Reggie's Yukon pulled up to the house. In a city, no one would have bothered. The driver's door protested when he opened it and got out. He wasn't in uniform. Instead, he wore athletic shorts and a moisture wicking tee.

"Why didn't you tell me you're off duty?"

He folded his arms once he reached her. "I promised your brother I'd watch out for you. What happened?"

Maybe he hadn't received the pictures.

"It was on the front door."

She followed him as he walked up the steps, took in the scene, and then looked at the pictures she'd taken.

"You know how to bring the creeps out."

"If only that's all this is."

"Let me get some things from the Yukon," he said. "I'll call Mack too. He's on shift. That way, this is official."

"And the sheriff?"

"He's fishing at the coast. Want me to call him?"

"No." Maybe she said it too quickly. "I prefer you didn't. I know what he'll say." Sheriff Hutchins said he was harmless. Did Reggie share his opinion? She didn't want another lecture about letting the old man be.

Reggie was a professional. Whatever he thought about his boss, he kept to himself.

"Maybe this turns out to be nothing, a nasty prank. But Mack and I, we'll take the steps. These words on the paper, disturbing."

Mack came by. Both he and Reggie put gloves on. Everything went into evidence bags and vials. They dusted the door and the railing for fingerprints.

They did a walkthrough of the house, the cottages, and checked the overall property. Nothing else seemed amiss.

Reggie asked, "Have you seen anyone lurking about?"

Rose thought of her encounters with George. Every interaction. The cemetery. The cafe. That feeling in the woods that someone was watching her. She shuddered. Last night before bed, for a fraction of a second, she thought she saw a light in the woods. She hadn't seen him on the property.

"No one." She held her breath. "I worry about my run-ins with George Hindley."

Reggie looked down and swore before meeting her eyes. "Should have known. He's the sheriff's least favorite topic."

"Something's not right with that. The safety of his citizens isn't Sheriff Hutchins' priority."

"I'm well aware of the sheriff's priorities."

That wasn't an answer.

Reggie said, "Hindley was still locked up when I got off shift yesterday. Can you think of anyone else?"

She tilted her head, debated about what she'd seen last night. The lights. A trick of her imagination? "Nothing."

Reggie closed his notebook. "Your ancestors had a few enemies. I've heard the stories. I'll talk to Broome as well. The Elders. See if they can think of someone."

Broome called soon after Reggie left. She'd sent another photo of the demented poem. "Got your texts. I'm driving up."

"No, don't do that," she said. "I'm fine. Reggie and Mack were here. What did you find out about the camera?"

"I've got footage of someone in a mask, a baseball bat coming towards the lens. I'll get someone out there to fix it today." She heard his frustration through the phone.

"Thanks, Broome."

Rose scrubbed every panel of the painted front door as if the entire door had been covered in bugs rather than one spot.

It didn't seem to be enough.

The door looked naked when she finally stepped back. Mack took the white wreath in for evidence. Something about boot prints.

Chapter Forty-Four

When Rose woke the next morning and checked the weather, she groaned. The predicted forecast was a bad one. Three days of high winds and too much rain. Storms this severe usually dissipated before they hit Evers Hollow, but everyone had to be ready. The radio and news stations broadcasted warnings for flash floods and landslides. Crews were out clearing the drainage grates when Rose pulled off Sixth Street to park at the grocery store.

It took her forty minutes to buy groceries. The shelves in the bread aisle were empty. All that remained in the dairy section was pumpkin spice coffee creamer, on sale. The line to check out stretched to the back of the store.

Her phone chimed as she left the store. A text. She looked down. It was Reggie. Her fingers tightened.

REGGIE

George Hindley's out. Over twenty-four hours ago. Be careful.

Twenty-four hours. The poem on her door. It could have been him.

She looked up and froze. Reggie meant to warn her, but the information was too late.

She could see for herself that George Hindley was no longer behind bars. He stood on the driver's side of her Jeep. He wasn't looking her way, but the shock of white hair was hard to miss.

Was his presence random? Or did he know the Jeep belonged to her?

Rose turned around and went back inside the grocery store. A furtive glance out the sliding doors told her he was still there. She wasn't about to walk back out alone. Biting her lip, she moved toward customer service. Carina Wellington, malicious town gossip, stood behind the counter, her hair bleached to almost white.

She hesitated. Word would circulate that she needed help to her car. So what? She lifted her chin and approached the counter. "Hello Carina."

The woman looked her up and down. "Rose Finch, as I live and breathe—all grown up and famous now." Her face sobered. "I'm so sorry about your gran-mama. She was a leader in our little community."

"Thank you."

"What can I help you with?"

"Can I get someone to walk me to my car? There's a man lurking about my Jeep."

Behind metal-framed glasses, Carina's eyes flashed with suspicion, perhaps a bit of glee as well. "Of course. We women can't be too careful these days, especially in the broad daylight."

Rose heard the dig, the lack of sincerity. Yes, it was late afternoon. People were all around, but during the Cracked Egg incident, only the staff helped her. Others who'd witnessed the incident had taken photos and video. Carina put the call out over the loudspeaker for carryout assistance.

While she waited, Louise Winston, the mayor's wife, approached the counter, carrying a grocery bag.

Rose felt the woman's eyes on her, the sneer the woman offered to most townsfolk. She wondered if the woman knew how to smile.

"Rose Finch," Louise said. "You should be more careful spreading rumors about innocent men."

She opened her mouth to respond, but Louise sliced her hand through the air. "No excuses. You've always been a pain in this town's derriere."

By the time Rose took a breath and counted to ten in her mind, Louise had effectively dismissed her. The snooty woman stepped forward, immersed in conversation with Carina, over a return.

A tall, gangly teenage boy in a blue apron appeared. He insisted on carrying her two bags to the car. George was gone. Every parking space around her Jeep was empty. The young man put her bags in the back. She thanked him and handed him a tip.

It wasn't until she sat in the driver's seat that she noticed the piece of paper beneath the windshield wiper. She hoped it was a flyer for a car wash. The local high school had them all the time. As soon as her fingers touched it, she knew—it wasn't a car wash.

In black ink, pressed into the paper hard enough to rip in some places, she read:

MAGGIE, YOUR WHITE NIGHTGOWN'S MY FAVORITE.

A drawn, crude angular heart with an arrow through it underlined the sentence. Dread encased her.

How was this her every day?

She drove straight to the police station. Sheriff Hutchins laughed when she handed him the note.

"You expect me to arrest someone because of a note with someone else's name on it?"

She wasn't that naïve. She wanted it entered into evidence.

"Maggie could be short for Magnolia. George Hindley was next to my car at the grocery. I heard you released him."

"Of course I released him. A judge set his bail, and someone paid it. You ought to be ashamed of yourself—destroying a man's future after he's done his time. I'm of the mind to think you wrote those poems yourself, you being a writer and all. Gotta be lonely there at the house with your granny gone."

It took everything inside her not to use every curse word in her memory against the sheriff. He'd throw her in a cell if she did. She moved to the door and turned back. "I guarantee you that if I were to write poetry and stick it on my own door, that it'd be better than that crap."

"Maybe you shouldn't be so quick to call my deputies. You're wasting taxpayer's money."

"Maybe you should assume you won't have my vote next election. This town deserves better."

Chapter Forty-Five

Rose made her last stop at Hanover Hardware for more batteries and lamp oil. She tried to tamp down her anger, but was certain it radiated from her. Mr. Hanover rang her up with only a few minutes of conversation. Smokie, the horror cat, looked better. Fresh sprouts of dark fur appeared in patches. His eyes still held menace and mistrust, but neither oozed.

She got the phone call when she started her car.

"Hindley's out," said Mack. "Someone paid his bail last night."

"Reggie texted me. Thank you Mack. I appreciate the both of you."

Debris kicked up around her vehicle as she navigated her way home. The rain began as she parked by the last cottage. It was closest to Briar House's kitchen door. She took her purchases inside, then pulled more wood into the house and onto the porch. Wind gusted as she fought to secure a tarp around the pile to keep it dry.

The power went out after she changed into dry clothing and brushed her hair. A text from the company predicted at least six hours before it would come back, maybe longer. Within minutes, she'd placed candles, lanterns, and flashlights in a few of the house's rooms. Outside, the sky darkened.

A glance at her phone told her she still had cell service, but no Wi-Fi. She checked the security app. The cameras powered by solar still ran despite the slashing rain. The one on the front door displayed nothing, having been wired to the house.

Without power and heat, she had to be practical. Losing both was inconvenient, but the wind worried her more. Sticks and leaves were already hitting the house. The surrounding trees— Magnolia said their strength lay in their numbers. Despite that, Rose didn't dare risk sleeping in her old room on the third floor.

The library. It would be the best room to wait out the storm and the warmest place to sleep. Before she lost natural light, she carried her pillows, blankets, and some firewood into the library. She'd light a fire once the sun set.

Back in the kitchen, she washed her hands, then sliced a loaf of rustic bread and put some on a plate. She pulled peanut butter from the pantry and jam from the refrigerator. A bottle of red wine sat on the counter. Who said peanut butter and red wine didn't go together? She should add some chocolate to the tray for her picnic dinner, and an apple.

Her phone rang.

It was Broome. He didn't waste words. "The cameras won't last long with the storm there. I'll come get you. You can stay with us."

A sense of unease slipped in with his words. It had been a severe storm that took their parents. People needed to stay off the roads, minimize the risk of accidents.

"You're not driving in this storm," she said.

From the sound of the wind and the flutter of debris hitting the house, there would be problems on the road with fallen trees.

Broome cursed. "I talked to Mack. I don't like that Hindley's out."

"Neither do I, but you can't keep everyone in bubble wrap."

"Believe me, I know, but—"

"I'll be okay." She forced confidence into her tone. "All the doors are locked. All windows latched. I checked the cameras when I got home. The solar ones are still going."

"Rose…"

"Broome."

After more back and forth, he agreed to stay off the road.

With a sigh, she hung up and pulled a knife from a drawer.

A hard knock came at the kitchen door. She yelped. The knife clattered to the floor. She picked it back up.

What if it was George? Her gut screamed. He'd tacked that poem to the door of the main house. She couldn't prove it, but instinct said it was him. The brave speech she'd delivered to Broome sounded hollow now. She stiffened when the knock came again until she heard her name said by a familiar voice.

With relief, she opened the door to Finn. And threw herself at him. Damp leaves whirled in.

"Stop. I'm soaked." Finn said, his words muffled against her until she stepped back.

"I wasn't expecting anyone."

"I got the next few days off," he said. "I heard about Hindley getting out. I'm worried." His cold fingers cupped her face. He kissed her with chilly lips then removed his rain jacket and shoes.

She wrapped her arms around herself. "I'll be fine—I grew up here, remember?" More hollow bravery. Her fear howled through the seams of the door.

"I know," he said.

"I'm all set. I've got batteries, oil lamps, and firewood."

"What if I also said I'm here because I'd love to be trapped in a storm with you?"

"Hmm," she glanced sideways at him. He was kind of adorable, wind-blown and damp, his words romantic. "Would you like to join me in the library? I'm having a picnic."

His eyes sparked mischief. "What kind of picnic?"

"A crackling fire, blankets, some nudity now that you're here. I'm planning to sleep in there. I even have snacks and sandwiches."

"So you're part of the picnic?"

With a little laugh, she smiled and moved away from him. She flipped her hair back and beckoned him with a come hither motion. "Why don't you lock that side door, follow me, and find out?"

His steps creaked on the floor behind her. His voice carried. "I've always wanted to do naughty things to you in the library."

F inn lay on his back, on top of the makeshift bed Rose had created in front of the fireplace. The fire had burned itself out, leaving the surrounding air chilled, but warmth radiated from Rose, who lay nestled against him, still asleep.

A hint of daylight outlined the library's drapes while the storm continued outside. Something hit the side of the house, a large branch probably. It was too distinct to be anything else.

He'd known about the approaching storm yesterday and assumed he'd be at the hospital in Asheville for the duration. The phone call from Mack between patients sent fear down his spine, for Rose. On a night when Evers Hollow would be rife with local emergencies, George Hindley had been released on bail. Finn knew little about the legal system, but even he knew this shouldn't have happened given the man's past crimes.

If trees came down and blocked the highway, it would be a challenge to get to Rose if she sent out a call for help. That scared him.

Thankfully, Dr. Walters had been in the staff locker room during his phone call with Mack. Finn hadn't minced words about his concern over the line. The chief resident overheard his side of the conversation and asked questions. Once Dr. Walters ordered him to leave, Finn wasted no time driving up here.

Rose stirred against him, her cascade of dark curls brushing over his arm and shoulder, as she shifted and nuzzled into him. She pressed her lips to his chest, murmuring, "Morning."

"The wind's died a bit." He ran a hand down her back, enjoying the feel of warm skin beneath his palm. She shifted more, sat up, and ran one hand through her tousled hair. "There's going to be a lot of cleanup."

There would be, all over town. They got up. He slipped on his jeans and rebuilt the fire.

She commandeered the t-shirt he'd worn last night and pulled it over her head. It hung loose on her, barely covering her bare ass. Her unbound hair flowed well past her shoulders.

The rain had eased some, but still fell. Rose opened the drapes, but the dark clouds and continued lack of power kept the room dim. Lit candles sat on the two desks in the library, away from the surrounding bookshelves. They reminded him of one of her books, the candles Ms. Tess had helped them make on another rainy day. They'd told her it was for a school project, but they'd also wanted to use them to explore the caves farther into the woods where they found a mystery.

Finn helped ferry breakfast from the kitchen into the library. Seated across from each other on blankets, they ate cinnamon muffins and pieces of fruit. Rose had boiled water on the kitchen's gas stove, and made coffee using a French press.

In between muffin bites, he said, "Thorne came by my apartment a few days ago."

"Why?"

"He brought me your books."

She stilled.

"He ordered me to read them."

She looked away. Her fingers were already in her hair, twisting the strands. "I didn't know he was going to do that."

"They're fantastic books, Rose," he said. "Made me feel like a kid again. Made me remember how we used to be. Criminy Mysteries."

"Inseparable adorables, according to your mom." She looked back at him, apology in her eyes. "I figured you knew. Thought someone told your pa. This is Evers Hollow."

Finn shrugged. "He doesn't read much. Why didn't you tell me about them?"

"Are you mad?"

He set his coffee down on the nearby hearth. "Why would you think that?"

"I never asked your permission." She looked down, her other hand twisted the hem of the t-shirt she'd borrowed.

He moved closer, grasped her shoulders. "Look at me."

She did, shifting in her seat as if she were in trouble.

He slid a hand to the side of her neck, tilting her head toward his. "I'm not Jed. You're not Ruby."

She shook her head. "But—"

He kissed her. "You wrote fictional stories for children based on us. Brilliant, but it's not the same."

Before she could argue, he added, "Besides, Ruby is bossy. Jed is smarter than me, braver."

Her eyes flashed. "Ruby is not bossy."

He'd hit a nerve. He couldn't resist. "Is too."

"She is not."

Suddenly, he found himself on his back, her atop him. He tensed as she dug her fingers into his sides in what he assumed was an attempt to tickle him. He resisted, grinning as he ruffled her hair. "She is. I like it. Your ideas, you always had them. I envied that."

She propped herself up, planting her hands on his bare chest. "You had ideas too, plenty of them."

He grimaced, shifting beneath her. "Small ones. The biggest one I had got you a broken arm."

One of his hands moved; his thumb ran over the slightly raised scar on the outside of her arm, where her bones once pierced her flesh. Her fingers traced the scars on his right hand.

She lowered her head. Her lips brushed his ear, her voice an intimate whisper. "Do you think I would have let you climb that tree without me?"

"No, but it was my idea," he said. "I'll never forget your scream when you fell."

"You were bleeding too. You could have run, escaped the raven."

He remembered his fear, trying to protect her from the angry bird. "What kind of person leaves his best friend? That scream of yours had to bring someone."

"You were my hero that day." She gave him a brief kiss. "My scream brought Chelsea's Aunt Norah. She thought someone had been murdered."

He rolled with her then, nestling himself between her thighs, wishing he'd removed his jeans. "Her cards foretold it along with the raven."

"At least she had one of those flip cell phones." Her fingers toyed with his hair.

The clanking bracelets Aunt Norah wore along her arms had announced her presence. Magnifying glasses perched on top of her head made her look like an absentminded professor instead of the mystic she preferred.

Rose giggled against him. "Remember her incantation, the way she waved her arms?"

He nodded.

In a somber tone, she lifted both arms and said, "Begone, you Stygian beast!"

"You're fucking adorable." He caught her hands and pressed them to the blankets over her head. He hovered over her, their mouths mere inches apart. Her large eyes, the hint of a smile on her defiant chin, was all he saw. This woman was it for him. He could already imagine a life with her, children with dark curls and her energy running around.

"I love you like this—tousled, beautiful, and wearing my t-shirt."

She blushed beneath his gaze.

He kissed her, melding his lips with hers. He wanted her again, to lose himself within her, preferably while she was still wearing his shirt.

Easing back, he played his fingers over her flesh, from the tips of her fingers to her inner thighs and then between. The way her body arched into his touch was a thing of beauty.

When at last he was within her and she fell apart in his arms, he couldn't hold back from speaking the truth against her ear. "I love you."

Chapter Forty-Six

F inn loved her.

Hearing him say the words with a rasp of pleasure against her ear was a tangible thing. Rose felt the words as if she could wrap her arms around them and carry them. She supposed she could, inside her heart.

A smile graced her lips as she slipped her feet into her daisy rain boots. Wearing gardening gloves, she worked alongside Finn to collect fallen branches and smaller pieces of debris downed by the storm.

I love you.

His words accompanied her as they traversed the partially flooded and obscured trail that led through the woods to Finn's childhood home. They repeated the cleanup process there until a small pile of branches lay at the end of the short driveway.

The three words echoed as they returned to the woods. They held power. Her former fiance had abused their meaning. She'd dreaded hearing them from him with his tone of condescension once they became engaged.

She hadn't said them back to Finn. He'd covered her mouth

with another kiss as soon as the last syllable left his lips. Was she ready to share her feelings with him?

A hint of blue sky beckoned ahead of them over the path they took toward town. The sound of distant chainsaws permeated the air. They saw downed trees on top of power lines while crossing Evers Hollow's main road.

As they walked, Rose asked him questions about his residency, the people he worked with, and his life in Asheville. He answered her, also telling him about the little boy next door to him who was determined to become a World Cup soccer player.

"Landon's having a birthday party in a few weeks. Want to go with me? We could stay at my place. You could meet some of my friends there."

"I'd like that."

She loved him. With Finn, things would be different—real, forever, what she'd always wanted with someone. She only had to say the words.

Everyone's power on Ash Street was out. A couple of blocks over, Firebrew's was on. The coffee house was crowded. Molly looked frayed by the time they got to the counter. A wide headband tied back her curls. The usual jewelry she wore was absent. Shirley appeared in a similar state. The baked goods in the glass case were nearly cleaned out. She and Finn each chose a muffin and coffee.

Rose grabbed a nearby table as soon as one became available.

Once seated, Finn asked, "Do I get to ask questions now?"

Rose lifted a shoulder. "With everything going on here, I feel you've heard too much about me."

"Not everything."

She picked up her mug. "Such as?"

"Why Criminy Mysteries?"

Nostalgia seeped into her. "Remember Mr. Munstead?"

"The gardener?"

"Yes. I helped him in the garden each time I came home."

He said, "You helped him when we were younger, too. Roped me into it a few times."

She nodded as she finished her last bite of muffin. "I told him all our stories growing up. He loved them. Suggested I write them down, see if they'd get published. One of my professors agreed."

"I'm happy for you. You've made a career with it."

"I still see Mr. Munstead," she said. "He moved in with his daughter and her husband after he retired. We meet for a meal from time to time. Sometimes at Briar House so he can keep an eye on the maintenance of his work. They found a new pair of rain boots for me recently. Wildflowers. A little big, but I figure I'll wear extra thick socks."

"Your rain boots—every time I see a pair, I think of you."

Her cheeks flushed. She pressed her fingers over the crumbs on her plate.

Finn asked, "What'd you do before that in New York?"

"I was a columnist for a ladies' magazine. Not very exciting, but I got my pinky toe in. The rest I had to work harder for. I wrote short stories in my spare time and had some published in magazines."

"When's your next book come out?"

"Beginning of next year."

"What's it about?"

"The dog."

He winced. "That'll be a hard one."

Rose reached for her mug again. "Yes. It's been a struggle to write it for a middle grade audience."

"I heard the cops solved it, caught the killer."

"Yes, it took awhile. They arrested someone in Florida. Lover's quarrel."

"How will you make it kid friendly?"

Rose set her empty mug down. "The dog will find a live person needing help."

"Its owner." Finn said.

"Exactly."

Chapter Forty-Seven

Finn ended the call on his phone. He braced his hands on the counter inside his apartment. The house hadn't been on the market long.

They had an offer.

Correction.

Pa had an offer. For more than the listing price. Rare for Evers Hollow. Houses like theirs didn't sell well, especially with the new subdivisions going in. Pa's was too outdated, with too many updates needed.

It had to the affordable housing shortage in the area. The local construction companies couldn't keep up.

The offer came from a couple expecting their first child. Willing to pay extra for a speedy closing. Three weeks.

He'd drive to Wylder. Tell Pa in person. He knew what he would say.

Chapter Forty-Eight

Too many parts of Rose's body ached to single out one muscle. The family and some of their friends had been at it most of yesterday, moving specific pieces of furniture out of the main house, along with the packed boxes. Willow took the dining chairs, three at a time, to her garage with Ada's help. Broome took most of his inherited pieces in his pickup. Thorne made two trips, one with Aspen's boxes and the few pieces of furniture she'd inherited. She'd rented a storage facility in Asheville, a choice that didn't quite make sense. She and Gavin had a large house fifteen minutes up the hill in the Opal Point subdivision. The second trip had been Thorne's stuff.

Finn helped load items into Broome and Thorne's pickups, but he hadn't been able to stay. He'd made a special trip to help for a few hours amongst a round of night shifts.

Mack Daggett and Zane Sheffield showed up to help early afternoon, staying for pizza after the pickups and cars were loaded. Ada joined them as well. Rose coordinated a date with Broome and Thorne to move the last of her furniture from the cottage.

Once everyone left, Rose locked the doors, set the alarm, and climbed the three flights of stairs to her childhood room. She'd promised Broome she'd live in the house from now on. She hadn't mentioned where she'd be sleeping.

It'd been almost two years since she'd slept in her twin bed, when she'd first returned to Evers Hollow. It felt too small. She tossed, turned, and tried to recapture the position she used to sleep in within this room.

When she drifted off, nightmares came, twisted ones, of the gruesome moments from the past weeks. She woke. Sweat clung to her. Her chest felt tight. Her heart pounded in her ears. A glance at the alarm clock made her curse. It was just after midnight.

The moon must be up, close to full. Pearly light leaked around the edges of the curtains.

She reached for her water bottle. It wasn't on her bedside table. She must have left it downstairs. Slipping from her bed, she grabbed her robe. In bare feet, she left her room. A glass of water or a cup of chamomile tea would settle her, wipe away haunting memories of decaying teeth and a vice-like grip. She held onto the handrail as she went downstairs, then headed toward the kitchen.

The faucet squeaked as she filled a glass. She stood at the sink; her gaze focused on the cottage she'd lived in for almost two years. It looked lonely, less welcoming. The mums she'd planted in the pots outside the door were fading.

The bright moon edged the tips of the forest, enough to remind her the trees stood just as they had for every Everson that got up in the middle of the night for a glass of water.

She should go back to her room, get another six hours of sleep. Around her, the house was a combination of eerie quiet and creaky loud. As if each wall needed to settle a microscopic amount at night.

Glass empty, she placed it in the sink. She glided out of the kitchen, toward the foot of the stairs.

A single loud thump came from the front door. It startled her. She wrapped her arms around herself as if that alone would save her. Her steps came to a halt in the moonlit room. Was the doorknob turning?

Another thump, louder. She flinched. The middle of the door flexed as if someone shoved against it. Its wood protested but held.

She backed away, her eyes fixed on the door as she did so.

Her cell phone was upstairs, in her room. The table at the base of the stairs held a cordless phone for the landline. Her fingers wrapped around it. She tore her gaze away from the door to dial 9-1-1. She hunkered down behind a nearby chair and waited.

"9-1-1, what's your emergency?"

Her words were brief to the woman on the other end of the line. She'd have help in minutes.

Another thud. Sharper. A crack of wood followed.

The house alarm triggered its shrill, repetitive sequence.

Rose sprang up and ran for the closest room, phone still in hand. She scrambled into the library. There was no lock on the door. She glanced at the secret hidden nook she used to hide in behind the bookshelves. Only a child could fit in there. She looked around for another option. She crawled beneath one of the heavy desks, pulling its chair toward her a tad. Then waited.

She should have gone upstairs. It held multiple hiding places. She could disappear for hours.

Her heart pounded in her ears as she waited for the next thud, another impact that cracked the door. Unlikely that she would hear it from here over the alarm, but still she listened.

She clutched the phone, her other hand over one ear. Sound pulsed outside the room. "I'm under a desk—in the library."

"Smart thinking. Stay on the line. Cops are one minute out."

"Okay. Sorry about the alarm."

"No worries. Stay hidden. They'll be there soon."

She listened, ignoring the emerging kink in her neck as she hugged her knees to stay as small as possible. All she heard was the sound of her own breath, the alarm in the distance, and occasional reassurances from the feminine voice on the line.

The crunch of wheels on gravel reached her ears. And the slam of two car doors.

"Cops are on site, miss."

Zane Sheffield and his partner, Ashley, found nothing but footprints and scuffs around the house. Along with a single crack in the door.

Zane said, "Good thing this is made of actual wood."

Rose didn't ask what would've happened if it'd been made of something else.

He looked above the entrance to the security camera, over the door. "Does that work?"

"Yes." She hadn't checked the feed yet. The security company had replaced the broken front camera after the last incident. She'd objected to the ugly wire cage encasing it, but Broome convinced her the cage would be temporary.

"Know where the feed goes?"

"I can access it on my phone and my computer. Broome can too."

Zane shone a light upward as if to check something. "From here, the wires look good. Let's look at your phone. See if you got some footage of your intruder."

Intruder. But he hadn't gotten in, at least not through the front door. Was there such a word as an *outruder*?

She tamped down a sudden desire to laugh. Tears would be more appropriate to the situation, but she felt depleted. A snort came out of her.

As if he understood, Zane gave her a pitying look. "Can I call someone for you? Broome's not that far away."

"No, I'll be okay. Don't call him. He needs his sleep. His toddler is teething."

Zane seemed hesitant to accept her answer, but nodded. "I'll get a patrol car to drive by the place on their rounds. We'll check every building on the property before we leave."

Zane and Ashley were thorough, like Reggie and Mack days before. The house was empty, as were the cottages. The garden shed held only varmints. Recent activity from the cameras showed a tall, dark hooded figure. They wore gloves and never looked up at the camera. A large wooden planter lay on its side, dirt spilling out onto the front porch. The footage confirmed it'd been used on the door. Zane bagged it as evidence.

It took her time to settle back into her childhood bed, to calm herself enough to close her eyes. She told herself no thief would relish climbing three flights of stairs to find her, not when the pricey valuables were on the lower floors.

Rose woke late the next morning, groggy from last night. After a cup of tea and some yogurt, she entered the woods for a morning hike. She passed other townsfolk, running or walking their dogs. She greeted each one.

Her clothes clung to her skin as she exited the woods and moved toward the house. Sweat burned her eyes. She used the hem of her tank top to wipe her face and neck.

She took the front steps and almost tripped before she grabbed the railing. Nausea filled her as she took in the latest addition to Briar House's front porch along with the sickly smell of sweet and decay. It hadn't been there last night. Reversing her steps, she pulled out her cell and walked around to the kitchen side of the house.

If this crazy kept up, she would be on a first name basis with the entire police department.

When she hung up, she emptied her stomach into the pink azaleas across from the kitchen steps.

She lowered herself onto the steps and curled her fingers into her hair. This had to stop. There was no space in her life for continual fear.

Her phone pinged. She removed it from her pocket, expecting a text from Reggie or Mack.

Damn. Her editor. She'd forgotten to email Elise her revisions.

She tapped a quick response.

ROSE

Will send revisions soon. Dead animal on my porch. Waiting for cops.

As she expected, her phone rang. She touched decline. Seconds later, it pinged.

ELISE

What the hell is going on there?

Rose slid her phone back into her pocket. Elise would have to wait. The revisions were done. Elise would have thoughts on them, the sort that'd be rough to hear. She rubbed two fingers against the side of her temple. What her book needed seemed out of reach, locked inside her amongst her grief, fear, and anger. And her feelings for Finn.

An EHPD vehicle spit gravel as it tore into the drive. Mack was at the wheel.

Chapter Forty-Nine

After his fourth night shift, Finn slept for four hours, then drove toward Evers Hollow, collecting his pa along the way.

He sat beside Pa at a table with Ray, the buyers, their agent, along with others associated with the title company. The paperwork for closing sat in a stack before them. The explanations, the turning of pages, felt therapeutic even though it was Pa who held the pen with his fingers.

Their buyers had come by last time Finn had spent time at the house. A couple in their late twenties. The wife was pregnant, within a month or two of delivery if he could hazard a guess. Chelsea popped over, introduced herself to her future neighbors. She'd asked the young woman about her pregnancy, shared that she was a nurse and available if they needed anything. He learned the husband worked in construction, and that he planned to redo the siding himself. He answered questions about the house to the best of his ability.

Genuine interest and excitement shown in their eyes. Was this how his parents acted the first time they saw this house, knowing it was about to be theirs?

The wife asked, "Is it too late to plant daffodils? They're my favorite."

His mom would have liked this woman. Her question softened Finn's heart. The rock that lodged inside him over the sale of his childhood home began to crumble. He pointed out all the places his parents had planted daffodils and hyacinths. In the walk around the perimeter with her, he decided everything was as it should be.

When they left, Chelsea gave him a hug. "This is the right thing, Finn. Your mom would be happy."

"I know." Meeting them, seeing their joy over this little house, hearing their plans to fix it up—the house would be well-loved and cared for. A new beginning. Better than what he himself had managed these past years.

Pa signed his name on one of many lines designated for his signature and initials throughout the documents. Finn rolled a pen beneath his fingers even though he wouldn't be signing.

His phone buzzed twice inside his back pocket. He ignored it. Then it rang. He should silence it. He pulled it out, glanced at the screen.

The texts were from Mack. So was the phone call.

He pushed back from the table, stood. "Excuse me. This might be important."

Finn stepped out the open door, touched the screen to answer. "I'm here."

Mack said, "You in town?"

"I am. What's going on?"

"I'm at Briar House. Get over here as soon as you can."

He stepped back into the room. "I'm on my way."

Pa looked up. "What's going on?"

"I need to leave. Something's come up. You don't need me here to finish this. I'll come back for you."

Ray asked, "Where are you headed? I can bring him to you when we're done. It's no trouble."

Gratitude leapt to his throat. "I'd appreciate that. Let me text you, though. I'm not sure what I'm walking into. Cops are involved."

His father studied him. "It's her, isn't it?"

"I think so."

Pa began to stand. "I should go too."

Finn set his hand on his father's shoulder and squeezed. "You've got paperwork. I'll find out what's going on. Make sure she's okay."

The ten-minute drive felt more like twenty. A cop car and the coroner's vehicle sat parked in Briar House's driveway. Finn jumped out of his SUV and rushed forward.

Rose stood alone, facing the house, her fingers circled her long braid of hair. She wore cut-offs, a tank top, and a faded flannel shirt. Her other arm wrapped tight around herself.

His shoes dislodged gravel as he stopped in front of her. Her face was pale, her eyes bracketed by something rare to see in her expression.

Fear.

"Rose, what happened? Are you, is everyone okay?" He may have imagined her flinch, but he didn't imagine her white-knuckled grip around her hair.

She didn't look at him. Her gaze fixed on the main house, as if she expected something to crawl out of it.

"Rose, is it Tess?" She'd retired, but…

Her eyes flickered. "No. Tess is fine."

"Then who?"

She said, "I had a delivery."

The way she spoke raised hackles on his skin.

A second EHPD SUV pulled in behind the other vehicles. Reggie and a short, black-haired female climbed out and walked towards them. Both were in uniform.

He looked at Rose. "Where?"

Without inflection, she said, "Front door again."

Reggie motioned to the petite female beside him. "This here's Clare." The young woman gave a nod before following him to the porch.

Rose remained where she stood.

Finn wanted answers, glanced at the van near the house. "Why is the coroner here?"

They both heard the curse Reggie gave when he reached the porch.

"What the hell?" Finn asked.

"Dead raccoon."

He was missing something. If it was a raccoon, why all the vehicles?

She let go of her braid and faced him, her face still pale. "Someone planted flowers in it."

His jaw fell open. Her words made no sense. It must have shown.

"Go see for yourself."

He did and regretted it.

F inn walked back to her, looking green. One would think he'd outgrown his childhood nausea around dead animals issue with his medical degree, but maybe some things never changed.

Concern and anger radiated through his posture. His lips were thin. There was a tightness in his jaw. "You okay?"

Before Rose could answer, he pulled her into his arms. Whether for his or her comfort, she didn't know. His anger helped, though. Made her feel less alone. She wrapped her arms around his waist and clung.

He hugged her so tight that her heart performed a tiny flip amongst her fear. She wished she could feel anger, but she was scared.

They stood like that until Reggie and Clare joined them. The deputy's jaw looked as fixed as Finn's. Clare looked a little pale.

Reggie said, "We don't get much like that here."

Finn's hold eased, but he didn't let go. His arm remained around her. His voice carried an edge when he spoke. "Wakefield boys used to kill things for fun."

"Whole family's gone. Moved away. After the lumber mill shut down. Michigan."

"The flowers?" Finn grimaced.

Rose spoke, her words shaky. "Gardenias. Their sweet smell. I never cared for them. I prefer carnations. Glad he didn't use those. Would ruin them forever."

Finn's hand squeezed hers. "Pink ones. I remember. My mom liked them too. Pa would bring them for her on payday."

Reggie pulled out a notebook. "You two done? Can we talk about the dead raccoon?"

"Of course. Can we go inside?"

Reggie glanced back at the people on the front porch. "As long as you stay away from them."

"That won't be a problem." As if she wanted to see the poor creature in that box again.

Rose led them into the house through the kitchen door.

Reggie insisted on being the last one in.

She grabbed a pitcher of raspberry lemonade out of the large fridge and some glasses. "Have a seat."

Clare helped her carry the filled glasses. They all took seats. Clare and Reggie sat on one side, she and Finn on the other. Finn laced their fingers together.

The new deputy made an attempt at small talk. Comments about the day's humidity fell short. Reggie kept quiet, as if he knew everyone needed a few minutes to enjoy a cool beverage.

A knock on the screen door broke those minutes.

It was the coroner, Quincy, and his brown-haired assistant.

He said, "We've got the animal and the evidence. You'll

have the necropsy report as soon as we finish. We've got an autopsy ahead of this." After delivering that information, they left.

Reggie whipped out his pen and notebook. "Is it common knowledge you don't like the white flowers?"

Rose shook her head, playing with the hem of her cut-offs. "Gardenias? I'd guess not. Usually, dates bring me roses because of my name."

"You think this was a romantic gift?"

She felt the color leach out of her at the thought. "I hope not."

Finn squeezed her hand, then asked, "Anything else like this happen before?"

Rose said, "No."

Reggie shifted in his seat. "Actually—yes. It got set aside because of the circumstances. More serious crimes needed atten-tion. The coroner reminded me when he saw the scene."

She turned to him.

"Your grandmother received a similar package."

"When?" Rose blanched. No one told her.

"A few days before her stroke."

Rose launched out of her seat, her fingers leaving Finn's. She needed to pace, but there was no space. Her arms wrapped around her waist. "Tell me."

"Same spot on the porch. Pink bow. Flowers."

"What kind?"

"Daisies, white ones."

She froze. How dare he! Fear morphed into rage. The thought of Magnolia finding that. Daisies. Too cruel. Magnolia named her firstborn Daisy, the woman Rose called *Mom*.

She spun. "Why didn't she tell me?"

Reggie cleared his throat. "She didn't want to worry you."

Her fingers curled. Stubborn woman. "Any others?"

"Not on my watch. Forest Service found a few dead animals

in the past months, but that's not unusual during fire season. The recent one we had—some miles away."

Finn asked, "Arson?"

"The report's not available to the public yet. Nothing like your raccoon."

Her raccoon.

Not hers, but her heart ached for the little animal. Why would someone do something like this? George Hindley had gone to jail for arson. He'd been released on bail. Did he like to hurt animals too?

She swallowed and sat straighter. Reggie's words. They reminded her of something. She pressed her fingers to her temples. What was it?

Fire.

No one had mentioned a recent fire.

She remembered.

"Cat."

The others in the room looked at her with curious eyes.

Reggie's voice carried a soothing tone, as if he needed to treat her carefully. "That's right. The animal left for your grandmother was a cat."

"No." She needed to make sense. "Smokie. Mr. Hanover's cat."

Again, that soothing voice. "I wasn't aware Bud Hanover had a cat."

Rose rushed through her next words. "He rescued one. You need to talk to him. It was in a fire. On purpose." She took a breath. "Someone hurt it."

"Your raccoon wasn't in a fire."

She gritted her teeth. Could he stop referring to the raccoon as hers? It made things so much worse. Another breath. One, two. "You just said you found other animals in the woods."

"There was a fire south of town, state forest."

Finn said. "Pa and I saw it the day of the funeral."

"Have you talked to George Hindley?" Rose had to ask.

Reggie ran his fingers over his jaw as if in thought. "I haven't. No one except you has seen him since his release."

"What about his parole officer?"

Reggie's lips thinned. "Same." Then he looked at Finn. "The old man who went to jail for the barn fire here. You remember him?"

Finn said, "Only his photo in the paper."

"They released him on bail. Sheriff's adamant that he's innocent."

"What else?"

Reggie said, "George went to jail for arson, had a history of it. Nothing on his record about animal mutilation."

The barn fire. The Murray's son. Lady. Her nails bit into her palms. "Because of him, Boone Murray ended up in a burn unit. His family almost lost him. My—Magnolia lost her favorite horse that night. We—we've never forgotten."

Rose could still see the smoking horse as it ran from the burning stable straight towards Magnolia, a glowing chain trailing behind her. She heard the horses' screams that night. And her own.

"It tore Magnolia to pieces—what she had to do that night." The memory of the gunshot sent a shiver through her.

Reggie sighed. "I'm sorry. All that happened before I moved here."

Rose's hands became fists. "However they justified his release, that man's still a monster."

"The courts tried and convicted him for that. He served time."

Rose said, "Not enough."

"That's not up to me or you. I'm investigating the situation we have now."

Rose swallowed. "All of it. It has to be him."

"Dang it, Rose, I have no solid evidence other than your statement at the cemetery and the witnesses at the cafe."

"The cameras. They should have caught who put that poor creature there." She'd handed him her phone after pulling up the security app. She couldn't watch the footage.

Reggie frowned. Shook his head. "Whoever did it, they know a little something about the coverage area. The box appears from the left side. Looks like they used a long handle, maybe a broom, to push it where you found it. Nothing else came up on the others."

Rose sank back into her seat. "Damn it."

"Don't give up on us yet. We're still here, working the case. And I promise to talk to Bud Hanover about his cat."

She nodded.

Gradually, the police cars disappeared with the promise of a regular patrol.

Finn pulled her back into his arms. His chin rested atop her head. "I'm staying here tonight."

She didn't object, but what happened when he went back to the hospital for his next shift and the one after that?

He couldn't protect her forever.

Chapter Fifty

The next morning, Rose walked into Cracked Egg Cafe and headed straight for The Elders' table. Her heart should have warmed at the sight of the two empty chairs between the Conroy's and Dr. Cook, but the raccoon incident was too fresh in her mind. Even a cheerful greeting escaped her.

Jeremy saw her first. Something in her expression must have alarmed him. He stood.

"What's wrong?"

She took the seat closest to Brigette. "Give me a minute. Willow's on her way."

Brigette put her hand over hers and squeezed.

Her mood must have carried. The table was silent. Florence stopped by her chair.

Rose said, "I could use a bear claw this morning, Florence."

Notepad in hand, she looked her up and down. "And maybe a small bowl of cinnamon crumb topping on the side?"

Rose managed a small smile. This town was full of people who knew her, recognized when things weren't right. "Thanks, I'll save it for another day."

"Eleven-year-old Rose would have jumped at the offer."

"Eleven-year-old Rose isn't herself today."

Florence pressed a hand to her shoulder. "Very well, sweetie. Next time."

Willow appeared and took the seat beside her. "Morning, all." She placed her order. "Can I get the oatmeal with pecans and blueberries?"

"Of course. Both of you want coffee?"

Rose nodded. Willow too.

Brigette nudged her. "Don't keep us waiting. Something's happened."

Rose shared the recent events. Willow knew all of it, but it was new to the rest. They reacted with a mixture of anger, shock, and concern. She appreciated their compassion, but she needed something else. She made eye contact with each of them, took a breath and said, "I believe George Hindley's behind all of this. I need you to tell me everything you know about him."

They exchanged looks among themselves, as if they were having a private conversation. The mayor cleared his throat and looked away.

Brigette poked her husband's side. "It's time, love."

Jeremy sighed and gave a single nod. "Hal, you start."

Hal waited until Florence came by for refills, then began. "Most of us went to school together. We were a close bunch: your grandparents, me and Martha, the mayor, and Sam. Brigette's a mite younger, but when she and Jeremy married, they joined us too. Hiking, canoeing on the river, dinners—we did all of it together. It was the same in high school."

"Back then, Nola's father, Malcolm Everson, offered summer jobs to teens as part of a rehabilitation vocational program after serving time. George Hindley was in that program. Your grandfather gave him a job working on the grounds. Nola was supposed to be overseas the whole summer with her mother, Angelika, and her other siblings. Her mother changed her mind last minute and rescinded the invitation. Malcolm had already agreed to help with the program."

"I worked in the Everson stables then. Malcolm felt he couldn't back out of the agreement. He'd found jobs for half-a-dozen young men in this community. Most were respectful, thankful for the opportunity to turn their lives around. Only Hindley caused him concern."

He paused while Florence set their orders on the table.

Hal continued. "Malcolm asked me to watch over Nola. He didn't like the way Hindley looked at his daughter. I saw it too, the way he watched her. Disturbing. Weeks in, Hindley approached Malcolm and asked his permission to court her. Malcolm lost it, fired Hindley, and sent him back to that ranch he'd come from."

"I figured he was gone for good. Sam, Jeremy, and I—we enlisted in the military after graduation. When we returned after a couple of tours, Nola was up at college in New York, studying—"

Brigette interrupted. "They don't need a local history lesson, Hal. They need the tale out and over. As do I. I hate what happened."

Her words didn't offer comfort.

Hal sent Brigette an irritated look. He reached out, patted Rose's hand twice before pulling it back as if preparing his next words.

"Fine. Weddings happened. Kids happened. Years went by."

Rose asked, "How many?"

"Over twenty. After Devin passed."

Beside her, Willow pressed her lips together.

"It was a chilly night in February. I was at home watching a movie. My phone rang. It was Nola. Someone was inside her house. She'd called the cops, but also called me. I called Jeremy and Brigette, then raced out my door."

Jeremy spoke next. "I arrived first. Poor Tess was knocked

out on the kitchen floor. She told us later, she'd been on her way out the door for the night. Neither woman knew Hindley was waiting outside. He'd come back to town and started bothering Nola. She didn't tell us."

"I wish I'd been there for her, but someone needed to watch Aidan and Ethan," said Brigette. "Nola refused to talk about it. She felt horrible that Tess ended up with a concussion."

"Nola knew her house, though," Jeremy chimed in, "all its hiding places. By the time he found her, Hal and I were inside. The others were just seconds behind."

"She was in the ballroom, behind the heavy drapes," said Hal. "Not sure what gave her hiding place away."

Rose blanched at the thought of Magnolia trapped, unable to get away. "You told us you stopped him from hurting her. Was that a lie?"

Brigette swallowed, looked at Jeremy, the others.

Jeremy heaved a sigh. "It wasn't a lie. He got a hold of her, had ill intentions."

A whimper came from Willow. She covered her mouth with her hands.

The mayor spoke, his voice too loud. "See here. There's no easy way to say it. This man was in love with Nola, wanted her to marry him."

Brigette turned so quickly her seat squeaked. "Clyde Winston, are you trying to give this story a happy ending?"

He blustered. "I don't want these girls—"

"What happened can't be undone, Clyde. These girls are adults. They can handle the truth. Jeremy, love, tell them the rest."

"Yes, dear." He looked at Hal and Sam as if for guidance. They both nodded as if agreeing. "That night wasn't what we'd call our best moment."

Hal said, "I wanted to kill him. Tear him into pieces."

Dr. Cook said, "I felt the same. He intended to force her, that was clear."

"They stopped him before he could," said Brigette.

She and Willow must have looked traumatized. With calm, Brigette leaned over, took both their hands and said, "Look at me, girls."

Rose met her eyes, saw Willow raise her head.

Her voice was so calm. "George didn't rape Nola, but he sure as hell tried. The men sitting at this table—they got to her in time, stopped him before he could."

Jeremy nodded. "Sam here tackled him. Then Hal tried to tear him apart with his bare hands."

"I stayed with Tess, called the paramedics," said Clyde.

Anger bracketed Jeremy's eyes, along with sorrow. "He never should have put a finger on her. Why the hell he thought she'd marry him is beyond me. The man was crazed."

With disgust in his voice, Dr. Cook said, "He looked at her like she was something to own, a possession."

Rose asked, "What happened next?"

"The cops showed up after we dragged George outside," said Jeremy. "They arrested him."

Willow asked, "They showed up after?"

Disgust lined Jeremy's voice. "You could say that. They made excuses. I'm guessing there's something in the records that justifies the delay. The truth is—they didn't believe her. Nola told us after that she'd made multiple complaints about Hindley days before for harassment, trespassing…"

Brigette interrupted. "The last time she complained, the new sheriff made lewd comments about the way Nola dressed, implied it was her own damn fault."

Rose pressed her palms to her coffee mug. "Hutchins?"

Hal nodded. "He'd been elected the year before. Your grandfather was still alive at the beginning of his campaign, but refused to back him."

Willow's voice was stricken. "That's total petty crap! How is he still the sheriff?"

Brigette turned to the mayor. Her voice oozed saccharine. "Yes, Clyde, you want to tell these girls why you continue to support Hutchins' re-election campaigns?"

The mayor's face turned an angry red. "He's a good police officer. I was there too that night. George was arrested and served time for what he tried with Nola. The police department did its job."

Brigette taunted. "They should have done it faster. Did you ever think about Nola's trauma? The station is on Center Street, closer than our house."

Jeremy wrapped an arm around his wife. "Calm yourself, love. We were there for her when others weren't."

The mayor's face turned a darker shade. He stood. "I don't have to listen to this." He reached out to catch the arm of another server. "Get me a to-go box."

Chapter Fifty-One

Rose left the house library with full arms. She'd spent the last hour opening bills with the dragon letter opener and writing the checks to pay them. Juggling the latest magazine issues from the mail along with personal items, she climbed the stairs. When she reached the second floor, she heard the front door creak open. She whirled, heard the thunk of items hitting the carpet as she moved. Not her phone again. The case was already chipped.

Thorne's voice called out. "Rose, you home?"

Relief overwhelmed her. She'd gotten in the habit of locking all the doors, something she never worried about when she was younger, despite Magnolia's lectures about home security.

Her siblings had keys.

She called down, "I'm upstairs, give me a minute." She picked up her phone. An ink pen lay next to it. How had that ended up in her arms? She saw nothing else on the carpet, but thought she'd heard more things fall.

Thorne said, "Take your time. I'll be in the kitchen."

She shook her head. His hand would be in the cookie tin

before she got back down. His love of homemade cookies never ceased.

She climbed the next set of stairs quickly, dropping the magazines on her bed. Then she went downstairs, her phone in her pocket.

Thorne held a handful of ginger cookies, one already balanced between his teeth.

He ate it, then said, "Great cookies! Can I take some back with me?"

"You have four others in your hand, unless you ate more before I caught you."

He smirked. "Never know."

Tess called him the cookie culprit. He might be twenty years older now, but he was still the sibling to blame when cookies disappeared off a sheet fresh from the oven. At least Rose had the wisdom to hide another dozen in the pantry, out of his sight.

She snagged one for herself and leaned against the counter. "I didn't know you were in town."

"Broome called me. He set up a meeting regarding my part of the will."

She took a bite. "No envy here. I'll take a collapsed ceiling over the pandering you'll have to do."

He gave her a playful punch in the arm. "No need to be mean."

Thorne finished the cookies, then opened the fridge and asked, "What's under the foil?" He didn't wait for an answer, pulled the covered bowl out and lifted the foil. "Yum. Leftover bacon mac."

He looked at her with hopeful eyes, reminding her of a salivating dog. With a sigh, she said, "Fine. You can have some, but not all."

"I knew there was a reason you're my favorite baby sis."

Her eyes looked toward the ceiling. "Brothers."

"That's right."

Thorne microwaved a sizable portion before sitting at the table. "You should join me. We can catch up before I ask if I can stay in the cottage for a few days."

"A few days. Starting tonight?" She sat down on the long bench at the wooden table. This brother had never been one to plan ahead. At least she'd kept the cottage clean since she'd started sleeping in the house.

He nodded as he chewed. After he swallowed, he said, "This town needs more medical resources. Doc Mason struggles to keep up with his current patient load. With the new subdivision, it'll worsen."

Her phone buzzed.

FINN

There by five. 🩶

The heart made her smile. She tapped a quick response and sent it.

Thorne cleared his throat. "Finn?"

She set her phone on the table. "Maybe."

He snorted and cracked his knuckles. "I visited him, helped him understand a few things."

She folded her arms. "What did you do?"

Thorne forked another mouthful before answering. "He still has his nose."

She sent her right foot into his shin. He flinched.

"Damn it, Thorne—I don't need your interference."

The last thing she needed was overprotective siblings.

"After asshole Brentwood," he said, "you don't have a choice when I'm around."

She sat again. "Caleb was a mistake. I'm allowed to make those."

Thorne leaned forward. "Back in high school, after I broke that nose of his, I ordered him to stay away from you. I wasn't here for you when he ignored my mandate."

Her brother had been in Mexico when she'd gotten engaged. When he found out, she received a phone call from him that was worse than her argument with Finn. By the time his educational exchange ended and he came home, Rose had broken her engagement.

She said, "Finn isn't Caleb."

He nodded. "I know. Brentwood never deserved you. Finn does."

Chapter Fifty-Two

A storm was coming. George could feel it. He'd seen the shadows, the dark sky. It was time.

The house was visible from where he stood in the woods. The porch light was on. So was a light on the second floor. Her room. He'd watched her from this very spot, many times from the dark. The first time, she'd been a vision, all in white. A glimpse before the curtain fell.

He dreamed of her then. He dreamed of her now. The past, the future he'd planned for them. Her hair as dark as a scorched forest floor.

George told Maggie's father he wanted to marry her. He'd been about to turn eighteen. Malcolm Everson had laughed at him. Told him to stay away from his daughter. Then he'd up and fired him, sent him back to the prison ranch he'd come from.

Another placement in another state. Until he aged out of the state's vocational program. They'd helped him find work in construction with a company that paid in cash.

The job took him to other cities, other states. Each time a job came up in western North Carolina, he found his way back to Evers Hollow.

His Maggie had moved away. Malcolm Everson held a shotgun the night he'd knocked on the front door of the big house to ask about her. She would come back. He felt it, knew she did too. He could wait a little longer.

Five years later, George attended Malcolm's funeral alongside his half-sister and her family. His Maggie had a husband, and a freckled, brown-eyed daughter. Inconvenient.

He continued working for the construction company, bided his time, and made plans.

The kid grew up and moved away. When Maggie's husband died, he thought he had a chance and took it. Her refusal, her interfering group of friends, put him behind bars. For ten years.

Tonight, things would be different.

He'd learned from past mistakes, planned. He had a shovel in hand, a rusty knife in his back pocket. It had come in use on his way here. The knapsack he carried held the rest of his supplies. He'd stolen what he needed. He'd had to pay a teenager to buy kerosene.

He rubbed his hands together to chase the chill away. His coat was old and worn. Maggie would buy him a new one.

Someone moved inside the second floor curtains, a feminine shape, a familiar one. He had to swallow the saliva that filled his mouth.

He'd seen the cameras on the front and back of the house. They were tests, ones he passed with stealth and the guise of a shadow.

To be sure, he'd visited the local hardware store earlier. The fool owner didn't notice when he slipped the can of spray paint into his coat pocket. He was too busy scolding the boys George had paid to create a distraction. He moved in shadow around the house until he coated the cameras in color. The camera's lights still blinked. He smiled. They wouldn't see him. Only Maggie would be granted permission. He was darkness and flame.

As he moved around back, his watch face showed he was on

schedule. Even better, he remembered his safety measures. The bucket of water he carried hung heavy in one hand. He wouldn't need it; he'd tested his plan on a cabin deep in the woods. Still, he set it within arm's reach.

Camouflaged by mud and greenery, a metal trashcan lay on its side, mere feet from the house. Like the bucket, he'd found it in a yard of overgrown weeds. He pulled it from its hiding place. A layer of dry leaves and sticks filled the bottom.

He set it on the terrace, as close as he could to the house under the window he'd chosen. It made little sound. Both the lights on the porch and on the second floor went out.

Once more, he went back to the woods. His knapsack was full of useful things. He turned it upside down. Everything fell out, some items with a clunk. With his hands, he picked up the clothes dryer fuzz from his sister's guesthouse and twisted bundles of old newspaper. In they went. He opened the bag of Fritos he'd bought at the Gas n' Go shop. They lit real well. One chip went into his mouth before he dumped the rest inside.

Next, the batteries. He opened the coffee can he found in a garage. The dry leaves cushioned their fall.

Last, he grabbed a bunch of pinecones from the ground. Tossed those in, too. Dad used to throw them into the fire. Mom always hated the popping sound, fearing the whole place would go up. To him, it added percussion.

George breathed on his hands before rubbing them together. He did a quick stretch, a few jumping jacks. A limber and loose body was vital to his success.

His pet would be asleep now. Dreaming of him. About their future. Together. His gifts. The flowers. His poetry. Women loved pink ribbons and poetry.

George glanced at the watch on his wrist and frowned. He was three minutes behind.

He reached into the pockets of his nicest pants. The match-books broke into song as he took them out, all four of them. He crooned as he lit each book and dropped them in. Quiet like. He couldn't have her hearing and calling the firetrucks. Not before he saved her.

He saw yellow, heard a pop. Started counting.

*1, 2, 3, 4...*all the way to six-hundred.

He checked the trashcan. Flames swirled at the bottom. One last step. He picked up two large rocks. Two was greater than one. The window in front of him shattered. The smoke needed to enter the house, make Maggie think she was in danger, just like her horse in the barn.

He jogged to the front of the house, shovel in one hand. The wind kicked up, messing up the hair he'd smoothed with gel. He pressed it back into place. Then made sure his button-down shirt was tucked in, his belt buckle centered, the laces of both his boots tied.

His hands became fists when he saw the front door. He'd never been allowed entrance that way. He'd tried the other night. Failed.

He'd been inside once, through the side door. The memory rushed through him, heated his blood. The way Maggie felt beneath his hands that night. He'd held her down and told her she would marry him. What happened after—he hadn't forgotten those who stopped him.

Her friends wouldn't be able to save her this time. He'd made sure of that. He pulled the rusty blade from his pants and examined it. Flecks of black rubber clung to its rough edge. He wiped it on his knapsack and returned it to the cardboard he'd wrapped it in, shoved it back in his pocket.

Lights came on in another building on the property, the old gardener's place. Bitterness assaulted him, congealed inside him like Mother's gravy. Maggie lied to him at the cafe. She'd hired someone. She'd pay. The gardener's job was his.

He heard the slam of a door, a male voice. He picked up his shovel and crouched out of sight.

A man appeared, a baseball bat in hand. George's mouth gaped. It wasn't possible, but his eyes didn't lie. Malcolm Everson himself, reincarnated, walking toward him. The dead man opened his mouth to speak.

George rushed him, hit him with the shovel.

Malcolm Everson fell.

George clutched his hand to his chest. Euphoria hurt, made his knees shake. The music came louder, its pops, its crackles. The greatest symphony he'd created.

Then he remembered. Maggie waited. He needed to hurry. The fire would go out soon.

He used the metal edge of the shovel to pry the seam of the front door. The surrounding frame cracked, giving way along the side. He kicked the maroon door three times. It swung open.

George stood in the middle of the house at the base of the stairs. They went up and up, into darkness, to her. The wall lights blinked like Christmas bulbs. He was inside the place that should have been his long ago. Now it would be.

Haze filled the space above him. So pretty in the dim light. His eyes misted.

He brushed off his sleeves, adjusted the tie he'd picked for this occasion. Then reached out, gripped the smooth wood of the handrail. He climbed. Two steps at a time. Up and up.

He reached the second story. Her door—the one that matched the window he'd seen her in. Joy rushed through him at the sight. Victory tasted like the smoke he created.

Only seconds now. She'd be his. He couldn't wait to slide his fingers through her dark hair.

George turned the doorknob, threw the door open, and rushed in. He shrieked. Flames licked up the far wall.

No. No. This wasn't right.

The bed had caught as well. Yellow and orange fingers wound around the posts.

No, no, no.

He rushed towards it.

This was wrong. Heat moved over his arms as he reached for the covers. He had to save her.

He pulled them away. Horror struck. The bed was empty. She was gone.

The canopy overhead showered sparks. He felt the pinch of each one on the back of his neck.

A crack sounded. The canopy fell. More pinches.

All wrong.

He'd practiced. At the cabin. The flames never left the metal trashcan.

The rest of the bed caught.

Despair, rage, and pain ripped through him.

He was on fire.

George ran from the room, slapping at his pants, his sleeves. He reached for the railing that led back to the stairs. He had to get out. Make a new plan. Find her.

Voices reached him.

He looked up and froze.

Maggie.

She stood in the smoke. The other side of the stairs.

Her long hair, a swirl of black around her face. His bride.

Their eyes met across the falling sparks. Like glitter.

They would be together after all. He only had to save her.

Then he saw she wasn't alone. A man held onto her. He'd seen this one before, in the woods. Not Malcolm, but he'd have to die as well.

The pain upon his back receded.

Beside him, something black sat on a small table. He reached for it. An old phone. It would do.

Chapter Fifty-Three

Rose tried to roll over, but couldn't manage it. Something heavy hovered. Something wrong.

Her eyes flickered open. She took a breath and immediately coughed. Fog surrounded her as if she were outside in the early dawn amongst the trees. Was this a dream?

Then she heard it.

The fire alarm.

Briar House's original fire alarm, clattering like something out of an antique movie. Or an antique home. Her room wasn't full of fog.

Smoke.

Fire!

She grabbed Finn's shoulder, called his name. His eyes were open. She scrambled out of bed.

"The house—it's on fire."

Finn swore. He stood, pulled his jeans on, and grabbed hers. She dressed quick as she could. Finn opened a dresser drawer and pulled something out. Then grabbed her water bottle by her bedside, using its contents to dampen the clothing.

He handed her one of her own t-shirts, now damp. "Try to keep this over your face."

On impulse, she jammed her socked feet into the new pair of rain boots Mr. Munstead and his daughter had given her. They were too big, but with the situation, they were better than nothing. Finn wore wool socks.

He handed her his wool sweater. "Put this on."

The smell of smoke crept in stronger through the seams of the drafty closed door. Both of them coughed, even with the damp tees against their faces.

She touched the door, then pressed her palm against it. "It's warm."

Beside her, he tapped the doorknob. "Same."

Even if it had been hot, they didn't have a choice. They were on the third floor. She dashed to her window. There were no fire trucks on the gravel drive.

He crouched down, pulling her with him. "Stay low— straight for the stairs if we can."

She nodded, swallowed, and tried not to think of what could happen.

"Ready?" He looked at her with concern as he slipped his fingers through hers.

She nodded and squeezed his hand. "Together."

Finn opened the door. It swung inward. A burst of heat hit their faces. It came from below. She turned her face away in reaction, pressed the cloth harder. The 1920s fire alarm continued to clang, louder now that the door was open. The newer up to code fire alarms emitted their shrill screams, background singers to the ancient one.

She and Finn edged out of the room and made their way toward the stairs. The wall sconces flickered like candles. The stairs so far were untouched. Smoke bellowed below, making it hard to see its source.

Halfway down the first set of stairs, the smoke cleared enough for her to see.

Magnolia's bedroom door stood open. Fingers of flame licked the edges of the doorway as if searching for fuel. Fire and smoke swirled within the room, hungry and loud.

"No."

Finn's expression was grim as he tugged on her. "Come on. We're running out of time."

He kept hold of her hand as they moved toward the second floor as low as they could manage.

That's when Rose saw him, the man who'd caused too much turmoil these past weeks. He skittered out of Magnolia's room. His white hair alone identified him, a contrast to the sight of flames on his legs, his back.

The one the sheriff called harmless.

The one who claimed Magnolia was his.

The man responsible for Boone Murray's injuries. And for the death of Magnolia's horse, Lady, all those years ago.

She froze at the sight of him, forgot what all the smoke, the glowing colors, and crackling sounds around her meant.

Finn's voice brought her back as he turned her to face him. "The floor's unstable. We've got to make a run for it!"

She felt it too. The slight tremble beneath her feet.

They were so close to the second floor landing, just a few feet from the next set of stairs.

But so was George.

He'd spotted her. Even across the smoky space, a chill encircled her wrist.

"Evie, don't look at him. I've got you. Go!"

The second they went into motion, everything blurred.

She heard a roar.

Something hit them.

Her breath left her as her body slammed against the hard

floor. She heard another sound, a sick thud. Felt more pain as Finn landed on top of her.

Trapped beneath his weight, a moment of silence followed, one in which he didn't stir.

"Finn—Finn—damn it! Answer me!" Louder. "Finn!"

He didn't answer, didn't move.

But someone else did.

Dark boots came into view. A foot from where they lay. Sound rushed back along with the overloud beat of her heart.

A sinister voice. "Come out, pet. He can't have you now."

No.

Her heart, her mind. Both screamed. Not Finn. She'd lost enough. She couldn't lose him, too.

The smoke was thicker, muffling the surrounding light. She coughed. Wished Finn would. Then she'd know he was alive.

His weight shifted. His chest against her back. Just a tad.

His hand lay against her side—his fingers, they curled. He was alive.

The icy voice came again. "Come out of there, Maggie. If I have to pull you out, your husband goes over the rail."

Husband? Finn wasn't her…

It came to her. He'd called her Maggie. Damn it.

She needed more time, time for Finn to come all the way around. Even if she could manage it, she didn't think he'd enjoy being dragged down the stairs.

She felt heat on her face. Pinpricks of pain as the flames moved closer. She had to get herself and Finn out. Get rid of the man who threatened them.

Hopefully, the fire department was outside now. Working to help before their time ran out.

"Pet!"

A warning. A word that should never describe a human being. Anger flooded her. If this was the end, she wasn't going down without a fight. With a lot of grunting and effort, she wriggled out from beneath Finn. She grabbed one of the railing spindles and got to her feet. The spindle came with her.

With a choked breath and a cough, she faced the man that had terrorized her and, likely, Magnolia in her last weeks of life.

Rage took fear's place, along with a desire to protect Finn. Love like theirs was hard to find. The two of them had waited long enough. She refused to let him go.

They'd never been in a situation this dangerous. This was no DIY adventure from their youth. This villain's grip was ice and steel. She doubted she could win a fight against him.

For herself, for Finn, for Magnolia, for the rest of her family —she had to try.

The house suffered more damage. She could hear it, feel it. Her home was in pain.

She wished ghosts were real, that they could fight alongside her. Lady with her sharp hooves. Old Macintosh with his supposed shovel. The civil war soldiers. They could use reinforcements.

Finn still lay on the ground unmoving, although she thought he'd shifted again.

There was no sign of rescue. Fire never played soft. Monsters didn't wait for the injured to recover before attacking.

It came down to her and George.

The spindle wasn't what she considered a weapon, but in this moment it was better than nothing. She gripped it tight, hoping it would be enough.

Then—

A flash. A glimmer.

Against the wall, close enough to reach, its blade reflected the flames.

Magnolia's dragon letter opener.

She switched the spindle to her left hand, crouched once more, and reached for the blade. It wasn't as sharp as a knife, but it didn't matter. Her fingers closed around the handle; her fingertips brushed over its emerald dragon eyes. It felt natural as she adjusted her grip, like a dagger, blade side down.

She wanted to survive. With Finn.

Magnolia's words. *I want you to have your happy ever after.*

They deserved that. Whether or not Finn heard her, she vowed, "We are not dying in this house."

She shifted and spoke over the crackles, the heat that inched closer. "I told you—I'm not Maggie."

Hunched over as if ready to strike, George broke into a grin that reminded her of the Cheshire cat mating with a piranha. "I'm going to have fun with you, pet."

With a cry of rage, he rushed toward her. His single-minded purpose had him on a specific course.

Her.

She swung the blade and spindle as hard as she could, let go when she felt the impact, the knowledge she'd stabbed him. She then dove out of the way in some semblance of a self-defense move Thorne had taught her.

George crashed through a section of railing.

His weight, his fall, changed things.

The floor of the landing splintered and pitched downward with a slow groan. Rose slipped, began to slide. A scream tore out of her. Her legs were no longer on a surface.

Hands clamped over her forearms. Finn's face appeared above her, smeared with blood and soot. His eyes were dark, but open.

"I've got you. I'll pull you up."

She kept her eyes focused on him. Even as more embers singed her arms. She wanted to get out of this. She wanted everything with him. Why hadn't she told him yet?

"I love you."

He gave her a hard look. "We're going to make it, Evie." He pulled, evidence of strain on his face. Her body moved upward. Hope pitter-pattered within her heart.

A second set of hands latched onto her. She screamed again as pain exploded through her left side. The weight that came with it took her backwards, along with Finn. His grip slid to her wrists, both hands locked tight, set determination on his face.

Finn said, "I won't let go."

George hadn't fallen.

She tried to kick, but the left didn't respond. Too much weight. Her right leg, though—she kicked as hard as she could manage. And hit something. She couldn't see, didn't dare try. Only knew she had to get this monster to let go of her. Before the rest of the landing went with nothing but dead air beneath.

Crack!

The floor gave way; she was yanked downward. The pressure on her leg was unbearable. More pain lashed up her body. She cried out. She heard a scream, felt a popping sensation in her leg. Her pain eased. She struggled to take a breath.

Finn pulled. She found herself sprawled on top of him, in his arms. There was no time for celebration. They were still on unstable ground. The stairs couldn't be trusted. She tried to crawl. Her left leg wouldn't work right. Finn stood. Despite the blood running down his face, he picked her up and threw her over his shoulder.

With extreme caution, they moved toward the other bedrooms on the second floor. The fire hadn't travelled to Willow and Aspen's old rooms. Upside down, she noticed the bridge was wet.

She heard the squawk of a radio from below, the sound of someone calling their names. Finn paused, pulled her off his shoulder, and answered the call.

"We're up here. Second floor."

A firefighter emerged from Willow's childhood room. He must have come through the window. Only his eyes were visible, but she recognized him. Aidan Conroy.

His voice was serious, near angry. This wasn't the first time he'd helped them out of trouble. "This time, you two have gone too far." She would have hugged him if they weren't still in danger.

Another firefighter appeared.

"Aidan, let's get them out. You can scold later."

Smoke from the house cast an eerie fog around them. Beside Finn, Rose sat on the tailgate of someone's truck, a blanket wrapped around her shoulders. Her leg had been dislocated. The paramedics popped it back into place.

Finn hadn't let go of her. She hadn't let go of him. They'd come too close to death.

He wrapped his arm around her and held her tight.

She leaned against him. "I thought he'd killed you."

"I thought he killed me, too. With a fucking telephone."

They were both treated with oxygen. Each of them had sporadic bouts of coughing. Both had given Reggie and Clare their statements after. Mack and Zane were close by.

Thorne sat on a nearby tree stump with an icepack on his head. A firefighter found him unconscious on the ground. He'd come round but was fuzzy on what happened. They'd go over it again tomorrow.

Finn looked down from where they sat and asked, "Where's your other boot?"

Rose glanced down. One of her wildflower boots was gone. Her left. Given everything that had happened, she hadn't noticed. Had the paramedics removed it? She didn't see it.

George had been holding onto her left leg, likely her boot as well. His weight had dislocated her leg. The boot was a size and a half too big. She could visualize how it'd happened. He'd taken it with him when he fell.

She shook her head in disbelief. "I think that rain boot saved my life."

Her eyes closed. She'd have to thank Mr. Munstead and his daughter.

Finn brushed her hair out of her eyes. "And the fire department? You giving them any credit?"

"What do you think?" She pressed her side against his.

Quick steps sounded on the gravel. Broome broke through the smoke, a look of terror on his face as he rushed into the area. Rose slid off the tailgate and winced. Finn followed, supporting her left side. Thorne eased himself up to stand and moved closer. He slipped an arm around her as well.

With near violence, Broome grabbed all of them into a hug.

Rose squeezed him back. He sounded as if he were crying. An impossibility. He held them for the longest minute and then released them. Then swore and wiped his eyes. She pretended not to notice.

The men and women of EHFD were doing their best to save what they could of the house. The fire wasn't out. They'd kept it from spreading. Occasional flames still flickered amongst the plumes of smoke.

In uniform, Reggie stood beside the fire chief as Ladder 1 arced water over the roof. Yells and squawks came through a nearby radio.

With a splintering sound, a corner of the house collapsed. Rose broke into sobs at the sight. A smaller section followed soon after.

Finn didn't let go of her. Neither did Thorne.

One ambulance left the property. With George Hindley. Firefighters had found him on the first level. They hadn't shared whether he was alive or dead.

Reggie approached, gave each of them a fierce look before turning to Broome. "Thought you should know. They all denied a trip to the hospital by ambulance." He motioned to Rose. "Even this one with her dislocated leg."

She glared at him. "Crud. You would have to say something."

Broome shook his head and gave each of them the *I practi-*

cally raised you look. "All of you know better. Two of you doctors."

He clapped a hand on Reggie's shoulder. "Thanks man. I'll take them in."

Broome moved his SUV closer and opened its doors.

As he helped her into the back seat alongside Finn, Sheriff Hutchins came through the smoke. He looked disheveled, as if he'd thrown yesterday's uniform on.

He asked, "What's going on here?"

Reggie nodded to them and stepped back. "Take them to the hospital. I've got this."

His movements looked militant and controlled as he turned and placed his hand on his service weapon. Rose watched him motion to Mack, Clare, and Zane to join him. Together, the four officers walked toward the sheriff. They surrounded him. Reggie's lips moved. The sheriff's expression turned ugly. Mack held onto his arm as if to keep him there.

A dark SUV came down the driveway fast enough to spit gravel. It braked behind a fire engine. Both doors opened.

A disheveled Louise Winston appeared in the mixture of light and lingering smoke. Her husband, the mayor, followed close behind, looking near as bad.

Broome turned away from Rose. Thorne still stood outside the car, one hand on the passenger door.

Louise Winston ran toward the four police officers. The mayor struggled to keep up.

The woman stopped outside the circle of cops, closest to Sheriff Hutchins, speaking loud enough to hear. "Darin Hutchins! You inept fool! Where is my brother?"

Was she yelling at the sheriff?

Whatever Hutchins said wasn't audible, but Louise clearly didn't like his answer. Through the tiny gap between Reggie and Clare, she struck the man's chest with one fist. "You promised me you would take care of him."

This time, the sheriff's voice carried. "You told me he stopped setting fires. The house behind you—that's his doing."

"Where is he? I'll take him home, take care of him."

Rose exchanged looks with Finn, Broome, and Thorne. She'd never known Louise Winston had a brother. Their families weren't close. It took little thought to connect her brother's identity.

One of them must have told her what happened to George. Louise shook her head as if in denial. Behind her now, the mayor tried to gather his wife into his arms, perhaps to console her. She clearly wasn't having it. Rose's mouth fell open when Louise turned and shoved her husband hard enough to make him fall to the ground.

Then she shifted and attempted the same with the sheriff.

He stumbled back, but Mack still had a hand around his arm. It kept him from falling.

The mayor got to his feet with help from Clare. "Louise, stop this."

Louise said, "Where is she? The little bitch. It's her fault. Her face. I'll take care of her once and for all."

Reggie reached for Louise. It appeared she reached for him. She collided with him, then spun, using the cop as a springboard. A weapon lay in her hand—a gun.

Reggie cursed and dove for the woman as she came towards Broome's SUV. Reggie caught her free arm at the same time she raised the firearm.

Rose's eyes met hers. Louise's face twisted into something ugly. There was no mistaking the level of hatred the woman directed at her.

"Fuck." Thorne's voice.

The world around her slowed. Her car door slammed, as did Thorne's. Broome moved, perhaps taking cover. Finn curled over her in the seat. She waited for the sound of gunfire.

It never came.

Chapter Fifty-Four

Smoke filled clothes lay discarded on the bathroom floor attached to Broome and Simi's guest room. Finn fell into bed beside Rose after a quick shower. She was already asleep.

He glanced at the nightstand on Rose's side of the bed. A digital clock read five a.m. Despite their ordeal, he hadn't fallen asleep. Too many what ifs. He kept his arms snug around her. Each rise and fall of her chest against his hand reassured him they were alive. That she was alive.

He'd almost lost her. He'd never forget those moments, opening his eyes to see Rose facing off with a madman. Her slide backwards. The fear he wouldn't reach her in time. His head ached, but the pain seemed nothing compared to how close he'd come to losing her.

Her love of rain boots had saved her life. Who would have thought?

She shifted in her sleep, made a small noise. The straps of her leg brace rubbed against his knee. The hospital had given her an injection for pain, but she continued to fret in her sleep.

The threat afterwards, Louise Winston holding a gun, seemed minor compared to what happened inside the house.

Sunlight trailed over the room's curtains as Finn drifted off. Dreams came.

Not of the nightmare of the recent hours, but of a night years ago when he'd been only eight.

The barn fire on the Briar House estate.

This time, he wasn't a participant. The nightmare played like a movie.

He and his parents showed up to help. His parents moved forward, took their places on the bucket brigade. He rushed to find Rose and Thorne, along with their siblings, all in pajamas and nightgowns. A younger, wide-eyed Chelsea stood beside her aunt. He'd forgotten she'd been there. Their neighbor, Ty, gave them a task. To help the bucket brigade. They ran the empty buckets back to the beginning of the line by the creek.

Sirens cut through the night. The firetrucks pulled in. Swirling lights illuminated all the people helping. The bucket brigade retreated once the firefighters rolled out their hoses and set up.

He saw himself, the other kids, gather around his mom, Ms. Tess, and Aunt Norah. All of their gazes fixed on the burning barn.

They pulled a person out of the barn, thankfully still alive. He'd later learn that Boone Murray had been watching over a mare about to foal. He'd been taken quickly away by ambulance.

The horses were evacuated, tied to trail posts on the edge of the woods. Except for one. Lady. She hadn't come out with the others. The flames grew.

Some said later that the beautiful horse Lady shouldn't have been able to walk, let alone run at full force out of the stable. Not in the condition she'd been in.

No one stopped her. They may have been too scared.

He heard the scream as he had then. Witnessed again the moment Lady erupted from the barn, her coat smoldering. A long, glowing metal chain struck the ground behind her. Alongside the other frightened kids, he watched the dark horse come to an abrupt halt in front of Ms. Magnolia. A man stood in front of her as if ready to protect her.

Love was like that. He'd witnessed how Lady stuck to Ms. Magnolia as if she'd been the one to foal her.

When the beautiful mare went down to her knees, Ms. Magnolia went with her, running her hands over the horse's head and along her neck. Someone hosed Lady down with water. Others stepped up to help guide Lady down to her side as gently as possible.

Even then, at eight years old, he knew. No horse came out like that and lived. His mom's arms fixed around him, Rose, and Thorne.

Her shaky voice, thick with tears, said, "Close your eyes."

He could hear Tess' soft voice saying the same thing, her arms wrapped around Willow and Chelsea.

He'd closed his eyes, just like Mom said, but it grew so quiet as if a wind had blown all the sound away. Then he'd heard it, the cock of a single gun, just like Pa's. His eyes opened. He couldn't look away.

He watched Ms. Magnolia point a gun at her own horse, the one Rose called her favorite. A man stood behind her, his hands over hers.

Even from where he stood, he saw Ms. Magnolia was crying. Finn felt sorry for her. Did they really have to—

The gun fired. His younger self closed his eyes as if doing so could erase what he'd just seen. It hadn't. For weeks, he relived that sight in his nightmares. Both his folks sat with him each time, explaining that the horse had been in considerable pain, that it had been a mercy. He understood what they were saying, but the nightmares didn't stop. He relived that night again and again. For months.

He woke on his back, covered in sweat. Rose slept quietly beside him.

It had been years since he'd watched Lady die. He had felt and seen all that his younger self had. But there was more.

For the first time, he noticed the identity of the man who'd had his hands around Ms. Magnolia's when the gun fired. The same man who held a sobbing woman in his arms, just like Pa held Mom after.

He moved closer to Rose, curled an arm around her, and drifted back into sleep.

When Finn fully woke a few hours later, he remembered the nightmare. Questions swirled. Could one trust the images seen in flashback dreams? If so, the man holding Ms. Magnolia, had the two of them ever been involved?

Chapter Fifty-Five

R ose hobbled out of Broome's guest room around noon, wearing the blasted oversized leg brace the hospital had given her. Her steps were slow and careful, a steadying hand on the hallway wall. She didn't remember undressing or climbing into bed, couldn't remember what time she and Finn had been discharged from the hospital. Had it still been dark?

Exhaustion, trauma, and the pain injection the hospital gave her combined to send her into a deep sleep. She'd woke once, the brace around her leg tangled in the sheets. Finn helped her get settled, but sleep had been difficult after.

Images of their brush with death flickered against her closed eyes. Every synonym for fear tumbled through her mind while she lay in an unfamiliar bed. Anxiety, panic, terror…she felt them all as she drifted back to sleep.

She entered the kitchen in the borrowed clothes Simi had set out for her. Too short baggy pants and an oversized floral tee.

Finn sat in the kitchen nook, on a cushioned wraparound bench, a plate of untouched food on the table in front of him. She studied him. He looked worn, a little pale.

Her voice came out raspy when she asked, "How's your head?"

He met her gaze with his own. "Heavy. You?"

"I've had better nights." She moved closer and ran her fingers through the hair on the back of his neck. "Is this okay?"

He bent his neck forward. "Please."

She continued. A hum of content came from his throat. She stopped when Broome entered the kitchen.

"Afternoon, Rose." He pulled a chair out for her. She took a seat, stretched her left leg out in front of her at an angle. He poured himself some coffee and brought the pot over, holding it up in question.

She nudged the stemmed coffee mug towards him. "Please."

"Glad you're awake." He glanced at Finn, seemed to take in how full his plate was. "How do you feel about food, Rose?"

"I'll try." Eggs would work, but she wasn't so sure about the chewy bacon she saw on Finn's plate. Her throat felt raw, sore. The hospital ran bloodwork on her and Finn to make sure everything was okay. She hadn't coughed up gray or black mucus, a sign she hadn't swallowed soot.

Finn pushed his plate away and said, "Sorry, Broome— something about the eggs. Too yellow."

Rose caught the amused uplift of her brother's expression.

Concern lined his next words. "Toast? I also have crackers Simi uses for morning sickness."

Finn grimaced. "A piece of toast should work."

"Simi made you both honey tea for your throats. It's strong, but it's a miracle worker."

He stood and grabbed a teapot from its warmer. Poured them both a mug. The tang of the honey was mixed with chamomile. It didn't pair well with coffee, but she got it down.

Broome put a half-filled plate in front of Rose, made toast for Finn, then joined them.

He ate his own bacon, eggs, and fruit. "George Hindley is dead."

Finn spoke first. "Good."

Rose had no words. Not any that would be sympathetic. Even as she recognized he too had a mother and father that loved him. Tears gathered in her eyes. That monster had almost killed her, along with people she loved. Now he was gone.

Broome put a hand on her shoulder. "Rose, did you hear me?"

She looked at him. "I heard you. He's dead. He can't hurt anyone now."

He studied her. Then squeezed her shoulder. "How's the leg?"

"It hurts." At least she'd been able to sleep some.

"We can pick up the pain prescription."

"No, I'm fine with what I have."

"Also," Broome said. "Jeremy called this morning. It looks like Hindley slashed a few tires on his way to you. His truck, Sam's sedan, and Hal's pickup all had flats. Only Brigette's SUV and the mayor's vehicle lacked damage—both were garaged."

Rose shook her head, "They helped Magnolia before, kept George from raping her. And he thought she was me."

Broome ran a hand over his jaw. "Seems so."

"What else?"

He continued. "Both the sheriff and Louise Winston are in custody. Turns out, Reggie's been working with the Asheville Police Department to investigate some inconsistencies in George Hindley's release and his recent bail hearing. They found enough to justify Hutchins' detainment."

Rose had a memory of Louise with a gun. Then something about her on the ground. "Did Louise try to shoot me?"

Broome nodded, his expression filled with torment. "Yes. Clare stopped her. Louise has been charged with attempted murder."

Rose looked up. "Wow."

Finn uttered one word. "Winston?"

"Devastated. Cooperating as best he can with the investigation."

Rose ate her eggs and drank her tea.

Broome said, "I took the day off. Aspen and Willow will pick up Thorne once he's discharged. That should be in the next few hours. I don't want you seeing the house alone. We'll face it together."

She had no objection. Her mind felt fractured. Images, the fear of last night, the house in flames around them. Had any part of the house survived?

She turned to Finn. He'd finished his toast. "What about you? Your next shift."

He gingerly threaded his fingers with hers. "I called last night while you were in the exam room. I'm here for you. Doc Walters said I'm out for a bit with this minor concussion. Driving not recommended."

She used the slightest tease in her voice. "And you're going to listen?"

"Funny." He squeezed her hand.

Late afternoon, Rose stood beside her loved ones, all together in a jagged line on the gravel driveway. Simi, Broome, Thorne, Aspen, and Willow, all beside her along with Finn, his arm around her waist. In one hand, she held the handle of a sturdy cane, one Simi kept for her dad when he visited. Broome's hand wrapped around Thorne's upper arm as if to insure he remained upright. Thorne hadn't complained yet.

Sunlight teased through wispy clouds overhead. Briar House stood before them, now a haphazard Victorian puzzle. Smoke clung to its remaining walls, and those that had fallen.

A single fire engine remained. Two men were assigned to make sure nothing would re-ignite. The fire investigator had been present when they arrived.

There was no question about the cause. The investigator pointed out the metal trashcan that had been used to start the blaze. Chills went through Rose. Years before, George Hindley was convicted for using a similar metal trashcan in the barn fire.

Tears ran rivulets down Willow and Simi's faces. With his other arm, Broome pulled his wife closer, pressed his lips to her temple. His expression held strength and determination. As if he could fix this latest blow to their family.

Aspen stood alone, pale, one hand pressed to her stomach. Gavin hadn't shown, not at the hospital last night or here today. Thorne's jaw clenched as he stood beside Broome.

Rose's sorrow echoed what she felt when they lost Magnolia. The house was an extension of her, its walls one more piece of what she'd given them years before. Her love, a safe place, a home.

Alongside a firefighter, Finn, and Broome, Rose picked her way to the threshold of the morning room with the help of the cane. Finn remained close by to help her maneuver through the ruins. Its walls looked like oversized splinters, as if an angry hand axed them to shreds. All the room's windows were gone, along with the ceiling. The blue sky above them matched the original color of the room. All that remained were the stones of the fireplace. The mantel and the wall above it had burned, along with the spot Magnolia's prized painting of Lady hung.

Thank goodness Willow had noticed the crack in its frame, had taken it with her to get it repaired. Such a small detail in the scheme of things, but Rose was thankful the painting still existed. She saw it in her mind—a new frame, above a rebuilt mantel on a sky blue wall.

Nothing remained of Magnolia's bedroom that she could see. It had stood just over this spot, the wrap-around view, the best outside of the morning room.

The space where the ballroom once stood looked as if a giant excavator had scooped it right off the back of the house.

Broome's bedroom and a bathroom were also gone. Thankfully, his had been transformed into a guest room years ago. All his personal items went with him after he'd married.

The family regrouped in front of the house. All looked at what remained. It reminded Rose of the first time she'd seen the house, when they'd come here to live. At six years old, she'd been unable to look away as Broome kept hold of her hand while they approached the front door for the first time. The many windowed house didn't resemble the pictures in her book of fairytales. There was no moat, no drawbridge, no stone wall around it. It looked solid, honest. She reached out to hold on to the wooden rail above the front steps and gripped the front post. And felt connection, a whisper of undefined magic, a hug around her heart.

Rose couldn't leave the house like this. She turned to those who stood beside her.

An array of emotions ran across their faces, but they weren't looking at the house anymore. They were looking at her.

Thorne spoke first. "What do you want to do with the house, baby sis?"

As if there were ever a question whilst she walked amongst what remained and what was lost.

Briar House had its own story. As did every person who'd lived within its walls.

More chapters waited to be written.

"I'm going to rebuild her. We need her as much as she needs us."

Broome gave a single nod. Approval shone in his tired eyes. "I'll help you make the phone calls."

Aspen nodded as well, her face still shiny with tears, but she sent Rose a glance. "I'll help too. She was right to leave it to you."

Chapter Fifty-Six

In the days between hospital shifts, Finn drove back to Evers Hollow. He stayed with Rose in the cottage while they continued to heal both mentally and physically from their respective injuries.

The cottage on the Briar House estate looked and felt different now. Less like Rose. Maybe it was the boxes she'd stacked in the entryway that hadn't moved because of the fire. Perhaps it was the absence of pieces of furniture he'd helped move to the big house before the fire. Some were lost in the blaze. Those that survived awaited professional cleaning from smoke damage.

Finn's nightmares hadn't gone away. Recurring, they were a mix of the past and present. Some nights he was on the landing over the stairs, opening his eyes and watching his Evie fall. Others, he dreamt of Lady and the barn fire. On the stairs, sometimes he lost Rose to the swirl of flames below; sometimes they both fell. The barn fire one remained the same every time.

He'd been in Asheville this past week, working, transitioning back to full time as the distance from that horrible night lengthened. He realized his apartment wasn't a home; he'd missed waking up beside Rose. Yet he had over a year left of his residency.

He wanted to spend forever with her. He saw the rest of their lives together. Children, hopefully, a dog or two. And moments of rescuing her in the rose garden. She'd snagged a pair of cargo pants last week before he'd left for Asheville.

"It's not my fault. The wind did it, sent the branches right into me."

Funny how the roses stayed still while he unstuck her from their barbs.

A curse came from the bedroom. Doc Mason insisted she continue to use a leg brace and had prescribed her physical therapy.

He found her seated on the edge of the bed, fastening the plastic buckles around her leg.

Unlike the rest of the cottage, her bedroom still looked like her. Multiple pillows leaned against the headboard. A stack of books sat on her nightstand. She stood as she wound a hair band around the long braid of her hair.

"I'm ready. Are you going to tell me where we're going?"

"No." Finn pulled out his phone, typed a brief text and hit *send.*

His nightmares drove him to make this phone call.

These past weeks, he and Rose talked about her birth story, and the lack of information around it. Finn wanted answers for her.

Despite her recovery progress, she seemed off kilter. It wasn't just her leg, or the obsession one man carried for her. Nor was it the fact that she'd lost someone vital to her life.

Rose didn't like unfinished puzzles. Her birth story was one of them, the identity of her father another. Her childhood drive to find answers hadn't diminished, but she needed the next clue.

The question of Rose's birth father was one of those.

Together, they locked up the cottage and climbed into his

SUV. She held the cane Simi loaned her. He could tell she was trying not to use it.

Before he buckled his seatbelt, she asked, "Are we going to another birthday party?"

If only. Two weeks had passed since he'd driven her to Landon's eighth birthday party. Rose had taken to the little boy along with Dare, Kendra, and the twins. The hug Kendra gave her implied the family felt the same. They'd left with promises to get together in the future.

He said, "We're meeting someone." He didn't want to say who. She'd talk him out of it.

Finn left the gravel drive and turned toward town. As they passed Cracked Egg Cafe, he spotted The Elders inside, at their usual spot by the front window.

They reached the north edge of town, passing the turnout for the newer subdivisions. He took a right onto Cemetery Road. Almost bare trees whipped by his vehicle. Fallen leaves swirled around them, curve after curve. He slowed, took a steep, paved driveway up and parked when it leveled off.

A squarish split-level cabin stood in front of them, likely built in the fifties. Yellowed wood planks covered the outside. A short wooden staircase led to a green door. Finn stayed in the car, hoping they wouldn't have to wait long. A glance at his phone gave him his answer.

"Who lives here?"

"Patience." His eyes turned to the rearview mirror.

Minutes later, another set of tires came in behind him. An old pickup pulled into a carport off to the side. Finn got out.

Rose followed, eyes curious.

Finn moved to her side, clasped her face in his hands, and kissed her gently before putting an arm around her. Her leg may have improved, but she still needed TLC.

A tall figure in a barn coat climbed out of the pickup.

Finn's arm tightened around her when her steps faltered.

"Hal?" She looked at Finn. "I don't understand. Why didn't we go to the cafe?"

Hal motioned toward the front door. "Come on in." He held the door, motioned toward the table. Rose sat.

Finn moved a chair so she could elevate her leg if needed. He knew he hovered, but he needed to.

Hal closed the door and hung his coat up. "I'll make some coffee." He moved past them into a hallway kitchen. "Make yourselves at home."

Paneled walls the color of honey stood behind a sagging burnt orange couch along one wall. Embroidered pillows sat at either end. A dark brown recliner sat catty-corner to it. Framed photos of wildlife hung on the wall. A few more of Hal and his wife sat on the mantle of a stone fireplace.

Hal pulled out three mugs from a cabinet while the coffee maker percolated on the counter. He set a cracked yellow sugar bowl and a can of powdered creamer on the table. Rose sat quietly, looking around the room. The yellow and maroon wallpaper looked from another time. His mom would have liked the yellow.

Hal filled the mugs, then folded his tall frame onto one of the wooden chairs. "What's this about?"

Finn glanced at her before answering. "We have some questions about Magnolia."

Chapter Fifty-Seven

Rose glanced between Hal and Finn. What was this?

"We've answered every question she and her siblings have asked," said Hal. "Nola's gone. The loss hurts all of us, but we can't change it."

His sorrow was visible. The Elders were a tight-knit group, a fixture in their small town for as long as she could remember.

Finn leaned forward. "I'm sorry to bother you about this, but I've been having nightmares."

Hal studied him. "That's normal, after what both of you lived through."

Finn nodded, swallowed beside her. "Some of them are about the barn fire, the one that—"

"—No need to say it. I've never forgotten that night."

Rose reached out and took Finn's hand. "Why didn't you tell me?"

But she already knew the answer. She still had nightmares as well about the recent fire and hadn't wanted to talk about them.

Finn shrugged. "I remember when Lady died—that you helped Ms. Magnolia pull the trigger."

Surprised by his admission, she said, "You never told me that. We were supposed to keep our eyes closed."

"Trust me, I regret opening mine. Why you, Hal?"

The older man toyed with the handle of his mug. "I was the veterinarian. Also, I knew Nola. A bit of her died that night, knowing what she had to do. I didn't want her to feel alone with her pain."

Rose froze mid-sip, her mind gathering questions.

Hal continued. "When she lost her husband, it took her a long time to heal. I understood what she was going through when I lost my wife. I used to come and sit with her. Sometimes, we'd ride horses on the trails. There was no need for talk."

The merest of smiles graced his lips. "Then I came across Lady at a place up north, near the Virginia border. She had a suitable temperament for Nola. So, I bought her and brought her to Briar House."

This man had bought Lady as a gift for her birth mother?

He chuckled then, lost perhaps in the memory. "It was love at first sight, so strong that Nola couldn't refuse the gift. It vexed her."

Her voice sounded off when she spoke. "I never knew that."

"It was awhile ago. Did you know I took her to prom?"

"Brigette mentioned something about all of you asking her out, but she didn't mention prom."

He laughed once more. "Brigette was so besotted with Jeremy that I could have brought my horse to the dance without her noticing."

Rose couldn't help but ask. "Were the two of you together?"

He nodded, looking lighter than she'd seen in weeks. "We actually did, in secret, back in high school. No one knew, not even our closest friends. I had to get permission from her father about the prom. Malcolm knew my character; he trusted me with his horses, and gave his consent for prom. He also made sure I knew his future plans for his daughter would never involve me. It didn't stop the way I felt about her."

Malcolm Everson sounded like a snob.

Rose blinked as she tried to process his words.

They'd dated in high school long before she came along. She didn't see the relevance.

Yet she noticed the way Hal's hands tightened around his mug, the slight slosh of coffee over its edge, and the tightness in his voice when he spoke again. "I graduated the year before her. America got involved in another war. All of us men felt compelled to enlist except Clyde. He was the only one who had family money for college."

"Nola went to college, well versed in her father's expectations for her. We made no promises to each other. We exchanged letters during my first tour. After my second, I came home and learned she'd married Devin Brooks and moved to New York City."

Hal stood, got more coffee. Even though his mug still held plenty.

"After my tour, I received tuition assistance and went to university. I majored in Animal Science. Got my veterinary license. Met Martha. We married after I opened my practice here in Evers Hollow. Nola inherited the house when Malcolm passed. She and Devin moved down here. Daisy was a toddler. Adorable kid. Brown pigtails, freckles, much like your sister, Willow."

He paused. They were used to Hal's long winded stories and the pauses. His gaze locked on something outside the window. What did he see out there?

"Nola and I decided we could exist as friends. She and Devin were happy. All I wanted was for her to be happy."

There was another pause before he said, "You look so much like her."

"Brigette says the same thing."

He looked towards the mantle. Half a dozen frames of him and his wife sat up there.

His next words came out strained, as if they were difficult ones to say. "If Devin had been less of a man, I would have resented him. He was a good person though, made her happy, a solid friend to us all. I loved Martha, but I never forgot how I felt about Nola. She was my first love."

Rose's next breath felt sharp. All the tumblers slid into place. Not just a first love, but maybe the last as well. The words came out before she thought to stop them. "You slept together."

He didn't need to answer. The answer was on his face, in his eyes. "We did." Hal hadn't moved. Both his hands circled his coffee mug. "Again, we kept it to ourselves."

Finn laced his fingers between hers.

She studied Hal. Thought about the timing. Had they been together when she was conceived? She couldn't find herself in his features. But it was possible. It was naïve of her to ignore the men who were closest to Magnolia. Brigette herself had said all of them had asked her out at one time or another. That she'd refused them all. Except Hal. He'd taken her to prom.

She gathered her words. "Magnolia's not my grandmother. She's my mother."

"You don't say." An automatic response given without thought. It was clear when he realized what she'd said.

Hal's eyes narrowed as he focused on her. She held her breath.

"Your mother—how is that—?" His expression changed to confusion, then to one of astonishment. "You can't think I'm— no—Martha and I couldn't have kids."

Finn asked, "Is it possible that only Martha couldn't have kids?"

Instead of answering, Hal pushed himself away from the table and stood. "I—I need some air."

Finn stood too, wrapped his hand around his upper arm as the man swayed. Hal sank into his seat, shock evident on his face. Then he put his head in his hands. A wrenching sound of anguish escaped him. His shoulders shook with near silent grief.

Rose moved closer to him and placed her hand on his shoulder.

He lifted his head a tad. "She came to me, told me she had to leave town, asked me to take care of the horses. So sudden, no explanation. I had no way to reach her. No idea of where she'd gone." The worry he'd felt then showed on his face.

Rose had known none of this. She said, "She went to England. There's a cottage there, near her sister. She stayed there for a time."

He went on as if he hadn't heard her speak. "I'd asked her to marry me. Told her I still loved her. She told me she couldn't marry me. That she couldn't go against her father, even in death. I never knew what she meant, but I assumed there were conditions, ones that kept her from being with someone like me. She was gone for months, stubborn woman. When she came back, she looked thinner, like she'd been sick. I tried to talk to her. But she was distant."

Rose said, "Tess was awful worried about her. I found out recently."

He sighed, shook his head. "I'm sorry. That must have been difficult for Tess. They were like sisters. Nola didn't come to breakfast at the cafe. Not for a long while. I continued to care for the horses after she returned. Checked on her like I'd promised Devin. She resented that, but never told me to stop."

He pulled a worn bandanna from his pocket and wiped his eyes. "Then the car accident happened. Poor Daisy and Clark, poor all of you. Another blow. I remember the day you moved in." He ran both his hands through his hair. "I tried to pay condolences for your, I mean, your…"

"Mom and Dad." She smiled at him. "Daisy will always be

my mom. Magnolia's my Magnolia. It's what she preferred I call her. Now I know why."

"We should do one of those DNA tests to be sure." He cleared his throat. His face flushed.

Finn said, "I can arrange that."

Rose explained all she'd learned these past weeks about Magnolia.

Hal shook his head. "I can't believe she kept this from me. If she were still here, I'd have strong words. Couldn't tell her what to do once she made her mind up. Too stubborn for her own good."

Then he stood steady on his feet this time. She did the same.

He put his hands on her shoulders. "I would have loved to call you daughter."

Tears came to her eyes as she wrapped her arms around him to hug him. "I'd say there's still time."

Chapter Fifty-Eight

Rose cuddled against Finn on the bench outside the cottage, a quilt tucked around both of them. The sun still lit the sky above them, but soon it would drop below the treeline. The sleeves of her sweater covered her hands, her fingers curled around their hems below the quilt.

It felt strange moving back to the cottage. It no longer felt like her place. She'd moved most of her belongings to Briar House. Some had survived; some hadn't. A stacked row of boxes sat in front of her bookshelves in the family space.

The back and forth with insurance had been maddening these past weeks. She'd applied for grants through regional historic preservation societies. The last of the estimates had come in from the construction companies she'd reached out to. She was closer to deciding who would do the rebuild. She'd consult with her siblings at their next family dinner.

Since the fire, Finn had bounced between his apartment and Evers Hollow. Rose sometimes accompanied him.

A gust of wind threw a flurry of leaves upward. They clattered as they whirled and settled to the ground.

Finn shifted beside her and said, "I found something I want to share."

He reached inside his coat pocket to pull out a leather bound book. It looked well-loved, its pages swelling thicker than the spine allowed. A piece of a leather belt secured it, keeping it together. A wide green ribbon stuck out of the top as if it were a bookmark.

He said, "With the downtime, I've been going through more of my mom's things."

Her brow wrinkled, but she removed her hands from beneath the quilt to touch the worn cover. "What is it?"

"Mom's journal," he said. "Before we moved here, she was a labor and delivery nurse in Winston-Salem."

He undid the belt. It sprang open, revealing pictures and scraps of paper tucked inside its pages.

"Why are you showing it to me?"

He kissed her once, gently. "Patience, Evie. It's my turn to tell a story."

She couldn't help but kiss him back. "Are there dragons?"

"No."

"I'm listening."

"Mom loved babies. She believed every life brought into the world was special. This journal contains the stories of those she helped deliver, first names only. The pictures in here, all taken with parental permission and a signed promise that she'd never use them for ill purposes. Some parents declined, but some sent her a birth announcement with a thank you card. They're all in here, some taped, others loose. She described the night I was born as unique."

Rose raised an eyebrow. "Aren't all babies' births unique?"

He pressed a finger to her lips, then tapped the book. "She told me about mine repeatedly. Like many children who'd rather be on adventures with their best friend, I ignored the story."

His hand slid over the cover of the book. "Good thing she wrote it down, so I'd have the story forever."

Rose reached out and touched the cover. It was a beautiful thought. How many infants had his mom helped deliver?

Finn continued. "You can read it yourself. I arrived a few weeks early, surprised both of my parents. When her water broke, she was on shift."

"That must have been frightening."

"Before she went into labor, a woman came in alone. Her water broke while she was driving, sent her into labor…she had a baby girl."

He intertwined their fingers, looked into her eyes. "Turned out the birth mother had set up an adoption."

Her eyes widened. "Are you saying—"

"Let me finish." He swallowed. "After you got engaged, I—I avoided town, avoided news of you. I didn't want to hear about your husband, two and a half kids, your dog. I assumed you had the perfect life."

Her life hadn't been close to perfect. Not even the dog.

He said, "Then I found that stack of pictures in my mom's things. She wanted you to have the pictures. She'd put your name on them. I…"

His eyes mirrored what she felt. "Finn."

"The conversation I had here—Ms. Magnolia mentioned a favor my mom did for her. That she wished to repay a debt."

"I don't understand."

"Neither did I. It took a bit to put the pieces together." He opened the journal to a page with the green ribbon. Then pointed to a section of cursive writing. "Start here."

First, she noticed the date. January 18th. The day after she was born. The same date after Finn was born. Feminine handwriting filled each line, each word a form of artwork.

When she hesitated, he put his hands around hers and tilted the pages toward the porch light. He read aloud.

My heart broke for the mother and her babe. So much smaller than my Finn, but her cry made up for it. The mother told me the babe would be better off with the couple she'd chosen. I looked the other way as the woman seemed to imbue her love for the child in a single kiss on the forehead.

Chills moved through her. Was it even possible? "Surely you can't think…"

"Turn the page."

She did.

The first line.

She named her Rose.

"Criminy." She reached toward the page as tears trailed down her cheeks. Her fingers traced the four words.

Finn said, "I came across this journal the same day I found the pictures of us. I didn't read it then. Took me till recent to pick it up."

Emotion clogged her voice.

Finn continued. "The day I brought the pictures here, Ms. Magnolia mentioned the favor my mom did for her, how she hadn't gotten the chance to return it. She didn't tell me what it was. Pa refused to answer my questions about it."

At that, Rose tilted her head.

Finn said, "This never occurred to me. Not when you told me the truth about your birth mother. Not when I learned we shared a birthday. Your birth certificate, though, it looked familiar. I pulled mine up on my computer and learned we were both delivered at the same hospital. Then I remembered the day I met you, what happened when we came to the Memorial Day BBQ."

"What do you mean?" She recollected seeing him, how he ignored her, until she took matters into her own hands.

"The look on Ms. Magnolia's face. She went white as a sheet when we approached her. Pa reached out a hand to steady her. He thought she was going to faint. When I asked what was wrong, my folks told me to go play. I ran off, but when I looked back, Ms. Magnolia had disappeared. I could tell Mom was upset. Pa was holding her. Then I read Mom's journal."

Her gaze returned to the bound book. Below her name, affixed by yellowed Scotch tape, sat a photo of two babies, one with dark hair, one with red. Whoever held each of them was hidden, but they stood close enough that both babies' fingers appeared to be entwined together.

"Is this—" She couldn't finish. She sniffled and pressed the soft hem of her sleeve to her eyes. "This is—things don't happen like this."

He slipped his free hand around hers. "This is us. This has to be what Ms. Magnolia meant. Mom kept her secret. Never told a soul as far as I can figure out. She wrote more about the woman's care, and yours. This was an unusual photo to take, but perhaps my mom and yours forged a bond of sorts that night. We'll never know."

She leaned back into him, her head on his shoulder. "Your mom was a special person. So was Magnolia. I wonder if they ever talked about it?"

He shrugged. "I don't know."

"The thing is, after I found the pictures, I came back to Evers Hollow because of them. I came back here for you." He laced their fingers together, turned to face her. "You know I love you. That I have for a long time. I can't say I was mature about it."

She teased, "Definitely not." But neither was she. Maybe

they needed those years apart to figure out who they were without each other.

She raised a hand, brushed her fingers over the slight stubble along his jaw. Sparks trailed up her arm, through her shoulder, then wound their way around her heart. She needed to make sure he knew how she felt.

With a deep breath, she said, "I've always known there was something about you, something that drew me in. I believed you when you told me the first time, but know, deep in my heart, I love you right back. I can't imagine my life without you."

Chapter Fifty-Nine

Dr. Sam Cook lived in a Craftsman bungalow on Poplar Street. The exterior was well-maintained, freshly painted. The landscape was the same. Trimmed shrubs, cut grass, and potted evergreens on either side of the front door. Finn pressed the doorbell.

Sam ushered him through the house onto a screened porch. Doctors Simon Mason and Thorne Finch were seated, drinking from coffee mugs. Finn shook their hands and took a seat.

Sam did the same. "Let's get this meeting started. Simon, do you want to start with the interview?"

Interview?

Simon sat taller, cleared his throat.

Finn couldn't help himself. "Who's being interviewed?"

Thorne smirked with a chin tip. "You're the only one who needs a job."

This made no sense. He was still in residency.

Simon said, "I'm planning ahead. I'd rather talk to you here instead of in the office. No interruptions from my staff."

His words made sense, but interview? He could have

prepared, studied, worn something besides shorts and a t-shirt. At least his paint stained jeans were in the wash.

The other three exchanged looks, reminding him of a hive mind.

Thorne asked, "Do you remember the night we found Camille after the soccer game?"

"Of course." How could he forget coming across a classmate in labor after her car had bounced off a guardrail and ended up in a ditch?

Simon rested his elbows on his knees. "I've heard the story, but not from you. Did you change your clothes?"

"Excuse me?"

"Before you helped Miss Crane. Did you change your clothes?"

Finn shook his head. "No. She needed help. She was injured. Her baby was coming. Best we could do was pour water on our hands and use hand sanitizer."

"Who delivered the baby?"

"We—" He paused. He'd been sixteen, Thorne seventeen. He'd considered it a team effort, as if both of them had caught the kid when she pushed him out. Except Thorne stayed by Cam's head, letting her hold on to him while she screamed and pushed.

"It was me. I delivered the baby." Thorne stood in for the person who should have been talking Cam through her contractions.

Simon nodded. "I did a wellness check on Connor Crane last month. Eleven years old. Camille told me the two of you handled the situation in a calm, straightforward manner. Especially considering your ages."

Finn shook his head. "We were lucky that night. Neither of us knew what we were doing. If there'd been complications…"

Thorne straightened. "There weren't. Connor's doing great."

Finn knew. Camille was friends with his old neighbor, Chelsea. She kept him up to date on Connor.

Simon said, "Tell me more about your residency. What's your life goals? Your perfect job when you feel you've earned the title of doctor?"

What was this? "I don't understand. I have a year and a half left."

Simon folded his arms. "I have an increasing number of patients. It's only going to rise with the new subdivision going in. I'm behind already. I have a waitlist. Sam helps two days a week, but he's also determined to help the refugees in the campground. He's supposed to be retired."

Sam grunted. "As long as I can make Thursday breakfast and play golf once a week, I'm happy."

Simon appeared to ignore him. "I need another doctor in my practice."

Finn looked at Thorne. He was a fully fledged doctor, an ideal choice.

Thorne said, "I've got a job and a second, bigger task at hand."

Finn said, "I can't accelerate time, Simon, but I'm honored by the ask."

"I know." Simon heaved a sigh. "I'll need references, of course. We'll have to do a formal interview, but unless things change, you have a job offer if you want it."

He didn't know what to say. His dream was to be a doctor here in Evers Hollow.

"I don't know what to say."

"Yes would be a great answer."

What would Rose think of this? Things were wonderful between them, a dream he didn't want to question. They hadn't talked about forever yet.

"Can I think about it?"

"Of course. This is a casual conversation."

Thorne stood. "It's not the only reason you're here."

"Oh?" What else could there be?

"My grandmother tasked me to do my damnedest to reopen Hollows Hospital."

That got Finn's attention. "I thought they declared bankruptcy. How does a hospital come back from that?"

"It's a process. I'm in conversations with the Department of Public Health, the hospital's most recent board of directors, potential investors, and hospital systems that might be interested in a partnership."

"Why you?"

Sam cut in. "The Everson family was one of the original investors. Nola held a seat on the board, along with Lancet Hughes and Gerard Roche. She wanted Thorne to take her place."

"I see." Not really.

Thorne said, "There's one more thing, Finn, that concerns you, your family," Thorne said.

"What's that?"

He pulled an envelope from his pack. "Broome wanted to be the one to hand this to you, but his schedule didn't line up. If you have questions, call him. He'll meet with you."

Finn accepted the parcel. His fingers traced over the sealed flap.

"What's in there—not a done deal. Talk with your dad. I promise to make it possible. It's what Grandmother wanted."

Finn stood, even more confused. He wouldn't open the envelope here. The curiosity tormented him as he drove back to Rose's.

In her cottage kitchen, he scanned the first page, then read it again, more slowly. Then again. Understanding crept in.

Clara did something for me once. I always hoped I would get a chance to return the gesture.

The contents of this envelope. It would make Pa cry. It made him cry. He reached for the box of Kleenex.

The next morning, backpack over his shoulder, Finn dropped by Wylder to see his pa. He showed him the contents of the envelope. He was right. Tears trickled over Pa's cheeks as he wiped a handkerchief over his eyes.

"They want to name a wing after my Clara."

"Yes, the women's and children's wing," said Finn.

He sniffled, wiped again. "She would've tried to talk them out of it, but secretly, she'd love it. She loved her work. Delivering babies and taking care of children."

Finn would let Thorne know they loved the idea.

"I need to tell you something else."

Pa folded his arms where he sat. "Then you might as well say it."

"I got a job offer."

"But you haven't finished your residency yet."

"It's for after graduation, contingent on my completion of the program."

Pa shifted in his seat, unfolded his arms. His face turned stoic. He was trying not to react. "Guess that means you'll be moving, then."

"Yes, I think so."

"How far away will you be?"

It was written all over his father's face. Pa missed him, would miss him more if he was far away.

"The job's here, Pa, in Evers Hollow, with Doc Mason. He took over for Sam Cook."

"I know who Sam Cook is. Why would you want to come back here?"

Finn sat down across from him, looked Pa in the eye. "You already know the answer."

"For Rose Finch. You're serious about her?"

"I'm in love with her." It'd always been her.

"I can't stop you. Your mom wouldn't either. She always said the two of you belonged together. I disagreed."

Finn stood, moved to his backpack, and pulled out a wrapped brown parcel. He handed Pa his gift. "Maybe this will help."

Pa held the package by one corner as if it had wriggly legs. "I don't need anything."

Finn smiled. "This is something different."

He unwrapped it. Studied the item in his hand. "This is a children's book."

His smile became a grin. "I know. It's one of Rose's books."

"You think one of her books is going to make me feel better when she breaks your heart?"

"I think it'll help you realize she loves me too, that she has no intention of breaking my heart. It won't hurt you to read it and find out." Pa opened the book, with a perplexed look on his face.

"Enjoy." Finn hugged him before he left the room.

It had always been Rose he'd imagined his life with. He'd let that dream go after she told him she was engaged. Forgot about marriage, a life with her, a daughter with green eyes, maybe a son. A whole dog. And let go of all the adventures he'd dreamed they could have as husband and wife.

Today, everything felt possible.

Finn had one more thing to do in town before he met up with Rose. He got back in his SUV, drove into town, and parked. Brick Wall Books displayed a poster in the window, advertising Rose's upcoming release and the reading she'd do for it. He left the store with a grin on his face as snow flurries danced across his windshield.

Chapter Sixty

January brought snow to Evers Hollow. Snowflakes fluttered against the windows of the bookstore like confetti. The children in attendance sat on their chairs, talking and waiting.

They quieted as Alec came up the few stairs to the stage to introduce her. Usually, they started a few minutes late. Tonight, though, her reading began on time.

Rose looked out on the crowd often as she read, smiling at the occasional child who met her gaze. It was habit. The pair of eyes she most wished to see was absent, like every time before. Finn was on shift. There had been no way for him to get out of it. A doctor on leave, one out sick. There had been a list of reasons.

There would be other books, other readings. She'd waited this long. Another book wouldn't matter.

She continued reading aloud.

"I can't see the paw prints anymore," said Jed.

Ruby studied the ground. "We've lost the trail. We should go back to our bicycles, to the path where we found the paw prints. Look for more clues."

Jed folded his arms. "We need to eat."

"Lunch is in my bicycle basket. We'll eat and then look for clues."

They ran back to their bicycles. Her basket was empty.

Jed said, "Oh no! Someone took our lunch."

Rose closed the book. As soon as she did, the children clapped.

Alec came up the short stairs to stand beside her. "Ready for questions?"

Rose nodded as she looked over the seated children and those standing behind the chairs. Had the audience grown? More people than she remembered stood outside the rows of chairs.

She'd known all The Elders would be here. They were four rows back, speaking amongst themselves.

She squinted. Was that Mr. Hanover in the back corner? Beside the Evers Hollow librarian? A man sat in front of them. Maybe she needed glasses. The man looked a lot like Charlie Murphy. Impossible.

Alec's voice pulled her back. "Great. We'll get started then."

He turned to the crowd. "Thank you again for attending Miss Briar's book reading. We here at Brick Wall Books are very excited to welcome her back. She's ready to take questions now before we head upstairs for refreshments."

Hands went into the air before Alec moved from her side.

She called on a boy wearing a backward baseball cap.

"Why is there such an ugly dog on the cover?"

Youthful voices launched into an uproar. They debated back and forth.

"He's not ugly."

"Is too."

"Is not."

Rose raised her hand for silence, then cleared her throat. "Each of you has your own opinion about the dog. There's nothing wrong with that. I happen to think he's cute, but he sure could use a bath."

The crowd laughed.

A childish voice, clearly someone who'd already read the book, said, "But Rusty hates baths."

"Can I get another question?"

A girl with long dark hair stood toward the back. One she recognized too well, Aliya. Her own niece didn't just raise her hand, she stood atop a chair while doing it. When had she arrived? Was that Simi sitting on the chair beside her? And Broome behind them, against a bookshelf?

She blinked. A dark-haired woman stood beside Broome with a baby in her arms. She looked an awful lot like her oldest sister. Aspen hadn't attended a reading since her first book release.

Rose glanced over at Alec. He quirked an eyebrow as if questioning if she was all right.

She cleared her throat and called on her niece. "Aliya."

Aliya looked so delicate and innocent, but even from the small stage, she recognized the saucy look the girl wore when she was up to something. With the slightest hint of a British accent, she asked, "Are Ruby and Jed going to get married someday?"

Rose's jaw fell open a tad. Her own niece dared to ask the one question she hated answering at every reading. It felt like a betrayal. Even now she could see the red-haired girl who'd asked the same question at the last book reading. The teenager displayed a wickedly gleeful expression on her face.

All the children were staring at her. She had to answer. But didn't get the chance to.

Sounds of commotion came from the front of the store. Those standing parted and shifted, as if stepping aside for someone. She spotted Finn alongside Broome, tossing off his coat, his hair unruly, melting snowflakes sparkling in its strands.

A breathy sound came through the speakers. She realized she'd been the one to make it. Finn had shown up after all.

With a teasing smile, he came forward, made his way up the stairs and whispered, "How about I take this one?"

What? She opened her mouth to speak, but he pressed one finger to her lips.

"Never mind. Don't answer. I've got this." Then he lowered his finger and winked.

What the hell was going on?

All she could do was stare at him. It was much the same for the audience. Heads turned this way and that as if they too wondered what was going on. Snowflakes continued to fall outside, but she still seemed to be the only one who noticed.

Aliya remained standing on her chair, Broome now behind her. She patiently waited for the answer to her question.

Had Finn just nudged her over, so he was centered at the podium? Nothing like this had ever happened before.

His voice trembled through the microphone. He sounded off a bit, gravelly even. "Can you repeat your question again?"

With her prominent, saucy grin, Aliya yelled. "Are Ruby and Jed getting married someday?"

He cleared his throat and glanced at her. Did she really have a choice? Maybe he would have a better answer. Rose gave him a slight nod.

Finn appeared to think about it for a moment before he spoke. "Ruby and Jed. They're what—twelve years old in this book?"

Many in the audience nodded in agreement.

"A little young to think about marriage."

Exactly! At least his answer was consistent with hers.

But he went on. "Who knows what will happen as they get older?"

What was he doing? She reached out and curled her fingers on his forearm in warning.

Finn kept talking. "This is the first time I've been to one of these. Do adults get to ask questions, too?"

More nods. What was he up to? She tried to nudge him, but he stayed put.

The red-headed teenager, Colette, stood and frowned. "Who are you?"

Finn didn't miss a beat. "I'm a friend of Miss Briar's. I have a question for her."

Broome's second oldest, Aliya, made her way to the stage, carrying a book. Mara followed close behind, hiding something behind her back.

Up the steps they came. Mara stumbled into her, holding up a bouquet of pink carnations to her. "For you. Pink."

Aliya handed the book to Finn. Both her nieces stepped to the side of the stage.

Finn stepped back from the podium, faced her, and asked, "Will you sign this for me?"

She looked down at the book in his hand. It was a copy of her latest in hardback. Dust jacket pristine as if it had just come fresh from a box.

A murmur went through the crowd. She heard the comments.

"Not fair."

"Who does he think he is?"

"He should have to stand in line."

And these were from nine to fourteen-year-olds.

Finn said one word. "Please." He held the book out.

She looked at him and found herself caught. There was something in those caramel brown eyes she hadn't seen before. Along with the shadows below him. He'd worked multiple shifts this past week. Night ones. He should be sleeping. But he was here. For her.

She glanced at the podium—no pen. They were at her table upstairs in the loft.

She felt a nudge on her elbow. Alec. Holding out an ink pen.

With murmured thanks, she took it.

Then held her hand out for the book. He handed it to her. She opened the cover.

And froze.

In the middle of the page, a small square had been carved out. Inside, within folds of pink velvet sat a beautiful ring. Silver rose petals surrounded the diamond in the middle.

It stole her breath. She looked at him, unable to even open her mouth to speak.

Finn no longer stood beside her. He knelt on one knee in front of her.

He winked. "I have another question."

"Criminy."

The word carried through the microphone. Giggles and laughter came back from the crowd. Her nieces were laughing, too.

"Evie, will you marry me?"

"Yes."

He rose quickly and lifted the ring out of the book. Her hands shook as he clasped them in his and slipped the ring on her finger.

Cheers and applause erupted in front of them.

Finn pulled her into his arms and kissed her. Then kissed her again.

Alec cleared his throat.

When they separated, her hand lifted to his face, resting against his jaw. "I love you, Finn Murphy."

He kissed her again. "I love you back."

Surrounded by cheers and congratulations, Rose couldn't help but grin when she heard a familiar redhead yell, "I knew it!"

Epilogue

The front door of the cottage opened and closed. Finn's voice carried down the hall, announcing his return.

Rose sat with folded legs on her cold bedroom floor, the nearby window cracked open enough to allow the sounds of scrambling squirrels and chirping birds to drift in.

Her nightstand drawer sat open. A packing box nearby held a few of the items she'd pulled from the drawer. Old journals, near-empty lotion bottles, and too many tubes of lip balm.

A wrapped rectangular box sat in her hands, one she'd forgotten about after Magnolia's death. She'd found it behind the stack of filled journals in her nightstand.

Magnolia's lawyer had given it to her after the reading of the will, near eight months ago. The feel of the paper wrapping, its edges, brought a tumult of emotions—a mix of nostalgia, grief and memory.

Finn appeared in the doorway, holding two cups of coffee from Firebrew.

As if he sensed her feelings, he asked, "Everything okay?"

"I started packing and found this. I received it after Magnolia passed."

Finn moved into the room, sat on the carpet across from her, and held out her drink. "What's inside?"

Rose accepted her mocha. After a sip, she said, "I don't know. The night the will was read, the letter from her—it was too much."

He scooted closer. His fingers slipped just inside the gaping tear in her overalls above her knee. His palm felt warm against her skin, loving.

"You never opened it?"

"No. I put it in this drawer, thinking I'd open it later that day…"

He offered a wry smile. "But your world turned to chaos."

She nodded. He knew her too well. These past months—Magnolia's death, inheriting Briar House, learning that Magnolia was her birth mother—was only the beginning. The night George Hindley set fire to the house, his obsession over Magnolia, then her, still gave Rose occasional nightmares.

Seeing the reconstruction of what the arsonist tried so hard to destroy helped. The sounds of hammering, the buzz of the saw cutting new wood, restored her belief that Briar House would stand complete once again. Rolling wet paint over new walls healed her, along with the refinishing projects Willow devised for the two of them.

Finn asked, "Do you want to open the box now?"

Once more, Rose turned it over and over in her hands. Her fingers traced the folded edges on either end.

"I have to open it. It's been eight months. I know the others received their manilla envelopes. Aspen wears a necklace and earrings she said came from Magnolia. Willow has a cameo that's come down through the Finch side of the family tree."

"They never asked what you received?"

Rose shook her head. "No. It would have been intrusive. And vice versa."

"I get that."

She sipped her hot mocha and studied him. He wore his old paint-splattered jeans and an old tee. She found the combo mouth-watering, and her thoughts turned to the passions of the night before, the parts of her that still felt tender from their lovemaking.

She took another drink, licked her lips, and set her coffee on the nightstand.

"Stop looking at me like that," Finn said. The words came out in what she'd decided was his sexy voice. "We've only got three days left to pack."

The main house, under reconstruction these past months, would be ready in four days. Her family, their friends, were coming to help move the items here along with all they'd had to put in storage during the rebuild. She well knew boxes didn't pack themselves. Yet, she couldn't resist edging closer to him. "One kiss. To tide us over."

His eyes narrowed, as if he didn't trust her to stick with one. "One kiss. Then you open the box." His hand around her knee tightened.

Her insides flickered as their lips met, more than once. Desire flared as if they hadn't spent much of last night making love. Her fingers threaded into his hair while his moved higher beneath her overalls. She forgot about packing and the box in her hand.

He broke away first. Restraint edged his voice. "That was more than one kiss. We'll continue this later. Open the box, Evie."

Breathless, her fingers made quick work of the rose print wrapping paper. She lifted its lid and frowned.

A single metal key on a long waxed cord lay secured around a flocked jewelry card.

Her brows furrowed as she pulled the tiny tab to lift it from the box. Nothing lay underneath.

Finn said, "There's something written on the back."

Rose turned it over.

Three words and numbers—in Magnolia's handwriting.

Your next mystery
#1862

He asked, "What does it mean?"

Rose didn't know whether to laugh or cry.

A quest. Magnolia had left her a quest, with only a key and four numbers to lead them.

She lifted the key up to the light, felt its serrated edge, a pattern that would unlock something. Exactly what she didn't know, but she'd figure it out. And Finn would help her.

"We have a new mystery to solve," Rose said.

The light in Rose's eyes reminded Finn of the little girl he'd followed through the woods long ago. The key clutched in her hand was old. Its brass color and square teeth reminded him of a jack-o'-lantern he'd carved back in elementary school.

She stood. "There are numbers on here. I need my magnifying glass."

Rose disappeared from the room, returning a moment later with her magnifying glass. She moved to stand by the window, focused on the key in hand.

"I was right," she said. "There are numbers. Tiny ones. Near impossible to read."

She wore a purple tank top underneath a faded pair of overalls. The light illuminated her hair, wound in what she called a messy bun, loosened after their kiss. Tendrils fell over her face as she nibbled her lower lip.

His fingers curled against his thighs. This woman was going to be his wife. In twenty-eight days.

Rose spun and moved to sit beside him, showing him what she'd found.

"Read the numbers out. I'll write them down so we don't need the glass," he said.

"There's paper and pens in my nightstand."

Seconds later, they studied the numbers on a small notepad. Nine of them.

"The key's old, based on the teeth."

He had a thought. He'd never had one, only seen them in movies. Seeing as her family was wealthy and had lived in the area for generations, he asked, "Does your family have a safe deposit box?"

"I don't know. No one's ever mentioned it."

"Whatever this unlocks, I don't think it's in Evers Hollow."

Rose's true identity had been a well-kept secret. He didn't think it was too much of a leap to guess this key echoed that secret.

She set the magnifying glass on her bed and pulled out her phone, corded key dangling from her fingers.

"Morning Broome. Do you know if Magnolia kept a safe deposit box?"

Finn stood, moved to the edge of her bed. He watched her, but only heard her side.

"I see," she said. "I forgot about the gift. I shoved it in a drawer."

Rose twirled her hair around her fingers as she listened.

"Do you know where it is?"

"What do you mean I'll have to figure it out?"

After another exchange, she hung up.

She moved toward Finn, wedged herself between his legs. "The family had a safe deposit box. Broome won't tell me if it still exists or where it would be. He said that this puzzle is for me to figure out."

Finn bracketed her waist with his hands. Tilting his head back, he said, "So, Ruby and Jed are back in play."

She smiled. "Ha-ha. I'd say with our years of experience, we'll be the smarter pair."

They exchanged another kiss. He pressed his forehead against hers.

"Can we get into trouble with the locals?"

Her fingers scraped against his scalp. "Only if broken bones aren't involved."

———

Broome gave her one clue.

The numbers are key.

How cute of him to use the object's word in the clue.

She and Finn moved to the small dining table in the cottage's kitchen. She pulled out lemon poppyseed bread while Finn used her blender to make berry smoothies.

Once seated, Rose said, "Nine numbers engraved on a key. It might be associated with a safe deposit box or not. Any ideas?"

He spread lemon blueberry jam on the poppyseed bread. "I think we can rule out the nine rings of the Nazgul from Lord of the Rings."

She rolled her eyes. "That's a given."

After a few bites, Finn silently counted off something on his fingers. Nine. He did the same a second time.

He said, "Social Security numbers and phone numbers come in nines."

"I think we can assume the number is something else." It wouldn't make sense to engrave a phone number on a key.

"Maybe the safe deposit box still exists," he said. "According to the movies, it would be inside a bank."

"What movie?"

"The one with the bank," he said.

With sarcasm, she said, "Thanks. That narrows it down quite a bit."

"It was an action movie."

She stood to retrieve her laptop from her desk. "We're not getting our research from movies."

He set his coffee mug down with a smile. "I've got it. *Bourne Identity*."

She shook her head and began typing.

Finn moved his chair closer. "Are you pulling up a video clip from the movie?"

"I am not. Jason Bourne won't help us solve this. If I remember right, that movie took place in Paris. I'm looking up what the numbers mean."

"Practical," he said. "Maybe we can do a Bourne movie marathon soon."

She pressed Return on her keyboard. Results popped up, including locksmith sites and links to purchase engraved keys. Nothing about what nine numbers meant. Finn leaned close enough to see the screen.

"Maybe focus on the key related to safe deposit boxes."

She typed in new search parameters and waited for the information to fill the screen. First, the internet recommended reaching out to banks to find out if Magnolia had a box.

Finn pointed to the screen. "Click on this one."

She did. Some keys had a routing number on them. All she had to do was enter the numbers.

Finn reached across the table, picked up the piece of paper with the sequence, reading it aloud.

She hit the *enter* button with gusto. As the info came up, she said, "Of course."

"What's it mean?"

She leaned back and smiled. "It's a routing number for a

bank in Asheville. Thanks to Magnolia's note, we know the box number."

He finished his smoothie then picked up his coffee. "Does this mean we don't get to terrorize every bank in Buncombe County with our questions?"

"Yes."

"How close is it?"

She pulled up her maps app and entered the destination. "Seventy-one minutes without traffic."

He rose, took his dishes to the sink and rinsed them off. "Let's delay the packing a few hours. We can grab lunch on the way back."

She took a moment to think. Briar House was days from being ready for occupancy. Her family was coming to help her with the move.

She looked at her watch, thought of the travel time. Four hours to solve a mystery, if all went well.

She decided, closed her laptop. "Okay. We'll go."

An hour and a half later, she and Finn stood inside a room surrounded by safe deposit boxes. The bank had taken her key, retrieved the Everson family's box for her and set it on a counter.

With caught breath, she opened it.

A small envelope sat on top, her name in Magnolia's script across its front.

Remembering the last letter she'd received from her birth mother, she opened it with shaking hands.

My dear Rebel,

I knew you would find your way here. Forgive my antics. Consider it a bit of sweet revenge for all the phone calls I received regarding my "hoyden" grand—

daughter.

You know the truth about your birth now. I hope in time, you'll forgive me for misleading you all these years.

I made my choices from a place of love, for your protection, for my own, and for the Everson legacy.

Inside this box, you'll find that which pertains to you and only you, along with any remaining answers you might seek.

With all my love,
Magnolia

Only when Finn brushed a thumb across her cheek did she realize tears had fallen. She tilted her head back, collected herself, swiped her own cheeks and looked into the box.

Two numbered jewelry boxes sat inside. Twine criss-crossed around each.

She picked up the first one. A small note was attached to the twine.

My grandmother gave these to me when I graduated from college. They belonged to her mother.

Inside sat a bracelet, one Rose recognized. An elegant piece that she remembered admiring as a child, on Magnolia's wrist. She'd asked to borrow it for first grade show and tell. Magnolia had refused, declaring it improper to bring to a first grade classroom. Alternating square cut emeralds and diamonds sat within sterling silver. It wasn't the only thing in the box. Emerald drop earrings lay inside, a perfect match to the bracelet.

Finn kissed her shoulder. "You should wear them for our

wedding."

Rose could only nod as she wiped her eyes again and picked up the other box.

It was slightly larger than the first and taller. She bit her lower lip as she took in its contents. A small cloth bag lay on top. She pulled it open, tipped it. An oval locket fell into her hand.

The locket wore a tarnish. She was no expert on jewelry, but guessed it was either silver or silver-plated. It took her a moment to open it, but once she did, she smiled. A miniature image of Magnolia sat on one side. The other held the image of a young man.

It was a younger version of Hal Lawson, Rose's birth father. There was a resemblance, but the photo was small.

Rose hadn't seen the locket before. Had Hal given it to her?

Finn stood alongside her. She passed the locket to him.

He studied it before he spoke. "They look so young. I've never seen him without gray hair."

Rose returned her attention to the box. A flat index card atop a few photos remained inside.

Me with your father. Knowing you, you've already figured out his identity.

A photo strip lay on top, maybe from a local fair. Two teenagers with smiling faces, goofy expressions, and one kiss.

Rose could only imagine how they'd had to sneak time like this together, a secret from her father and friends.

Next was their prom photo. Magnolia wore a sleeveless, floor-length, light green dress with long white gloves. She wore her hair pinned up. Hal stood beside her in a tux consisting of a white jacket, white shirt, and black pants.

One thing remained.

Another photo, a Polaroid. When she pulled it out, she

gasped and reached out. Her voice felt breathless as she tapped his arm. "Finn."

He too took an audible sharp breath. "My mom."

The white border of the picture framed the image of two women. Both wore hospital gowns, seated and smiling with swaddled infants in their arms.

Magnolia Everson-Brooks and Clara Murphy.

She turned it over. In black ink, Magnolia's flowing script read:

Clara– The woman who helped deliver you. Hours after, she gave birth to her own child. Her compassion, her coaching, and her companionship during those precious days were the sort I've cherished and never forgotten.

Rose leaned against Finn in wonder as they both stared at the two women and their babies.

"There's no way they could have known they would see other again. That we would become friends."

"And husband and wife." Finn wrapped an arm around her. His lips pressed over hers.

She returned his kiss and gazed into his eyes, the photograph held tight between her fingers. "Twenty-eight days."

"Twenty-eight days," he said.

"I love you."

ENJOYED LINGERING FLAMES?

Thank you for reading Rose and Finn's story.

If you enjoyed this book, I would love your help in sharing *Lingering Flames* with other readers by leaving a review on your favorite books site. Reader reviews help others discover new books and they mean the world to authors.

Would you like to know what happens next? Read on for the opening of:

Hidden Peril

Book 2 in The Everson Legacy Series

Coming Winter 2026

www.annaaugustbooks.com

HIDDEN PERIL

Book 2 in The Everson Legacy Series

PROLOGUE

Dressed in a sleeveless lavender dress made of chiffon, Willow Marie Finch walked down the aisle a dozen steps behind her sister Aspen. Piano and flute music accompanied their steps. Her fingers tightened around the small bouquet of lavender sprigs and rosemary amongst roses and carnations. The scent of the blooms calmed her as she pivoted and stepped into her assigned spot in front of the newly constructed wooden arbor before Briar House's rose garden.

One of Rose's friends, Becks, took her place beside Willow, also in lavender.

Family and friends filled the folding chairs in front of them, except for four in the front row. Small wreaths of carnations, roses, and rosemary lay upon those chairs in memory of Grandmother, Mom, Dad, and Finn's mom, Clara Murphy.

As Ada, the maid of honor, took her spot, the two flower girls appeared.

Broome's oldest, Aliya, in dark lavender, took precise steps towards the arbor, her floral filled basket perfectly centered on her delicate frame. Pink and lavender rose petals fluttered through her fingers at regular intervals down the aisle. Behind her, in a similar dress, three-year-old Mara wove side to side, tossing her own collection of petals from her basket.

Willow pressed her lips together when a handful landed atop the little floral crown Mara wore, then stifled a giggle when the little girl twirled and almost tumbled with another handful. When Mara stopped and turned the basket upside down over her head, Aliya stepped back and took her sister's hand, leading her over to stand in front of the bridesmaids.

All stood when Rose appeared with Broome's arm tucked around hers. The musicians began playing an Enya song about love. Willow's eyes misted at the sight of her sister walking down the aisle, looking devastatingly beautiful in a boho wedding dress with a chiffon skirt that looked like something from an ethereal forest. Flowers nestled amongst the curls atop her head, accenting the bouquet she carried. The lace sleeves just past her elbows suggested she could still climb trees if she wished.

Broome kissed Rose on the forehead, then took a seat beside his wife Simi and their two younger children in the front row.

With a tender look, Finn wrapped his arm around her. Together, they stepped forward to speak their vows. The ceremony ended with their first kiss as husband and wife. Then they shared a second one, as if their first kiss hadn't lasted long enough.

Night overtook the setting sun as guests moved in and out of Briar House's ballroom.

Rose and Finn's first dance as husband and wife had Willow's eyes shiny, a damp handkerchief clutched in her palm.

Four songs later, Willow put a hand to her heart as she left the dance floor. The many toasts and two glasses of champagne made her feel floaty, lighter, and in need of fresh air.

First though, she stopped by the dessert table, picked up a

second floral themed cupcake and napkin before stepping out onto the recently rebuilt large stone terrace. The cloying humidity swirled around her, bringing the scent of citronella with it from the torches around the edges.

To her surprise, only one person stood outside—a man, tall and lean with dark hair, facing away from the house. He didn't seem to notice her.

The railing outlining the terrace beckoned and offered her something to hold on to. She steeled herself against needing it, but her feet had other ideas. She moved quietly away from the man, hoping the loud music inside masked the sound of her one-inch heels on the stone.

The cupcake in her hand disappeared, one bite at a time, the frosting light and decadent on her tongue while happiness spilled from the ballroom behind her.

For the past days, hours, Willow had reveled in it, ecstatic for the happy couple.

Rose and Finn deserved every stitch of love binding them together.

Too close they'd come to losing their chance at that, in the fire that threatened their lives and burned a good fraction of what stood behind her, rebuilt these past months.

She wished their sort of bond was contagious. She too, wanted a forever with someone and at thirty-two was thinking it might be out of reach.

With that thought, Willow perched her bare arms on the railing and sighed.

The reception line had been a small torture, full of intrusive questions dropped like unsecured thread on a runaway spool.

When do we get to see you walk down the aisle?

Have you met my son? He's just divorced. He needs a new mom for his twin boys.

You should eat more. Who wants to marry a toothpick?

Her fingers closed around the cupcake wrapper. And the ever present reminder that her biological clock was ticking.

Sigh.

Thankfully, the wedding dinner and the many toasts provided a barrier between her and the local matchmakers, along with their offers, to set her up on blind dates. She shuddered at the thought of one more stranger who assumed *date* meant automatic naked time.

A glance sideways told her the tall guy realized he wasn't alone. He'd moved toward her.

If she were ultra-athletic, she'd use the railing as a springboard and disappear before he could say whatever he planned to say.

She braced herself as he stopped beside her, not too close. She appreciated that.

A glance told her he looked a tad familiar, that he wore glasses, but she couldn't place him.

"Willow, right?" A glass of beer, half-full, cradled in his palm.

"Yes, that's me." Her index finger ran over her thumb, along the edge of the rail.

He nodded. "Thought so. I've heard about you."

She bristled. From who? Who'd been talking about her? After Rose's experience with a stalker who loved setting fires, it was wise to be careful.

Hoping her words didn't come across as rude, she said, "You have me at a disadvantage. Do I know you?"

If anything, his posture straightened. "Not really. Rose mentioned you. But I believe you've bought me coffee."

He had a connection to Rose. Hmm. She nibbled her lower lip. "I buy many people coffee." It was her way, without fail, every Tuesday.

He leaned closer, one hand wrapped around the railing, an

inch from her own. His voice lowered, almost intimate. "I didn't like it when you did it for me."

The scent of cedar and something else, like a memory, reached her. She swallowed and managed a shrug. "You're the only one to object."

He raised an eyebrow. "We argued about it."

As if that would help. She never argued. There were moments she felt she needed to start. "That doesn't help. Do you have a name?"

"It's not important."

"But you know mine."

"I should go." He glanced around the space, seemed fixed on the double doors that led back into the ballroom. "Last thing I need is my gran seeing me talk to you."

That stung. She turned to face him, her fingers tightening around the railing. He seemed too close now. "You approached me."

He met her eyes with his own. His dark blue eyes. Sapphires. She had seen him before.

Firebrew.

They had argued. He looked different then. Unkempt.

Now he looked clean and crisp, attractive even, in a pair of slacks and a button down white shirt.

He said, "Gran's a matchmaker."

And he didn't want to be matched. Not the first time she'd heard that excuse. Her brother, Thorne, seemed to consider it his personal motto.

Despite his words, she felt his gaze on her. Her breath caught.

He bristled when he spoke again. His voice held irritation. "You're lovely. Rose never mentioned you were lovely."

Stunned, no one had ever—

The lightest warmth, a singular caress, touched the outside of her hand, like butterfly wings, so brief she wondered if she'd imagined it.

He cleared his throat. "I don't d—"

Laughter spilled from the ballroom as the nearby doors swung outward. He stepped back with a furtive glance toward the house.

Like a flash of lightning, blue eyes no longer stood beside her. He did exactly what she'd contemplated when she'd first spotted him.

He went over the railing and disappeared. Try as she might, she could no longer see him.

Had he really called her lovely? And meant it?

"Willow dear." Said in a familiar voice.

She turned to see silvery-haired Emmie Kincaid walking towards her in a sparkly long sleeved dress. Her husband, Lou, accompanied her.

"You look beautiful, dear."

Before she could thank her for the compliment, Emmie took both of Willow's hands with a smile and looked up at her. "I have wonderful news."

Threads of hope curled inside her.

The woman's smile became a grin. "Belmont's agreed to sell his storefront to you."

Belmont agreed to sell.

Willow's breath caught. "For real?"

She said, "I would never jest with you, dear."

Her months long fixation with the empty storefront beside the local bookstore wasn't a waste. Her pursuit of learning more about it, her conversations with this sweet, sparkling blue-eyed woman, led one step closer to fulfilling her dreams.

The older woman's voice held amusement. "I assume that means you're happy with the news?"

Willow couldn't help herself as the news sank in. She hugged

Emmie with a squeal. "Happy doesn't come close. I'm—in the clouds."

She released the woman and took her hands. "Thank you so much. This means the world."

Emmie squeezed back. "I remember what it's like to have dreams. The bookstore was ours. The moment I saw you, I saw that same spark."

After another hug and tentative plans to connect tomorrow, the older couple stepped back into the ballroom.

Willow put her arms back on the railing and closed her eyes.

Her sketches, paint swatches, the storage unit with all the pieces she'd gathered and refinished since moving back to Evers Hollow—her efforts weren't for nothing. Her imaginings of mannequins in that gorgeous bay window wearing her hand-sewn pieces could become reality.

This called for another cupcake.

COMING THIS WINTER 2026

Acknowledgments

This book began fifteen years ago in North Carolina. It was handwritten for the most part, filling multiple composition notebooks while my husband worked at the nearby US Air Force base and my kids were at school. It was inspired by my love of trees, the mystery books I read as a child, and a love of romance novels. I knew when the first words fell onto the page, that it had to be set in the mountains of western North Carolina with an old Victorian in a small fictional town close to Asheville.

To my husband, Mike, thank you for being wonderfully supportive of this journey toward my dream. To my two adult children, Erik and Meghan, thank you for all your support. All three of you have witnessed my efforts these past years at turning this book into a published reality. I love each of you to the moon and back.

To the two women who encouraged me to get started on this journey sixteen years ago, thank you to Francisca Ruger and Margaret Mihoerck. This book wouldn't exist without you both.

To my editor, Lynn Mapp, thank you for all your edits, for reading this book four times, and for sharing your feedback in a way that made me more likely to laugh than cry. You are a gem.

To Kari March Designs for the beautiful book cover.

To my daughter, Meghan, for my author logo.

To my Wednesday coffee group for answering all my questions about publishing and for being so supportive. Thank you, Lynn Mapp, Judith Keim, Kate Baray, Joanne Pence, Peggy Staggs, and Niki Mitchell.

To Janis McCurry and Stephanie Berget for their advice and answered questions.

To James Dayton, Sarah Evans, and Kate Castro for providing information on century old homes.

And lastly, thanks to "Flying M Coffee" in downtown Boise for being such an awesome place to drink coffee, think, and write.

Thank you to all the readers who took the time to read my book!

About the Author

Anna August writes romantic suspense and contemporary romance. She enjoys writing imaginative characters with complicated backgrounds. She cherishes books with plot twists, humor, and happily ever after's.

Born and raised in California, Anna has also lived in Illinois, Texas, North Carolina, Idaho, and England. She served as a military spouse alongside her active duty husband in the US Air Force for twenty-one years. She holds a bachelors degrees in English and also in Geology, after discovering her love of rocks during a camping trip to a gold mine as a child.

When she's not writing, she enjoys spending time with her husband and two adult children at their home in Boise, Idaho. She also enjoys gardening, gluten-free baking, and random home improvement projects.

Find her at www.annaaugustbooks.com

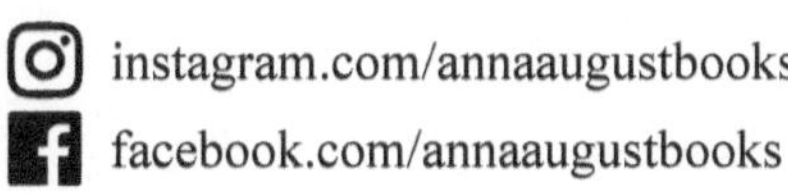